WEST AFRICAN FOLKTALES

▼▲▼▲▼▲▼▲▼▲▼▲▼▲▼▲▼▲▼▲▼▲▼▲▼▲▼▲▼

W·E·S·T AFRICAN FOLKTALES

▼▲▼▲▼▲▼▲▼▲▼▲▼▲▼▲▼▲▼▲▼▲▼

COLLECTED AND TRANSLATED

BY JACK BERRY

EDITED AND WITH AN INTRODUCTION

BY RICHARD SPEARS

Northwestern University Press ▲ Evanston, Illinois

The publisher wishes to acknowledge the assistance of Mrs. Jack Berry in the publication of this book.

Northwestern University Press
www.nupress.northwestern.edu

"Spoken Art in West Africa" copyright © 1961 by Jack Berry.
West African Folk Tales copyright © 1991 by Northwestern University Press. Published 1991. All rights reserved.

Printed in the United States of America

First printing, 1991
Second printing, 1993
Third paperback printing, 1994
Fourth paperback printing, 1996
Fifth paperback printing, 2008
Sixth paperback printing, 2011
Seventh paperback printing, 2011
Eighth paperback printing, 2013

ISBN-13:   978-0-8101-0979-7 (cloth)
ISBN-10:   0-8101-0979-4 (cloth)
ISBN-13:   978-0-8101-0993-3 (paper)
ISBN-10:   0-8101-0993-X (paper)

Library of Congress Cataloging-in-Publication Data

West African folktales / collected and translated by Jack Berry ;
edited and with an introduction by Richard Spears.
p. cm.
Includes index
ISBN 0-8101-0979-4 (cloth). — ISBN 0-8101-0993-X (paper)
I. Tales—Africa, West. I. Berry, Jack. II. Spears, Richard A.
GR350.3.W45 1991
398.2'0966—dc20   91-24282
                                             CIP

♾ The paper used in this publication meets the minimum requirements of the American National Standard for Information Sciences—Permanence of Paper for Printed Library Materials, ANSI Z39.48-1992.

CONTENTS

▲▼▲▼▲▼▲▼▲▼▲▼▲

PREFACE

▼▲▼▲▼▲▼▲▼▲▼▲▼▲▼▲▼▲▼▲▼▲▼▲▼▲▼▲▼▲▼

SPOKEN ART IN WEST AFRICA

JACK BERRY

Serious collecting of folklore in West Africa can be said to have begun around the middle of the last century with the publication of Koelle's Vai and Schlenker's Temne stories.[1] Since those times somewhat systematic collections have been made among a number of tribes, and a considerable corpus of West African literary material has accrued. We owe to Melville J. and Frances S. Herskovits a rather complete bibliography of these studies published in 1936 as an appendix to their *Suriname Folklore*.[2] This bibliography, except for a few notable omissions, is still entirely adequate since, as Herskovits himself rightly remarks in a later, recent volume,[3] not many collections have been added to our resources in the past twenty years or so (a fact of some significance, to which I shall later have occasion to revert).

Although the area is by no means covered by existing material (it will be one of my main concerns here to assess the adequacy of the documentation), much has been gained to give us a better knowledge of the subject. There is, however, a paper by Bascom[4] in which he voices the frustration that is surely felt by all anthropologists and linguists when confronted by the complexity of the so-called primitive cultures of the Guinea Coast. What, in that paper, is relevant to us here is his comparison, in the field of folklore, of the number of tales and proverbs actually recorded for a single tribe with reasonable estimates, by anthropologists and others, of the numbers known and in use at the present time. For example, collections of folktales numbering two hundred from a single tribe have yet to be published. But Bascom's estimate for the Yoruba-speaking peoples is five thousand tales, "with more of a chance of being too low than too high." Similarly with proverbs. Collections published as commercial ventures for sale to West Africans (without, therefore, translation or notes) frequently contain three thousand or more proverbs. Of these, Christaller's[5] is perhaps the best example. But more adequately edited collections—one thinks immediately of Herzog's for the Jabo or Rattray's for the Ashanti[6]—rarely attain a third of that number. Rather clearly, then, present records represent only a relatively small sampling of the total artistic resources of the area.

In these circumstances, generalization of any kind is risky. Especially risky is *argumentum ex silentio*; we cannot assert with accuracy that a form or a theme, for example, is not found in a given area, and we cannot, therefore, as yet delineate our subprovinces by motifs that do or do not occur.

Nevertheless, a basic unit is apparent throughout the region, and it is possible, I think, to speak safely in fairly general terms about some aspects of folklore in West Africa. This I now propose to do.

Prose narratives, proverbs, riddles, and songs are the chief forms of oral expression found among the West African native peoples. I am exonerated, I assume, by a carefully chosen title, from any consideration of the last-named form, and I turn with a clear conscience and considerable relief from a field in which I have no competence. But there are unfortunately areas of indeterminacy between what is quite clearly spoken art and what is more properly the concern of the ethnomusicologist. Borderline cases of this type are usually called verse or poetry by West African folklorists and are said to be recited or chanted. Only in a very few cases have these terms been expanded and the techniques of recitation described. It may be pertinent in this respect to remark that the terms for "song" and "verse" are, in most West African languages, significantly the same.

Through the courtesy of D. Arnott I have had an opportunity to hear examples of the Fula Gimε and Gimi, which he himself recorded in Gombe and Upper Volta. These would appear to be verse sequences in the main composed by professional verse-makers, and they have the important, though not exclusive, function of aiding the memorizing of genealogies and historic events; they are frequently recited in honor of chiefs and other important individuals. From the point of view of outer form, at least two types were clearly distinguishable. The first could be described as true chant and exhibited most of the to-be-expected features of cantillation without instrumental accompaniment. A second type—declaimed, I should say, rather than chanted—was characterized by striking departures from the normal utterance, in respect of rate, pitch, and stress features. In both cases, especially the latter, it would seem more profitable to regard the form as a type of speech utterance, perhaps with rudimentary musical characteristics, rather than a species of song.[7] The Akan funeral dirge in one of its forms as described by J. H. Nketia would appear to constitute a similar problem.[8]

Reverting now to forms that are unambiguously spoken, I shall attempt some subdivision of the main categories I have listed. In so doing, I am not unmindful of the eloquent pleas made on occasion by Margaret Green,[9] for example, among others, that we should respect indigenous canons of genology. But classification and definition have posed problems from the outset of the study of verbal art. Herskovits, who is at pains in a recent work[10] to elicit the categories of narrative established and identified by the Dahomeans themselves, admits that they are often hard put to give a categorical answer if asked the types to which certain tales belong. One of his informants rather distressingly named a fable or parable as falling with the proverb group. One instance of the difficulties of overall classification will suffice. A type of narrative is classified by Bascom,[11] who gives an example from the Bura of Nigeria, as dilemma tales. Entirely comparable tales are classified by Klipple,[12] following Stith Thompson, as tales ending with a question (Z. 16). The Sefwi analogue of one of Klipple's tales (from Vai) was identified by my informants as a "long riddle." A variant of another common dilemma is recorded in *Dahomean Narrative*,[13] where it appears incorporated in a straightforward tale.

Prose narratives are part of the cultural tradition of all West African peoples. A first and generally valid dichotomy would appear to be one between fictional and nonfictional narrative. Under the latter heading I would subsume what have been variously considered as myths, legends, and chronicles. These are distinguished from tales proper—that is, from fictional narrative—by the fact that they are regarded in context as true. Ethnographically at least, they are history. Myths, chiefly stories of the deities and the origins of natural phenomena, are especially important throughout West Africa, and a large body of mythology has been record-ed.[14] Legends that recount the origins of families or clans and explain the rituals and taboos of the ancestral code are less well documented. Under-standably so: they are told only for instruction within the group, rarely to outsiders.[15] Fictional material includes, in the main, serious explanatory and moralizing tales, humorous trickster tales, and tales developed wholly or essentially in human society.

By far the best documented of West African prose narratives is the animal trickster type. The protagonists in these stories vary with the fauna of the area in which they are found. While in the dry savannah to the north Hare is the hero of a large cycle of tales, we find that farther to the south first Spider, then Tortoise, takes his place.[16] The same tales are told of all three actors, as well as of human tricksters and trickster deities, and the primary trickster of one area elsewhere figures in a secondary role. In at least one part of West Africa it is possible to observe the actual process of transference from one actor to another. Cardinall[17] has drawn attention to the spread of Anansi, the Akan culture hero, in Togoland. There he ap-pears to be usurping the position of Soamba, or Hare, among the Dagom-ba, in whose tales he figures with increasing frequency as Patinnarega. The character of Spider (he is everywhere selfish, vindictive, and cruel) and his function as a symbol of freedom from physical limitations and moral restraints, has received considerable attention. The matter of his compan-ions and family (he has a wife and adopted son) perhaps deserves more emphasis. Spider is frequently accompanied by a secondary trickster of a less malignant (at times almost lovable) character, as in Sierra Leone. There he is called "Cunnie Rabbit" and is identified with the Royal Ante-lope. Everywhere as foils for the tricksters are Elephant, strong but slow, and Deer, who is helpless and stupid. Hyena is the buffoon of the animal world and the dupe of all.

Although a complete list of all the trickster incidents has not been compiled so far as I know, it is fairly clear that a certain number are found practically wherever the trickster cycle occurs. Most widespread of all, perhaps, is the well-known Tarbaby or Stickfast theme (Type 175). Vari-ants of this incident have been recorded from all areas and adequately illustrate the transfers from one actor to another. Hare or Rabbit, Spider, and Tortoise, in their respective versions, are trapped by a wax maiden, a rubber policeman, or a limed figure. But in Togoland, versions are reported in which an Ashanti soldier plays the role that is elsewhere trickster's, and he is trapped by an old man of Zilimon, who has acquired much magical power from the god Bruku.[18]

An imbalance in our records of West African narrative has been remarked repeatedly and may be due, as has been suggested,[19] in some measure at least, to the influence and fame of the Uncle Remus stories. The predilections of earlier collectors for animal trickster tales are glaring, and undoubtedly they have long been thought of as the typical African tale, with a consequent exaggeration of their importance in terms of both category and character. Cardinall,[20] discussing the spread of Anansi among the Dagomba, somewhere makes this significant remark: "How far this adoption of Anansi is real and how far Anansi has been made the hero especially for European listeners—for all Negroes know we expect the spider to be the hero—cannot be determined."

More recent collections and larger samplings have done much to redress the balance. It is now clear that in some areas the less-well-known human tricksters and trickster-deities are of almost comparable importance. Herskovits has recorded from Dahomey a cycle of tales in which Yo, a trickster of gross sexual appetite, and Legba, a trickster deity, youngest son of the Creator, are the protagonists; and among the Yoruba, according to Bascom, the deities Eshu and Orunmila or Ifa have roles in the narrative cycle analogous to that of Tortoise.

Not all tales involve tricksters. Everywhere are found tales of ogres and other supernatural beings.[21] Very widespread, too, are cycles of tales centered on the adventures of children-born-to-die, twins, orphans, and the precocious child born with magical powers, whom the Akan call Kwaku Babone. A leading actor in another cycle is Hunter, who (sometimes with the help of the long-haired little men) defeats not only the dangerous animals he encounters, but Sasabonsam, the forest monster in the silk cotton tree, and other supernatural spirits.[22]

Two examples of types of tale having a very wide distribution in West Africa are very reminiscent of Thompson's C. 441 (tabu: mentioning the original form of a transformed person) and 563 (the magic objects). In the first type of tale, a vegetable or animal agrees to become the child of a barren woman on condition that its antecedents are never mentioned and returns to its former shape when the bargain is broken. In the second type of tale, there is a magic food-producing object (most commonly a calabash or pot, but sometimes a drum or horn) and a magic beater (nearly always a whip) that punishes the one who steals the former.

Formula tales have been recorded in several areas. Examples of chain and cumulative tales in Malinke, Twi, and Hausa, for example, are to be found in the collections of Frobenius, Rattray, and Tremearne,[23] respectively. (Among the Fulani, Arnott[24] has noted somewhat comparable "chain-rhymes" having a very marked regularity of rhythm, which justifies their being treated as verse rather than prose.)

I have already had occasion to mention one type of formula tale, the unfinished tale or tales ending in a question. If classified as tales, these undoubtedly belong with the miscellaneous groups of motifs (Z. 16) of the Thompson Motif Index of Folk Literature. A widespread example, for which I have personally noted variants among the Vai, the Dangmeli, and the Akan, is very reminiscent of the Four Skillful Brothers (Type 653), because three men working together do what no one alone can do, and because the tale leaves the audience presented with a dilemma. Briefly outlined, the tale is this: Three brothers are on a trading expedition. One acquires a magic mirror in which he sees that the chief's daughter, with whom all three are in love, has died. The second has a magic hammock (or basket or mat) which takes them back before the girl can be buried. The third resurrects the princess by means of a magic medicine. Each claims her as a wife, and the judge, to whom the case is referred in the Vai version, is unable to decide who has done most toward saving her. In an Adangme variant, the tale ends quite simply with the question, "Which of the three is the greater magician?" No solution is suggested. Each person in the audience must give his views and an ad hoc solution is accepted at each telling, depending on the consensus of opinion of those present and the weight of the arguments advanced.[25]

Intimately associated with narrative forms, often as integral parts of them yet distinct and with their own franchise in the life of the people, are riddles, proverbs, and praise-names.

Collections of riddles for the area are relatively meagre, possibly because of the erotic double entendre so frequently associated with them. True riddles (by which term I mean riddles that are logically solvable), riddle-questions (that is, riddles that can be answered only by the initiated), and conundrums or riddles that involve puns and plays on words, are all found. Functionally, there appear to be two main categories of riddle: besides the normal, "polite" riddle commonly heard at children's storytelling sessions, a second "indecent" type is used in certain tribes as a form of abuse. A relateable example from Sefwi, roughly translated, is: "I saw two oranges rolling on the path before the King," which has the implication: "It was your father's two-facedness that got him executed."

Stylistically, the West African riddle is characterized by exaggeration and reference to the grotesque, the incongruous, and the forbidden. As to form, we may say that the enigma is developed generally, though not universally (as we shall see later), through the opposition of two apparently inconsistent declarative sentences. The answer is commonly stated in very simple form.

A widespread and characteristic feature of the riddles of the area is the giving of proper names (sometimes quite meaningless) to the character or object whose identity is to be guessed: Odere, for example, in the Yoruba riddle cited by Bascom:

Q.   "I look here, I look there,
      I don't see my mother, Odere."
Ans. "Ear."

Somewhat similarly, among the L'élá, Nicholas[26] notes the metaphorical use of expressions like "Grandfather" and "children of my mother's hut" to indicate proximity or close resemblance. Toponyms are also employed to suggest long or short distances. Interesting, but, I suspect, minor forms of riddle, based not on visual but acoustic images, have been noted among the Gio of Liberia, the Fulani, and Yoruba.[27]

For example:

Gio: "Wɔzɔ." Ans. "Sound of a falling anana tree."
Yoruba: "Huh" (guess that!). Ans. "Dumb mute" or "Understanding
        of your belly."
Fula: "Kerbu kerbu njolla." Ans. "The sound of goats' feet on hard
        ground."

In recent papers Simmons[28] has described two types of riddle in use among the Oron, Ibibio, and Efik that are not widely paralleled elsewhere.

In the first type, multiple questions (not, it would appear, statements) are posed and similarly answered in multiple form:

Q. "What is kpai kpai, what is kim kim, what is an herbalist under a tree, what is a signal drum, what is ekoŋ play?"

Ans. "Coconut, palm fruit, cocoyam, yam, maize."

The second type Simmons calls "erotic tone riddles." With these, the listener attempts to provide an answer that has one-to-one correspondence tonally with the question posed. The answer may be a proverb, an eroticism, a curse, a sentence, or a nonsense sentence.

The proverb has been treated perhaps more systematically than any other form. Closely related types, the proverbial phrase, for example, which permit change in number, person, or tense, undoubtedly exist, though the distinction between these and the proverb proper is not always stated explicitly in the earlier collections.

"Wellerisms," or quotation proverbs, are known but are probably rare. An example from Hausa I owe to F. W. Parsons,[29] roughly translated, is: "Indifference of the butcher [as] the vulture [said when she] saw the carcass of a motor car."

Almost entirely unstudied, though everywhere existing, is the subclass of *blasons populaires,* of which, again from Hausa, we may quote a single instance: "Katsina, home of genteel poverty, one eats a dimesworth of groundnuts and washes one's hands."

As for proverbial comparisons and clichés, insofar as they have been recorded at all, these are to be found only in the grammars and dictionaries of individual languages, from which they may be elicited by those who seek to make special studies of these forms.

Longer and more involved than the proverb proper is a form noted by Arnott in his paper on the proverbial lore of the Fulani.[30] The form which he calls an "epigram" is very reminiscent of the fifteenth-century European priamel, in that it appears basically to be an accumulation of superficially unrelated ideas united in some unexpected way. These "epigrams," it is to be remembered, are in the main the sophisticated products of professional versifiers in a society much influenced by Islamic culture, and to that extent at least, marginal.

Finally, praise-names, or titles—known, for example, as *kirari* among the Hausas, *oriki* in Yoruba, and *nsabran* by the Akan—are recited throughout the area in honor of deities, chiefs, important individuals, animals, even of inanimate objects, towns, and places: they also figure significantly in the prose narrative.[31] A rather complete collection of the *oriki* of the Yoruba *orisha* can be found in Pierre Verger's monumental work "Notes sur le culte des Orisha et Vodoun."[32] And for the same people, Ulli Beier has published (unfortunately in translation only) additional material in his recent *Yoruba Poetry.*[33]

Having thus briefly outlined the main genres of the area that have so far received the attention of West Africanists, I again revert to a closer consideration of the existing documentation in this field. I have already hinted at marked deficiencies in quantity and quality and suggested possible reasons to account for them. But completely to appreciate the inadequacy of the corpus demands some understanding of the intellectual climate of the period in which the earlier collections were made, the type of collector, and the purely technical difficulties that confronted him.

The earlier period of collecting was much influenced by historico-comparative theories and diffusionist preoccupations in their crudest form. Given such views and such predispositions, content is all; a bare abstract of plot and dramatis personae suffices. Unhappily, the marked swing from this general theoretical standpoint in the last thirty years has not led (as was reasonable to hope) to improved techniques in collecting, but to an almost total neglect of the subject.

At the same time, and perhaps oddly, a somewhat static view of oral tradition led to the preference we have already noted for "purely African" material, unaffected by assimilative and adaptive processes. This is much to be regretted, since innovation is more readily observed in spoken than in other arts. Herskovits[34] has a relevant comment on the facile adjustment from cowries to modern currency effected in Dahomean narratives. A more extreme example I owe to E. C. Rowlands, who tells me that in Yoruba tales Tortoise now attends adult literary classes and hopes ultimately to achieve a white-collar status. Closely related to this static view of folklore is the earlier prevalent misconception of the "correct" form. Both misconceptions have deprived us of much-needed variant versions.

Most of the recorded material that we now have we owe to the pious labors of the amateur collector. Of these, by far the greatest number were, I believe, missionaries. To acknowledge that their interests were somewhat restricted by sensibilities entirely proper to their persuasion is in no way to belittle their very real contribution to our studies. But it has meant that our records are not nearly so representative as they might have been. Typical of the special attitude they held is a passage from the introduction to "Cunnie Rabbit" in which Cronise and Ward speak quite frankly of "another class of tale such as a missionary would not care to hear or record."

It is only with reluctance that one would speak critically of such collectors. Their collecting was done before the advent of the portable tape recorder, in languages laboriously learnt and little studied. Two techniques, it would appear, were largely employed: dictation (out of context) by a native either in his own language or in a translation ad hoc and in situ into English, French, or German. Or, alternatively, direct transcription by literate native speakers, often, as Rattray[35] remarks, in special forms of the local language, unidiomatic, curiously uniform, and pseudoliterary.

The ultimate products of both methods are never more than abstracts, however full, and, as such, undoubtedly serve certain folklorist purposes well enough, as do translations into European languages. But we have had altogether too much translation, and it is difficult to see how, at this stage, the recent publications of, say, Gurrey, Beier, and Herskovits[36] are to be justified other than by appeals to the exigencies of the commercial market.

To preoccupation with translation I would further suspect is due the neglect of such common but minor types of West African verbal art as tongue-twisters and set-verbal formulae, incantations, and the like. These forms are not readily susceptible to, or at least lose their effect in, translation.

The considerable research that has gone into the collection of folklore, and the analysis of plot and theme, is understandable and not, of course, without value. But it can be contrasted only regretfully with the little that has been done to indicate stylistic traits and functions in this area. For what we have been looking at so far are all examples of "literary art in nonliterate societies." They are art in the sense that all of them show a concern for the forms of expression over and above the statements and simple needs of day-to-day communication—a concern that manifests itself at all levels of linguistic structure and analysis.[37]

There are a few exceptions—Bascom's study of "Literary Style in the Yoruba Riddle,"[38] for example—but on the whole scholars have tended to neglect this aspect of style in these, as in other, areas. Yet everywhere there is evidence of stylized and required features. Introductory and closing formulae to the riddle and the tale are universal, and almost as general is the greater freedom of variation in respect to the latter.[39]

Throughout the area the mystic pattern number three features the style. We recall the three brothers of the formula tale outlined earlier, and the tripartite proverbs and riddles of Fulani.[40] In this language, too, the items enumerated in "epigrams" are commonly arranged in threes or multiples of threes.[41]

Repetition figures widely as a stylistic device in all forms. J. H. Nketia has drawn attention to patterns of rhythmic repetition in the heightened language of the Akan funeral dirge.[42] These may be repetitions of sounds, syllables, words, phrases, or tone groups. Coherence of the dirge is achieved primarily by this device; its parts are held together by repetitions functioning as links between the separate thematic statements. Rather similarly, in Fula literary style Arnott has noted the significant repetition of key words and assonance, which in this case is also a form of repetition, deriving from the excessive use of identical suffixes. A related device he calls "parallel phrasing"—that is, again, repetition—but with variation of the key words only.

Arnott has also listed the special grammatical features that characterize Fula proverb style. These may be summarized briefly here as two: first, simplified sentence structures (the anomalous use of nominals or nominal groups, for example, without stabilizing verbs, and the not uncommon use of verbs without subjects); second, special features of the verbal system (the subjunctive tense, for example, used without time reference). Parallels for both these features could be found in many languages of the area. Attention has been drawn to a third feature, the significant absence of connectives in the Yoruba riddle and in one type of Hausa proverb, by Bascom and Parsons, respectively.[43]

Also very common, at a different level, is the device in narrative forms which I myself remarked on some years ago in my transcription of a Ga folktale, whereby identification of an important character is withheld until after the outline of the action is well established and understood.[44] Herskovits, too, has a comment on this feature in *Dahomean Narrative*.[45]

As to vocabulary, there appears to be less unity of practice. Archaisms are noted in the proverbs of many tribes, and in the heightened language of poetry figurative and allusive expressions are commonplace. Especially noteworthy is the stock of poetic clichés within each language, reminiscent of Homer's fixed metaphors or the word-hoard of the Anglo-Saxon bards.

In these it would seem to myself, an outsider, that the metaphorical is neither wholly realized nor wholly missed, belonging to the professional ritual language of poetry and much used in improvisations on traditional themes by skilled amateurs or by professional reciters and raconteurs. Apart from such occasional departures, however, the somewhat unexpected comment is frequently made by students of West African literary forms that the language of both poetry and prose, like the characterization of the tales, is simple and straightforward.[46]

Hand in hand with the view we have taken of folklore as art necessarily goes the recognition that it is spoken art. And since it is spoken rather than written, the reactions of the audience and the mode of expression of the speaker are intimately intertwined. The literary style functions in a highly stylized social setting. Throughout the area, tales are told only at night, and usually after a traditionally institutionalized period of riddling, although among the Akan I have heard tales told in the daytime (but only on special occasions, such as the funeral rites of one who was himself a famous storyteller).

Audience participation and response are an integral part of all West African spoken art, especially of narration. Listeners may be asked and reply directly to questions from the storyteller or, on their own initiative, interject exclamations of assent and approval by way of encouragement. So important to narrative tempo are these interpolated interjections that, if too long delayed, the narrator will frequently substitute his own exclamations of "Good" and the like.[47]

More strikingly effective, perhaps, and equally general is the interpolation of songs and structured jingles at key points in the narrative. I have described the procedures and formulae involved in "cutting" a story (as it is commonly termed) among the Gamei in the paper I earlier mentioned, which was published some years ago. Entirely analogous practices are recorded throughout the area.

As to the creative role of the raconteur in West Africa, testimony to his skill as a literary artist comes from all parts, and many descriptions are to hand of his virtuosity in mime and mimicry. Rattray has described the closeness with which the telling of tales may, on occasion, approach dramatic art. By a rather elaborate makeup, leprosy was simulated with white ash and lumps of clay in the impersonations that accompanied the telling in his presence of Anansesem among the Akan.

Everywhere the subdialect features of nasality and consonantal variants, used for the chief protagonists of the animal-trickster tales, provide opportunities for exploitation of the raconteur's mimic talents. These are well-known features. Spider, for example, among the Hausa is said to "lisp."[48] His speech is characterized phonetically by the palatalization of consonants. In one recording I heard some time ago, I noted the following transcriptions (IPA):

ʃauja (i.e. saura)
ʃu: ne: ʃuka (i.e. su: ne: suka)
ajja (i.e. Alla)
kje: ɓo: ɓji (i.e. ke: ɓo: ɓi)

Among the Akan and peripheral tribes, like Tortoise among the Yoruba, Ananse is envisaged as "speaking down the nose"! Indeed, the Akan version of our English proverb "You don't teach your Grandmother to suck eggs" is roughly translated as "One doesn't teach Spider's children to talk down the nose." Phonetically this well-known speech defect of spiders is most commonly interpreted by the raconteur as nasalization of all vowels that would be oral in more normal speech. A random example from Sefwi transcriptions I have in my notes is of Spider congratulating Asɔyaa. My transcription of this personal name reads: àsɔ̃jã̀:.

Having said that we have much testimony to the virtuosity of the skilled amateur or professional raconteur, I must now go on to say that we have little evidence. This is regrettable but at the same time understandable. Technically perfect and imaginatively and stylistically creative renditions of folktales are unlikely to be obtained in the artificial contexts in which so many of our transcriptions have obviously been and, for that matter still are, elicited. Translations, of course, unsupported by vernacular texts and frequently of an inferior and suspect nature, inevitably result in the loss of much or all stylistic and artistic quality. Nor have we as yet the much-needed variant renderings of the same tale by different raconteurs of acknowledged merit. These would surely give us rewarding insights into narrative art. In this respect, the recent suggestion made separately but coincidentally by my friends W. Whiteley and M. Gilbert Rouget in Oxford and Paris, respectively,[49] will commend itself to us all, whatever our views as to its practicability: that we should, in future collections of African texts, recognize the individual performer as far as is possible, even to the extent of issuing accompanying records as supplementary material.

Finally, after these all too brief observations on content, form, and style, we turn to the social function of these arts within the area—one aspect, at least, of West African folklore that is better understood and documented than most, largely, I imagine, because of the special interest it has always held for the anthropologist and sociologist. Rarely in West Africa is pure entertainment on the artistic level the only motivation. Some other obvious points or sources of motivation will be found embodied in our previous observations: the self-evident function of praise-names as indicated by the term employed to classify them, for example, and the role of myths and legends as sanctions of custom. A ritual or social distinction, or a behavior pattern, often has its origin explained by a myth or legend, and a moralizing fable will show what happens to those who disregard the tribal taboos. The Ifa divining cult among the Fon and Yoruba is, of course, a special case, showing that folktales can be essential parts of religious ceremonies.

Simmons has recently given a rather full list of the functions of riddles in Efik society.[50] Not only are they a source of amusement, but they also function: as greetings (when used by intimates instead of the traditional formulae); in explanation (the answer of the riddle supplies the explanation of a person's action); and (a function we have already noted among the Sefwi, too) as a form of indirect cursing (a riddle is said which implies a derogatory answer). Again, with somewhat similar motivation, they may be used: for erotic double entendre (to embarrass and insult women); or, more respectably, for educational purposes (memory training for children and to sharpen their wits); and finally, along with proverbs, as nicknames (originally men were summoned on the signal gong, hence the use of very familiar forms as names).

Many of these functions are duplicated in the case of proverbs. As is well known, in West Africa these enter into almost every form of interaction.[51] Proverbs are used inter alia as literary devices (for thematic statement in poetry and heightened or elegant prose);[52] in argument, quite simply, to influence others (they are cited much as lawyers cite precedents); or as stereotyped sarcasms (a culturally recognized means of expressing resentment without danger of incurring legal redress). Children in West Africa are taught proverbs and are taught *in* proverbs, and their educational function is nowhere better typified than in the Akan proverb *about* proverbs, which says, "A wise child is talked to in proverbs."

The role of proverbs in the nominative procedures peculiar to and characteristic of West Africa, deserves, I believe, a closer study than it has so far received. Not only are proverbs the basis of many praise-names and titles, but also of more mundane matters: lorries and canoes, cloths and headkerchiefs, and the style of tying and wearing them, are all frequently named by proverbs. Proverb-based names of this type have the especially important and interesting function of expressing—publicly but allusively— resentment, defiance, and derision, or, conversely, approbation and congratulation. An instance from Akan practice will explain. Among the Ashanti, a senior wife who is jealous of a junior co-wife may name a domestic goat or fowl "Ɔkomfo bɔne," alluding thereby to the well-known proverb "ɔkomfo bɔne na ɔhwɛɛ yarefo ma ɔkomfo pa bɛto no" ("the bad 'fetish priest' looked after the sick man till the good one arrived"). In calling the fowl, she recalls the proverb a hundred times a day.

Conversely, among these people, one who has successfully survived impending disaster may assume or acquire, for that reason, the by-name "Abuburo Kosua" (that is, "doves' eggs"), and when so addressed he will respond with the second part of the proverb, "nneɛma a bɛyɛ nsɛɛ" ("things which will be all right, don't spoil").

My main intention, as I stated at the outset, has been to indicate and assess the present state of folklore studies in West Africa. The picture I have so roughly sketched is by no means reassuring. Briefly to summarize the position, among the emergent facts the following are salient.

1. The more traditional aspects of the study—analysis in terms of the provenance, history, and diffusion of narrative incidents, proverbs, and the like—are hampered by the still relatively small available sampling of the total resources of the area. Largely for this reason, I suspect, Klipple, who has made a very exhaustive study of the foreign analogues of African tales,[53] while establishing that versions of a type are often widely distributed over Africa, could reach no very definite conclusions. We still cannot delineate with any conviction the areas of Africa as a whole nor, within the putative areas where we operate today, the minor provinces and subprovinces.

2. There has been a tendency in past collections to concentrate on folktales, and folktales of a special kind, to the exclusion of other minor but no less interesting forms of spoken art—such as tongue-twisters and set-verbal formulae, oaths, incantations, charms, and the like.

3. About certain aspects of form we are woefully ignorant. This is especially true of much of the so-called poetry of the area. The position with regard to Yoruba poetry, as recently summarized by Ulli Beier,[54] is

entirely representative. Whereas Beier can recognize, or claims to recognize, many characteristic features of inner form (his inventory is not markedly different from the general one I myself have given earlier in this discussion), on the other hand he finds outer form difficult to analyze in the absence of European-type meter and rhyme.

4. Studies of the spoken arts in terms of traditional stylistic devices are meager. Here, too, the paucity of texts and the nature of those available are the accounting factors. Especially in the study of the important role of raconteur and verse-maker, we are hindered by lack of suitable transcriptions and/or readily accessible systematic recordings.

After a hundred years of collection and scholarly effort, we are, then, in reality only at the beginning. But there are grounds for optimism. Not least of these is the growing interest of West Africans themselves in their own traditional spoken arts. The political quest for the African personality is reflected elsewhere in a growing preoccupation with African modes of expression, and some stimulus has undoubtedly been provided by the critical acclaim accorded in Europe to recent literary efforts by West Africans that have drawn deeply on the traditional repertory of their cultures.

Whatever the motivations may be, the increased interest and attention of Africans will be welcomed by all in the field. Especially valuable for the fresh insights that will surely derive from them, and, on that account, especially to be hoped for from scholars speaking a West African language as the mother tongue, are contributions in the study of stylistics. Whoever tries, for example, to feel and measure the metaphoric intentions of African poem or poet, will be acutely and continuingly conscious of the intimacy with which both language and literary convention must be known. To such an intimacy, alas, only a very few of us in Europe at the present time can ever hope ultimately to aspire.

December 8, 1960
University of London

NOTES

1. S. W. Koelle, in *Outlines of a Grammar of the Vai Language* (London, 1851); C. F. Schlenker, *A Collection of Temne Traditions* (London, 1861), texts with translations, to which is appended a Temne English vocabulary.

2. Melville J. Herskovits and Frances S. Herskovits, *Suriname Folklore* (New York, 1936).

3. Melville J. Herskovits, *Dahomean Narrative* (Evanston, Ill., 1958).

4. W. R. Bascom, "West Africa and the Complexity of Primitive Cultures," *American Anthropologist* 1, no. 1 (Jan.–Mar. 1948).

5. J. G. Christaller, *Twi Mmusem Mpensa Ahansia Mmoaano* (Basel, 1879).

6. G. Herzog, *Jabo Proverbs from Liberia* (Oxford, 1936); R. S. Rattray, *Ashanti Proverbs* (Oxford, 1916).

7. Cf. D. Rycroft, "Melodic Features in Zulu Eulogistic Recitation," *ALS* 1 (1960): 60–78, on a comparable form in other fields.

8. J. H. Nketia, *Funeral Dirges of the Akan People* (Achimota, 1955).

9. M. M. Green, "Unwritten Literature of the Igbo Speaking Peoples of SE. Nigeria," *BSOAS* 12, pt. 344 (1948): 838.

10. Herskovits, *Dahomean Narrative*.

11. W. R. Bascom, "African and New World Negro Folklore," in *Standard Dictionary of Folklore Mythology and Legend* (New York, 1950).

12. May Klipple, "African Folktales with Foreign Analogues," Ph.D. diss., Indiana University, 1938.

13. *Miscellaneous Tales*, No. 154.

14. Of especially wide occurrence, for example, is the mythological motif of the Raising of the Sky (A. 625.2): originally the sky was near, but the Sky God is annoyed by an old woman who throws hot porridge at him (or knocks him with her pestle as she pounds fufu) and withdraws in anger.

15. These are everywhere regarded as esoteric and sacred: knowledge of a family's totemic myths is believed by some tribes to give power of life or death over its members; cf. R. S. Rattray, *Akan-Ashanti Folktales* (Oxford, 1930): "the historical myths . . . unlike märchen, are the sacred and guarded possession of a few selected elders of the tribe."

16. Typical Spider stories are found among the Akan, Hausa, Vai, and Temne, to name no more. They are markedly absent from the folklore of Calabar, Ikom, and Yorubaland, where Tortoise figures more prominently, and from that of Senegambia and Guinea, which favors the Hare.

17. A. W. Cardinall, *Tales Told in Togoland* (London, 1931).

18. Ibid., p. 233.

19. By Bascom, Herskovits, and Simmons (op. cit.), among others.

20. Cardinall, p. 150.

21. For example, the tales in Hausa of Dodo, whose role is often interchangeable with a witch's. A distinct class of ogres is that of "half-men," as in the Cronise and Ward's Temne story "Marry the Devil and There's the Devil to Pay" (*Cunnie Rabbit, Mr. Spider and the other Beef,* London and New York, 1903), which intro-

duces the recurrent theme of a girl who, after refusing many suitors, is at length won by a devil in the disguise of a handsome man.

22. R. S. Rattray, *Religion and Art in Ashanti* (Oxford, 1927), has some notes on Sasabonsam (p. 28) and on "the little people" (p. 26).

23. Frobenius, *Atlantis,* no. 12 (June 1926): 97ff.; R. S. Rattray, *Ashanti Folktales* (Oxford, 1930); A. J. Tremearne, *Hausa Superstitions and Customs* (London, 1912), pp. 237ff.

24. D. W. Arnott, "Proverbial Lore and Word Play of the Fulani," *Africa* 27, no. 4 (Oct. 1957).

25. This story is very widespread throughout Africa as a whole. It has been noted in the Congo by Dennett (*Notes on Folklore of the Fjort,* 1898) and, in Junod's collection of "Chants et contes des Baranga" (Bridel, Lausanne, 1897), it appears under the title of "Les Trois Vaisseaux." A. Werner (*Myths and Legends of the Bantu,* [London, 1933], p. 320) considers it an importation from the east coast, "whether from Arabia, Persia or India" she is unable to say.

26. Nicholas, "L'élé Riddles from the Haute-Volta," *Anthropos* 49, nos. 5/6 (1954).

27. W. R. Bascom, "Literary Style in Yoruba Riddles," *JAF* 62, no. 243, pp. 1–16.

28. D. C. Simmons, "Specimens of Efik Folklore," *Folklore* 66 (Dec. 1955): 417–24; "Erotic Ibibio Tone Riddles," *Man* 56, no. 78 (June 1956): 79–82.

29. Personal communication.

30. Arnott, "Proverbial Lore," pp. 379–96.

31. Cf. the introduction of Folktale 21 in Rattray's *Akan-Ashanti Folktales,* p. 71, in which the titles of the rock hyrax, the chameleon, and the owl are rehearsed.

32. *Mémoires de l'Institut Français d'Afrique Noire* (Dakar, 1957).

33. (Lagos, 1959.)

34. Herskovits, *Dahomean Narrative,* p. 71.

35. R. S. Rattray, "Some Aspects of West African Folklore," *JAS* 28 (1929): 2.

36. Phebean Itayemi and P. Gurrey, *Folktales and Fables* (London, 1953); Ulli Beier, *Yoruba Poetry* (Ibadan, 1959); Herskovits, *Dahomean Narrative* (1958). All the authors complain of the difficulties of translation and of how much is lost by it: not one offers so much as a fragment of original text by way of support or example.

37. Cf. W. R. Bascom, "Verbal Art," *JAF* 68 (1955): 245–52.

38. *JAF* 62, no. 243 (1949): 1–16.

39. The formulae connected with the folktale are well known and well documented. Less well known perhaps are the formulae for "riddling." Especially interesting are the "surrender" formulae, by which anyone who fails to solve a riddle must "surrender" a town or village to the person posing it. Arnott (p. 382) gives in

detail the Pankshin version of the Fula surrender formula. The name for riddle among the L'élá (it is a compound of two nouns and a nominal class prefix, having the rough translation meaning "tale-village") probably alludes to the forfeiture of a village by one who fails to solve a riddle.

With regard to the greater freedom of variation in the closing formulae of tales, compare, for example, Herskovits, *Dahomean Narrative,* p. 541: "But a story-teller often plays with his ending. . . . "

40. Cf. H. Gaden, *Proverbs et maximes peuls et toucouleurs* (Paris, 1931), Nos. 209, 392, 393, 394, 404, etc. Riddles in Fula, as elsewhere, usually have a single theme, but tripartite riddles do occur: Arnott, p. 384, n. 1.

41. As, for example, in the epigrams cited by Arnott which begin: "Three exist where three are not" and "Three are like three."

42. Nketia, *Funeral Dirges of the Akan People.*

43. W. R. Bascom, *Literary Style in Yoruba Riddles:* "A noteworthy characteristic of Yoruba riddles, particularly since the enigma is generally developed through the opposition of an apparently inconsistent declarative sentence, is the absence of 'but' (sugbon), 'and' (ati), 'or' (tabi)." F. W. Parsons (personal communication): "Usually one part (of the tripartite proverb) consists of a string of nouns, without any connectives, other than the genitive copula, and the other part of a normal sentence with a verb in it."

44. J. Berry, "A Ga Folktale," *BSOAS* 12, no. 2 (1948).

45. *Dahomean Narrative,* p. 50: "Again [in No. 107] the name of one of the characters is given only after the outline of the action is well understood."

46. For example, Nketia, pp. 103–4. "Apart from allusive and occasional figurative language consistent with the poetic form of the dirge . . . much of the language is ordinary and straightforward. . . . "

47. *Dahomean Narrative,* p. 52: " . . . in the absence of an audience, or where the interjection is too long delayed, the narrator himself pauses to exclaim 'Good.'"

48. A. Werner, *African Mythology* (Boston, 1925), p. 324: "A peculiarity everywhere attributed to the Spider is his inability to pronounce words in the ordinary way. In Hausa he speaks with a lisp and says shaki for sarkin ['chief'] and doyina for droina ['hippopotamus'], &c."

49. W. Whiteley, *African Literature* (Oxford, 1960); G. Rouget, personal communication.

50. D. C. Simmons, "Specimens of Efik Folklore," *Folklore* 66 (Dec. 1955): 417–24.

51. Cf. especially J. B. Christensen, "The Role of Proverbs in Fante Culture," *Africa* 28, no. 3 (1958).

52. The moral precept of an apologue is often pointed by concluding the tale with a proverb. Conversely, the meaning of a proverb may be derived from a

folktale in which it occurs. Of the many proverbs throughout the area of the pattern

"Tortoise says——"
"Goat says——"

some are, no doubt, originally quotations from characters in folktales.

53. Klipple, "African Folktales with Foreign Analogues" (n. 12 above).
54. Beier, *Yoruba Poetry,* pp. 8–11.

INTRODUCTION

▼▲▼▲▼▲▼▲▼▲▼▲▼▲▼▲▼▲▼▲▼▲▼▲▼▲▼▲▼▲▼

RICHARD A. SPEARS

Storyteller: Now this story—I didn't make it up!
Audience: Who did then?

The foregoing is a typical opening formula for storytelling in the Sefwi language of Ghana, and it might well serve as the opening formula for this book. It is the peoples of West Africa who are the authors of these tales.

This book contains stories about animal tricksters, moralizing tales, how-and-why tales, and tales that instruct. The original settings in which these were told involved singing, acting, using a variety of voices, and, above all, audience participation. One may note with some regret that typical Western literature excludes almost all of the storytelling devices found in West African spoken art. Westerners are obliged to indicate these things through choice of vocabulary, style, metaphor, and other literary techniques.

The tales have been edited and arranged to make them readable by, or tellable to, non-Africans with the fewest possible obstacles to the tellers or the audience. One of the goals of the arrangement has been to keep the actual texts of the tales as free of distracting encumbrances as possible. Following Jack Berry's lead, an attempt has been made to focus sharply on the story line of each tale by placing all explanatory and supplementary materials at the back of the book, in the Notes and Index sections.

No titles were provided with Berry's tales. Those which appear here I devised expressly for this book. They are intended to pique interest in the reader and reveal some aspect of the major theme of the tale they introduce. The tales are not grouped according to language or motif but are ordered so that one can read the book straight through, encountering variety as one goes. In this form, each of the tales is suitable for reading or telling without digressions to explain the names, opening and closing formulae, audience participation, songs, and other operatic devices that are an integral part of the African cultures in which these stories are told. Through this conversion to Western patterns and expectations, the original simplicity, purposeful innocence, directness, and moral tone of the original tales have been preserved. No attempt has been made to doctor or censor the tales for the sensibilities of a Western, English-speaking audience.

This book is unique in the care and accuracy that have been applied to its translation and in the conversion from African to Western folk traditions. The tales are as enlightening for modern American adults and children as they are for African adults and children. In fact, in reading them, one can begin to see, not the differences in our cultures, but the similarities.

THE TELLING OF A TALE

There is a considerable difference between a West African folktale told in situ and its simple narrative or story line. All of the tales in this book occurred originally in a setting where the storyteller and the audience interacted, both parties having specific rights and obligations. The actual setting typically includes a group of people who take turns telling tales. Each storyteller begins the tale with an opening formula, essentially announcing that a tale is about to be told, and the audience follows with some sort of response. At the end of the tale, the storyteller brings the tale to a formal close, usually with an ending formula, and may call upon the next storyteller to begin. During the telling of a tale, it is not uncommon for someone to interrupt with some totally irrelevant remark, or perhaps a correction. Many tales include songs that are sung by the storyteller or by the entire group. Next to being there in person and participating, only a video recording could provide a satisfactory record of all the events that are part of the traditional West African storytelling session.

This collection does not attempt to reproduce the performance elements, which can be quite complicated and require a significant amount of specific knowledge of a number of different West African cultures and languages. This is not because the collector of the tales, Jack Berry, was not conscious of or interested in these details. A reading of his professorial inaugural address of December 8, 1960, reprinted as the preface to this book, will reveal just the opposite. However, although these matters were of great interest to Berry, they are not the subject of this book. The story lines of these folktales have been extracted from the storytelling setting and presented in a way that makes the folk motifs evident for simple reading pleasure. By the way, such extraction of the story lines of tales is not wholly foreign to West Africa: missionaries have used folktales in printed form for the purpose of literacy training for decades.

There are very good storytellers, and very poor ones too. The best add a sense of drama—careful timing, appropriate voices—and sustain a dynamic relationship with the audience. The worst leave out parts of the story, put story elements in the wrong order, mix elements from different stories, and rush through the whole performance.

ABOUT THE TRANSLATOR

Jack Berry was one of the cofounders and the first chairman of the Department of Linguistics at Northwestern University. He was a specialist in West African languages and culture, and throughout his career he collected folktales from Africans in Africa, England, and the United States. During the last decade of his life—up to his death in 1980—he devoted a considerable amount of time to translating, editing, and preparing this collection of tales for an English-speaking audience. This book contains the finished collection. His thoughts on West African spoken art—narrative, proverbs, and riddles—are documented in the Preface.

This collection constitutes the first phase of an African folktale project begun by Berry in the 1950s. The phase represented by this book consists of a variety of West African folktales translated and edited to show the important elements of each tale with a minimum of embellishment and elaboration. The second phase was intended to be an analysis of the folk motifs and story elements of these tales and a comparison of these motifs and elements to those found in folktales told elsewhere in Africa and in the rest of the world. This ambitious project was to include a bibliography of previous publications of the same or similar tales, as well as citations of all relevant points from existing folk-motif indices, and was sadly interrupted by Berry's death in 1980. At that time, the second phase consisted of marginal notes on an early typescript of the tales and a set of his own bibliographies showing the type of material he was consulting. The marginal notes were too incomplete and sketchy to be included in this volume. But the material remains in the Northwestern University Archives awaiting the resumptive energies of a successor.

Although the methodology used in gathering the material must have varied over three decades of collecting, Berry strove to have as much "naive" African input as possible, hoping, one supposes, to avoid a "pseudoliterary" style in the telling of the tales. Furthermore, Berry, unlike many of the earlier collectors and translators, was very much aware of the stylistic devices and folk motifs found in West Africa and would not allow any significant story element, no matter how subtle, to be lost in translation. This book must be viewed as an outgrowth of an attempt to catalog the distribution of known folk motifs in West African languages. It is most regrettable that Berry did not live long enough to complete the task.

COLLECTION AND SOURCES

Jack Berry collected versions of West African folktales in West Africa starting in the mid-1950s. Many of the tales that appear here are traditional and well known in many African countries. In addition to the firsthand collection of tales, Berry also collected a number of printed versions of the tales—both in the original languages and in translation—when they were available. His edited versions of the tales were based on material collected directly from Africans, but it is almost certain that some of the previously printed versions were used to corroborate his work.

The bulk of the material on which this book is based was collected during the early 1970s as part of a project for the training of American doctoral students in fieldwork in West Africa. Berry and the students were in Ghana at the time, and they worked with informants as well as with Africans associated with African universities. Much of this work was concerned with verifying material in the Akan languages previously collected by Berry. The versions of Ga and Yoruba tales told by Kotei and Abimbola were recalled by these two Africans—graduate students at Northwestern University—who participated with Berry in translating the tales.

A smaller number of tales came into Berry's possession from colleagues who were aware of his project and his interest in the tales. Berry himself was very active in collecting tales in the languages that were his primary interests: Ga, Twi, Sefwi, and Krio.

THE NOTES

Information about particular tales can be found in the Notes section that begins on page 199. The number of each note corresponds to the numbering of the tales. The language in which the present version of the tale was told is listed after the title, followed in parentheses by the country where the tale was told. In the few cases where this information is not available, the language is almost certainly one of the Akan languages of Ghana. The set of initials that follows the language indicates the name of the person who most recently corroborated the tale. Those individuals are fully identified in the Acknowledgments below. This information is not available for all the tales. Many tales begin and end with traditional opening and closing formulae, which are given in the notes at their first use. Tales with similar themes are cross-referenced in the notes, and bits of information that may help the reader to understand the tale are included in some notes.

THE INDEX

The Index is a combination of a number of different types of indices and includes entries for each character name, an indication of pronunciation for foreign words and proper names, subjects, themes, motifs, and entries for each language represented in the book, with a list of the tales in that language. This integrated approach, though not complex, allows easy access to the recurrent character names and motifs of the tales both for the casual reader and for those who have a professional interest in folklore. Annotations within the index allow it to serve as a simple encyclopedia explaining the non-Western terms and concepts encountered in the tales. Cross-referencing is a further aid to identifying related terms and dialectal variants.

Many of the tales contain names and words from various African languages. All of these words appear in the Index, and each is followed by suggestions for pronunciation set in a type of phonetic respelling. It should be emphasized that these pronunciations are not necessarily the way the word or name is pronounced in a particular African language, but only a convenient guide for English speakers. A Guide to Pronunciation explaining the phonetic respelling system follows the Index.

One can easily find the numbers of all the tales told in a particular language by looking up that language name in the Index. One can also find all the stories about Spider or Tortoise by looking up those subjects. Other widely known West African folk motifs, such as the pineapple child, also have entries. If "Pineapple child" is consulted, one will find listed all the tales having this motif, as well as a reference to a similar theme, the fish child.

ACKNOWLEDGMENTS

The authorship of these tales lies with the people of West Africa. For each of the tales, Berry had, in addition to his own versions, corroborative versions either in translation or in the original language, as well as versions collected or verified by other persons.

Here are the full names of corroborating individuals and their roles:

A.S., tales told in Mende (Sierra Leone), Augustine Stevens

B.J., tales told in Larteh and Twi (Ghana), Bruce Johnson

C.G., tale told in Cameroon Pidgin (Cameroon), collected by Charles Gilman

D.A., tales told in Fula and Hausa (Nigeria), collected by David Arnott

E.J., tale told in Krio (Sierra Leone), version from Eldred Jones

G.A., tales told in Ga (Ghana), collected by Gilbert Ansre

G.I., tale told in Mandinka (Gambia), collected by Gordon Innes

G.O.B., tales told in Twi (Ghana), Godfrey Ofasu Bekoe

H.M., tales told in Twi (Ghana), Helaine Minkus

L.L., tales told in Ga (Ghana), Lantei Lawson

L.T., tale told in Krio (Sierra Leone), version from Lorenzo Turner

N.A.K., tales told in Ga (Ghana), retold by Nii Amon Kotei

S.M., tales told in Krio (Sierra Leone), version from Salakor Maxwell

T.Y.E., tales told in various Akan languages (Ghana), collected by T. Y. Enin

W.A., tales told in Yoruba (Nigeria), retold by Wande Abimbola

W.G., tale told in Avatime (Ghana), Winifred Gadzeti

Stevens is a speaker of Mende and Krio from Sierra Leone whose tales were recalled from childhood. Johnson collected tales in Ghana from various informants as part of his doctoral training. Gilman collected a tale in Cameroon previous to his doctoral training. Arnott, a former colleague of Berry's at the School of Oriental and African Studies, University of London, collected the Fula and Hausa tales from informants in Africa. Jones is an African scholar who provided a version of a Krio tale. Ansre is an African scholar who provided a version of a Ga tale. Innes, one of Berry's first doctoral students and a former colleague of Berry's at the School of Oriental and African Studies, University of London, collected the Mandinka tale in situ in West Africa. Bekoe and Lawson are Ghanaians who submitted tales collected from informants. Minkus collected from informants in Ghana as part of her doctoral training. Lawson is the source of a number of tales in the Ga language. Turner's work provided a corroborative version of a Krio tale. Kotei retold a number of tales in the Ga language. Maxwell provided versions of two tales in Krio. Enin did a considerable amount of fieldwork—collecting and translating—of versions of various tales. Abimbola retold a number of tales in the Yoruba language. Gadzeti told one tale in Avatime.

Jack Berry was fluent in all of these languages except Fula, Hausa, and Yoruba, although he had a thorough linguistic knowledge of these three. He oversaw the final translation of each tale into English and saw the tales through their first typed draft. At the time of his death, he had begun to correct the typescript and make notes and comments in the margins. I undertook to bring the work to its current form, following Berry's lead where it was apparent. In order to make this volume stand independently as Phase One of the project, a few additional editorial tasks had to be undertaken. An attempt was made to reduce the amount of cultural material that required elaborate explanation. Adjustments—mentioned in the Notes—were made to stories having untranslated songs. Occasionally some license has been taken with Berry's translations to make the elements of wordplay clearer. Other significant deviations are mentioned in the Notes section. The spelling was converted from British English to American English. Seven tales in the collection were not used for various reasons.

A panel of readers—faculty and students of the linguistics department—was asked to appraise the flow of the story lines and general interest of the selected tales. Their comments were valuable to developing the Notes and the Index. Thanks are due to the following people—faculty and students of the Department of Linguistics, Northwestern University—who volunteered to read the tales and to comment on them: Scott Allen, Rosemary Buck, Terrie Byrne, Abraham Demoz, Kate Dowe, Duke Ferguson, Steve Forsythe, David Frayne, Karen Frayne, Morris Goodman, Bob Gundlach, Kathy Harris, Judy Hochberg, Steve Kleinedler, Rebecca Lee, Judy Levi, Linda Llano, Talke MacFarland, Sharzad Mahootian, Judith Markowitz, Rae Moses, Lisa Orlandi, Regina Paik, Brad Pritchett, John Reitano, Julie Schiltgen, and Gregory Ward.

WEST AFRICAN FOLKTALES

1 The Scarecrow

Once upon a time the Spider, Anaanu, made a huge yam farm, together with his wife Kornorley and his son Kwakute. When the time for harvesting was drawing near, Anaanu called his family together, and when they had all assembled, he told them that he believed he was about to die. He told them that his wish was to be laid in a coffin, after his death, and for the coffin to be left in the middle of their beloved farm. The lid of the coffin was not to be nailed down. And inside the coffin, to accompany him to the land of the dead, his family were to put a grinding-bowl and ladle and all the other cooking utensils.

Three days later, Anaanu died. His family had already found a coffin and all the cooking utensils. His instructions were followed faithfully, as is proper when an elderly person, and particularly the head of a family, departs from this world. The coffin was taken to the farm unsealed and left in the middle of the place, right there among the yams.

In the middle of the night, Anaanu got up, came out of the coffin, uprooted some yams, and cooked and ate them. Then he retired to a well-fed rest inside his coffin.

In the morning, when his family came to the farm, they noticed that some of the yams had been uprooted, but they said nothing.

That night, Anaanu did just the same, and the following morning his family again noticed that more yams had disappeared. But again they went away in silence.

This went on day after day and night after night, with Anaanu stuffing himself, and his family getting more and more worried about the way the yams were disappearing.

When the yams were almost all gone, Kwakute said he couldn't let things go on this way any longer. He had thought up a plan by which they might be able to do something about the thefts. The family made a scarecrow, a man's figure, of sticky, gluey rubber and left the figure on the farm.

At night, when Anaanu came out of his coffin as usual to eat the yams, he saw this human figure standing among the yams. He was annoyed and shouted, "Who are you?" The figure didn't answer. Anaanu wasn't going to leave it at that. "If you do not answer me," he said, "I'll slap you with my right hand."

The figure didn't say a word, so Anaanu slapped it with his right hand, and the hand got stuck in the glue. Now he said, "If you don't let go of my right hand, I'll slap you with my left." The figure didn't move. So Anaanu slapped it with his left hand, and that got stuck, too. And now, more furious than ever, "Unless you let go of my hands immediately, I'll kick you with my right foot." The figure didn't move. So Anaanu kicked it with his right foot, and that became stuck even harder than his right hand. With furious exclamations, Anaanu kicked with his left foot, and that got stuck, too.

Finally he threatened loudly, "Unless you release me at once, I shall push you down with my stomach."

The figure didn't move. So Anaanu drew his belly back and swung it forward with great force. But now he was completely stuck to the glue, spread-eagled on the scarecrow.

In the morning, when Kwakute, Kornorley, and the rest of the family came to the farm to uproot some yams, there was the thief stuck to the scarecrow. "We have got him, at last!" they shouted and rushed forward to take down the thief and start beating him. But when they got near, who could it be but their own father and husband, the dead Anaanu!

They slowly pulled him loose from the scarecrow. But Anaanu was so ashamed of himself that he could not stand around. As soon as his feet touched the ground he ran away home, and even there he didn't stop until he had hidden his face in the eaves of the roof, where the darkness is.

That is why the spider always stays in the eaves of the roof.

▼▲▼▲▼▲▼▲▼▲▼▲▼▲▼▲▼▲▼▲▼▲▼▲▼▲▼▲▼▲

2 The Wise Fool

A poor peasant woman bore many sons. All except one lived normal, useful lives and did well. Naturally their mother loved them. One of them was born a fool, and he was neglected and left to shift for himself as best he could. All day long he worked on a large patch of sandy soil, not far from the village. Everybody laughed at him all the time.

One day the mother went to her garden and there found a baby with very long hair lying on its back under a big tree. It was crying and kicking. It looked hungry and neglected. The woman fed and nursed it, and soon it fell asleep. She worked all day on the farm and no one came for the baby. When night began to fall, the woman took the child home with her. Again the next day nobody came for the baby, so she cut its long hair.

Soon afterward, a troupe of fairy people came to the village to claim the baby. When they found that its hair had been cut, they demanded that it be put back. This, of course, was impossible. They demanded that if the woman could not make the baby's hair grow again, she was to be taken away and killed. The chief and the elders did everything in their power to appease the fairies. They offered gifts—gold ornaments, land, slaves—everything to no avail. The fairies were adamant. The woman must die!

Further discussion seemed useless, and the meeting was just about to break up when the fool walked up and demanded to be heard. "Listen to me," he said. "The fairies say my mother should die. It is a fair punishment for her crime. But the fairies walked across my land as they came to the village. I demand that they rub out their footprints before they are allowed to take mother away." It seemed a foolish, meaningless demand, and everyone said, "How simple!" The fairies agreed.

At sundown the fairies were still working on the sandy plot. Two days went by. And a week. And another. Because just as one set of footprints were got rid of, another set appeared. By the end of the second week, in fact, the fairies had covered the entire plot with footprints. At last they gave up and let the woman live.

That is why even today, children who do not do well are not cast out, but treated fairly. Wisdom hides in many places.

▽▲▽▲▽▲▽▲▽▲▽▲▽▲▽▲▽▲▽▲▽▲▽▲▽▲▽▲▽▲

3 Why We Tell Stories About Spider

In the olden days stories were told about God, not about Anaanu, the Spider. One day, Anaanu felt a very strong desire to have stories told about him. So he went to God and said, "Dear God, I want to have your stories told about me."

And God said, "My dear Anaanu, to have stories told about you is a very heavy responsibility. If you want it, I will let you have it, but first you must prove to me that you are fit to have it. I want you to bring me three things: first, a swarm of bees; second, a live python; third, a live leopard, the King of the Forest himself. If you can bring me these three things, I will allow the stories that are told about me to be told about you instead."

Anaanu went away and sat down and thought. For three whole days he sat and thought. Then he got up, smiling, and took a huge calabash with a lid. He put some honey in this calabash, set it on his head, and he walked into the forest. He came to a place where a swarm of bees was hovering around some branches. Then he took the calabash off his head, opened the lid, and started saying loudly to himself while looking into the calabash, "They can fill it; they can't fill it; they can fill it; they can't fill it."

The bees heard him and asked, "Anaanu, what are you talking about?"

And Anaanu said, "Oh, it would be nothing if it were not for that foolish friend of mine. We had an argument. I said that, despite the honey in the calabash, there is still enough space for the makers of the honey to go into the calabash. But he said you are too many, that you cannot go inside the space that is left. I say you can fill it; he says you can't."

Then the leader of the bees said, "Ho! That is easily proved. We can go inside." So he flew into the calabash. And all the bees flew in after him. As soon as they were all inside, Anaanu clapped the lid onto the calabash, very tightly, and took the calabash to God. He said, "I have brought you the first thing, the swarm of bees." And God looked inside the calabash and said, "Well done, Anaanu, but where are the python and the leopard?"

Anaanu went away into the forest and cut a long stick from a branch of a tree. He scraped all the bark off this stick so that it became a long white pole. Then he went deeper into the forest, carrying the pole and shouting to himself, "It is longer than he; it is not longer than he; it is longer than he; it is not longer than he."

Now the python, who was very proud of his length, for which he was feared throughout the forest, was lying down curled up and resting. When he saw Anaanu, he said, "What are you talking about, Anaanu?"

And Anaanu said, "Oh, it is nothing but an argument that I had with a very ignorant and foolish friend of mine. Do you know that when I told him that you are longer than this stick, from the black mark to the other end, he refused to believe me, and said the stick is longer than you? I say you are longer; he says you are not."

The python growled and said, "What! There is nobody in this world longer than I. As for that stick, bah! I shall soon show you who is longer."

So saying, Python stretched himself beside the stick, putting his head on the black mark. Anaanu said, "To be sure I get the correct length by which you exceed the stick, let me tie you closely to the stick so you won't wiggle and seem shorter." So Anaanu tied Python firmly to the stick. But as soon as Anaanu had finished doing so, he lifted the stick onto his shoulder and said, "Now, my friend, we will go on a little journey." Then he took the python to God and said, "I have brought you the second thing, the python."

And God looked at the long pole with its burden and said, "Well done, Anaanu, but you still have to bring me Leopard, the King of the Forest himself."

Anaanu went away and dug a deep pit in the forest, on Leopard's path, and covered the pit with sticks and leaves. Leopard, who was going hunting for his food, soon came along the trail and fell into the pit. He was trapped and couldn't get out. Anaanu soon appeared, as if by chance, and said, "Eh, is this King Leopard himself? Well, well, well! But if I am kind enough to bring my family to help me get you out of this pit, you will reward us by eating us all."

But Leopard replied, "How can you talk like that, Anaanu? How could I do such a thing after you have saved my life? I promise that, if you get me out of this pit, no leopard will ever eat a spider again."

And Anaanu said, "All right, I believe you. I will call my family to help get you out of this pit." So Anaanu brought his family and also a heavy stick and a lot of rope. He threw the stick into the pit and jumped in after it. And he told Leopard, "Since you are so heavy, we will have to hoist you out with this stick and some ropes." So Leopard took hold of the stick between his four paws. Anaanu tied first his two front paws to the stick and then his two hind paws, all very firmly. Then his family hoisted them both out of the pit. But as soon as they came out, Anaanu jumped off and grabbed the tail end of the pole. He told Leopard, "Now we will go and visit someone you know." So saying, he dragged the stick with its load to God and said, "I have brought you Leopard, the King of the Forest himself." And God looked at Anaanu and said, "You have done very well, Anaanu. You have achieved the impossible. You deserve to have stories told about you. So from today I decree that the stories that were once told about me shall be told about you."

And that is why stories are told about Anaanu, the spider.

▼▲▼▲▼▲▼▲▼▲▼▲▼▲▼▲▼▲▼▲▼▲▼▲▼▲▼▲▼▲

4 How Tortoise Won by Losing

Tortoise and his wife had no food to eat. Tortoise therefore decided that he would approach his father-in-law and beg for food. He did so, and his father-in-law was very happy to offer Tortoise yams, corn, and vegetables. He took Tortoise to his farm and showed him all around it and let Tortoise take what he wanted.

Within a few days, Tortoise and his wife had finished the food given to them, and they became very hungry again. They wanted more food, but Tortoise was ashamed to go back to his father-in-law to ask for more. He decided to help himself. Tortoise left his house at midnight and went straight to his father-in-law's farm. There he took yams, corn, vegetables, and other things, packed them in a big basket, and tried to lift the load onto his head, but the load was too heavy, and he could not lift it. He kept on trying and trying until morning, when his father-in-law saw him and seized him.

The father-in-law then tied Tortoise to a tree by the side of the road where everybody would see him. When people saw Tortoise disgraced thus, they asked his father-in-law what he had done. He told them that Tortoise had stolen his crops. Then they praised him for being able to catch such a sly thief as Tortoise. But the same people who had praised him in the morning were returning from their farms in the evening and found Tortoise still tied to the same tree, and they went to the father-in-law and asked, "Is Tortoise not your son-in-law? Why should you tie a man with ropes to a tree from morning till evening, even if that man is a thief? Do you want to kill him? Surely you have shown yourself to be more evil than the thief."

So in this way Tortoise's wrongdoing was shifted to his father-in-law.

This is an example of how someone can make himself unpopular by placing his rights before his human feelings.

▼▲▼▲▼▲▼▲▼▲▼▲▼▲▼▲▼▲▼▲▼▲▼▲▼▲▼▲

5 The Power of the Temper

Once upon a time there lived a woman who had no child. This woman was very rich, but she was barren, and she had always wanted to have a child.

One day the woman went to the seashore. She saw something lying on the sands as if it had been washed up from the sea. She took this thing home with her.

When she got to her room, the thing started talking. It asked her what she wanted most in life. The woman said she most wanted to have a child. Then the thing told her that her wish would be granted.

Soon afterward the woman had a child. She named the baby Dede, which means "satisfaction" or "salvation."

The woman loved her baby very much. She was so fond of the child that, as it grew up, she could never bring herself to correct it no matter what it did wrong.

But one day Dede did something that was very, very bad. Then her mother scolded her harshly. Dede became angry, cried, and threatened to return to where she had come from. Her mother begged her over and over again not to go. But still Dede cried and said she was going.

Then suddenly a mermaid appeared. And Dede went to her. The mermaid took Dede on her back, and they both went back into the sea.

Soon afterward the woman began losing her money, and she became very poor. Because of her temper, she lost both her baby and her fortune.

▼▲▼▲▼▲▼▲▼▲▼▲▼▲▼▲▼▲▼▲▼▲▼▲▼▲▼▲▼▲

6 The Contest Between Fire and Rain

A very, very beautiful young girl was being wooed by all the men in the neighborhood. Although she was of age, she would not agree to marry any of them. Two of the principal suitors of the young girl were Fire and Rain. The young girl could not decide which of the two renowned young men she should marry. Then she said that she would marry whoever succeeded in beating the other in a contest.

A date was named for the contest, and Fire and Rain gathered together all their friends, relatives, and admirers in order to show how powerful they were. Rain boasted that he was going to win the contest. Fire boasted that he was going to win instead.

On the day of the contest Fire set out to burn all the bushes and all the rooftops. He started to burn all the trees and grass, robbing the birds of their nests, driving all the animals from their burrows, and destroying their paths in the forests. He started to burn the farmer's crops and to lay waste to the whole area of the contest. Everybody thought that Fire would win the contest.

They all sang: "Look at Fire! The bright one! The very tall one!"

Suddenly dark clouds gathered in the sky, and they grew, and they gathered until they formed a thick mass. Then torrents of rain began to fall. The contest had started in earnest.

Then the spectators again sang: "Look at Fire! The bright one! The very tall one! Look at Rain! The black one! The falling one! Which will you choose?"

And the beautiful young girl answered, "Instead of choosing Fire or Rain now, I will wait for the end of the contest."

Fire grew higher and brighter. The showers of rain grew bigger and bigger, and Rain fell and put out all Fire's life and energy. Of course, when Rain started to fall in great torrents, all the spectators fled for their lives. They ran away and hid until Rain was over. When Rain stopped they found that the beautiful young girl was nowhere to be seen. Rain had carried away his bride in thunderous torrents of water.

As the people returned to their homes, they sang: "Here is Fire, the bright one, the very tall one. Here is Rain, the black one, the falling one. Rain conquers Fire, and the contest is over."

▼▲▼▲▼▲▼▲▼▲▼▲▼▲▼▲▼▲▼▲▼▲▼▲▼▲▼▲▼▲

7 The Constant Parrot

One day a very brave hunter went into the forest to hunt for animals, but after hunting in the forest the whole day, he still had killed nothing.

He then saw a parrot and decided to kill that, just so he wouldn't return home empty-handed. But as he pointed his gun at the parrot, it started to speak. The parrot begged the man not to kill him, but to spare his life. And it promised that if the man did not kill it, it would reward him on another future day. The man took pity on the parrot and spared its life.

Many years afterward, this same hunter was involved in a very difficult situation. He was charged with murder because he had unknowingly shot a man whom he had mistaken for an animal in the forest, and he had killed him. The man that this hunter killed was a very popular man in the town, and pressure was brought to bear on the king to sentence the poor hunter to die for his crime. The hunter had been brought before the king of his town and had been imprisoned.

The day of a festival in the town was the time the king had set to execute the hunter, but he said that he would spare his life if the hunter could pass a test. The hunter would have to recognize the king on the day of the festival.

When the day of the festival came, the hunter was brought before a very large crowd of people who had come to watch. The hunter was asked to pick out the king of the town from among the guests of honor at the occasion. Some of these guests wore very costly garments, others had very costly crowns on their heads, some had beaded walking sticks, while others had only rags to cover their heads. Some were naked to the waist, others wore masks, and all of them were supposed to be the important guests of honor at the festival.

The hunter was brought before the crowd and was asked to tell who was the king. At that very moment the hunter noticed a parrot alighting on top of a tree close to him, and the parrot was singing this song: "Hunter, hunter, goodness has its reward. Continue to do good. The one who has the beaded walking stick is not the king. The one who wears a very costly garment is not the king. The one who is in rags is the king."

At first the hunter did not know what the song was about, but after some time he remembered that many years ago he had met a very strange parrot singing with the voice of a man in just the same way. He listened more carefully, and again he heard the parrot sing: "Hunter, hunter, goodness has its reward. Continue to do good. The one who wears a very costly crown is not the king. The one who wears a very costly garment is not the king. The one who has the beaded walking stick is not the king. But the one who is in rags is the king."

Then he remembered the promise that the parrot had made to him when he had spared the parrot's life. He walked straight into the crowd and touched the guest of honor who was in rags and proclaimed him to be the king.

Many people started to laugh at him because of the man he touched, but when the face of the man was uncovered, everybody was surprised to see that the man in rags was indeed the king.

So the life of the hunter was spared and, in addition, the king and all the guests of honor gave him many presents for his wisdom in being able to recognize the king.

This story teaches us that we should be kind to our fellowmen, and that we should be kind to all the animals and the birds because, for a kindness done even to a bird, there could be a reward.

8 Aja and the Enchanted Beast

Once upon a time there lived a woman called Ajanye, and she had a son called Aja. Aja could do many magic things. For instance, he could find water when all the rivers were dry, and things like that. And he was a very good hunter, too. But in the bush around where Aja and his mother were living was an enchanted beast, a bad one, and he had the same sort of magical powers that Aja had. This enchanted beast liked to change into an antelope to deceive people.

One day Aja was hunting in the bush when he saw an antelope. Bang! He shot it, and it fell down. But it didn't die. No, it changed into a man. So Aja shot the man, too, and this time he killed him. The man was really the enchanted beast who lived in the bush. Aja cut open the man and took out his heart. He buried the rest and took the heart home with him. He gave it to his mother to look after for him, and he told her to put it in the sun each day and keep it very dry. No water should get to the heart at all, or something bad might happen.

His mother looked after the heart for Aja for quite a long time, and she always did what he had told her to do. But one day she put the heart out in the sun and forgot about it when she went to market, and it rained. The heart got wet. Soon it was changed into a beautiful woman. All this happened when nobody was around, so nobody knew about it. When Aja came home and went to get the heart, it wasn't there, and he knew at once what had happened.

This beautiful woman went to town, and everybody admired her. Yes, even the chief. She was so beautiful, she soon had many suitors. She couldn't decide which to marry. She told them all she was going to test them. She went and got seven bags full of sand and stood them all together. What she had in mind was that if anyone could shoot an arrow through all seven bags of sand, he was the one she would marry. All the men came to try. Even the chief came with his bow and shot a lot of arrows. He couldn't do it. No one could.

Now, Aja heard of all this, and he went to the town to try his luck. But before he shot his arrow, he cast a spell. He pulled a hair from the woman's head, wrapped it around the arrow and said, "It should go through one. It should go through two. It should go through three. It should go through four. It should go through five. It should go through six. It should go through seven."

Then he shot the arrow, and it went through all seven bags. But nobody believed that he had really shot an arrow through seven bags of sand. He was asked to do it again. He pulled another hair from the woman's head, wrapped it around the arrow and said, "It should go through one. It should go through two. It should go through three. It should go through four. It should go through five. It should go through six. It should go through seven."

And the arrow went through all seven bags. So Aja got the woman, and the woman learned who it was who had enough strength, skill, and magic to slay the enchanted beast disguised as a man disguised as an antelope. She therefore planned her revenge.

Aja married the woman and took her home with him. But Aja didn't sleep in the same room with the woman. Not once, even though they were married. This was because Aja knew what the woman really was and what kind of calamities were likely to befall him.

One night it happened this way. Aja was resting on his bed. He saw the woman turn herself into a lion and come toward his room. So Aja turned himself into a sheet, and the woman thought he wasn't there.

Another night the woman turned herself into a deadly snake and slithered toward Aja's bed. Aja turned himself into a tiny gnat that the snake could not see.

This sort of thing went on night after night, but the woman could never catch Aja asleep.

Now, one day, Aja had gone to his farm and had asked the woman to bring him food. When she got there and found Aja was alone, she turned into an eagle and began to attack Aja. But Aja turned into a fire and the eagle could not get close to him.

That is why whenever the bush is on fire you see the eagle circling over it. The eagle looks for Aja.

9 The Elephant, the Tortoise, and the Hare

All the animals living in the forest wanted to know who was the fastest, so they picked a day for a footrace, and all the animals in the forest entered the race.

At the first trial it happened that the Elephant was the animal that led all the other animals in the race. Then at this stage Tortoise appeared. He said that he could run faster than all the other animals put together. Then Hare challenged him, saying that he could run faster than both Tortoise and Elephant. So another day was named and on that day the three animals, Elephant, Hare, and Tortoise, were present. Judges were appointed and marks were made on the ground for the start of the race.

When the race started, of course Hare ran faster than Elephant, and Elephant ran a thousand times faster than Tortoise. But at the end of the race it was Tortoise who led the other two animals. Everybody was surprised. Tortoise was not.

What Tortoise did was to gather all his children and all his brothers and all his other relatives, and hide them at regular intervals of a mile along the track. He started the race, but it was one of his uncles who finished it. Since all Tortoises are very much alike, however, nobody could tell that the one who started the race was not the one that ended it.

▼▲▼▲▼▲▼▲▼▲▼▲▼▲▼▲▼▲▼▲▼▲▼▲▼▲▼▲▼▲

10 The Snakebite Medicine

Once upon a time there lived a very poor hunter. He was so poor that he had only one set of clothes, and he had to go hunting every day.

One day when he was hunting, he came upon a huge hole in the forest. In the hole were many animals who had been trapped there. The animals begged the hunter to release them, and at first the hunter did not want to listen to them. Then he saw a man in the hole who had also fallen there. The man begged the hunter to release him. The hunter thought a bit.

Then he got a long pole and released the man and all the animals from the hole.

When the creatures came out of the hole, they were very happy and very grateful to the hunter. Each of them brought him some presents. He received much gold and silver, and many precious jewels. He became a rich man. Snake, who was one of those released, brought him some medicine that could cure any snakebite. Snake said it was the best he could give, and it should be very useful for a hunter.

Now the chief of the village also had some jewels. And one day he found that all his jewels had been stolen. He sent out messages about his jewels. A friend of the hunter's heard this message, and he went straight to the chief and told him that he knew where the jewels were. He said they were with the hunter. The chief sent people at once to ask the hunter whether he had any jewels in his possession. When the hunter said yes, they immediately took him to the palace and condemned him to death.

Just as the hunter was about to be executed, some people came in and said that the chief's daughter had been bitten by a snake. Now the palace was thrown into confusion, for no one could do anything to save the chief's daughter from dying. The chief was mad with grief. Then the hunter remembered the medicine that Snake had given him. He gave it to the chief's daughter and cured her. The chief was very pleased with him and set him free.

The friend who went to tell the chief that the hunter had stolen his jewels was arrested and taken to the palace and beheaded.

▼▲▼▲▼▲▼▲▼▲▼▲▼▲▼▲▼▲▼▲▼▲▼▲▼▲▼▲▼▲

11 What Spider Learned from Frog

A long time ago, Frog and Spider were the best of friends. They went everywhere together and they did everything together. All the same, Spider used to treat Frog badly, even though he was his friend. For example, he would always eat most of the fish or meat in their food before serving the meal to Frog. Frog wasn't like that at all. When he shared a meal with

Spider, he always gave him a fair share of the meat or any other especially good part.

One day, Frog decided he had had enough of this sort of treatment, and he thought of a way to teach Spider a lesson. He told his wife to get a meal ready for Spider and himself, and he especially asked her not to put too much salt or pepper in the stew. By evening, Frog's wife had finished everything and had set out the food on the table. As they were waiting for Spider, Frog pretended to think of something. He told his wife, "Look, I've forgotten my hunting knife. I left it at the farm, and I think I had better go back and get it. If Spider comes, welcome him and don't wait for me—serve the food immediately." When his wife went back to the kitchen, Frog jumped in the stew and hid there.

Along came Spider shortly after, and he was given the message and was served the food. The first thing Spider did was to fish out all the meat from the stew and gobble it down greedily. Doing this, he ate Frog, too, without even noticing.

When he had finished Spider got up to go, and he was just about to take leave of Frog's wife when he heard, "Greedeep! Greedeep!" in his stomach. He was frightened and began to run, but the faster he ran, the more the noise came from his stomach. "Greedeep! Greedeep!" This went on for forty days. It kept him awake at night, and he had no sleep and could eat no food. Spider could stand it no longer. He lay down and got ready for death. Then, suddenly, Frog jumped out of his mouth and said to Spider, "I have known for a long time about your greedy ways, and this should be a lesson you will never forget."

From this you should remember that when you are invited to share food, let the one who provides serve it and divide it among the guests.

▼▲▼▲▼▲▼▲▼▲▼▲▼▲▼▲▼▲▼▲▼▲▼▲▼▲▼▲▼▲

12 The Magic Contest

A long time ago there were two very powerful magicians living in the same town. Each of them could perform wonderful feats of magic.

One day there was a big celebration in the town, and the chief, as part of the festivities, promised a reward for anyone who could do something unusual. So one of the magicians climbed a palm tree, using only his knees, and cut down a palm nut, using only his leg to do it. But before the palm nut could fall to the ground, the other magician had caught it on his head.

Which of the two magicians do you think was more deserving of the reward?

▼▲▼▲▼▲▼▲▼▲▼▲▼▲▼▲▼▲▼▲▼▲▼▲▼▲▼▲▼▲

13 The Greedy Dog

I wasn't living at the time, but once there was a man who raised dogs and other animals. One day he left the door of his house open and went to town. While he was away, one of his dogs climbed on the table and took some meat in its mouth. There was a mirror in the room, and the dog saw its reflection in it. It thought, "Eh, eh! There is a friend in the room with some meat, and I will get that meat, too." It jumped at the mirror, and the mirror fell down on the dog and wounded it so badly that it died.

For that reason, what is given to you is what you must accept. Don't say, "It isn't enough; it isn't enough."

▼▲▼▲▼▲▼▲▼▲▼▲▼▲▼▲▼▲▼▲▼▲▼▲▼▲▼▲▼▲

14 Adene and the Pineapple Child

Once upon a time there lived a man and his wife who had long wanted a child but could not have one. So they went to an old woman and asked her to help them. The old woman told the wife, "Go down the road that is straight in front of you, and when you have gone some distance you will come to a fork. Take the left path, and you will at last see a plantation full of pineapples. One of these pineapples will say, 'Pluck me, pluck me.' Do not pluck it, pluck rather the one that says, 'Don't pluck me, don't pluck me.' Take it home and hide it behind your water pot. In three days' time you will hear a voice saying 'mama, mama,' and you will see a child crying behind the water pot. Take the child for your own."

The man and his wife did exactly as the old woman had told her. When the third day came, she heard the child crying behind the water pot, and when she went to look, she saw a beautiful baby girl hiding there. She took her up in her arms. Both she and her husband doted on the child, and they reared her carefully until such time as she could walk and talk and could be safely trusted.

One day, the father and mother and an older girl named Adene who lived with them set out for the farm, leaving the child at home, sitting in a bath of water playing with a gourd that they had made for her. Their intention was that the girl should fetch firewood and return home immediately to look after the child. The child, meanwhile, having played for some time with the gourd, polished it nicely and set it aside on some firewood that someone had gathered into a heap.

Not long afterward Adene came back from the farm carrying on her head a bundle of firewood. She was completely tired out by the work, so much so that she didn't look at the heap of firewood, but, Crash! She threw down her load on top of the child's gourd and broke it into little pieces. When the little girl saw what had happened she burst into tears. Adene turned to the child and said, "What are you making such a fuss about? What is the matter with you? Are pineapple children always so fussy?" The little girl was very hurt that Adene should speak like that to her, and she began to sing this song and set out to look for her father and mother: "Adene was carrying a bundle of firewood, Adene let it fall on my gourd."

Adene said, "You can tell your parents if you want."

The little girl sang: "Adene said I wasn't a human child. Adene said I was a pineapple child. So I'm going to the land of the pineapples where I belong, Adene. Adene, oh, Adene."

About this time the father and mother had left the farm and were on their way home. They heard the singing, stopped, stood, and listened to it for some time. Then they realized that it was the voice of their own child.

They met Adene at the gate and asked her what was wrong. She had told them that it was really nothing, that the child had only gone out of the gate. From what he had heard of the song the man realized that Adene had offended his child deeply, and that was why she was running away. Then the father began to run as fast as his legs could carry him toward the place where the song was coming from.

As he ran he could hear the song more clearly and could make out the words. Soon, he could see the little girl's back as she was walking off into the distance. When the child saw her father running after her, she too began to run, and she reached the pineapple plantation just as her father was on the point of catching her. Her father stretched out his hand to grab her, but he could not hold onto her. He did, however, grasp her hair just as she got to her old place on a pineapple plant. Some of the hair was left in his hand, and he clutched it to his breast in grief over his lost child.

That is why man has hair on his chest.

▼▲▼▲▼▲▼▲▼▲▼▲▼▲▼▲▼▲▼▲▼▲▼▲▼▲▼▲▼▲

15 Sasabonsam's Match

A hunter went hunting. He wandered all day without firing a shot. He decided to give it up, but just as he was turning for home he saw an antelope that he then shot and killed. He found some vines and was starting to tie the carcass up when he heard a voice behind him.

"Hunter, cut off the animal's legs."

The hunter turned around and was horrified to see a man as tall as a silk cotton tree. His limbs were thin, and his hair reached down to his knees. His eyes were huge balls of fire, and his teeth were like red-hot spears. The hunter was so terrified that he could neither move nor speak. Once more he was ordered to cut off the animal's legs. He managed to do as he was told. The monster picked up the rest of the carcass, swallowed it whole, and without another word, vanished. The hunter went home with what was left of the antelope.

On the following day he went to another part of the forest, and the same thing happened. And again the next day, too. And the day after that. And so it went on for several weeks until the hunter's wife, who was pregnant, decided to find out why her husband only brought home legs, and what he did with the rest of the meat.

She made a tiny hole in her husband's powder box and filled the box with ashes. Early the next morning when the hunter set off from his village he left a trail of ashes. His wife followed him to his usual hunting grounds. She hid behind a tree. Presently, along came a black duiker. The hunter lifted his gun. *Bam!* The duiker fell dead.

"Hunter, cut off the animal's legs."

The hunter, by now, had no will of his own left, and he did what he was told. Sasabonsam swallowed the animal and shouted again, "Hunter, cut off the animal's legs," this time pointing to the tree behind which the wife was hiding. Thinking that a stray bullet had killed some other animal, the hunter went to do as Sasabonsam ordered. What do you think he found there? Of course, his wife. She had fainted from fright. Sasabonsam stood there, his eyes flashing—his mouth pouring smoke. "Cut off the animal's legs!" he ordered. The hunter couldn't move. Sasabonsam became angry and picked up the woman to swallow her. But as soon as he got hold of her, her belly opened and out jumped a baby that grew at tremendous speed. It was soon as big as Sasabonsam himself, and only then did it stop growing. The child blew fire and smoke from its mouth and nostrils.

These two giants now began to fight over the woman's body. They howled and roared. They tore up tall trees by the roots and used them to club each other. The dust from their feet, as they stamped, rose high into the sky. All the animals in the forest ran away. The fight was fierce and lasted a long time and neither seemed to be winning. They were so evenly matched the fight could not go on much longer. They both lay down on the ground gasping for breath. But as the wonder child lay watching Sasabonsam he saw a little hammer hanging from his belt. Quick as lightning, he grabbed it and hit Sasabonsam on the head with it three times. Sasabonsam reared up and stretched high into heaven to tell the Sky God Nana Nyamee Kwame that one of his children had wounded him. But he couldn't reach the Sky God. He fell full-length on the ground and turned into a great river. His arms and legs became the streams that flow into the river. As for Akokoaa Kwasi Gyinamoa—for that was the child's name— he went back into his mother's womb and lay there waiting to be born.

16 The Jealous Wife

Two women were married to one man, a chief. One of the women was called Aloko. Aloko was very jealous and talkative. She used to go on at her co-wife all day long, and she never gave her husband any peace.

She wanted to get rid of her rival, so she made a plan. She forced her husband to treat the other woman badly so that when he came back from the fields he wouldn't visit her hut, nor would he send her any meat when he killed an animal. She was left to fend for herself.

When Aloko was satisfied that her rival was quite fed up with things and couldn't stand to be married to such a bad husband any longer, she persuaded her to join in a suicide pact. Both women agreed to hang themselves on a certain day at an appointed spot.

The day arrived. The women, wearing their best clothes, left their huts unnoticed. When they arrived at the place where they were to die, they prepared their individual ropes, put them around their necks, and said goodbye in great sorrow to each other.

The moment arrived. They kicked over the stools on which they were standing, but Aloko had hidden a small, sharp knife in her headdress. With it she quickly cut the rope. She soon recovered and went back home.

A few days later Aloko's rival was found hanging from a tree not far from the village. After the funeral Aloko moved from her own hut into her husband's compound, which was much bigger and more comfortable. She chose a room deep in the middle of the compound because she was afraid of the ghost of her rival whom she had murdered.

One night, when the moon was high and all was silent in the village, a voice was heard singing: "Where is my sister, Aloko? I seek the company of my friend. Aloko, I think you are close by."

The front door of the chief's house was opened by an invisible hand.

The voice again sang: "Where is my sister, Aloko? I seek the company of my friend. Aloko, I think you are close by."

The second door of the chief's house was opened by invisible hands. Aloko had heard the voice and recognized it as that of her dead rival. She trembled all over and crept into a corner of the room and covered herself with rags and leaves.

The voice sang again; more doors opened. At last the ghost of the dead woman stood face to face with Aloko. She sang: "Here is my sister, Aloko! I have found the company of my friend. We will be together, always."

The ghost stopped singing and stared deep into Aloko's eyes.

"So it is you at last. You who deceived me into taking my own life. I looked for you a long time in the land of the dead, and when I did not find you I realized you had tricked me. So now I have come to the land of the living to find you."

She opened her mouth, and when Aloko saw the hair that was growing in it she too fell dead, and her ghost accompanied the rival to the country of the dead.

That is why a woman should not be too jealous.

▼▲▼▲▼▲▼▲▼▲▼▲▼▲▼▲▼▲▼▲▼▲▼▲▼▲▼▲▼▲

17 A Mother's Love

There were once two wives of the same husband. It happened that one of these wives was barren, but the other had a daughter. The barren wife tried in every way to have children, but all her efforts failed. She therefore turned her energies to wickedness. She was as wicked as a witch.

The other wife, who had an only daughter, was kindhearted, loving, and pleasant. She loved her only daughter more than her own life. One day she was going to a distant market to sell things, so she had to leave her child behind. She decided to leave her with her co-wife. But she left sufficient provisions—eggs, yams, soup, and vegetables—for her daughter and left everything in the hands of her co-wife. She did not return until the seventh day.

While she was away the co-wife ill-treated the little girl. She sent her on long errands and gave her hardly any food at all to eat. On the fifth day the girl had become so weak and so miserable that she started to cry. She wept and sang, wept and sang. Her song was: "Travelers to the market of Ojeje. Oh! Travelers to the market of Ojeje. If you see my mother in the market, tell her I'm dying of hunger and thirst. Tell her that I have little food to eat, but plenty of work to do. Tell her that her co-wife eats all the yams, all the eggs, all the vegetables, and all the nice things she left behind, leaving only the skins and rinds for me."

As she was singing she started to sink into the ground, and her voice grew faint and more and more sorrowful. But she went on singing.

Soon she was waist-deep in the ground. In a few days she was neck-deep in the ground. It was then that her mother appeared on the scene. She too was weeping and shouting. She begged her daughter not to go away from her. She promised her she would give her many nice things to eat if only she would come back to her. The gods took pity on the poor mother. All of a sudden the ground cracked, and her dear little daughter came back to her.

▼▲▼▲▼▲▼▲▼▲▼▲▼▲▼▲▼▲▼▲▼▲▼▲▼▲▼▲▼▲

18 Spider Finds a Fool

This is about Mr. Spider and his nephew, Obleku, the coucal. One day Spider went around the town saying that he was looking for a fool to be his partner in setting a trap. He shouted and called out in the town for a fool to help him in setting the trap, but he couldn't find one.

Then Coucal said, "Why is it that my uncle is so anxious to find a fool for a trap? I will go with him." And so Coucal went with Spider, and they went and cut the sticks used for setting the trap. When they had set the trap they left it and went home. The following morning they went to look at the trap, and it had caught an animal. The animal was a squirrel. Spider called out and said, "My son, come and look at the animal we have caught."

Coucal went and looked at the squirrel and said, "This is called a squirrel." Spider said, "So, what animal shall we catch tomorrow?" And Coucal said, "Tomorrow we shall snare the grasscutter." Spider said, "But isn't a grasscutter bigger than a squirrel?" And Coucal said, "Yes, it is bigger." And Spider said, "All right, in that case, you take the squirrel today, and tomorrow when we catch the grasscutter, I will take that." So Coucal took the squirrel home and ate it.

The following morning when they returned, indeed there was a grasscutter in the trap. So Spider called to Coucal and said, "Come and see, indeed we have got a grasscutter." Then Coucal said, "Yes, and tomorrow we are going to trap a duiker." Spider said to Coucal, "But a duiker is bigger than the grasscutter, isn't it?" And Coucal said, "Yes, it is bigger." And Spider said, "All right, in that case you take the grasscutter, and tomorrow when we trap the duiker I will take it." And so Coucal took the grasscutter.

When they got home, Spider's wife, Konole, asked him, "After all the traps you have been setting, hasn't your trap caught any animal at all?" Spider said, "Have heart, be patient. The day I trap an animal and bring it to this house you will be very happy." Konole said, "Go and look at the coucal; his wife is curing meat, unheard-of meat. You know, the other day they caught a grasscutter. Today they caught a duiker." Spider said, "You just be patient."

So Spider went and asked Coucal again, "What animal will we catch tomorrow?" And Coucal said, "Tomorrow we will catch an antelope." The following morning they went and looked at the trap, and indeed they had caught an antelope. Spider said, "What animal are we going to catch tomorrow?" And Coucal said, "Tomorrow we will catch the biggest antelope." Spider said, "All right, in that case, take this antelope, and tomorrow when we get a real antelope, the biggest antelope, I will take that." So Coucal took the antelope home.

The following morning when they went to the trap, there was a real antelope in it, the biggest antelope. Spider said, "Aha! After this antelope, what can we catch again?" Coucal said, "Oh, tomorrow we can catch a bush pig." And Spider said, "But the bush pig is bigger than this antelope." And Coucal said, "Yes, it is bigger." Spider said, "All right, take the antelope. Tomorrow when we catch the bush pig I will take that." So Coucal took the antelope away and ate it.

Now, Spider's wife, Konole, was feeling very distressed and irritated at the way Coucal was bringing home meat every day when she wasn't getting any meat at all. In fact, she lost her temper and had a little quarrel with Spider about it.

In the morning when they went, there was a bush pig in the trap. Spider said, "What animal are we going to catch tomorrow?" Coucal said, "We shall catch a wild cow." Spider said, "But a wild cow is greater than a bush pig." Coucal said, "Yes." And Spider said, "Then take the bush pig."

This game went on for some time between Coucal and Spider, Spider who said he was looking for a fool to be his partner in setting a trap. They went on with this game, animal after animal, until at last they trapped an elephant, and then Spider asked Coucal, "What animal are we going to catch tomorrow, after this elephant?" And Coucal said, "Tomorrow, the animal we shall catch is called I-overwhelm-anything-even-an-elephant." Spider said, "If its name is I-overwhelm-anything-even-an-elephant, then it must be greater than an elephant," and Coucal said, "Yes, it can overwhelm an elephant." And Spider said, "In that case, Coucal, you take the elephant, and tomorrow when we catch I-overwhelm-anything-even-an-elephant, I will take it." And Coucal said, "All right."

So Coucal took the elephant away. The next morning when they went to look at the trap they had caught a mouse, a small mouse with a very long nose and a very bad smell. This kind of mouse stinks so bad that when it crosses the path in front of you, you almost fall down and die. That was the animal they caught. So Spider shouted to Coucal and said, "Coucal, Coucal, Coucal! Come and see what animal we have caught!" So Coucal went over there, looked at the animal, and said, "Oh yes, this is the animal that is called I-overwhelm-anything-even-an-elephant." So Spider said, "After this animal what animal can we catch again?" And Coucal said, "Oh, we trapped all the animals, and there is none left that we can trap again that is of a magnitude greater than this mouse." So Spider said, "In that case I will take this animal." Coucal said, "All right, you can have it."

So, it was only with that mouse that Spider was able to take any meat home so his wife could see that he too had brought some meat home from the trapping. So when Konole saw the mouse that smells she said, "Take it away! Take it away! We don't want this animal here in this house." So in shame and grief Spider took this mouse and ran away with it and scurried up the wall and went and hid in the eaves of the roof.

Because of this, if you are ever going to do any work with a partner, you yourself ought not to go around saying that you are looking for a fool to be your partner in the work. You should just do the work with your partner without cheating so you both can succeed.

19 The Locust-Bean Seller

There was a time when locust beans were very hard to find. That was unfortunate because they were an important ingredient of people's soup. So this shortage of locust beans made the locust-bean sellers very rich. They got very rich indeed—richer than almost anybody else—but they were still very stingy.

One day one of these locust-bean sellers went to the river to wash her locust beans to prepare them for market. Despite the fact that she had many servants and slaves, she did not take anyone to the river with her. She decided to go alone, in case her servants and slaves might steal her locust beans.

In the river she washed her locust beans neatly and very carefully, so that not a single bean dropped into the river. But as she lifted her calabash from the ground, one of the beans dropped into the river and got carried away by the water. The stingy locust-bean seller jumped into the river and went after it. She swam downstream with the current, saying, "One locust bean, one locust bean, if you go to the sea, I'll follow you there."

The current of the river took her farther and farther away, into the deep part of the river, until she was seen no more. She went after her one locust bean until she lost her life.

Such is the fate of stingy people.

▼▲▼▲▼▲▼▲▼▲▼▲▼▲▼▲▼▲▼▲▼▲▼▲▼▲▼▲

20 Magotu and the Devil

There once was a woman named Magotu. When it was time for her to marry she said she wouldn't have anyone but the most handsome man in the world. Many suitors came to see her, but she was attracted to none of them. Needless to say, her parents were quite concerned about this matter.

Then a devil named Kpana, hearing about this affair, went to the most handsome of the young men and took from them their best features. He got new arms, new feet, new teeth, and extremely nice eyes. There was to be a great ceremony where Magotu, at the urging of her parents, would choose a husband. Many suitors came, and Magotu went among them. She refused them all except one, and that one was Kpana, the devil in disguise.

Later Kpana and Magotu went to Kpana's hometown. On their way a small dog followed them.

Kpana said to Magotu very mysteriously, "Wait for me, wait for me." Then, suddenly, he disappeared. He came back with legs swollen by elephantiasis. He said to Magotu, "Hee, hee, hee! It is I, your husband!"

Magotu began to tremble and weep, "Mommy, Daddy, come take me away, take me away!"

The devil growled, "What are you saying? Stop your shouting!" Poof! He was gone again.

At this time the small dog begged Magotu to run away and hide. So Magotu and the dog ran and ran until they came to a distant village where they hid in a goat hut.

Kpana returned to the place in the road where he had left Magotu. This time he had only one eye, which he used to look all over for Magotu. He started tearing through the bushes, sniffing the air in search of Magotu, saying, "Where is Magotu? I'm ready to eat that nice juicy woman."

He came to where Magotu and the dog were hiding and passed them by without seeing them. But he stopped and said, "If I go into that village, I will find them."

Just then one member of a set of twins came to Magotu and the dog and said, "If you want to be free of this devil, take a banana, eat it, and lay the peel on the road in front of the devil. When he comes he will slip on it and fall into his hammock and be so comfortable that he will never come after you again."

So straightaway they did that. No sooner had they finished than the devil came along, and he slipped and fell comfortably into his hammock.

Magotu thanked the clever twin and returned home. There the family gathered and gave thanks to God, and there was much feasting, dancing, and celebrating. Afterward the elders gathered around and listened to Magotu's story.

They said, "It is not good for a woman to be so particular in the choice of a mate. It is also wise to give some degree of respect to small dogs."

21 Leopard and the Son of the Hunter

Once there was a Hunter who would go out and hunt all kinds of animals. One day he killed Leopard's son. He took him and put him in the enclosure where he kept the animals he had killed. Leopard heard about this, and he went to Hunter's village, where he met Hunter's son.

Leopard said, "Where is your father?"

The boy answered, "He has gone out hunting, so he isn't here."

"Well, when he comes back will you tell him I want to talk to him about something?"

The boy agreed, "All right."

So that night when Hunter returned, his son told him.

The next day, Leopard came back and said, "Where is Hunter? I want to speak with him."

And the boy said, "He has gone out hunting again, so he isn't here."

"Well, tell him that I will come back tomorrow at this time to speak with him about something."

"All right."

So that night when Hunter returned, his son said to him, "Leopard came again today to talk to you. He said he would come back tomorrow." And Hunter said, "It's all right, tomorrow I will be going hunting again."

The next day Leopard came to the village and asked for Hunter. Then Hunter's son told him, "He has gone out hunting, so he isn't here." Then Leopard said, "You be sure to tell him to be here tomorrow when I come. There is a matter I want to discuss with him. If he isn't here, I will kill you. Do you hear?"

So that night when Hunter returned, his son told him what Leopard had said, and he begged his father, saying, "Please stay home tomorrow, father, because Leopard is getting angry, and he frightened me." And the father said, "It's all right. Tomorrow I will be going hunting again."

So the next day Leopard came and said, "Where's Hunter?" The boy said, "He's gone hunting, so he isn't here." Then Leopard roared and began to chase him. BOOM! Hunter stepped from behind a tree and shot Leopard and killed him.

The moral of this story is this: You shouldn't frighten Hunter's child.

22 Spider's Bargain with God

Kwaku Ananse, the spider, went to Sky God Nana Nyamee and asked whether he could buy the stories told about Him so they would be told about Ananse instead. Nana Nyamee said, "Yes, provided you bring me the following things in payment."

Ananse said, "I am willing. Just name them."

Nana Nyamee said, "Bring me a live leopard, a pot full of live bees, and a live python." Ananse was afraid, but nevertheless he agreed to provide them. He went home and sat down and thought and thought.

At last he took a needle and thread, and set out toward the forest where the leopard lived. When he got to the stream where Leopard got his water, he sat down, took out the needle and thread, and sewed his eyelids together. He waited. When he heard the footsteps of Leopard coming to fetch water, he began to sing to himself: "Hmm. Nana Nyamee is wonderful. He sewed my eyes and took me to his palace. Then I began to see wonderful things, and I have been singing of them ever since. Beautiful women, palaces, rich and delicious food, and a wonderful life."

Leopard came up to him and asked Ananse, "What were you singing about?"

He replied, "Hmm. Nana Nyamee is wonderful. He sewed my eyes and took me to his palace. Then I began to see wonderful things, and I have been singing of them ever since. Beautiful women, palaces, rich and delicious food, and a wonderful life."

Leopard said, "Eh, Ananse, what is it, are you dreaming?" "No," said Ananse, "there is a beautiful woman here."

Leopard said, "Please Ananse, sew my eyes shut, too, and lead me to Nana Nyamee so that I, too, may see all the wonderful things."

"No, I know you, Leopard, when you see her and all those other beautiful creatures you will kill them and eat them up."

"No, No, No," Leopard growled. "I shall not. Rather, I shall thank you."

Ananse took his needle and thread and sewed Leopard's eyes and led him to Nana Nyamee's palace. He said, "Nana Nyamee, here is the first installment. Keep it."

Next day Ananse took an earthenware pot and went to a place where he knew there were honey bees. As he came near the place he sang, "Oh bees! Oh bees!"

The bees said, "Ananse, what is all this murmuring about?"

Ananse replied, "I have had an argument with Nana Nyamee. He says all of you together won't fill this pot, but I say you will, and so I came to find out."

They said, "Oho, that is easy," and they flew into the pot, buzz, buzz, buzz, until the pot was full, and every bee had flown into it. Then Ananse quickly sealed the pot and carried it off to Nana Nyamee as his second installment.

For two days he could not think how to get the third—a live python. But at last he hit on a plan. He went to the forest and cut a long stick, a stick as long as a tree. He carried this off to the forest, singing to himself, "I am right, he is wrong! He is wrong, I am right."

When Python saw him he said, "Ananse, what are you grumbling about?"

He answered, "How lucky I am to meet you here. I have had a long and bitter argument with Nana Nyamee. I have known you for a long time, and I know your measurements both when you are coiled, and when you are fully stretched out. Nana Nyamee thinks very little of you. He thinks you are only a little longer than the green mamba, and no longer than the cobra. I strongly disagree with him, and to prove my point I brought this pole to measure you."

Python was very angry, and he began stretching himself out to his greatest length along the stick.

And Ananse said, "You are moving! You are moving! Let me tie you to the stick so I can get the measurement exactly right."

And Python agreed. As Ananse tied Python up he sang a little song, and when he had Python securely fastened to the stick, Ananse carried him off to Nana Nyamee.

Nana Nyamee was very pleased with Ananse and forthwith beat the gong throughout the world that all stories should be told about Ananse.

That is how Ananse became the leading figure in all Ananse stories.

23 Python Meets His Match

One day some big chimpanzees were going for a walk. One of them went off on his own and came upon a giant python. As soon as he saw it he called his friends to come and look. When they got near the place where the python was, they got into single file and marched in step like a military guard. At first the python didn't see them, and by the time he did, they were already on him. They fell on him. Some held his head, and others held his tail. They pulled him in opposite directions, as though he were the rope in a tug-of-war. Soon the length of the python doubled. They threw him to the ground, and any part of him that moved was beaten with sticks until it stopped.

After the chimpanzees had finally killed the python they returned to the forest.

It has been said that pythons fear ants most. Now it also can be said that strength overcomes strength, and chimpanzees can be very strong.

▼▲▼▲▼▲▼▲▼▲▼▲▼▲▼▲▼▲▼▲▼▲▼▲▼▲▼▲▼▲

24 Big Man and the Chimpanzee

Once upon a time the people of a town were being threatened by "Big Man," the leopard. The hunters wondered what they could do about the threat. One of them suggested that they set a trap for the leopard at the crossroads of the town. The plan was agreed upon, and they made an iron cage, into which they placed a smaller cage. One of the hunters said, "Let us put a dog in the little cage, and when the leopard comes, he will enter the big cage to get at the dog."

It was agreed upon, and after they had put the dog in its cage, the hunters went home. At midnight a chimpanzee was out walking, and when he saw the trap he went inside, and immediately the trap was sprung.

He couldn't get out. The chimpanzee saw the dog in the little cage, but he could do nothing. He just sat down quietly in a corner of the cage.

When the leopard came, he saw the dog, but not the chimpanzee, because the chimpanzee was black and the cage was dark. As the leopard prowled round and round the cage, seeking a way to get at the dog, his tail accidentally got into the cage. The chimpanzee caught hold of the tail, got a good grip on it, and held it fast. The leopard did not know who or what was holding his tail. He struggled to get away, but the chimpanzee held on tightly. The leopard was more puzzled than ever.

The next day some people passed the cage and saw the leopard, but not the chimpanzee. They sought the hunters and informed them, "A big man has come to town." The hunters came with guns, and when the leopard saw them he tried to free himself, but the chimpanzee held him fast. The hunters did not know that the chimpanzee was keeping the leopard from attacking. They shot him twice, and killed him. As the hunters came closer to the cage, the chimpanzee was still holding onto the leopard's tail. When the hunters saw him inside the cage they were surprised. They asked, "Is that really a chimpanzee inside the trap?" They opened the cage and let the chimpanzee out. Everybody shouted, "Chimpanzee, come out, do. You gave us Big Man today!"

Which is the more powerful, the chimpanzee or the leopard?

▼▲▼▲▼▲▼▲▼▲▼▲▼▲▼▲▼▲▼▲▼▲▼▲▼▲▼▲

25 The Sacrifice

One day all the people in town noticed that some dirt had fallen on the town, and they declared that the town would have to be purified. The purification they decided on was that every household was to give up one of its sons. That is what they decided to do to purify the town. A woman there had only one child. This woman said, "My son is my only child, so if I take him and give him up, where will I get another?" Someone said she should hide her son away, far inside the forest.

She took him away. She and her son built a secret room in the roof of a house, and she put her son there. He lived there, and every morning his mother would go and visit her son and give him food. She would mash the food and then go give it to him. As she approached the house, she sang a song to let her son know she was coming. When the child heard the song, he came out to meet her. Each morning, then, she called the child.

"My son, my son, my son, my son. I came to the grave. I didn't meet that empty room. But the sun sets on white man's shining. And come and take something to eat, quick, quick, quick."

Then he would answer her and say, "Yea, my mother, Yea I am at the empty grave. I didn't meet that empty room. But the sun sets on white man's shining. Come and give me something to eat."

Then the child would come down from the secret room and take the food, eat it, and let his mother go. About evening time she came to give him food again.

"My son, my son, my son, my son. I came to the grave. I didn't meet that empty room. But the sun sets on white man's shining. And come and take something to eat, quick, quick, quick."

Then he came to her and said, "Yea, my mother, yea I am at the empty grave. I didn't meet that empty room. But the sun sets on white man's shining. Come and give me something to eat."

Then the child came down again to take the food and eat it, and his mother went. One day she came and called him in the evening time and said, "My son, my son, my son, my son. I came to the grave. I didn't meet that empty room. But the sun sets on white man's shining. And come and take something to eat, quick, quick, quick."

But the son didn't come, and the son didn't come, and the son didn't come. She said, "Why does not my son come when I call?"

"My son, my son, my son, my son. I came to the grave. I didn't meet that empty room. But the sun sets on white man's shining. And come and take something to eat, quick, quick, quick."

She sat down quietly. The son didn't answer. She started singing again.

"My son, my son, my son, my son. I came to the grave. I didn't meet that empty room. But the sun sets on white man's shining. And come and take something to eat, quick, quick, quick."

She waited, but the son didn't answer. She hadn't been waiting long, when a bird passed overhead and started calling to her, "Look to the house, look to the house, look to the house!"

The bird kept up its calling, and the woman took a stone and threw it at the bird. It just kept on saying, "Look to the house, look to the house!"

After she had come with food for her son and had gone away, witches had come and sung the same song she had sung. The boy had come out and opened the door, and the witches had caught him and butchered him and shared the meat. When the woman looked round, she thought she saw some water standing under a tree. When she looked carefully, she saw that the water was red. They had washed their hands and everything in the water. She looked inside. Her son's head was lying inside the house.

This was why the bird came to her and told her to look in the house when the child didn't answer. When she went to look in the place, she said, "Oh! All people gave their sons, and I didn't do it. If I had known, I would have given up my son for the purification. I have only hidden my son to feed the witches."

▼▲▼▲▼▲▼▲▼▲▼▲▼▲▼▲▼▲▼▲▼▲▼▲▼▲▼▲▼▲▼▲

26 The Cruel Mother

There was once a mother who had a very beautiful daughter. This girl was kind and gentle. But the mother was harsh with her, always flogging her and putting her to shame.

This beautiful girl was betrothed to a man in the neighborhood. When she came of age, she started to ask her mother to buy clothes and trinkets and all the other necessary things in preparation for her wedding day. But the mother didn't buy a thing. She kept on deceiving the girl by telling her that she had a basket of clothes, trinkets, and other things for her, and the poor girl believed her statements.

On the day of her marriage, the girl asked for the basket of clothes and trinkets promised by her mother. Then the mother went in and brought out a big basket. But when the basket was opened, they found leaves of different kinds, and ropes made to look like beads and trinkets. The mother then said, "My dear daughter, when we were living together you were very lazy, and headstrong and nasty. Now we will live together no more.

But here is your reward for everything. These things are for you—your clothes, your beads, your rings, and your trinkets."

When the daughter heard this she started to cry. She cried and cried and cried until her tears made little torrents of water. Her eyes were red. Her face was pale. Then after some time she started to sink into the ground. Her mother did not notice what was happening until the child was waist-deep in the ground. Then she started to plead with her daughter, "Oh! My daughter, my very dear daughter, come out of the ground, and I will give you plenty of money, plenty of beads, clothes, rings, and trinkets. I will give you plenty of everything." But the daughter sank deeper and deeper, until only her hair was above the ground. When the mother saw that her daughter was about gone, she clung to the hair, weeping and begging and wailing. But it was too late. Very soon the daughter had disappeared, never to be seen again.

This story teaches us that we should never be cruel to our children.

▼▲▼▲▼▲▼▲▼▲▼▲▼▲▼▲▼▲▼▲▼▲▼▲▼▲▼▲▼▲

27 The Orphan's Revenge

I was not there at the time, but there were some children, and their mother died, and not long afterward their father died, too. They were orphans. Their guardian married another woman. One day, this woman told the children to go fetch firewood. When they got back they were hungry, so they went to wash their hands and came to eat the food the woman had prepared for the family. She told them their hands were not clean, and sent them off to wash again. And when they came back, the same thing. Over and over again, the same thing. She kept sending them back to wash their hands until, at last, her own children had eaten all the food. The orphan children stood this as long as they could. Finally, they said they were going to find their father.

The next day they left home. They traveled for some time, till they came to a place where they sang a song: "We have nobody. Our mother died, our father died. We have nobody. We don't know where we are going." Then one of the children died.

The rest began to sing: "We have nobody. Our mother died, our father died. We have nobody. We don't know where we are going." They went on, and another child died. They buried him, and continued their journey. They met a magician. He turned them into fully grown men—just like that! Then they returned home, killed the woman who had treated them badly, cut her up in pieces, and put the pieces on a platform outside their house. Then said to everyone who came to their village, "Take some meat!"

Anyone who took some meat was a bad person. Anyone who took no meat was a good person.

Even if you are entrusted to a guardian, the guardian should look after you.

▼▲▼▲▼▲▼▲▼▲▼▲▼▲▼▲▼▲▼▲▼▲▼▲▼▲▼▲▼▲

28 The Sacred Bowl

There was a certain sacred carved wooden bowl in the palace of the king. This bowl was very precious to the king. It was so precious that he commanded each of his wives in turn to wash, clean, and paint the bowl every day.

One day as one of the wives was washing the bowl, it fell to the ground and broke into many pieces. Now this woman was a very sly and wicked person. She immediately rushed to the palace and announced that Qlere (another wife of the king) had broken the sacred bowl. The king called his advisers together and announced that the sacred bowl had been broken.

The king's advisers immediately ordered that whoever had broken the sacred bowl must die. Qlere was tried and convicted, and the king's executioners beheaded her and buried her near a river.

A few months later the women who went to the river to draw water noticed that a shrill, small voice was always singing near the river: "It was another person who broke the sacred bowl, but I was wrongly convicted, killed, and buried here."

When the song persisted, all the people in the town went down to the river to hear it. So the king was forced to reexamine the case of the broken bowl. But this time there could be no mistake. The name of the wife who actually broke the bowl had been mentioned by the strange voice singing in the river, and all the available evidence supported what it had said. The real criminal was therefore beheaded.

Sly and wicked people get what they deserve.

▾▲▾▲▾▲▾▲▾▲▾▲▾▲▾▲▾▲▾▲▾▲▾▲▾▲▾▲▾▲▾▲

29 The Wise Child

Once there was a boy called "I'm-wiser-than-a-chief." This boy played with the children of a chief. One day, the chief asked his children the name of their playmate. They said they didn't know his name. So the chief said, "When he comes tomorrow morning ask him his name and tell it to me." The next morning they asked him his name, and he said he was called "I'm-wiser-than-a-chief." The children went and told their father. The next day the boy came again. The chief asked him his name, and the boy said he was called "I'm-wiser-than-a-chief." The chief said, "Is that so?" The boy said, "Yes."

Now the chief said the boy should come and cut his hair for him. The boy said, "All right, I will, but you, for your part, must first find corn and roast it, and for every hair I cut, you must give me a kernel of corn to eat." The chief said, "What is corn?" So the boy went off to find corn and roast it himself. The next day he came back with it and told them, "This is corn. Each time I cut a hair from the chief's head you are to give me one kernel of it to eat." And so they began. One hair, one kernel of corn. Soon the supply of corn was finished, and the boy told the chief that he wouldn't be able to cut any more hair. The chief told the boy to put those he had cut back on his head. The boy said he would if the chief would put the corn back on the cob.

"All right!" said the chief. "Debt cancels debt, but I never want to see you again." The boy said, "All right."

The next morning the child returned and cut off the branches of the shade tree that stood behind the chief's house. The chief asked him if he wasn't the boy he had said he didn't want to see again. The boy said he forgot. So the chief had his executioners put the boy in a sack to take him out to sea and drown him.

When the executioners reached the shore they left the child while they went to get their canoe. There was a hole in the sack, and the boy could see out. He saw an old man nearby and called him to come. The old man said, "What's all this about?" The boy said, "The chief of our town said I should marry his beautiful daughter, and I said I didn't love her." Then the old man asked him, "When you marry the beautiful daughter how much are you to pay?" "Nothing. I'm getting her free. They said if I don't marry her they will throw me into the sea."

"Where are they?" asked the old man.

"They have gone to get a canoe." The old man said, "Oh, as for me, I love her already, so let me get into the sack and then you tie it up again." The old man untied the sack and got inside. The boy left. Very soon after the executioners came. As they were carrying the old man off, he cried out, "I love her! I love her!" The executioners said, "Fool, whom do you love? What are you talking about?" They drowned him in the sea.

The very next day the chief was holding a celebration to celebrate getting rid of the boy. He was sitting in state when the boy came in. The chief said, "Where are you from?" The boy said, "Listen! That place where you sent me under the sea—there is nothing but money there. Nothing but money. If you like, send your wife there to see for herself, and she can come and tell you about it." The chief said, "Is that the truth?" The boy answered, "Yes, but be careful. Perhaps your wife won't come back because of all that money."

So the chief sent his wife. The next day the boy appeared and said, "You see, she didn't come back after all. I warned you." The chief said, "Oh, if that's the case I'll go myself," and he had them put him in the sack and tie it and throw him in the sea.

The boy became chief of the town. He said he was wiser than the chief, and it was true.

30 The Headstrong Bride

There was a very, very beautiful young girl who always took her mother's things to the market to sell.

As time went on, she came of age, and many men wanted to marry her. Her parents constantly nagged at her, wanting her to choose someone. But this girl always said that she was not ready to marry because she had not yet seen the man of her choice. One day, in one of the markets, while she was selling her things, a handsome young man came and bought a lump of butter from her. After the man had gone, she started to think about how beautiful he was. Even while she was thinking, the young man reappeared and sat down beside her. So she asked him who he was, and where he came from.

The young man said that he came from a town far away. Right then and there this young girl decided to take him for her husband. She told him that she was prepared to follow him to his town, and the young man agreed. But after they had traveled a few miles away from the girl's own town, the young man started to complain, saying that the girl should go back home, and that he would come to see her on the following day. But the girl would not go back. She insisted on going with him to his home.

After they had traveled for another few miles, the young man, with a frown on his face, cautioned the girl to go back home. But instead of going back home, the young girl started to weep, saying that she was prepared to follow the young man to the ends of the earth.

Then the young man started to sing: "Young girl, go back home, go back home. The elephant is going into the forest. The mahogany is going into the river. The python is going into the sea. Young girl, go back home."

But the young girl would not go back. After traveling for another few miles, they came to a forest, and suddenly the young man's arms disappeared. They disappeared because he had borrowed them from a fairy in that forest, and now he had to give them back.

He started to sing again: "Young girl, go back home, go back home. The elephant is going into the forest. The mahogany is going into the river. The python is going into the sea. Young girl, go back home."

But the young girl would not go back. Then they came to a place where they had to cross a river. Here both the young man's legs disappeared, and as he jumped into the water he turned into a python. Now, the girl did not know what to do next. She sat down near the river weeping and crying until the next day. On the next day, her parents, when they could not find her, had begun to look everywhere in the town. She was nowhere to be found. Nor could they find their daughter in the neighboring villages and towns.

Then one of the girls who had been in the market the day before told her parents that the missing girl had followed a man out of the market, and that they had set off going west. So the parents of the girl and all the people helping them to search for her started out westward. After traveling for a whole day, they found their daughter still sitting near the river. They picked her up and took her home.

The story teaches us that young daughters should not marry without first consulting their elders.

▼▲▼▲▼▲▼▲▼▲▼▲▼▲▼▲▼▲▼▲▼▲▼▲▼▲▼▲▼▲

31 The Pact

This is a story about two boys and their mothers. The mothers ate a great deal of their scarce food until one day the more cunning of the two boys said to his friend, "Let us make a pact. We will take our mothers and eat them."

"How will we do it?" his slow-witted friend asked him.

The wise boy said, "You must kill your mother, and I'll kill mine. We'll eat yours first until she's all gone, and then we'll start on mine."

The friend said, "Yes, I agree."

The cunning one then said, "We live in the same section of town, and my house is just up the street from yours. On the day when the rains begin, watch the rainwater that flows down past my house and by yours. When you see something red in the water, you will know that I have cut off my mother's head. Then you, too, must go catch your own mother and kill her."

Again his slow-witted friend agreed, "Yes, I will do it."

When the first day of the rains came, the boy who had thought up the scheme went out and found some grass and some plantains that are good to cook with food and put them all into a pot. Then he went to the chemist's shop and bought a certain medicine that was as red as a person's blood. When the rainwater began to flow past his doorway, he took some of the medicine and poured it into the water. The red water flowed down toward his friend's house.

The dull boy said, "Well! My clever friend has killed his mother. I, too, shall kill my mother." So, he went into the house and cut off his mother's head. Then he, too, went out and found some plantains and put them in a pot. He cut his mother into pieces and put her in the pot and cooked her. At the same time, his clever friend was cooking grass with the plantains, pretending that he was cooking his mother. He cooked the mixture until he thought his friend's mother would be ready to eat. Then this cunning boy went to his friend's house and said, "My own is done."

His friend said, "Yes, let's eat mine first." So they went down to his house and ate and ate until they had finished his mother.

When they were through, they went to the house of the cunning one to eat the second meal. After a few bites, the friend said, "I don't understand. Why does your mother's flesh taste so bad?"

His cunning host answered, "Perhaps it's because she was so old."

As they ate the friend said, "Your mother may have been old, but mine was good."

The cunning one replied, "Well, my mother never was as good as yours." This clever boy had dug a hole in the ground and had taken his mother there. He would cook food and bring it to her. When he came with food for her, he would sing: "Come out, Mother, take food and eat. Come out, Mother, take food and eat. I fooled my friend, he killed his mother, but I hid you here. Come out, Mother, take food and eat."

Then his mother would come out and eat and would hide again. Every day when the two friends ate, the crafty one would eat half his food and leave half. He would say, "Since you are a little older, dear friend, let me take the garbage out."

He would go to throw the food away at the place where his mother was hiding and sing: "Come out, Mother, take food and eat. I fooled my friend and brought you here. Come out and eat."

His dull-witted friend began to be suspicious and said to himself, "Why is he so eager to take the garbage out every day? The next time he goes I will follow him and see what he does."

The next time the boy went to take food to his mother, his friend followed him, and hid in some nearby bushes. He heard his clever friend sing, and thought to himself, "Is that how it is, then?" He watched the mother come out and eat, and then he went back home. Things went as usual for a few days, and then he said to his clever friend, "I'll throw out the food this time, since you always do it."

"All right," said the crafty boy. "Do it then." The dull boy went out with the peelings and sang in his own deep voice. The mother said, "That's not my child's voice. I won't come out. That's not my child's voice."

He began to think of a good way to kill his cunning friend's mother. He had an idea and went to the house of the smith, who fixes knives and swords.

He told the blacksmith, "Here is my problem. I made a pact with my friend, and I killed my mother, but he took his mother and hid her. Now I want my voice to change and be like my friend's, so that when I go there and sing she will think it is her own child."

The smith fixed a special potion for him. Then the smith told him, "This is a very strong potion. Be careful with it. When you reach the fence, don't touch the wood."

The boy agreed, and went out and walked until he reached the fence. As he was crossing he fell on the other side and accidentally touched the wood. He hurried home and cooked some food and ate it quickly, then said, "I'll take the garbage out."

"Go ahead," said his friend. The slow-witted boy who had killed his mother went out and sharpened his cutlass. He walked to the place where his friend's mother was and sang: "Mother, come out, take food and eat. Mother, come out, take food and eat. I fooled my friend, he killed his mother, but I hid you in the ground. Mother, come out and eat."

The mother came out, thinking it was her child who sang. As she was coming out the boy raised his cutlass and cut off her head. Her head fell on the ground, and her body fell back into the hole. The boy was very happy and went home and rested.

The next day the boy who had been so clever took the food out and sang. But nobody came out. Again he sang: "Come out, Mother, take food and eat. Come out, Mother, take food and eat."

He looked and looked, but still no one came out of the hole. A voice said, "Look up, look down. Look up, look down." He looked up and saw the head of his dead mother, and below he saw the skeleton left in the hole by the rats.

He cried and went back to the house. He began to cook with his friend and cried some more. His friend said, "Why are you crying?"

He said, "It's nothing." But still he cried.

His friend again asked, "Why are you crying?"

And again he said, "It's nothing." But at last he knew that his friend had killed his mother, so they separated, and never saw one another again.

▼▲▼▲▼▲▼▲▼▲▼▲▼▲▼▲▼▲▼▲▼▲▼▲▼▲▼▲▼

32 Adele and the Pineapple Child

Once upon a time there was a hunter who had two wives. The younger wife had no child and always worried about this. One day, when the hunter and the younger wife were going to their farm, they met a very old man in the forest. The old man asked them what they wanted most, and the hunter said his wife wanted a child.

Then the old man bent down among some pineapples growing nearby and uprooted one. He set the pineapple down in front of the wife, and it turned into a baby girl. The old man told them to take the baby home since it was exactly what they wanted. And he told them that when the child grew up, she must never be told that she came from a pineapple.

When the younger wife brought the baby home, she was very, very happy. She stayed constantly in the house, spending long hours feeding the baby, singing to her, adorning her, and playing with her.

The older wife became very curious about where the baby had come from. She was jealous that the younger wife was so happy. So when the mother was playing with her baby in the room, she would often stand outside the hut and listen to them through the eaves of the thatch.

One day, she heard the younger wife playing with her baby, and laughing and saying, "Oh, my wonderful baby, my wonderful, wonderful pineapple baby."

The younger wife did not have another child. So when the baby grew into a girl, her mother spent even more time decorating her and giving her even more things than before. This made the older wife even more jealous.

One day, the younger wife had to go with the hunter into the forest to collect some firewood, and she left her daughter to the older wife to look after. When they had gone, the girl said she wanted a drink of water, and the woman gave it to her. Then she said she wanted something to eat, so the woman gave her food. Then she said she wanted something else. The woman's patience was now gone, so she shouted at the girl, "Why are you so spoiled? Be quiet and give me some peace! After all, you are nothing but a pineapple child."

As soon as the girl heard this, she began crying, left the house, and went toward the forest. As she went, she sang plaintively: "Adele does not go for firewood. Adele does not call me a human child. Adele calls me a pineapple child. Adele m-m-m-m, Adele!"

Soon afterward, the hunter and the younger wife returned, and the woman asked for her child. Then the older wife said, "I only called her a pineapple child, but she is running toward the forest weeping and wailing as if I had done something terrible."

When the hunter heard this, he immediately ran after the girl. He heard her wailing, and, guided by the sound, he reached her at the place where they had met the old man. When he saw her, she had just gone and stood on the spot where the old man had uprooted the pineapple from the ground. As she stood there, she started sinking into the ground, and as she sank, she began to turn into a pineapple.

The hunter rushed forward and plucked at her head, to pull her out of the ground. But she had almost completely turned into a pineapple. Only her hair remained, and this peeled off into his hands. Weeping, he grasped the hair, held it tightly to his breast, and there it stuck.

That is why man has hair on his chest.

33 The Voice of the Child

There was once a man and his wife. The man was a hunter, and they were very happy. Then one day the woman became ill. All the important fetish priests were consulted, but she didn't get well. When she was given food, she wouldn't eat. Her husband went to the bush and brought home the choicest meat, but she wouldn't eat.

One day the hunter sat in front of the hut in which the sick woman lay. A small voice spoke to him, "Bring the elephant, bring the elephant." He rose up and stood there. He looked this way, and he looked that way, but he could not see the owner of the voice. The voice spoke again, this time more urgently. He took his gun and went to the kingdom of the animals and brought back the elephant. Now the elephant was the most powerful medicine man in the whole world. When he arrived, every chair on which he sat broke immediately. Finally, all the chairs were broken and no more chairs could be found for him. The hunter stood there looking round for a seat for Elephant.

A dirty-looking little child all covered over with yaws said, "Elders, if I may say a word."

"Get out of our way," the men shouted. They would not listen to him. An old woman sitting near the fire said, "It is the ring of a child which doesn't fit a man, but not his food and certainly not his word." So they listened to the dirty-looking child covered all over with yaws.

"Get three broomsticks and tie them into a tripod. Sprinkle ashes in a circle around it and let Elephant sit on it." His advice was followed, though with many jeers and a good deal of murmuring. The elephant sat down. Whump! And all was well.

The elephant then began to make medicine. He waved his magic switch three times over the sick woman and listened attentively.

He nodded, cocked his ear, and said, "My right ear has heard, my other ear has not heard." He cocked his left ear and said, "My left ear, too, has heard. My fetish, Bruku, has not heard." After a long pause while he listened intently, he said, "My fetish, Bruku, has now heard. Now listen, all of you. This woman who lies here has been bewitched. She has been given a strange and dangerous longing for unobtainable foods. Let her husband hear. If your wife is to live she must eat the liver of a live elephant, eat the tongue of a black cobra, and drink water from the river Duku."

The hunter at once set out to seek the liver of a live elephant, a cobra's tongue, and water from the river Duku. After wandering through the forests for a long time, he saw a herd of elephants.

He raised his voice and sang: "My wife Kwaso Adwa is dying. I'm left alone. They gave Kwaso Adwa food. She wouldn't eat. Kwaso Adwa wants elephant liver. Elephant ee. I'm afraid oo. Elephant liver. I'm afraid oo."

One old elephant came to him and said, "My son, you tell a sad story. Come enter my belly. Cut what you want, only you should not touch my heart."

He got inside the elephant's belly and cut enough of the liver to make a broth. He came out and thanked the elephant. When he arrived home he made a broth with the elephant's liver and gave it to Kwaso Adwa. She ate it all and got a little better.

Now, he set out toward the grove in which flowed the waters of the river Duku where no man had ever been before. When the grove was in sight he stood there and cried. Then he raised his voice and sang: "My wife Kwaso Adwa is dying. I'm left alone. They gave Kwaso Adwa water. She wouldn't drink. Only Duku water. They go to Duku, they don't return. Only Duku water. They go to Duku, they don't return."

The god of the river Duku rose up out of the water when his ears heard. He sprinkled Duku water on the hunter to purify him. He led him to the grove where a white-robed servant of the river collected a calabash full of Duku water for him.

When he returned home he gave the water to his wife to drink. She got much better, but still couldn't get out of bed without help. They had to hold her hands like a little child. Only cobra's tongue would make her well enough to walk.

The hunter again set out on his third and most dangerous mission—to get the tongue of the live black cobra.

When he arrived at the outskirts of the country of the snakes he raised his voice and sang: "My wife Kwaso Adwa is dying. I'm left alone. They gave Kwaso Adwa food. She wouldn't eat. Kwaso Adwa wants Cobra tongue. Black Cobra ee! I'm afraid oo! Black Cobra's Tongue. Black Cobra! I'm afraid oo!"

And again and again he sang the song, but no help came. There was not a snake in sight, and he was afraid to enter the land of the snakes without permission. He sat there on the borders hoping a kind snake would come to help him. Day and night he watched and waited, but no snake came.

At last, weary and hungry, he lay down and gave himself up to sleep. As his eyes closed, he heard a small familiar voice, "Kwadwo the Hunter. Your wife Kwaso Adwa would eat Cobra's tongue. Black Cobra is coming! Black Cobra's tongue. Black Cobra is coming."

He opened his eyes. Only a few yards away from him a big black cobra stood on its tail, swaying to and fro. It shot out its forked tongue and said, "They gave your wife, Kwaso Adwa, food. She wouldn't eat. Kwaso Adwa would eat black cobra's tongue. Black Cobra ee! I've come!"

The snake swayed more and more and moved nearer and nearer the hunter. But the hunter stood there. He was too frightened to move. Just as the snake was about to strike, a magic arrow flew from nowhere and struck the snake in the mouth. Its tongue fell out on the rock. Its body fell to the ground.

The small familiar voice said, "Take the cobra tongue to your wife. She will live and grow well when she has eaten it. But as soon as she is strong enough, take her back to her father and mother, because it is dangerous for a woman to develop strange appetites."

Whom do you think the familiar small voice belonged to? The dirty-looking boy covered with yaws? But who was the dirty-looking boy covered with yaws? If it wasn't Akokoaa Kwasi Gyinamoa, then this my story which I have told you is a lie.

▼▲▼▲▼▲▼▲▼▲▼▲▼▲▼▲▼▲▼▲▼▲▼▲▼▲▼▲

34 The Yam Farm and the Problem Tongue

There was a certain Mister Spider who lived with his wife, Konole, in a certain town. And in the town in which they were living there was a great famine. One day Spider said he was going to look for sticks with which to weave baskets that he would go and sell. Going on and on, then, looking through the grass, he came upon a place where somebody had planted yams. It was a huge farm. So he took some trouble to find the owner. He shouted, "Mister Farmer, Hello! Hello! Hello!" Then at the third call the farmer replied, "What?" When the farmer appeared, he was followed by two other medium-sized young men, and they said this was their farm, and that they had planted the yams and were now looking for somebody who would help them to harvest them, and carry them away. If he would help, they would give him some.

So Spider came and laid out his carrying cloth, and he helped them haul the yams away the whole day until nightfall, and then it was time to give Spider his share. Now, one of them asked him, "Call us by our names, and we will give you what we are to give you." He didn't know the name of any one of them. So they took one puny little yam and gave it to Spider and said, "If you had known our names, we would have given you an equal share of the yams, but since you don't know our names this is your yam."

When Spider returned home he went and sat down for a long time and thought about this thing. Then he called his wife, and he said, "Konole." She said, "Yes?" And he said, "By luck I have found a farm with many yams growing on it. There are three people working there, and they need someone to help harvest the yams. I want you to go and help me." She said, "All right." And Spider told his wife, "When we get to the farm I will change myself into a very small boy, a baby, with huge testicles and all my head shaved clean, and you can lay me under the shed. Your task is to help carry the yams, and my task is to find out the names of those people." And so Konole and Spider started out and went to the farm. When they were almost there, Spider changed himself into a very little boy, a baby just about a week old, with huge testicles, and his scalp was shaved very, very clean. Konole took the baby and put him on her back, and she went forward and greeted them and said, "Hello!" And they said, "Yes," and then they came forward, all three of them.

She said, "Spider says I should tell you that because of the work he did here for you, he is not feeling at all well today, so I should come and do his work today." They said, "All right! Pick up your basket and go and carry some yams." And so she took Spider off her back and spread out a cloth under the shed and laid Spider on the cloth. Spider lay there for a long time, and then he noticed that one of the three young men was coming to the kitchen under the shed to drink some water. When he reached the shed he came upon Spider lying there, and he hadn't seen this before. There was a very small baby with huge testicles and all his hair shaved very, very clean. The one who came upon this scene shouted, "Ahihi!" Then the other one said, "What?" And he shouted again, "Ahaha!" and the other one said,

"What?" And he said, "Come and see, come and see!" And then, of those he called, one asked him, "Asogadagrija, what do you want?" And he said, "You come." Spider kept the three names in his head. Then they came and looked at the enormous testicles for a long time and the bald head of the baby, and then they went back. The one who was to drink, drank his water and went.

Then after Konole had carried yams the whole day till night, the three farmers asked her to tell them their names, and when they asked her this question, Spider, that is Konole's baby that was lying on the cloth, suddenly started shouting, "Ahihi, Ahaha, Asogadagrija!" in the hope that Konole might hear these names so that she might repeat them to the people. Alas! Konole didn't understand, and so when she, too, couldn't give their names, they took a puny little yam and gave it to her and said, "You see, you couldn't tell our names, but if you had found out our names we would have shared these yams with you equally." And so off Konole went with the strange-looking baby.

After they had gone a little way from the farm, behind a bush Spider jumped down from Konole's back and said, "Konole, aren't you stupid and foolish? All that time I was crying 'Ahihi, Ahaha, Asogadagrija!' couldn't you hear what I was saying, shouting all those names at you? You didn't listen, and you went on like that till you had done all that work for nothing. Now, tomorrow you can't come with me." That was what he said to Konole.

So they went home and slept, and the following morning Spider alone set out and went along little by little until he arrived at the farm. When he got there he greeted the farmers. When he greeted them they replied and said, "Yesterday you sent a woman here, and she said that you weren't feeling well at all." And he said, "Yes, that's true. Yesterday I didn't feel well at all, so I sent my wife on to come and do my work for me." And they said, "Ah, well, there is your basket."

Spider went and picked up his basket and started carting yams, and all the time he was carrying the yams away on his head he was repeating the names over to himself silently. He kept on doing this the whole day till quitting time came in the night—the time when farmers stop work. They lined up, all three of them, and said to him, they said, "Spider, you have finished the work. Tell us our names so that we can give you your share of the yams, and then you can go."

Spider said, "You, you are called Ahihi." And then the first one fell down, yes this one whose name he called fell down and died. He said, "You, there, your name is Ahaha." And as soon as Spider called his name, the second, too, fell down and died. Then Spider said, "And you, you are called Asogadagrija." As soon as his name was mentioned, he, too, fell down and died. Spider said, "Ho! Spider! You have come upon much valuable property? These three people are dead, and all their yams now belong to me. Right!" And so he dragged all three of them away and hid them. Then he went off to town to the chief's house and made them beat the gong. He said, "You know I have planted some yams, and this year they have fared very well, so I want all the people of the town to come with me to my farm to help me harvest the yams. Anybody who will come and help me will get his share."

And so they all went and helped Spider, and they carted lots of yams, lots and lots and lots of yams to his house. Spider became a very rich man because of the yams. He became a chief, in fact. It was therefore necessary for Spider to do something about the three dead bodies on the farm. After some time he decided that these bodies should be treated as the bodies of animals, so he must skin them as animals are skinned, and then he could eat them.

He went and got the bodies and peeled off their skins with hot water and cooked them. He and Konole cooked some yams, too, and then they served the yams and the meat. Spider took some of the boiled yam and the boiled meat. As soon as he put it in his mouth, and the meat touched his tongue, his tongue shot out of his mouth, and swelled up. It was a huge tongue, very swollen, bigger than the biggest table.

And he said, "Oh, Spider, what am I going to do with this huge tongue?" He thought about it for some time, and then he sent for his son, Kwakute. He sent his son to the chief's compound, and Kwakute went to say that Spider would like everybody, on the following Tuesday, to go and bathe in the sea. After returning from the swim in the sea all the people would go to his farm to pull up some yams. When the people got to the beach, they must pull out their tongues and lay them aside before going into the water to swim.

So the time came, and they all went to the sea, but when they set out to go there, Spider was the very last person to leave. All the people pulled out their tongues and laid them out, one tongue here, one tongue there, one tongue over there—tongues all over the place. Spider came at last, and when he got there he also took out his tongue and laid it down. Then he ran down to the water's edge, dipped his toes in the water, and immediately returned to where the tongues were and sorted through them. He looked and looked for some time and finally decided that the most beautiful tongue there belonged to the pig, so he took Pig's tongue and put it in his mouth and left his own huge tongue lying where it was. Then he himself shouted out, "It's time to go! It's time to go! We are going! Anyone who is late is a dirty bush dog!" And then he set out fast for the town.

Those who heard the shout, and those who saw that he was going, came out and also started taking back their tongues. This went on until there was only one tongue left. Meanwhile Pig had been looking for his tongue. He had looked and looked and looked and couldn't find his tongue. Finally he was faced with this single huge tongue, and out of disappointment and shame and tiredness, Pig said, "All right, I shall pick up this ridiculous and disgusting tongue and put it in my mouth, but with this disgusting tongue I will not be satisfied until I have eaten dung." And so, Pig picked up the tongue and put it in his mouth. That is why it is that when Pig has been roaming the whole day eating everything, its final dish—the dessert which it eats last—is dung.

▼▲▼▲▼▲▼▲▼▲▼▲▼▲▼▲▼▲▼▲▼▲▼▲▼▲▼▲▼▲

35 The River's Judgment

There once was a woman who had a very industrious daughter. She helped her mother in all the household chores and on the farm. She was excellent. When she planted anything it grew better than what her mother had planted. She had a green thumb. Many men sought her hand in marriage, but the jealous mother would not agree to let her be married.

One especially good season their farm was beautiful, and they expected an unusually large harvest. The plantains that were planted by the daughter were deep green, and the corn had big cobs. People who passed that way admired the farm, and all the talk among the young men of the village was of this girl.

Her mother, however, did not like this kind of talk. She grew very jealous and began to treat her daughter badly. She began to scold her all day long for no reason at all. Even when there was plenty of food she would give her only raw vegetables without meat.

In spite of this, the daughter remained as loyal and as industrious as before. At last the mother sought the aid of witchcraft and killed her daughter just as harvesttime was near. The mother then made a cottage on the farm and began to enjoy the fruits of the farm.

Even at that time, the spirit of the daughter was restless in the land of the dead. The daughter had to seek revenge against her mother. To find her mother, she had to cross seven different rivers. If she was ever to find revenge for the wrong her mother had done her, she had to appease and plead her cause with these seven rivers.

One day the ghost of the daughter set out with a dish of mashed plantain and eggs. When she came to the first river, she threw some of the food—first to the right and then to the left. Then she threw some into the river and sang of her grief and of her mother's treachery.

As she sang, she wept bitterly. The spirit of the river was moved. The river dried up where her path lay, and she crossed over to the side where the village was.

When she came to the second river, she took some of the food and threw it first to the right, then to the left. Then she took some and threw it into the river, and, weeping all the time, she sang of her grief and her mother's treachery.

The spirit of the second river was also moved to pity. Her path was made dry, and she crossed to the other side.

She continued to cast food and sing and weep at all the other rivers until she came to the last one, which barred the way to her mother's cottage. She threw some food first to the right, then to the left, and then into the river. She sat there on the bank and wept bitterly, for she saw her mother in the cottage cooking, and the smell of the food drifted to her across the river. It was good food—the very food that she had planted and raised and harvested.

She thought how good a wife she would have been, cooking good food, food she had grown with her own hands, if only her mother had allowed her to marry. But now she was only a ghost and could never marry.

The tears filled her eyes, and she stood up and sang sadly of her grief and of her mother's treachery.

Her mother looked up from her cooking, and there across the river she saw her daughter standing all white and beautiful. She threw away the cooking things and ran to meet her, whether from fear or from joy, I do not know. What I know is that the river that had dried up in the middle to allow the daughter to pass now flowed over both mother and daughter. The daughter rose to the surface and walked away—back to the land of the dead—but the mother was carried away by the river and drowned.

This is why when you have a daughter you must never be jealous of her. This woman was jealous of hers, and she lost a good daughter and her own life too.

▼▲▼▲▼▲▼▲▼▲▼▲▼▲▼▲▼▲▼▲▼▲▼▲▼▲▼▲▼

36 Who Has the Greatest Love?

A man was once traveling with his three wives when a snake bit him. In a short time, he died in the forest. One wife said, "My husband is dead. I can't live without him." She went to the snake and let it bite her, and she died.

Another wife said, "Since this place is full of wild animals, I had better stay and guard the bodies." She did not rest at all and did not allow even a fly to touch the bodies.

The third wife said, "My husband and my co-wife whom I loved are dead. I will not rest till I find a way to bring them back to life." She went immediately to an old woman and asked her to help. The old woman gave her an enchanted cowtail switch and told her to touch the bodies with it three times. This she did, and the husband and the dead woman came back to life and were just as before, just as if nothing had happened.

Tell me which of these three wives, then, loved her husband most.

37 Tortoise Buys a House

There was a very great famine. The people suffered, as did all the birds and all the animals and all the rivers and all the bushes and all the people. Everybody!

Tortoise wasn't bothered at first because he had stores of food close by. But after some time, when the famine wouldn't go away, Tortoise used up his food, and he became hungry like everybody else.

He thought of a hoax that could get him something to eat. He went and dug a very big hole near the place of a groundnut seller. He hid himself early in the morning in this pit and watched the groundnut seller sell her groundnuts. Suddenly he started to sing a very sweet and hypnotic song that went: "Hello, groundnut seller. Listen, groundnut seller: leave your groundnuts so that I may eat them. Dance from here and dance into the next big city. Dance from there into the next big city. Dance all over the country."

The tune of this song made the groundnut seller dance all over the city and into the palace of the king.

The king was puzzled about the whole business, and he sent one of his slaves to go and fetch the groundnut seller. In the palace the groundnut seller told the king what had happened to her, and the king sent one of his slaves with her to the place where she had kept her groundnuts. But when they got to the place they could not find the groundnuts. Then the slave of the king started to look everywhere in the forest trying to find where the tune was coming from that was making the groundnut seller dance. All of a sudden he came to the pit that Tortoise had dug and found that it was full of groundnuts. He then took a very heavy club and hit Tortoise on his back with the club. Since in those days Tortoise was a soft animal like a frog, he was easily overpowered and captured. After capturing him, the slave took Tortoise to the palace of the king.

In the palace of the king the tortoise was put on trial. Tortoise boasted that his song and his tricks would work on anybody. The king said that his song would not work on him. Then Tortoise hid in a corner of the palace and started to sing his hypnotic song. As he was singing the king began to dance all over his palace, and as the king danced, all his wives and all his slaves and all his elders danced also. They were all dancing everywhere. When they had danced and danced and danced, Tortoise went into the middle of the crowd and told the king, "Can't you see, now, that my spell has worked on you?"

It was then that the king himself came to his senses. To reward Tortoise for his talent, the king commanded that all his servants and all his messengers should take stock of all the properties he had in this world. He then divided all his wives, all his horses, all his clothes, and everything he had into two parts and gave one part to Tortoise.

Tortoise took the possessions and sold them. With the money he received from the sale, he went and bought a very hard shell. With that shell on his back, he would be safe from any attack with either a sharp object or a club, and no one would be able to capture him again.

From that time on Tortoise always had this very, very hard shell on, and whenever an enemy approached he would just pull his head and his legs inside it.

▼▲▼▲▼▲▼▲▼▲▼▲▼▲▼▲▼▲▼▲▼▲▼▲▼▲▼▲▼▲

38 Why Bush Pig Has a Red Face

Once upon a time a great drought crept all over the land. The animals looked very dirty, because they had no water to wash in. And soon, some of them even had no water to drink. Now they were all afraid that soon they would have no food to eat if the drought did not end.

Because of this, Anaanu, the spider, told them that they should all get together and make a huge yam farm. When the yams had ripened and been harvested, they should store them away in a safe place, so that they could eat some little by little till rain came to end the drought.

All the animals agreed, and they all came to make the farm. From the leopard himself, the King of the Forest, and the brave and mighty lion, down to the smallest and weakest grasscutter, they all put their strength into the work, and soon they had a huge yam farm. When the yams were ripe, they uprooted them and stacked them in a barn which Anaanu had made them build at the edge of the farm. Now they sat down to rest and enjoy the fruit of their work.

All this time, they did not know that Anaanu had dug a deep hole not far from where the barn was. He had carefully hidden away in this hole a coal stove, a frying pan, a sharp knife, a cooking pot, water, oil, pepper, salt, onions, tomatoes, and all the other ingredients for cooking yams. While the animals stacked their yams on the platforms in the barn, Anaanu, starting from below, removed the yams night after night and carried them into his hole.

Shortly after the animals had started resting and eating their yams from the top of the pile, they discovered that the lower platforms were empty and that the yams were almost gone. Now there was great consternation among them, each shouting at the top of his voice. Leopard and Lion were very angry, and they threatened to eat whoever took the yams. Suddenly someone noticed that Anaanu was nowhere to be seen. At once they suspected him of the theft, and they all went out looking and shouting for him.

Soon they smelled the scent of cooking coming from the hole. Anaanu had finished boiling some yams, and had now put a frying pan on the fire. He had put slices of onion and tomato in the oil, and was preparing stew. When the animals smelled the stew, they became very angry. Everyone shouted that Anaanu should be brought out of his hole. But the entrance to the hole was very narrow, and no one could squeeze through and go down. Anaanu just kept on cooking his stew and laughing at them.

At last the courageous Bush Pig shouted, "Friends, I will bring him out of this hole. I will push my long snout down the hole and bring him out. But since the hole is narrow, you must all push me from behind. If you see me push my hindquarters up, it means that the hole is getting narrower, so push me down harder."

With that, he put his snout down the hole. The animals pushed him down farther. But Anaanu was waiting for him. Anaanu took a knife and shaved a slice of flesh off the bush pig's nose. The slice of flesh fell straight into the frying pan, and Anaanu now had meat in his stew. The bush pig was in great pain, and pushed his hindquarters upward in order to get out of the hole. But as he came up, all the animals grabbed hold of his backside and pushed him down harder, as he had told them to do. He went down a second time, and Anaanu shaved off another piece of meat from one side of his face for the stew. Again Bush Pig pushed up, and again he was pushed down, and Anaanu shaved a slice of flesh off the other side of Bush Pig's face for his stew. This time, Anaanu took pepper and spread it all over the raw flesh on Bush Pig's face. Bush Pig could not bear it any more. With one mighty heave, he shot up and backward out of the hole, scattering to left and right the bunch of animals who had been pushing him down.

When the animals got up and looked at his face, they were astonished. With one voice they cried out, "Look how red Bush Pig's face is!"

And that is how Bush Pig got his red face.

▼▲▼▲▼▲▼▲▼▲▼▲▼▲▼▲▼▲▼▲▼▲▼▲▼▲▼▲▼▲

39 Spider and the Nightjar

Atendefianoma, the nightjar, was a fetish priest. Ananse was his assistant. One day they were invited to a village to make medicine for a sick chief. There wasn't the slightest reason to boast about anything, but Ananse is a strange person who loves being in trouble. When he is not in trouble his skin aches. So, loving trouble, he swore the great oath of the nation that he would never eat a bite of food until he had returned to his own village.

They were kindly treated at the chief's village. There was much to eat. The chief's wives and daughters brought delicious dishes. The fetish priest fed well. Ananse could not eat because of his oath. He became very thin.

Every day they had to dance for several hours. The fetish priest danced while Ananse followed him and threw powder at his feet and over his body. When the fetish priest was possessed, his fetish spoke through him in a strange language. Ananse, as assistant, had to translate into ordinary language what he said. Sometimes too, the fetish sent the fetish priest dancing through the streets, seeking out the evil spirits that threatened the chief's life. Once the fetish sent them tearing through the bush along the narrow paths, from which they pulled herbs, twigs, and even thorns with their bare hands.

It was after one such exercise that Ananse felt very hungry, hungrier than all the days of his fast put together. He knew that bean meal had been sent to their room for Atendefianoma. How his belly heaved and ached! How his mouth watered! He could almost feel the smooth, delicious bean meal sliding down his parched throat. The temptation was too powerful for him. In the middle of an unusually vigorous dance he asked for permission to visit the backyard.

He rushed to their room ready to take a few mouthfuls of beans. To his great astonishment, however, a feather from the nightjar's wing was stuck on top of the bean meal, dancing as vigorously as Atendefianoma was doing. Poor Ananse, what could he do? He had to go back to join in the dance. Ananse tried again and again, but each time there was, spinning knowingly, this magic feather. At last Ananse could no longer stand this sort of teasing. He went straight to Atendefianoma and shouted at him, "Look, concentrate on your dancing or else go back and eat your bean meal!"

Atendefianoma replied, "And you, concentrate on your task or you will break your solemn oath."

Ananse threw the plate of white powder at Atendefianoma and swore that if he ever saw him in their village, he would kill him. That is why the nightjar is seen only at night around the village and along the bush paths and not in the village itself.

▼▲▼▲▼▲▼▲▼▲▼▲▼▲▼▲▼▲▼▲▼▲▼▲▼▲▼▲▼▲▼▲

40 Spider Learns to Listen

There was a famine in the land, a very serious famine. There was nothing to eat. People even drank the juice of boiled pebbles. Some even chewed the tough roots of the bush trees that could be found far away, but few people had the strength to travel.

One day Kwaku Ananse decided to go away and try to dig some of the tough roots for his family. When he had gone half a day's journey from home, he saw a fancy earthenware dish lying by the roadside. He said, "That's a bit of luck, now I've got a fine dish!"

The dish spoke, "I'm not a dish."

"Then if you're not a dish," said Ananse, "what are you?"

"Food Pounder is my name," the dish answered.

"All right, if you can pound food, pound some and let me see."

As quick as a wink, every kind of food you could think of was there on the ground in front of Ananse. Kwaku ate as much as he could, packed the dish in his bag, and returned home. When the usual pebble broth was made in the evening, Kwaku refused to take it. He said, "It is the children who are important. Let them have it." For several days he refused to eat, always saying that the children needed food more. What he really did, of course, was this. Early in the morning before anyone else got up and late at night when the family was asleep, he would go to the secret room in which he kept Food Pounder and say to it, "That's a bit of luck! I've found a dish."

And back would come, "I'm not a dish."

Kwaku would then say, "All right, what are you?"

And the dish would answer, "My name is Food Pounder."

And after that, "If you know how to pound food, pound a little food for me to see." And food would appear, and Kwaku would fill his belly.

One day while Ananse was away in the bush, Endekuma, his eldest son, wandered into the secret room and saw the dish. He cried out in surprise, "Oh, what a beautiful earthenware dish father has here!" The dish said, "I am not a dish, I'm Food Pounder."

Endekuma was very much afraid when he heard the dish talk, but he managed to say, "All right, then, let me see you pound some food."

The dish pounded fufu and put it in a nice soup and made a lot of other sorts of food as well. The boy called his three brother spiders, Bighead, Bigbelly, and Thinlegs, into the room, and together they ate all the food. When they could eat no more they asked the dish what things were taboo to it.

"Red earth, the fiber of the plantain, and the fruit of the lime," was what the dish told them. So the three boys immediately went and got bits of each of these three things and rubbed the dish with them. Now the dish was powerless. It couldn't provide any more food. The boys ran away.

In the evening the usual broth was served. Ananse said "no." He went to his secret room. "That's a bit of luck! I've found a dish!" Nothing happened. He tried again. Nothing. And again he tried. Nothing. So he went back to the family very angry and very hungry.

The next day, at dawn, he again set out to fetch tough tree roots from a distant land. Around midday he saw a whip lying by the roadside. He cried, "I've found a whip!"

The whip spoke, "I'm not a whip. I'm Pounder."

Ananse in great delight, thinking of food again, replied, "All right, then, if you are Pounder, do a little pounding and let me see it."

The whip went into action—Thump, thump, whack, slash!—with Ananse crying, "Help! help! I'm dying! help!" Until a passing bird told him,

"Say Adwebreww." Ananse said, "Adwebreww." Then the whip stopped flogging him. He said, "This is just right for my children who ruined the magic dish."

He put the whip in his bag and carried it to the secret room. When the evening pebble broth was served, he refused it and went to the secret room.

The following day Endekuma and his brothers went to the room and discovered the whip. They said to it, "What a fine whip father has here." The whip said, "I am not called Whip." The boys asked, "Then who are you?" It answered, "I'm Pounder." How they licked their lips, and how their throats ached for a good meal! Food! Food! So they said, "If you are Pounder, pound a little and let us see."

You should have been there to see it. The whip beat and beat and beat. Then it flogged and flogged for a while, and then it went back to beating. The children cried and cried and cried. But there was no way out. They had closed the door. As the beating got heavier, Endekuma managed to climb the wall and escaped under the eaves. Bighead did the same, but he was so top-heavy that he fell, and his head dropped right off. Thinlegs jumped down, and his legs snapped off. Bigbelly fell on his stomach, and it burst. The whip went on flogging and flogging and flogging, and when it could get no one else to flog, it ran off and planted itself in good earth, where it grew up as the plant known as Old Woman's Razor.

▽▲▽▲▽▲▽▲▽▲▽▲▽▲▽▲▽▲▽▲▽▲▽▲▽▲▽▲

41 Tortoise and the Singing Crab

I wasn't living then, but Tortoise was, as were all the other animals. There was a big famine, and the animals went looking for food. They went to the bush and found a water yam vine. They scratched round it and found a water yam. They dug and dug and soon they saw a very big water yam. They dug it out. Then they asked themselves who could pick it up and carry it. It wasn't an easy decision. Someone suggested Tortoise. When he came forward they all agreed he was too little, so they let that idea go. Then lion. But he couldn't move it. He tried, but he couldn't lift it.

Tortoise went back. He picked it up, and all the animals praised him. But who would carry it home? Again no suggestions. Tortoise, being as full of wisdom as he was empty of food, said, "Let's cook it and eat it here!" So they peeled it, and they sent Tortoise off for water.

He went off walking, walking, walking. He heard a strange song being sung. Tortoise ran away from the song. He ran away for awhile and came back. Again he heard the same strange song. As he got nearer he saw it was a crab singing. He caught it and put it in a bag. When he got back to the other animals, they cooked the meal. They said Tortoise walked on the ground with his hands, so he should go and wash them before he sat down to eat. He went and did so. But when he got back, they said he had walked on the ground again, so he must go and wash once more. He said he wouldn't. He sat down. They were eating. They had prepared the yam with plenty of palm oil, and they were eating all of it. Tortoise clapped his hands.

The singing came out of the bag faintly. All the animals stopped and asked, "What is that? What is that?" But they soon started to eat again. Tortoise asked if he might join them. They said no. He asked again, but they said no. He clapped his hands harder, and the singing began again, much louder this time.

The animals ran away in terror, some fell down, some died of fright. Tortoise sat down for a while. Then he started eating. Antelope came. He said, "I beg you, give me a little food." Tortoise took a handful of food and said, "Come and get it." As Antelope came for the food, Tortoise threw it at him, and Antelope ran away. Tortoise went back, sat down, and finished the food. Then he took the crab who had sung the song for him, cracked its shell and ate it, too.

▾▲▾▲▾▲▾▲▾▲▾▲▾▲▾▲▾▲▾▲▾▲▾▲▾▲▾▲▾▲

42 Spider Meets His Match

One day Grandfather God gave Spider a cow. Spider said, "I'll not kill this cow, except in a place where there's not another living creature. If I kill it where there are people they'll get some of it to eat." He took the cow away into a big forest. He called and shouted for a long time, but nobody answered. He said, "There's nobody here, but perhaps there are some flies, so I'll break wind." He let go. Brap! And sure enough, there were flies everywhere. "Sure enough," Spider said. "I was right. There *are* flies about, so I'll not kill my cow here." He went deeper into the forest, and he broke wind again and again flies came. So he didn't kill his cow there either. He went on, into virgin forest and there he stopped. Brap! And there were no flies to be seen. "Yes! No living creature here. Not even a fly. Not even a greedy housefly! This is where I'll kill my cow."

He killed the cow. He cooked a delicious meal, and he was just sitting down to eat it when "Thump!" He heard something fall behind him. He said, "On my soul, that's a bit of luck! It's a monkey that has fallen down. I'm going to go and get it and add it to my meat." He got up and went to where the noise had come from, and what a surprise! It was Tortoise. He was about to return to his meal when Tortoise said, "Father Spider, don't leave. Take me with you." Spider said, "I'll not take you with me." Tortoise said, "If you don't I'll make trouble." Spider said, "Wait! I'm coming to get you."

Spider took Tortoise with him and later put some food in a broken dish and offered it to Tortoise. Tortoise asked him, "What's this for?" Spider said, "It's for you." Tortoise said, "Oh no! Why am I the one to eat from the broken dish? Spider, come and eat my food, and I'll have yours." Spider said, "No, I'm not giving you mine." Tortoise said, "All right, if you don't let me have your food, I'll make trouble for you." "Come and eat then." And even as I am talking, Tortoise falls on the food, and Slurp! Slurp! Gobble! Gobble! How yummy!

The next day when it came time to eat food, it was the same. And the day after that, too. That is just how it was, day after day. By now, Spider was almost starved. Only his good sense remained. He told himself, "I'll teach Tortoise a lesson." He collected slippery herbs and smeared Tortoise all over until he was slippery too, and Gulp! He swallowed Tortoise.

Then Spider made plans to vomit over a fire so that Tortoise would die in it. But because he was in Spider's belly Tortoise could see what was in Spider's head. So Tortoise said, "Come, let us go to your mother-in-law's village." Spider jumped for joy, saying, "Good! Let's kill two birds with one stone!"

Spider was tired out by the time they got to his mother-in-law's village. She received him well and cooked an excellent meal of goat meat and fufu for him. How Spider wanted that food. Food! His throat ached for it. He sat down and was just going to eat, when Tortoise said, "If you touch that food, I'll squeeze your heart." Spider said, "Ah Tortoise, is this any way to treat someone? And I am so tired and hungry. All right, I have to eat, and you'll just have to squeeze." Tortoise squeezed hard. Squinch! Spider yelled, "Eyauch! That hurts! Stop it, stop it, I won't eat." He called his mother-in-law to come and take the food. His mother-in-law said, "Son-in-law, is it that you don't like my cooking?" Spider said, "It was good, but I'm full."

During the entire eight days they spent in the village Tortoise wouldn't allow Spider a bite of food, though his mother-in-law cooked all the time for him. By now Spider had hardly the strength to walk. One day he heard his mother-in-law beating her children for stealing meat from her soup. Tortoise said, "Spider, say it was you who took the meat." Spider said, "You want to disgrace me, do you? You are in one of your treacherous moods again. I'll not say it." Tortoise said, "If you don't say it, I'll squeeze your heart again," and he did. Squinch! Spider said, "Mother-in-law, stop beating the children; I took the meat from the soup." Now look at Spider! He was ashamed, so very much ashamed.

It wasn't long before the queen mother of the village died. You should have seen how the executioners went on the rampage looking for a sacrifice for the queen mother. Strangers visiting the village hid in their rooms. Tortoise said to Spider, "Let's go to the funeral." Spider said, "Eh, you want them to kill me? See how all the strangers in town have gone into hiding." Tortoise said, "That's not my concern. Let's go. If you don't, I'll squeeze your heart." Spider said, "Go ahead, squeeze away if you want to. Death is death in whatever form." Squinch! Squinch! Then Spider said, "All right, all right! You villain! I'm going, I'm going!" He got up, put on his mourning cloth, and slipped into the palace. Thumpity thump, he tiptoed into the palace.

They sat for a while. Then Tortoise said to Spider, "Say to them I have lived too long. Make me the queen mother's sacrifice." Spider said, "Mm. So this is what we have come to at last. You have tricked me and deceived me and dragged me through the mud! I thank you for it. I have heard what you said, but you'll need a knife to open my mouth to get me to say it." Tortoise said, "So I'll squeeze." Spider said, "All right, go on and squeeze!" Squinch! Squinch! "Yauch!" cried Spider and was suddenly on his feet, addressing the mourners. In a faint voice he said, "Take me for your funeral sacrifice. Execute me immediately." The executioners were eager to do their job, they grabbed Spider and cut off his head. Chop!

That is why every man born of woman knows if you have something to eat, give someone a bit of it. Spider did not do that willingly, and he died a painful death.

▼▲▼▲▼▲▼▲▼▲▼▲▼▲▼▲▼▲▼▲▼▲▼▲▼▲▼▲▼▲▼▲▼▲

43 The Enchanted Loom

One day Ananse went to the bush to hunt. He wandered far into the thickest part of the forest without killing any animal. He sat down against a tree to rest. The forest was dark, but the sunshine peeped in here and there. He became drowsy, and in a short while he was asleep.

When he woke up he saw before him the finest cloth he had ever seen. It was soft silk woven in many colors. He picked it up and went home. He sold it for quite a sum of money.

The following day he returned to the spot to see whether he could find his benefactor and thank him for the cloth. He sat there a long time, but no one came. Finally he dropped off to sleep. When he woke up, there it was again! There before him lay another piece of cloth, much finer than the one he had found the day before.

Many days passed, and Ananse watched all the time, but he couldn't find his benefactor, although on every visit he got a piece of cloth.

One day after sitting a long time under the familiar tree, he thought he heard someone singing. He turned his head this way and that way to listen more carefully. There was no mistake about it. Someone was singing. He peered into the valley below him, for the singing seemed to come from there. He got up and went down the slope. The singing was now clear, and he could hear the words.

They were: "Carry me away, oh, carry me away. Swing ee! Carry me away. Carry me far, far away."

Ananse hid behind a tree and looked. He saw a most amazing thing. On a loom stretched between two trees across the valley sat a little fairy. He was swinging from one side of the valley to the other in big arcs, and as he swung, he sang and worked the loom and wove cloth.

Ananse watched for a long time and then crept back to his usual sleeping place. He fell asleep. When he woke up the cloth was there in front of him. You know Kwaku Ananse, how greedy and selfish he is. He was not satisfied with having the cloth. He wanted to be the weaver. So the next day he went to watch with a plan in his head. He stood and stood. When it was noon the little man climbed down from the loom and went away for awhile, after saying "Adwebreww" to stop the loom from swinging.

Quickly, Ananse climbed onto the loom and began to sing: "Carry me away, oh, carry me away. Swing ee! Carry me away. Carry me far, far away."

At once, like lightning, the loom moved and swung in great arcs. How pleased Ananse was, especially when he discovered that he, too, was weaving cloth! He sang louder, and the arcs of the swing got wider. He sang and swung; he swung and sang. The arcs of the loom climbed higher, reaching over the tops of the trees. Kwaku now gave himself up to complete abandon. He hung on the loom, first with one hand, then with the other. He hung from it like a bat by his toes. He lay full length on it. He jumped and bounced over it.

Before he knew what was happening, Kwaku had been carried high into the sky and over the wide sea. He couldn't stop the loom because he had forgotten the word for stopping it. He was carried to Europe where he still is weaving the best kind of silk cloth.

▼▲▼▲▼▲▼▲▼▲▼▲▼▲▼▲▼▲▼▲▼▲▼▲▼▲▼▲▼▲

44 How Tortoise Got Water

There was a drought in the town in which Tortoise was living. The shortage of rain was so great that all the streams and all the rivers in the area had dried up. There was only a water hole left, and this water hole supplied all the surrounding villages and towns with water.

But after some time, this water hole also began to dry up. Tortoise saw this was happening, and he thought about how he could get all the water that was left and store it in his own house.

He went to market and bought twenty big gourds for drawing water. But Tortoise realized that Elephant and Bush Cow, and all the other wild animals who were more powerful than he, were living very close to the stream. So he thought about how he could draw all the water in his twenty gourds without these wild animals seeing him. He tied the twenty gourds around his head, and, as he was walking to the brook, the gourds began to hit one another and make very nice music. To this music Tortoise sang: "I saw the Elephant in the bush, I met the Bush Cow in the river."

When Tortoise began singing, all the wild animals who were living very close to the water hole—including Bush Cow and Elephant—began dancing. They danced and danced and danced until they had danced many miles away from the water hole. Tortoise went to the water hole and drew all the water into his twenty gourds and carried the water home.

On his way home the Tortoise sang again: "I saw the Elephant in the bush, and met Bush Cow in the river."

The wisdom of Tortoise made it possible for him to drain all the water from the water hole, and he was able to have enough water to drink until the next rainy season. Everyone else lived in thirst.

▼▲▼▲▼▲▼▲▼▲▼▲▼▲▼▲▼▲▼▲▼▲▼▲▼▲▼▲▼▲▼▲▼▲

45 The Cloud Mother

Once upon a time there was a famine in the land. All the animals had agreed to share their mothers and eat them one by one. Many mothers had already been killed and eaten, and it was soon going to be Cunnie Rabbit's turn to kill his mother. He did not want to have her eaten, so he took her and hid her on a cloud. Well, every day after the animals had eaten, Cunnie Rabbit would take his mother a little bit of food he had saved for her. He would wait until all the beasts had gone, and then he would go off where no one could see him. He would call to his mother, "Send a chain, Mother, send a chain." Then his mother would drop a long chain down from the cloud. If his mother did not hear him, he would shout more loudly, "Send a chain, Mother, send a chain," until she sent the chain down from her cloud. Cunnie Rabbit would catch hold of the chain and call out, "Draw up the chain, Mother, draw up the chain." Once his mother could see that he had a firm grip on the chain, she would begin to pull it up. And in that way Cunnie Rabbit could go up and see his mother and give her the food he had brought for her. It was in that way, too, that Cunnie Rabbit managed to hide his mother until the animals had eaten everybody else's mother.

The other animals soon remembered that they had not yet eaten Cunnie Rabbit's mother, and they asked him about it. He kept saying that they had eaten her long before and had forgotten about it. The other animals couldn't remember eating her, so they decided to watch Cunnie Rabbit closely to see if his mother was still somewhere around.

One day when he thought no one was watching, Cunnie Rabbit went away and called to his mother as he used to do. The beasts heard him shout, "Send a chain, Mother, send a chain." Soon they saw the chain come down from out of the sky. Again they heard Cunnie Rabbit shout, "Draw up the chain, Mother, draw up the chain," and they saw him go up as his mother pulled on the chain. So they said, "Oho! Now we know where he hides his mother. He has been sharing *our* mothers with *his* mother all this time." So they decided that they would come early the next day and call Cunnie Rabbit's mother just as her son did, and when she sent the chain they would catch hold of it and have her pull them up. Then they would eat her where she was—on the cloud.

When the next day came they ran to the place, and one of them who had a light voice like Cunnie Rabbit's shouted, "Send a chain, Mother, send a chain." Immediately the chain appeared, and they were all delighted at how well their plan was working. They grabbed the chain, and the same animal as before shouted, "Draw up the chain, Mother, draw up the chain."

Cunnie Rabbit's mother began to pull up the chain. It felt very heavy, but she thought perhaps her son was bringing her a lot of meat, so she sweated and sweated to pull up the chain. It took her a long time because it was so very heavy. But she was lucky, after all, because just as the animals were getting near the cloud, and only a few more pulls would have got them there, Cunnie Rabbit himself arrived on his way to visit his mother. He saw the animals way up in the sky, and he knew at once that if they got to his mother they would kill her and eat her. He ran round and round shouting at the top of his voice, "Cut the chain, Mother, cut the chain." His mother heard him and guessed there was trouble. So she picked up a big knife, and she quickly cut the chain. All the creatures fell out of the sky. Some broke arms, some broke legs, some were killed, and some were never able to go hunting again.

Well, Cunnie Rabbit brought his mother down from the cloud and back to their house, and no animal ever gave him trouble again.

▼▲▼▲▼▲▼▲▼▲▼▲▼▲▼▲▼▲▼▲▼▲▼▲▼▲▼▲▼▲

46 Spider the Artist

Once upon a time there was a very serious famine! There wasn't any food for miles around, and all the animals went hungry and got thin. Anaanu, the spider, grew thin and felt hungry. This he liked least of all things in the world.

One day Anaanu went to one of the animals in the village and showed him his tongue, which had a beautiful design painted upon it. Anaanu told him that he could give him a design like that on his own tongue, and it would make him admired in the village because of its beauty, and it would also make him lucky and bring him food. So the animal agreed to have the design painted on his tongue.

Anaanu took him to the forest, and told him that he would have to be pinned to the ground for the painting to be done. The animal was pinned down. Then Anaanu painted a beautiful design all over his tongue. Anaanu told him that he would have to remain pinned down for some time, with his tongue stretched out, so that the design could dry and set, and then it would never come off with eating. Then Anaanu disappeared.

After some time, when the animal had become weak from lying on its back and dried out by the sun, Anaanu appeared with a knife, salt and pepper, and cooking utensils. He carved up the animal and cooked him and ate him. He went home looking very happy.

One by one, Anaanu went quietly to the animals in the village and offered to paint a design on the tongue of each. One by one, he led them to the forest and ate them. One by one, the animals in the village disappeared. While everybody became thinner and sadder, Anaanu grew fatter and more cheerful.

At last, Anaanu went to Lizard and offered to paint the design for him. Lizard accepted and was led to the forest and pinned down. When Anaanu disappeared, and the sun had scorched Lizard and dried his skin, Lizard, who was already hungry and thin inside it, could stand no more. So he simply shed his skin that was pinned down, and came out and crawled under some bushes and hid in the shade. Then Anaanu came back as usual with his knife and salt and pepper and cooking utensils, ready to cook a tasty meal and fill his belly. But Lizard was nowhere to be seen.

Suddenly, Lizard rushed out from the bushes to catch Anaanu. Anaanu dropped his things and ran for his life, with Lizard hot after him.

That is why the Lizard is always chasing the Spider.

▼▲▼▲▼▲▼▲▼▲▼▲▼▲▼▲▼▲▼▲▼▲▼▲▼▲▼▲▼▲

47 Ata and the Messenger Bird

A long time ago there was once a woman who had triplets. They were all boys, and she called them Lawe, Ate, and Ata. One day when these boys had grown up a bit—when they were about five years old—they decided to go and look for things to eat in the bush. Lawe said, "I shall look for sweet berries." Ate said, "I'm going to look for snails." And Ata said, "I hope to find some birds' eggs." They set off and soon came to a big river called Retse. The river said, "I'll let you cross me, boys, but on the way back you must give me something for that." The boys agreed and crossed the river safely.

Now Lawe found lots of sweet berries, and Ate got some snails, but Ata could find only one bird's egg. When evening came they all started back for home. Lawe came to the river first and said, "River, here are sweet berries that I found in the bush," and he gave the river some. The river said, "Thank you," and allowed Lawe to cross. When it was Ate's turn to cross the river, he said, "River, here are some snails I found in the bush. Take some and leave me some." And he, too, crossed the river and was soon near home. But when Ata came to the river, he had only one bird's egg, so he said nothing and started to cross. When he got almost to the middle the River Retse said, "Little boy, where is the something you promised me?" Ata said, "Oh, as for that, I only found one bird's egg so I can't give you anything." The river was very angry. Its waters rose and held Ata firmly. Soon the water was up to his neck, and then Ata saw a bird and he began to sing: "Oh, my father, my father, I am drowning. Oh, my mother, my mother, I am drowning, River Retse is taking me away."

He sang his song three times. The bird heard his song and flew to Ata's home. Now Ata's father was sitting outside his house and he heard the bird singing Ata's song.

Three times the bird sang: "Oh, my father, my father, I am drowning. Oh, my mother, my mother, I am drowning, River Retse is taking me away."

Ata's father understood the bird's song and cried out, "Did you hear? The River Retse is taking my son away. I must go rescue him." He ran to the river, but it was too late. The water was already up to the boy's head. Only the very top of his head was showing. The father rushed into the river and grasped his son by his hair to try to pull him out of the water. He couldn't. The boy's hair came away and his father clutched it to his breast in grief, and there it stayed.

That is how men came to have hair on their chests.

▼▲▼▲▼▲▼▲▼▲▼▲▼▲▼▲▼▲▼▲▼▲▼▲▼▲▼▲

48 Who Is the Greatest Thief?

Once a very long time ago there were two young men who met in a village. While they were waiting to speak to the chief, one of them who had been driven out of the East for stealing said, "There is no person in the East who can equal or surpass me in the art of stealing. I steal what I like, and no one can catch me."

His companion said to him, "You must be a very good thief indeed. In fact, you may be almost as good a thief as I."

The argument continued, and a large crowd gathered around them. When the people learned what the argument was about, they took the two young men before the chief where they explained the feud. It was the chief's idea that the two should enter into a contest to prove who was the greater thief. It was agreed upon.

The thief who had been driven out of the East saw an eagle in a tree nearby and told the chief that he would steal the eagle's eggs and bring them to him. He went out and climbed that big tree very cautiously without the eagle being aware of it. Very slowly and very quietly, he stole the eagle's eggs one by one and put them into his pocket. After he got the last one, he climbed slowly down to the ground.

The thief, very pleased with himself, came back to the chief. He said, "I have stolen the eagle's eggs and have them in my pocket."

The chief asked him to display them for his examination. When the thief put his hand into his pocket he found, not the eggs, but only a pocket full of stones. The chief was very angry about this deception and had the thief put in chains.

The second thief put his hand into his own pocket and pulled out the eggs. He had stolen them from the first thief, which greatly surprised the chief. Now, of these two, which is the greater thief?

▼▲▼▲▼▲▼▲▼▲▼▲▼▲▼▲▼▲▼▲▼▲▼▲▼▲▼▲

49 The Song of the River

One day a child was sweeping his father's house and found a ring. He said to himself, "I will take this ring and wash it only in the River Densu." He went off to wash it in the river immediately, and he had almost finished when the river took the ring away. But in its place, the river gave him a big fish. As the child was going off with the fish, a bird snatched it from his hand.

So he sang: "Bird took my fish. This fish from where? This fish from Densu. What was it Densu took from you? Densu took my ring. This ring from where? This ring from my father's house? Densu ei! House ei! Densu ei!"

But before he went off the bird gave him a feather, and then, as he was going, the wind took the feather. So—

"Wind took my feather. This feather from where? This feather from Bird. What was it Bird took from you? Bird took my fish. This fish from where? This fish from Densu. What was it Densu took from you? Densu took my ring. This ring from where? This ring from my father's house. Densu ei! House ei! Densu ei!"

Then the wind gave him a leaf. But as he was going, a sheep took the leaf from him. So—

"Sheep took my leaf. This leaf from where? This leaf from Wind. What was it Wind took from you? Wind took my feather. This feather from where? This feather from Bird. What was it Bird took from you? Bird took my fish. This fish from where? This fish from Densu. What was it Densu took from you? Densu took my ring. This ring from where? This ring from my father's house. Densu ei! House ei! Densu ei!"

But the sheep gave him two bottles of oil. On his way he came to a tree and both the bottles of oil broke against the tree. Again he sang his song:

"Tree, give me my oil! This oil from where? This oil from Sheep. What was it Sheep took from you? Sheep took my leaf. This leaf from where? This leaf from Wind. What was it Wind took from you? Wind took my feather. This feather from where? This feather from Bird. What was it Bird took from you? Bird took my fish. This fish from where? This fish from Densu. What was it Densu took from you? Densu took my ring. This ring from where? This ring from my father's house. Densu ei! House ei! Densu ei!"

The tree told him to dig under it and that he would find two sixpence there. The boy forced himself to dig, and he got his two sixpence. The tree told him that when he got the sixpence he must swallow them and then straightaway afterward go and vomit them back up. The boy said, "All right." When he had swallowed the sixpence, he saw a vulture passing, so he told him to go and tell his mother that she should make a plantain fufu and put codfish bones on top of it. Vulture said, "All right." So Vulture went and told the boy's mother, and she said, "All right." She started cooking and put fufu on the fire and put the codfish bones on top. She made the table, and put her son's food on it. When he got home he cut up the fufu, first one slice, then another, until the bones stuck in his throat and nearly choked him.

He began to vomit money. His mother took some of the money to her co-wife, but that woman said the money was not enough for her, and that she ought to have more. She didn't get any. The boy meanwhile said he was going to vomit more, but all he vomited was snakes and worms and many other things.

▼▲▼▲▼▲▼▲▼▲▼▲▼▲▼▲▼▲▼▲▼▲▼▲▼▲▼▲▼▲

50 The Most Suitable Name

Once upon a time Stingy, Greedy, and Nosey began to argue among themselves. Stingy said to Greedy, "You aren't nearly as greedy as I am stingy."

"Rubbish!" answered Greedy. "You have no right to say a thing like that to me."

"Of course I have," said Stingy. "And much more right than you have to say what you said. If you want to prove which of us is the best named, then let us travel about the world and let the people decide which of us is most aptly named."

But they didn't realize that Nosey was standing close by, listening to every word of their quarrel. When Nosey got home, he said to his wife, "Cook me enough food for a long journey. I'm off to keep an eye on Stingy and Greedy and see whose name suits him best."

His wife said, "Well, your name 'Nosey' suits *you* very well, for your nosiness is sending you off on a journey."

Next morning he packed up his food and went to where Stingy and Greedy were preparing to leave town.

Now, because he was so fond of begging, Greedy did not take any food with him—he was determined to compel Stingy to give him something to eat.

When it was light, they set off for a distant town. When Stingy was almost crippled by hunger, he said to Greedy, "Stop a moment! Wait for me here, while I go and relieve myself." In fact, he wanted to get away from them so as to eat some porridge without having to share it with anyone else.

Greedy was suspicious, and said, "Well, I wouldn't mind doing that, too, I'm full to bursting. Let's go off and relieve ourselves."

Nosey went after them, saying, "I must go and see what they're up to, even if they're only going to do as they say." So he followed them into the bush.

When Stingy saw that he couldn't cook his porridge and eat it, he carefully and secretly brought out his cake of pounded grain and put it in the sun to dry, so that he could pack it away, and Greedy wouldn't be able to see it, much less ask him for some. When he had put it out to dry, he paid no more attention to it, and a gazelle came along, picked up the dried cake of food, and ran off with it. When Stingy saw this, he ran after it, determined to recover his food.

Greedy saw it too, and Greedy said, "I'll go after this Stingy fellow, and when he grabs back the cake that the gazelle has taken, I'll ask him to give me half." This was just the sort of situation that Nosey had been wanting, so he ran after them saying, "I must see how Stingy manages to recover the cake from the gazelle."

So they all ran off, one after the other.

I ask you now, which of these three best lived up to his name—Stingy, Greedy, or Nosey, who went after them to see who won? If you say Stingy won, who in his stinginess ran after the gazelle that had taken his food, have you forgotten Greedy, who expected that Stingy would get his cake back from the gazelle, and he would be able to cadge some from him? And what about Nosey, who followed them to spy on them?

▼▲▼▲▼▲▼▲▼▲▼▲▼▲▼▲▼▲▼▲▼▲▼▲▼▲▼▲▼▲

51 Who Is the Most Helpful Lover?

Once there were three young men who all loved the same girl. She was very dear to them all. These young men had traveled together into a far land. One morning one man looked into his magic mirror and exclaimed, "Our loved one is dead and lying in state at this very moment!"

The second man said, "We shall go to mourn and bury her. But, we need to get there fast. We shall have to travel for many days, and she will be buried long before we reach home. I will have to use my special charm."

After he had touched the legs of the other two men with his charm, he asked them to sit with him with their backs against the wall of their hut. Instantly all three of them were in their hometown mourning with the family of their loved one.

The third young man pulled out his magic horsetail switch and hit the corpse, shouting, "Arise my love! Arise my love!"

She arose and passed a hand across her face. Now of the three lovers, who had helped the most?

▼▲▼▲▼▲▼▲▼▲▼▲▼▲▼▲▼▲▼▲▼▲▼▲▼▲▼▲

52 What Spider Knows

There was a severe famine in the land. All the hunting grounds had been deserted, and no animals could be found anywhere. Everything was dry and parched. One day Ananse decided to travel to a far country to do some hunting. For three days he wandered through the bush. Each day, he started early at sunrise and continued to walk until sundown. At last he came to a river. There was no canoe, and there was no bridge. He could not wade or swim across either. So, weary and bewildered, he sat down beside the river to rest. As he sat there a strange feeling came over him, as if someone had come to sit near him, but he could see no one.

Then a strange voice spoke to him. "Ananse, why is it that no one ever comes to my country and yet you have come?"

Ananse was startled, and he nearly fell into the river with surprise, but he managed to say, "There is no meat in my country, and I have come to hunt."

"All right. I have heard. Come with me." Before Ananse could get up, the voice said, "Huha!" and Ananse was across the river. There, sitting on a rock, was a tiny man, no bigger than a boy, but very, very old. He had a long nose that stretched away into the thick undergrowth.

"Sit down," the man said to Ananse.

"No, I'll stand," said Ananse, frightened and suspicious.

"Sit down, you fool!" said the old man. Ananse didn't want to, but he sat down on the grass. He was shaking all over, for never in all his life had he seen anything like this. This nose was as long and as big as the tallest of all the trees in the forest.

The man with the big nose said, "Ananse, you go carry the end of my nose as we walk to my hut."

Ananse obeyed. The nose, it is true, was long and big, but it was not heavy—at least, not as heavy as Ananse had thought it would be when he first saw it. There were strange things in this country. The trees were very thin, but very, very tall. The undergrowth was dense but rather low, and there weren't any of the creeping and climbing plants that intertwine among trees and make passage through the bush difficult. Furthermore, the whole place was teeming with game of every kind.

When they arrived at the hut, Ananse saw a long platform leading from the door into a clearing. When they went in the hut the old man asked Ananse to lay his nose on the platform. He told Ananse to cook a meal. After they had eaten, they lay down to sleep. At midnight the old man woke Ananse up and asked him to carry his nose for him, and they would go hunting.

They had not gone far when they came upon a herd of bush pigs. The old man directed his nose toward them and growled, "Huha!" Instantly, they fell down dead. Farther on, they saw some bush bucks. Again, "Huha!" and they all fell down dead. Within a short time they had gathered more meat than Ananse could have killed with his gun in a year.

Ananse feasted on the meat for a week. Then he asked permission to go home. The old man allowed him to carry what was left of the meat away with him. When Ananse's supply of meat was exhausted, he asked his wife and children to fetch clay from the clay pit. He built himself a great nose and baked it in the fire.

The rainy season was now at its heaviest. The trees were green. There were birds and beasts around again. Ananse asked Endekuma, his son, to carry his nose, for they were going out to hunt. They had not gone far when they met a rat. Ananse said, "I'll try my nose on the rat." He pointed his nose at it and growled, "Huha!" The rat fell dead. Ananse was delighted. His son marvelled at his father's new magical powers. They saw an antelope and a porcupine. With his "Huha!" Ananse killed them both. He was now convinced of his powers.

For a long time they saw nothing. Suddenly, right in front of them stood a tree on which monkeys of all kinds were playing. "Ha ha!" Ananse laughed to himself. "What a find!" He pointed his nose at them and

"Huha!" Nothing happened. Again he growled. "Huha!" Then he snorted more loudly. "Huha! Huha! Huha!" The monkeys were not in the least affected. They just stared down on the strange sight.

Then they began to chatter. "Yeew! Yeew!" "That's him! That's him!" They jumped down from the tree in hundreds and set upon Ananse. They beat him and tore off his big nose. Then they laid him down and walked all over him until he was quite flat. Taking him for dead, they left him and went off chattering.

That is why the elders say, "He who perseveres in asking his way does not go astray." For if Ananse had asked the old man to teach him all the secrets of his nose, he would not have come to grief.

▼▲▼▲▼▲▼▲▼▲▼▲▼▲▼▲▼▲▼▲▼▲▼▲▼▲▼▲▼▲▼

53 The Tale of the Enchanted Yam

At the height of the famine that raged in the time of our great-grandfathers, Ananse traveled to a distant land to buy food. He came to a cottage in which lived a grotesque old woman. Her back was covered with caked filth. Her eyes were watery. Her teeth were long, and they protruded like tusks. She said, "No one ever comes to this place. Why have you come?"

Ananse said, "You dirty old woman, do you think I would ever dream of coming to your filthy cottage were it not for hunger?"

She said, "Oh, if it is hunger, you need not worry. There is plenty of food here for both of us."

Ananse was very happy and said, "After all, you don't look so dirty. You are not so bad, after all."

The old woman asked Ananse to cook a piece of yam for their supper, but she added, "Peel the yam and throw the inner part away. Cook the peelings."

Ananse said, "Hyeaa! Do you think I am as crazy as you are? Who ever thought of cooking yam peelings?" So he put the yam in the pot instead, placed it on the fire, and threw away the peelings.

When he reckoned that he had allowed enough time for the yam to cook properly, he took the pot off the fire. To his astonishment, the yam had turned to gravel. He therefore collected the peelings and followed the old woman's instructions. When the pot was ready, he examined it and found that it contained a tempting whole yam.

The following day he continued his journey. All along his path grew many yams, and these yams talked to Ananse. Some called out, "Dig me up!" Others cried, "Don't dig me up!"

Ananse said, "Even if I were a fool, I would know that what you say gives me a hint as to which of you are ripe."

He dug up some of the yams that had said, "Dig me up." At the end of the day he made a fire and cooked the yams, but they turned into gravel, and he went without food.

Early at dawn he continued his journey. Again there were yams that said, "Dig me up!" and some that said, "Don't dig me up!"

He selected this time the yams that cried out, "Don't dig me up!" When they were cooked, they made delicious eating.

He crossed a stream that said, "Drink me, drink me, drink me!" and another that said, "Drink me not, drink me not, drink me not!"

When he drank the water of the "drink-me" stream, it burnt his mouth. It was very bitter. But he was able to drink the "drink-me-not" water, which was cool and refreshing.

So he came to the conclusion that he was in an enchanted country and a topsy-turvy land. He decided to act contrary to accepted and normal behavior in all things. In fact, this seemed to work.

On the outskirts of a beautiful town, he met a woman who took him to her house where she entertained him. This woman had a magic yam. When a piece was cut off for cooking, it grew back into a whole yam again. There was one condition, however. Whoever ate it must know its name. The woman cooked a piece of this yam and set it ready for Ananse to eat. She demanded that he tell her the name. Ananse called out names of various kinds of yams, but this magic yam that always grew back had a name that was not like any of them.

At last the woman said, "I shall eat my Dagraga."

She ate the yam, and Ananse got nothing but the knowledge of the yam's name. He repeated it to himself throughout the early part of the night—"Dagraga, dagraga, dagraga."

When a mosquito bit him, however, he stopped to curse it, "Death to the beast that has come to eat me!"

Then he continued to say the yam's name, but alas, it was now—"Digirigi, digirigi, digirigi."

For breakfast Ananse's hostess cooked some more of her special yam that always grows back. He was very confident now, for he was still repeating his "Digirigi." Both sat down to eat. Ananse, of course, had to name the yam, "Well, the yam is called Digirigi."

She shrieked, "No name, no food! I will eat my Dagraga." And so, with a great clicking noise, the woman ate the yam.

Again Ananse repeated, "Dagraga," to himself all day, but unfortunately he knocked his foot against a stone and in his agony slipped into saying—"Ragdaga, Ragdaga."

"Ragdaga!"

Again no food for Ananse. He decided to go back to the bush to learn properly the name of the yam. He repeated the correct name as he went along, for his hostess mentioned it before she ate the last meal of yam. "Dagraga! Dagraga! Dagraga!"

He was confident now, and he turned back to go to the house. Within sight of the village a bush fowl flew with a great flutter from the roadside and called, "Garada! Garada!"

The suddenness of the movement threw Ananse off balance. When he recovered he continued to repeat the name of the yam, but he was so confused that he now said, "Garada, garada."

Mealtime came round once more. A piece of the woman's special magic yam that always grows back was served. Ananse put on his best clothes and headband, for he was sure he was going to eat well today. The woman said, "Mention the name of the yam and eat."

Ananse said, as he rubbed his hands together, "Ho! It's easy, Garada." The woman said, "No name, no food! I will again eat my Dagraga!"

Ananse was very angry. When his hostess was away from the house he took the magical yam and cut it up into tiny pieces and scattered them all over the land. That is how yam spread throughout the world.

54 The Most Powerful Name

In the olden days, nobody called God by his present name, "Mawu." In those days His name was the same as the name of the number six, which is to say, "Adewu." And in those days anyone who said God's name aloud would die!

Spider was living at the time I am talking about, and he was very wise. He was called Wiseman. His brother was Lulu. They had built a farm settlement together. Now there was a famine, and people were needing food badly. Spider cleared land for a farm, and on the farm he made six mounds, and he sat on one of them.

There was Spider, then, sitting on one of his six mounds. Now, when ever an animal passed, Spider would call it over to him and ask the animal to count his mounds for him. If the animal counted five mounds Spider would say, "And how about this one I'm sitting on, too?" When it said six, it dropped down dead. If the animal counted, "one, two, three, four, five," and then went on to count, "six," it also dropped down dead. Spider would take the dead animal, roast it, go and find a little cornmeal for porridge, and have a good meal in no time. He went on doing this for some time.

Leopard had been sitting and watching Spider's doings carefully. "Who is this Wiseman? So wise!" He, Leopard, too, would watch and learn. He kept close watch until finally, the day came. Spider sat among his mounds, and Leopard left the trees and went to greet him politely, "My friend, how is everything here? Ah, so you have made a farm here? I did not know of your farm because I haven't been here before. Your farm is very nice."

Spider said, "My friend, come and look at these little mounds I have made here. Come and count them for me." Leopard started counting. "One, two, three, four, five." He said he couldn't count more.

Spider said he should include the one on which he was sitting, not knowing that Leopard already had got the idea. Leopard said he couldn't count. Spider pestered him to count to six, but he wouldn't. So Spider whispered, "Say six," and upon whispering the word for "six" Spider dropped down dead.

Now Leopard said that the way Spider had died and all the wisdom that he had seen was very impressive. He would eat Spider, except for his head full of wisdom. The head he would swallow whole. He took the head and swallowed it. At once, it began to swell in his belly.

He climbed a tree and sat in its branches. He couldn't breathe, his stomach ached so much, and he said, "Spider is the one who did this to me." And Leopard cried loudly, "Eeyaaooo! Eeyaaooo!" which is the cry that Leopard makes to this very day.

▼▲▼▲▼▲▼▲▼▲▼▲▼▲▼▲▼▲▼▲▼▲▼▲▼▲▼▲▼▲

55 The Return of Ananse

Many seasons ago Ananse and his wife, Aso Yaa, made a bean farm. It looked good and promised a big harvest. Both Aso and Ananse had worked hard. In rain and sun they had worked until their backs ached.

Now the crops were growing. The farm was a bean farm, but they had planted other crops, too. The plantains were tall. The yam vines were bushy and green, and you could tell there were some big tubers under the mounds. There were also tomatoes, okra, peppers, and eggplant. Ananse was very pleased with himself.

The weeks went by. The crops grew and ripened. The smell of sweet things was in the air. Ananse stood in the middle of his farm and studied the crops. They were fine specimens, especially the beans, which were Ananse's favorite vegetable. Now they were there, ripe and ready to be eaten. Ananse stood in the middle of his farm and watched the beans swaying on their stalks. He was making plans—plans to have all the beans for himself.

He said, "These beans will be good almost any way they can be cooked." He congratulated himself for having married Aso Yaa, who had worked so hard to get such a fine crop. Before he returned home he had completed his plans for having all those wonderful beans for himself.

A few days later he called his family together, and he said in a sad voice, "My wife and children, I can see now that I haven't long to live. I shall soon die. When I am dead, bury me on the farm so that my spirit won't wander. Put something to cook with in my grave so that my spirit may feed."

The family were all saddened by what they had heard, but they did not expect their father to die too soon. In two or three days, however, Ananse lay down on his bed looking seriously ill. Within a few days he was dead. According to custom, a man's last wishes should be fulfilled. So Ananse was buried in the bean farm. Plenty of pots and pans were put in the grave to please Ananse's spirit. For forty days, while the customary rites were being performed, no one visited the bean farm.

As soon as the funeral procession had left the graveside, Ananse worked his way out, for he was not really dead. He built himself a little hut on the edge of the farm and cooked himself a bean feast. By day he slept in his grave, but every night he got out and had a meal. By the end of the forty days there was very little left on the farm, for Ananse was a greedy man.

At the end of the forty days, after Aso had been purified, she went to the farm to collect some food. But what did she find? The farm had been stripped almost bare. She stood there and lifted her voice, "May he die whoever stole my beans! May he die alone in pain!"

A voice answered from far away: "Peace, Aso! Peace! She who has lost her husband should not complain over lost beans."

Aso cursed the thief again. Again the voice answered: "Peace, Aso! Peace! She who has lost her husband should not complain over lost beans."

Aso now understood, so she returned home. Early the next morning she went with her eldest son, Endekuma, to the farm. She had Endekuma cut down a tall tree that stood on the farm. When he had cut nearly through the tree, he asked Aso, "Mother, where is the tree likely to fall?"

She said, "Quick, run! The tree is going to fall on your father's grave."

When Ananse heard that the tree was going to fall on his grave, he rushed out, shouting, "Aso, Aso, here I am. I have come up from Ghost Land. You understand? From Ghost Land."

He was very, very ashamed and rushed into a nearby bush and hid under some dry leaves. That is why Ananse is always found among dry leaves.

56 Spider Gets Cured

I was not living at the time, but a certain princess was, and she had a daughter who was very beautiful. They offered one man after another to her, but each time she refused to marry the man. This went on for a long time. This princess—Ameyo—remained with her mother. Then one day the daughter said she was going for firewood. A spider said he would show her the place to get wood. He took her to get the firewood and helped her collect it. Just as they were leaving, she saw a cricket and asked Spider to catch it for her. Spider dug and dug and dug, and he put his hand inside the hole. No sooner had he put his hand inside the hole than he cried out, "What shall I do? A snake has bitten me!"

Then he said, "Aah!" and sang: "Ameyo said I must catch her a cricket. I tried to catch the cricket. And a snake bit me! If she took me home, perhaps that would stop the pain."

She took him home with her. They walked together slowly. Then he said, "Aah!" and sang: "Ameyo said I must catch her a cricket. I tried to catch the cricket. And a snake bit me! If she made hot water to bathe me in, perhaps that would stop the pain."

She put water on the fire for him and bathed his hand. But in a little while, more singing: "Ameyo said I must catch her a cricket. I tried to catch the cricket. And a snake bit me! If she would give me a bed to lie down in, perhaps that would stop the pain."

And then even more singing: "Ameyo said I must catch her a cricket. I tried to catch the cricket. And a snake bit me! If she would lie down with me, perhaps that would stop the pain!"

And finally, the last of the song: "Ameyo said I must catch her a cricket. I tried to catch the cricket. And a snake bit me! If she would let me make love to her, perhaps that would stop the pain!"

The girl let Spider make love to her, which he did, and then he recovered immediately.

57 The Wise Man Takes a Wise Wife

Once upon a time there were two friends, and one of them had no wife. The one who was married told his friend, "What kind of man are you who doesn't want to get married at your age? You must marry. This way of life of yours isn't good."

He answered, "I'll marry, too, but not yet. I have to gain wisdom before I get married."

The married friend had three children, all girls, and he asked his friend to travel with him to his village to see them. When the time came, the two friends got ready and left. They came to a big river and were so heated by the journey and the sun that they wanted to wash. The married one said, "My friend, I think we should wash here."

"Is this the end of the river?" asked the unmarried man.

The first man was very surprised and asked, "Does the river have to end before people can wash?"

His friend answered, "Since the river doesn't end here, you'd better go ahead. I won't wash."

So the married man washed, and they went on. They came to a big town where the people were mourning because a man had died. The married man said, "Let me leave you here and go see the man." The married man went to see the dead man, a fine young man, and then returned. He said, "My friend, I am sorry. Death is a bad thing. How can it take this fine young man?"

His friend inquired, "Friend, when that man died, did his image die, too?"

The married man kept that matter in his heart, and when they came to his house, his daughters came to welcome the stranger in proper fashion. Their father told them, "Make food for this visitor. We're hungry." The man's first daughter prepared a meal and put the food onto the table. She called to the guest and announced, "Master, come and eat now."

When he had come to the table and washed his hands, he asked the girl, "When I eat this food, shall I eat the plates?" The girl was shocked and said, "My mother's dishes? How can you eat my mother's dishes? No, if that's how it is, I won't agree to let you eat."

The stranger replied, "All right, then, take away your plates if you won't let me eat them with your food." So the girl removed the plates and the food went back. She came to her mother's kitchen and said, "That stranger said he wants to eat the plates with the food, so I refused to let him have anything."

The second one came to her mother and said, "I also must cook food. Maybe that man refused my sister's food to trick her." She said, "Master, come and eat." He answered, "Thank you, but if I eat that food shall I eat the plates, too?"

The girl shook with fear because she had borrowed those plates from another woman. She thought, "No. If that man eats the plates with the food, maybe I'll have trouble with the woman I borrowed the plates from." So she said she couldn't agree to let him eat her food. She said, "Master, if that's how you're going to eat—the plates along with the food—there can be no food." So he didn't eat, and the girl took her dishes to the kitchen and told her mother the same thing the first sister had said.

The third sister, who was very small, asked her father, "Why does that man refuse to eat my sisters' food?" Since she couldn't cook, she took the same food that had been refused and presented it to the guest again. She brought it to him, called, and pleaded, "Master, come and eat."

The man said, "I thank you, my child. You brought me this food. Shall I eat the plates along with it?" The little girl shook. She said since she was born she had never seen a man eat until he had even finished the plates as well. She said, "All right, if you think that when a man eats food he also eats the plates, you eat them, too."

So the man began to eat the food. He finished it and said, "All right, you can take the plates, now." When she brought the plates to the kitchen, her sisters were amazed. They questioned, "How did this man manage to eat your food?"

The little girl answered her sisters, "That man has wisdom. That man asked you a question, 'If I eat your food, shall I marry you, too?'"

The sisters said, "Ah!"

Her father called her over and said, "Maybe you have some special understanding of the man. He told me two things on the road that I didn't understand. I'll tell them to you and see if you can interpret them. The man and I were walking on the road when we came to a river, and he told me we couldn't wash because the river didn't end there."

She told her father, "He meant, if you and he washed in that water, wouldn't you make dirty water for the people who use the water downstream?" Her father said, "Ah! The second thing he told me was about a dead man I saw. He said, 'That dead man, did his image die, too?'"

She said, "Papa, the man wanted to ask you if the dead man didn't have children who looked like him." The father said, "It's true. You are wise, my child."

The stranger came and said, "That little girl is the one I will marry from your house here." So they bargained as they do in the country, and the man put money on the girl's head and took her as his wife.

She grew heavy, and they had a child, so one day the man thought, "I must leave my wife and go look for work on the plantation so I can finish paying my bride price." And he left his wife at the house. When he had been at the plantation one month, some of his friends wanted to go back to their village for a holiday. He said, "Let me give you something for my wife." The man took five fathoms of cloth and five shillings and tied them in a bundle and told them, "When you pass my house, give it to my wife."

The man came to the road and took out two fathoms of the cloth and three of the shillings and wondered, "Will the woman notice that something is missing?" When he passed the man's house, he gave her the things.

When the man had sent the things, he had put in a string with five knots tied at either end. The woman opened the parcel and saw the three fathoms of cloth and the two shillings, along with the string that had ten knots. She requested, "When you go back, pass by here so I can send news to my husband."

The people came back and stopped by the house. She said, "When you see my husband, tell him the fowl that he gave me had five chicks, the hawk took three and only two remain. The goat he left me had five kids, the leopard took two, so three remain."

When the people reached the woman's husband he asked them, "Did you take the parcel?"

They replied, "Yes, and she sent you a message, too: the fowl had five chicks, the hawk took three and two remain. The goat had five kids, the leopard took two and three remain."

The man said, "I did a good deed by sending something to my wife, and I thought you would do a good deed and help me. But when you came to the road you took two fathoms of cloth and three shillings." And he detained the people until they returned the money.

Those people sent the story back to their village to show how wise the man and his wife were. The chief said, "The man is very proud because he and his wife are so smart, but we'll see." And he began to wonder how he could manage to marry such a fine woman. He said, "But I'll take that woman from him, I swear it."

The man came back from the plantation and met his wife. The whole town talked of nothing but the wisdom of the couple. The chief thought until he knew what he would do. He sent news to the man that he must come to him. He said, "Friend, my hair has grown long. I want you to cut it like a young man's, like your own."

The man consented, "Yes, chief, I can do it well. Tomorrow I shall come to cut your hair."

He went and bought a razor blade and scissors and brought them to the king's house. When he came he brought two ears of corn as a gift for the king and asked that they be roasted for him. When it was time to begin the haircutting they roasted the corn and brought it. He gave one ear to the king and said, "Take it, king, and as you eat this corn so will I cut your hair." He didn't cut it like a young boy's, as the king had wanted, but he shaved it like a Hausa man's, first only on one side. When one ear of corn was finished the king threw it away, and the man gave him another ear. As the king ate the corn, the wise man cut the other side of his head, and when the king had finished that corn, the man had finished the job. The king said to himself cunningly that he would use the hair as a pretext to hold the man. He put his hand up and felt his head.

The king exclaimed, "How? I told you to cut my hair like a young man's! Put it back! Why did you cut it like a Hausa's? Put it back!" He called his servants and shouted, "Hold this man! He has ruined my head. I didn't tell him to cut my hair like that! Today we will put him in prison since he didn't do what I asked. He has shown how much sense he has."

The king's counselor said, "You must judge him first. You can't just put him in prison without judgment."

So they held court. The man pleaded, "The king told me to cut his hair. I gave him corn. As the king ate the corn, I cut his hair. He cleaned off one ear of corn, and I took the hair off half his head. He cleaned off another ear of corn, and I took the hair off the other half of his head. So if he thinks you can cut hair and put it back on the head, let him put the corn back on the cob."

As the judges sat they said, "This is a very hard case, and the man speaks the truth. We can't just put this man in prison." They told him, "We have dismissed your case because if the king wants his hair back, he must give you back your corn as you say." His wife was sitting at home fearing that he had been imprisoned, when he came back.

The people saw him and marvelled, "Oh, you have won again today." The king tried to make friends with the man again. He said, "After you caused all that trouble, did you think you could run from me?"

The man answered, "No, sir. I couldn't run like that, sir." The king advised, "You had better take a goat from me. I want that goat to prosper. Maybe you can bring me back two goats."

He said, "All right."

The king took a he-goat and gave it to him. He took it to his own quarters and kept it about a year. The king planned to say to him when he brought the goat, "Where is the child of that goat, then?" And that would be the reason to lock the man in prison for good.

When the time came, the man tied a rope around the goat's neck and brought it to the king and said, "King, here is your goat. I see that it won't bear."

The king responded, "You lie. You are a wicked man. You took those kids and sold them, or else you ate them. I want my goat and the kids, all of them."

The man said, "King, I am very sorry. I have plenty of trouble at home. My father, who lives with me, is about to have a baby." The king laughed until he fell off his stool. He said, "In all my life I have never seen a pregnant man. Is it true?"

The man said, "I just left my father's house. He is really going to have a baby." The king laughed. He said, "This is really a funny man. How can a man have a baby?"

The king's wives were present. The man simply said, "If you've never seen a man have a baby, why did you give me a he-goat, then?"

Everybody laughed at that business. That is the end of the story. The king couldn't do what he wanted to that young man because the young man had a little sense.

58 The Spoiled Bride and the Python

There once was a man and his wife who wanted a child badly but did not get one. They prayed and prayed and prayed for one, but to no avail. Many years passed, and they earned much money before they got a daughter. Because they were rich and spoiled their child, she grew into a badly behaved and disrespectful girl. When she was fully grown, many rich men came, seeking to arrange a marriage with their sons, but the girl said she would marry no one but the young man of her choice. So she lived many years without marrying. Her father and mother were always talking to her about the need to marry, but she would never agree to accept a husband whom she had not first seen.

Then one day, when they were all outside their house, they looked up and saw a young man coming toward them playing a musical instrument. As soon as the girl's eyes fell on him she jumped up and cried out that here was the man she wanted. Her father was grinding snuff at the time, and she snatched the grinding stone from him and hit him on the head with it. Once she had done this, she rushed to the young man and embraced him, saying, "I love you, and I will marry you."

The young man replied, "I love you also, and it is because of you that I have come. I shall make arrangements, and then I will come and fetch you."

The girl said, "No, whether you are ready or not, I will go with you now."

The young man argued and argued, but the girl would not listen to him, and at last he said, "Very well, if you will not wait, get ready and we will go."

Soon the girl's slaves had got everything ready for their journey. They took animals—cows and horses—and gold, and many other things besides, and if you could have seen them you would have known her to be a rich man's child indeed.

Once the preparations were completed they wasted no time in setting out. They walked and walked and walked through many towns and villages, and still they had not come to the young man's country. By this time the slaves and the woman were all tired, and no one talked to anyone else. When someone spoke to the young man, he would only say, "It's not far now, and we'll be there." And now the young woman saw that there were no more towns and villages, but only a forest ahead. Soon they were in virgin forest, the mere sight of which was enough to give a man goose-flesh. But they went on until they reached the very center of the forest, and the young man beckoned them to follow.

By this time the young woman was weeping. After they had gone a little farther, the young man told them to put down their loads, because they had arrived. The young woman looked around her and saw how thick the forest was, and she could hear the cry of wild animals, and she knew she was lost. There was a big silk cotton tree where they had halted, with buttress roots bigger than an ordinary room. The young man told his wife to put all their things in the tree's roots, and as he spoke he went inside. Her eyes followed him, and she saw that he had changed into a huge python.

She looked to heaven and began to weep. Her husband, however, called out to her that he was hungry, telling her to bring him a goat to eat. When the woman saw her husband there, coiling and uncoiling his great length, and heard what he was saying, she was panic-stricken. But she told one of her slaves to bring a goat. Standing at a distance, the slave threw it to the serpent, who fell upon it and swallowed it in one gulp. This went on each day, and soon the python had eaten nearly all the animals, even though the woman and her slaves went hungry. When the animals were all eaten, it was obvious that the snake would soon turn to human flesh.

So the woman told her slaves to get ready to run away before all the animals were eaten, and as soon as they could, they started out by night. They ran all night and were far away by the time the python got up from his bed. He called and called his wife. Silence. He lifted up his head. Nothing. Now he was angry and set off in pursuit. The people had been moving very rapidly and so were far away. But the man-python strength-ened his tail and swore that wherever they might be, he would catch up with them. He ran and ran and ran until he could see them in the distance. Since they kept looking back as they fled, they saw him coming after them in the distance, and they began to run faster.

It was touch-and-go now. The serpent swore that he would catch them, no matter what. But the woman and her slaves ran harder than ever before. Soon, they saw a town nearby. The serpent was gaining all the time, but they reached the town before he did and ran into a house. They quickly told their story and urged the townspeople to take up their guns to protect themselves. The strongest young men were chosen to go and stand on the road at the outskirts of the town. Soon the python arrived. When he got near enough, they fired their guns and killed him. They took him and cut him into little bits and scattered the pieces far and wide.

That is why our elders have the saying that if a child is told something over and over again and doesn't listen, he will meet misfortune.

▼▲▼▲▼▲▼▲▼▲▼▲▼▲▼▲▼▲▼▲▼▲▼▲▼▲▼▲▼▲▼▲

59 The Dishonest Wife

Once a husband had two wives. The older one was barren—as unproductive as a piece of rock. But the younger one was pregnant. Then an evil thought entered the mind of the barren woman. She said to herself, "I will pretend that I, too, am pregnant, so that I may be free from shame." She put a calabash bowl on her stomach and tied her wrapper around it so that it might appear that she was pregnant. Every month she increased the size of the calabash so that her stomach became bigger and bigger. In this way she was able to make the people of her area believe that she, too, was pregnant.

After some time, the young wife was ready to have her baby, and she started to assemble the necessary things for its arrival. The older wife did the same. On the day the younger wife delivered, the older wife went to her own room and started to groan as if she, too, were expecting a baby. At night when everybody was asleep, she went to the room of the younger wife, stole the baby, carried it into her own room, and invited the neighbors to come and see her new baby. She had smeared the baby with blood so that all the neighbors would believe that she, too, had delivered a baby.

After some time the younger wife discovered that her baby was missing. She began screaming and woke up all the neighbors. When she learned of the newborn baby of the older wife, she went to inspect it. After she had inspected the baby, she claimed that the baby was hers. Then a terrible fight erupted between the two wives.

When their neighbors could not settle the fight, they took the two fighting women to the king. The two women stated their cases before the king, and the king was asked to make a judgment. But before the king could say anything, the baby started to sing: "The one who puts the calabash bowl on her stomach to make people think she is pregnant is not my mother. The younger wife is my mother."

Then the king commanded that the older wife be beheaded for her crime.

▼▲▼▲▼▲▼▲▼▲▼▲▼▲▼▲▼▲▼▲▼▲▼▲▼▲▼▲▼▲

60 Ananse Is Put in His Place

One day Ananse said he would go find a girl in the next village who would be willing to marry him. He invited the white-thighed colobus monkey to go with him and seek a wife, also. The monkey said, "I am willing to go, but all my teeth are black, and the girls will not like me." Ananse said, "Never mind, paint your teeth with white clay."

Ananse next went to the Mona monkey and invited him to accompany him. The Mona monkey said, "I am willing to go with you, but my eyes are hollow, and no girl will have me." Ananse said, "Never mind, fill the hollows with wax."

He next went to the dog and asked him to come too, but the dog said, "I am willing to come with you, but my waist is so thin." Ananse said, "Never mind, get a pounding stick and shove it into your belly; it will fill the empty space at your waist."

Ananse then went to the bush fowl and asked him to come with him. The bush fowl said, "I am willing to come, but my legs and feet are red." Ananse said, "Never mind, paint your legs and feet with charcoal and make them black."

Ananse then said, "Now I am suffering from dysentery. Maybe I shouldn't go." They said, "Put a calabash at your backside to collect your excrement."

So it was a handsome, perfect group that set out to woo the girls of the next village. The girls fell for them immediately. Everyone got a wife.

When they had had a few days together, Ananse became dissatisfied with his wife and planned to take the wives of his friends from them.

Early in the morning when the animals were washing their faces, Ananse said to them, "The colobus monkey has bad breath. His black teeth give off a bad smell, so in order not to disgrace us, he should clean his teeth." They agreed and forced the colobus to wash his mouth out. The white clay was washed away, and the monkey cried, "No! No!" He then ran off into the bush, for his teeth were now black.

When it was breakfast time, and the girls were cooking, they had difficulty with the fire. Ananse said to the Mona monkey, "Go and blow the fire." He protested, "But the heat will melt the wax in my hollow eyes." But Ananse insisted. As he blew the fire, the wax melted, and, crying, "No! No!" he disappeared into the bush.

The plantain was ready to be pounded into fufu, and Ananse saw that the girls did not have enough pounding sticks, so he called the dog aside and demanded that he pull the stick out of his belly. Dog did so, and his waist returned to its original state. He ran away, crying, "No! No!"

When bath time came, Ananse washed the bush fowl's legs and feet, leaving them red as they had been before he painted them. He flew off into the bush, crying, "No! No!"

Now Ananse had succeeded in driving away all his friends, and it was not difficult for him to seduce their wives.

When the days of his courtship were ended, Ananse left the village. All his wives accompanied him to the outskirts. He was in a very happy mood, singing love songs as they went along.

Meanwhile, the friends whom he had betrayed decided to disgrace him, too. They smeared a portion of the path with a kind of slippery herb and hid in the bush.

Ananse stepped onto the path, slipped, and, whump!—he was flat on his back on the ground. The calabash at his backside broke into a thousand pieces, and its accumulated contents flew into the faces of his stolen wives. The air was filled with stench, and their cries and shrieks. You could hear the whomp, bash, clonk as all the wives beat Ananse. When he struggled free, he ran away into a corner of the ceiling crying, "Corner, corner! Hide me! Hide me!" And that is why Ananse is found in the corners of ceilings.

61 Wonder Child and the Talkative Woman

Once there was a town. It wasn't a big town, and in this town all the people who lived there were wise. There was nobody there at all who was a fool. They were all there until one day a great thinker was born who grew up to believe that he was wiser than everyone else in the town. He became the chief, and this chief introduced many laws and gave a great deal of advice to the people of the town, but every so often he would bring trouble on it with disputes and arguments. So all the people came to the conclusion that they should gather round and think about what they were to do with this chief.

After a time some assertive young men got together in the town and decided that they must find some way to unseat this chief and take his power from him. They tried and tried, but they couldn't succeed because there was always a group of spies in town, and if anybody plotted anything they would go and tell the chief about it. However, the people managed to unite. Then one day this chief decided that he was traveling to another town to confer with the people there. When he went away the people became one, chose a leader, and under their new leader the farmers and the other people all came together and unseated the old chief.

After some time a child was born in the town. He already had teeth when he was born, and he was wearing sandals. He had also grown a beard before he was born. This was very strange. So they took the child to the meeting place, and they beat the gong, and all the people in the town came and gathered round to look at this child who had so strangely appeared from nowhere. The townspeople were all surprised and astonished, and they decided that any child with teeth and a beard already at birth could only be taboo. So they decided that if any child were born like that, he should be killed. But then many chiefs came from many different towns. They came from all over, and they gathered together, and they thought about this. They came to the conclusion that this was not right, because it may be that a child can be born like that, but he may turn out eventually to be a good person and a great person, so they shouldn't kill him.

After some time, when the baby grew up, they noticed that if he spat on the ground, the spittle became a river. If he took a stick and stuck it in the ground, it immediately turned into a flourishing fruit tree with abundant fruit. If he took a knife and plunged it into the ground, nobody could pull it out. So they said, "Eh, what wonders are these?" So they decided that this person was someone they ought to worship, just as we worship Jesus, the Son of God in heaven. So they started worshipping him, and after some time he told them that if all the people of the town could unite and understand each other, he would make them a throne, and this throne would be for every chief of the town who would succeed him. If a chief sat on that throne it would bring plenty of money and gold into the town. So he told all the chiefs from all around that each of them should shave off hair from his head and from his private parts, and hair from under his armpits, and cut off his nails and bring them all to him. With this hair and with these fingernails, he would make the throne upon which they would sit to be chiefs over the town. Everybody would see that they were good chiefs, because they had a good throne to sit on.

All the chiefs came together, and they shaved off all the hair asked for and the fingernail shavings, and gave them to this wonder child. This wonder child did everything exactly as he had said he would, and made the throne. He performed all the proper rites, and cut off all his own fingernails, and shut himself in a room, and prayed and fasted for seven days while making the throne. Then all the chiefs came and looked at the throne, and it was a really wondrous throne, but they took it away and hid it. It was such a wondrous throne that they could not let any one chief sit on it forever. So they kept the throne hidden, and they would lead every new chief to the throne, and he would sit on it for a moment, and then they would lead the chief away.

Now, after some time a war broke out, and the wonder child told the people that before they could win the war they should make him a bed. They should lay a mattress out for him to lie on. He told them that he would lie on the mattress, and he would sleep for twenty-four days. When they watched him, even if they thought that he wasn't coming back to life they shouldn't cry; they shouldn't make noise, they shouldn't make any lamentations; and they shouldn't say anything out of the ordinary. They should just wait for him to sleep as long as he said he would, and then he would get up and come back. He told them that during the battle, if any of them was hit by a bullet he would be able to revive that person.

So it happened. All the people were staying there quietly and waiting, until one day a certain woman—one of those troublesome women—was going to fetch some water from the river. On the way she saw somebody who looked like the sleeping chief coming back to the village, carrying some things under his arms. When she met him she said, "Oh, Sosorisu! Isn't it you who was said to have died and about whom we've all been told not to cry?" And he said, "Oh you troublesome woman! Weren't you told—didn't you hear the announcement that you people shouldn't talk and shouldn't say anything? So you have talked to me, and now I am annoyed and angry, and I am going away and will leave your town. Henceforth, any time you have a war with other towns, those towns will defeat you, and your town will never be able to have any success or make anything of itself in the future."

And so the wonder child departed, and went and lay down, and he never woke up again.

▼▲▼▲▼▲▼▲▼▲▼▲▼▲▼▲▼▲▼▲▼▲▼▲▼▲▼▲▼▲▼▲

62 Greed Makes a New Friend

One day an old beggar was walking down the street. He knew that the people on that street were wealthy, and he wondered if they were content with what they had. It always seems that the rich want more.

This beggar began to preach about a man who lived in a fine green house. He said, "Inside this house lived a rich man. What do you think the man did? He bought a big ship and filled it full of things he hoped to sell in another country so that he could make more money. What happened? A storm blew up and sank the ship. So all he had was lost in the sea. He became a poor man." The beggar preached about another man, a rich neighbor of the man who lived in the fine green house. Not satisfied with what he had, the man gambled and lost all his money.

Just as the beggar had finished preaching, the Power-That-Makes-People-Rich appeared. The beggar was astonished to see this Power, which this time had assumed the shape of a beautiful woman. The woman said to him, "I've been waiting a long time to help you. Take these gold coins that I have been keeping for you. Open your bag, throw away everything in it, and fill it with these gold coins."

The beggar looked at the gold coins as if he were not satisfied with them. The woman warned the beggar, "If one of these gold coins I have given you falls to the ground, all of them will turn to dust. Remember what I tell you. Your bag is old, and you had better not put into it more than it can hold."

The beggar rejoiced and opened his bag and began to fill it with the gold coins. It got very heavy, and the woman asked if he were not satisfied. The beggar said that he was not. The woman asked him if his bag were strong enough to hold more gold coins. The beggar told the woman he was sure it was.

"Think! You are rich now," the woman said. The beggar replied, "I want a little bit more."

So the woman gave him a few more coins, warning him to be careful or the bag would burst. But, greedily, the beggar kept asking for more. Soon the bag burst, and all the coins fell to the ground and turned to dust. The Power-That-Makes-People-Rich disappeared, and the beggar was left with an empty bag.

When you point your finger at people, remember that their fingers are pointing at you. The head that is destined to carry stones will never wear a crown.

▼▲▼▲▼▲▼▲▼▲▼▲▼▲▼▲▼▲▼▲▼▲▼▲▼▲▼▲▼▲

63 How Crab Got His Shell

There was once a poor orphan girl who had been left in the care of her wicked old grandmother. The old woman was very cruel to the child. This mean woman would send her to fetch water in a sieve and things like that. She even refused to give the child enough food until the child had called her by her proper name, but the child didn't know her grandmother's name, and the grandmother wouldn't tell her. It was a hard life for the poor girl, and she would often go to the river and sit there weeping for her dead parents and her unhappy life.

One day she was sitting by the river, sobbing quietly, when a crab came out of its hole and asked her why she was crying. The girl told the crab her story, how her cruel grandmother would only give her enough food if she could call her by her proper name, and how she didn't know her grandmother's name, and didn't know how to find out because her grandmother wouldn't tell her. The crab said, "That is easy; I'll help you. Your grandmother's name is Sarjmoti-Amoa-Oplem-Dadja." The girl said, "Thank you, Crab," and set off.

On the way home the girl kept repeating the name to herself so she wouldn't forget. But halfway home she heard a bird singing a most beautiful song. She stopped to listen. She enjoyed the bird's song very much, but when she set off for home again and tried to say her grandmother's name, she found she had forgotten it.

So she went back to the river and found the crab and asked it to tell her the name again. This time, the crab refused to tell her. It explained why, saying, "I've been thinking about this, and I'm not going to say that name again because your grandmother will know who told it to you. She is a wicked old woman and will come after me." The girl pleaded with the crab, who was feeling really sorry for her, so he finally gave in and told her the name again: Sarjmoti-Amoa-Oplem-Dadja.

All the way home, the girl repeated that name Sarjmoti-Amoa-Oplem-Dadja, Sarjmoti-Amoa-Oplem-Dadja. Over and over again she said it. She got home safely and started to prepare food for the evening meal. As she prepared the food she said to herself, "Sarjmoti-Amoa-Oplem-Dadja." The old lady came home. As the poor child began to serve the food, her grandmother said, "And what is my name?" The girl appeared not to know, so the grandmother took all the food, and just as she was going to eat it, her granddaughter called her by her name, "Sarjmoti-Amoa-Oplem-Dadja."

"Who told you my name?" demanded the wicked old woman. The girl said, "I got it at the river," but she didn't mention the crab. The old lady grabbed a calabash and went straight to the river.

She went all along the riverbank asking everyone she saw, "Did you tell that girl my name?" Everyone she asked told her, "No, I didn't!" Then she came to Crab.

He was very much frightened and confessed that he had told the girl the name. Then he turned and tried to run away. Furious, the old lady chased

Crab, waving the calabash. She reached out and clapped the calabash down on the crab, and he ran off with it into the forest.

That is how the crab got the shell it has today.

▼▲▼▲▼▲▼▲▼▲▼▲▼▲▼▲▼▲▼▲▼▲▼▲▼▲▼▲▼▲

64 Tortoise and All the Wisdom in the World

Everybody knows that the tortoise is a very wise creature. In fact, the tortoise also thought of himself as the wisest creature on earth. One day the tortoise said to himself, "I will collect all the wisdom of the world in a very big gourd and keep it at the top of a tree so that nobody can get at it. Then I will be the wisest man on earth for all time."

The tortoise therefore took a gourd, and when he thought he had collected all the wisdom of the world in it, he sealed up the gourd, tied it with a rope to his chest, and started to climb a tree in which he wanted to hide the gourd full of wisdom. But the fact that the gourd was tied right to his chest made it impossible for him to climb the tree. Every time he tried to climb the tree he fell down again.

While the tortoise was trying very hard to climb the tree, the snail was watching him at close range. The snail laughed at the folly of the tortoise and said, "Tortoise, I think they say you are a very clever man, but I cannot see how a clever man can climb a tree with a big gourd tied to his chest. If you want to climb that tree, you should tie the gourd to your back, not to your chest."

When the tortoise heard this, he tried the suggestion, and it worked. It was then that the tortoise realized that he did not have all the wisdom of the world in his gourd.

No one can be so wise as to have all the wisdom of the world in his possession.

65 Dede and the Leopard

There was a certain young woman, and this young woman was called Dede. Many suitors had come to ask for her hand in marriage, and she had always refused them. Every man that came got turned down. When this one came she said no, when that one came she said no, until one day when she was feeling very happy, she called to her mother, and she said, "My mother!" and her mother said, "Yes?"

"Mama," she said, "the day that a suitor comes here whom I really like, that day I will pick up the stool you are sitting on, and I will throw it in your face." Her mother said, "All right." She called her father and said, "Father!" and he said, "Yes?" And she said, "The day that a man comes here whom I really like, and whom I accept, that day I will pick up your stool, and I will hit you on the ear with it." And he said, "All right."

A short time later one young man appeared, and he was wearing a beautiful velvet cloth and gold ornaments from head to toe. As soon as Dede saw him she said, "Aha! This is the man I really like." And so Dede immediately got up and ran and pulled out the stool from under her mother and hit her mother in the face with it. Then she ran and pulled out the stool from under her father and hit him in the ear with it. Her father and mother didn't say anything at all. They simply huddled together in a corner of the room. When the young man came forward and told his story, it turned out to be what had been expected: he wanted to marry Dede. So they told him all the customs he had to observe if he wished to marry her. He performed all the ceremonies and married the girl. So then the only thing left was for the bride to be sent to the bridegroom.

Now this girl Dede had a brother called Mensa who was a great medicine man, but he was also suffering from yaws. Now, when Dede was about to leave, Mensa said he would go with her, but Dede refused to take him. She said, "Look at your skin, all blotchy and swollen from yaws! How can I take you with me?" Mensa cried and cried and cried, but Dede said she would not take him, and so Dede went off alone to her husband.

Dede had been away from home a long time, and no word had been heard from her. Meanwhile Mensa, the medicine man who was suffering from yaws, decided he should go hunting. One day he went into the forest, and after he had been hunting and going through the forest for some time he came upon an anthill. He noticed that the area around the anthill had been swept very clean. He circled the anthill, and on the other side he suddenly came upon his sister. She said, "Mensa, how did you come here?" He said, "I was on a hunting trip and came upon this place by accident." She said, "Now that you have come here, you are as good as dead." He said, "Why?" And she said, "The husband who brought me here, I have never seen his face, but every morning when I get up, this man has already laid out plantains for me and meat from his hunting trips, and has gone away. But I have never seen him in person since the first day I came here with him."

Mensa said, "I will take you away." Dede said, "Really?" Mensa said, "Yes." So they set out on their way.

Now it so happens that the man who married Dede was actually a leopard, and the leopard had made up his mind that at the end of that very week he was going to eat Dede. When he came home about noon to check on Dede, nobody was there, so he set out into the forest to find her. He followed Dede and Mensa and followed them and followed them, and all this time Mensa was running away with Dede.

This leopard was very fast, and soon there were only about four yards left between them. Then Mensa took out a horsetail—a medicine man's enchanted switch—that he was carrying with him, and threw it down between them. Immediately the leopard changed into a stone. While the stone was lying there, they kept on running away, and they ran and ran and ran until they had put a great distance between themselves and the stone. Suddenly, the stone cast one of its spells and immediately turned back into a leopard and started pursuing them again. He pursued them until the distance between them was only about three yards. Then Mensa took out another horsetail and threw it down, and this time Mensa and Dede changed into flies. Because they were flies, the leopard couldn't see them, and they flew and flew, flew and flew, in the shape of flies until they reached home. Then they turned into human beings again. Then the leopard thought that he might catch them at home.

So the leopard followed them to their village, and when he reached the outskirts of the village he transformed himself into the same young man he had been when he had come looking for his bride. But meanwhile, Mensa and Dede had told the whole village everything that had happened to Dede since she was taken away, and what sort of husband she had found—

how he would leave her the whole day and come back during the night, and how every morning he would lay out pieces of plantain and pieces of meat for her, and how he would then disappear again and never be seen during the day. They had told how Mensa had found her and brought her home, and how her husband the leopard had chased them.

By that time the bridegroom had arrived, appearing in his human form. He did not know that the people had formed a plan for dealing with him, so when he came, and they gave him a stool, he sat down, and they talked to him, and he talked to them. By the time he had explained what business brought him there, all the people came out of hiding with guns, and they all fired at him. Bang! Bang! Bang! They shot him, and then they cut his body into little pieces of flesh and scattered them all around.

The lesson they learned from this was that if you are a girl going into marriage, you should not go and pull a seat out from under your mother and hit her in the face with it, and you should not go and pull out a seat from under your father and hit him on the ear with it.

The lesson they learned from Mensa's part of the story was that if anybody is going into marriage, one of her relatives should accompany her.

That is how the custom came about that if any girl is married, and she is being taken away on a journey to the home of her husband, then her aunt or her cousin or some other relative of hers goes with her, just to find out where she will be staying.

▼▲▼▲▼▲▼▲▼▲▼▲▼▲▼▲▼▲▼▲▼▲▼▲▼▲▼▲

66 The Master Trickster

One day soon after the rains had started, Gizo, the Spider, was thinking about preparing his farm for the new season. He was in no great hurry to go because he was not at all keen on doing any actual work himself.

He waited until everybody else had finished sowing their crops. Then he went to Koki, his wife, and said, "Hello, Koki, I've got good newth for you. I went out of town today and found that all the menfolk have finithed their thowing, and the cropth have now thtarted to thprout. And now, here are my inthtructhionth to you: Go and get thome groundnutth, take off their thells, fry them, and put thalt on them, tho that when I've thown them, and they come up, they'll be already thalted."

Koki said, "Oh, Gizo, that's a fine idea!" And she ran off, and didn't stop until she reached the market, where she went straight to the groundnut sellers. From them she bought several measures of groundnuts and brought them home, shelled them, fried them nice and brown, and sprinkled salt all over them.

Next day, as dawn was breaking, Spider came and took the fried groundnuts, and went off with them to the foot of a tree, where he sat down and ate groundnuts until he had polished them off. Then he went down to the riverside, scooped up some water and drank till he was quite full. After that he made his way to the foot of another tree where he lay down and fell fast asleep.

Some time later, in the afternoon, he got up, had a good wash, and put on his clothes and went back home. There he found Koki lying down resting and said to her, "Hey, Koki. A manth life ith a hard one. I went off to my farm today, and thtarted work, and thweated away right through till almotht the middle of the afternoon. Then I went down to the edge of the thandbank and had a bath, and here I am, only jutht back."

Koki said, "That's all right. This evening I'll put on some water for you, and when it's nice and hot, you can have a bath, and give yourself a good scrub."

Gizo said, "Fine!"

The days passed, and whenever the other husbands went to their farms, Gizo went to his farm. So it went on, with the other husbands going off to their farms, and Gizo going to his, until the time came for harvesting the groundnuts. Now Gizo, of course, had no groundnuts in his farm, so, if Koki, getting impatient, said she was going to the farm, Gizo would order her to stay at home.

Then one day Koki said, "Now, Husband, I see that lots of other husbands have harvested their groundnuts and are bringing them back home. You ought to make the effort and dig yours up, and bring them home so that we can lay in a good store."

Gizo said, "If God willth, not tomorrow, but the netht day, I'll go and get them up, and bring them right home. But you are not to go, Koki, becauth I don't want you to be theen in the farm grovelling for groundnutth like thothe common folk do."

Koki said, "All right, I'll wait till you bring them."

Two mornings later, at first light, Gizo went off and took a roundabout way till he came to the chief's farm, where he stole some of the chief's groundnuts. When he had pulled up as much as he could manage, he bundled them up, and brought them to Koki and said, "Koki! Here are your groundnutth!"

When she saw that the groundnuts were the first picking, which are often rather poor quality, she peeled one and put it in her mouth; but she couldn't taste any salt. So she said, "Gizo! Why haven't the groundnuts got any salt in them?"

He said, "There you are, back to your old wayth again. The reathon for thowing thalted groundnutth ith thith. When the nutth turn down into the ground, they bury themthelveth right under the ground, and you know that if white antth come along, they'll eat them up. But if they eat the thin outer thkin of the nutth, and it'th thaturated with thalt, they'll have had enough, and will go back underground and leave the nutth alone. And tho, of courthe, you won't tathte any thalt in the nutth themthelveth."

She said, "Yes, of course, that's true."

He went on, "And don't you thee, thothe who have thown their groundnutth without any thalt will be complaining that the white antth have damaged their cropth. But in my farm, the white antth haven't done any damage at all."

Then Koki was satisfied and even more pleased with her marriage.

▼▲▼▲▼▲▼▲▼▲▼▲▼▲▼▲▼▲▼▲▼▲▼▲▼▲▼▲▼▲

67 Asiedo and the Fish Child

There once were a man and wife who had no baby. They were not happy because they had no baby. All the women said, "She has no baby." All the children said, "She has no baby." She went to the river. She said, "River, give me a baby," but the river had no baby to give. She cried and cried and cried, and she had no baby.

One day the man and the woman went to work on the farm. They saw an old woman along the way. She said, "Where are you going?"

They said, "We are going to the farm."

The old woman said, "Where is your baby?"

The man said, "We have no baby," and his wife began to cry.

The old woman said, "I will give you a baby."

The woman said, "O please, give us a baby. We will be so happy."

The old woman said, "Listen to me. Go back home. When you reach the river catch the first fish that comes to you. Carry it on your back. Go home. Don't look back at the fish. Only when you get home can you look at the fish."

They turned to go home. They reached the river. They caught the first fish, as the old woman had told them. Then the woman put it on her back, and they went home.

When they got home the fish began to cry. It was no longer the fish they had caught. It was a lovely baby girl. The mother was happy. The father was happy. The baby was happy. They were all as happy as a family should be. Father bought a rattle for the baby, and she liked playing with it.

One morning Father and Mother went to the farm. Baby was playing with her rattle. An old woman named Mo Asiedo who was staying near the child broke the baby's rattle. The baby cried, and Mo Asiedo said, "Why do you cry?"

Baby said, "You are naughty. You have broken my rattle."

Mo Asiedo said, "Shut up, you fish child!"

Baby said, "What? I am not a fish child!"

Snarled Mo Asiedo, "Yes, but you are."

Baby cried more and went along the path to find Mother and Father. She met a woman. The woman said, "Baby, why are you crying?"

Baby said, "Mo Asiedo, Mo Asiedo. She called me a fish child. I am going back to the river."

The woman said, "No, don't go. You are not a fish child. Come, let us go home." But Baby would not go.

Now far away she saw her mother and father. She ran to meet them. They said, "Why are you crying, Baby?"

Baby said, "Mo Asiedo, Mo Asiedo. She called me a fish child. I am going back to the river."

The mother said, "Come, my baby. You are not a fish child. You are my baby and your father's baby. Mo Asiedo is lying. She is a bad woman."

But Baby ran. She ran toward the river. Mother ran after her. Father ran after her. All the people who saw what was happening came and ran after her. Mother reached her first. She put out her hand to grab the baby, but she jumped into the river, and all that they could see was a little fish swimming away. She looked very, very sad.

Mother said, "Mo Asiedo is a good as dead today."

So she ran to the village and found Mo Asiedo pounding corn. Mother seized Mo Asiedo. She hit her on the head and put her in the mortar. She pounded Mo Asiedo until she was like powder. Mother took Mo Asiedo's powder and cast it on the surface of the river for the little fish to eat.

This is why the elders say, "You should not involve yourself in matters that do not concern you."

▼▲▼▲▼▲▼▲▼▲▼▲▼▲▼▲▼▲▼▲▼▲▼▲▼▲▼▲▼▲

68 The Incredible Nose

Adeebenyasu, a hunter, had been hunting several days and was returning home empty-handed. Suddenly there appeared before him a strange copper-colored man covered with red hair. He was dressed in the usual manner of a hunter, that is, a loincloth with a cartouche and powder box, and he was carrying a gun of unusually large size slung over his shoulder. It was the much-feared Eborobofoe.

"Do you have a little tobacco?" he asked. "Yes, I can give you some," the hunter replied. "And flint?" "And snuff?" "And salt?" Adeebenyasu gave him everything but salt. This he promised to bring when next he came hunting. "You haven't had any luck on this trip, have you?" "No," Adeebenyasu replied. Eborobofoe gave Adeebenyasu a little black pill to chew and told him not to use his gun, but, when he saw an animal he wished to kill, to turn toward it and blow through his nose the magic sound, "Huha!"

Adeebenyasu thanked him and continued his journey. From then on it was "Huha!" "Huha!" all the way home, and the animals fell dead by the dozen.

The next day the hunter returned to give his new friend the salt he had promised him. Eborobofoe thanked him, then warned him never to reveal the secret of his new powers to anyone—not even his wife.

The days went by and weeks turned into months, the months turned into years. Adeebenyasu grew rich, and he grew haughty. One day there was a funeral in the village, Adeebenyasu drank heavily. He was surrounded by hangers-on who were flattering him—praising him to the heavens. Adeebenyasu bragged and swore. One who was there, who hated him, could stand it no longer and accused him of using magic to get his money. Adeebenyasu denied it, and there was a quarrel.

His enemy taunted him with a song: "Adeebenyasu is a liar, oh! Adeebenyasu is a liar, oh! Adeebenyasu has misled me, oh! You have deceived me, oh! Adeebenyasu."

Adeebenyasu beat his chest and swore more loudly, "Yes, all right! What about it? I use magic. And where do you think I got it from? Not from any human source. I am a brave man. I met Eborobofoe, and he couldn't do anything to me. Why don't you go and meet him, you coward? He will tear you into pieces."

As he spoke, his magnificent house crumbled before his eyes. His children disappeared. His clothes fell off him. At last, he was alone, standing in the middle of a forest, with nothing on him but his loin cloth, his old pipe, and his hunting things.

That is why we should always remember to keep secrets, even in the face of the strongest possible provocation to reveal them.

▼▲▼▲▼▲▼▲▼▲▼▲▼▲▼▲▼▲▼▲▼▲▼▲▼▲▼▲▼▲

69 Rat's Vanity

Once upon a time the Dove, the Sparrow, and the Rat were all married to one man. The man went about telling his friends, "As for my wife Rat, she is wonderful. She is the only wife for me. She is my favorite. If I were down to my last penny, I'd spend it on her."

The elders kept telling him, "This is blasphemy. A man should treat all his wives the same. No man should have a favorite wife. It will only make the gods and your other wives angry with you and her." But he would not listen. He went on praising Rat everywhere.

Dove and Sparrow, of course, did not need anyone to tell them that they were neglected. They labored all day in their husband's fields, harvesting his crops and carrying them home. In the evening they took turns cooking his favorite dishes and setting his table. But when he returned from the farm, he had happy words only for Rat, who had been staying home all day combing her hair. After eating his food, he had talk only for Rat, with whom he slept all the time, even when it was not her turn.

Within a short time, the man died, and all his relatives gathered in the house to arrange his funeral. His sisters called the widows and said, "Today our brother, your husband, is gone. Let us see how you mourn your loss."

Dove, who could not see anything because of her copious tears, cried aloud, "Oh my husband, father of my children, how can I live in this world after you are gone? I had better go with you to the land of the dead."

And her sisters-in-law mourned with her, and said, "Oh brother, how can you leave her so?"

Then Sparrow's high voice was heard, wailing shrilly, "Oh my husband, father of my children, how can I eat again when you are gone? I shall stay in the widow's room forever, and never wash off my mourning with seawater. Why did you not take me with you to the land of our ancestors?"

And her sisters-in-law mourned with her, and said, "Oh poor Sparrow, don't cry any more, for you know so well how to cry. We know your pain will never end."

Then they called Rat and said, "Eh, Madam Rat, come and let us hear you. We know you will speak last because what you have to say to our brother can never be finished. Did he not enjoy all the sweetness and fat of life with you? So that even now you look so soft and sleek? What other woman was ever so lucky as to be a bride all her married life?"

But Rat only shook out her fine fluffy hair and looked up at the ceiling with dry eyes—eyes that were as dry as bone. Then she said, "As for me, I do not like wearing black cloth and staying in darkness for three months. Why should I make myself lean and dry, when husbands are so easy to find?" And she shook out her hair again. "If he is dead, he is dead, and that is all there is to it." And once more she shook out her hair and left her sisters-in-law.

All the people were astonished. But the elders said, "This is a lesson from the gods. Special treatment is wasted on a spoiled person. A man should treat all his wives the same. No man should have a favorite wife."

▼▲▼▲▼▲▼▲▼▲▼▲▼▲▼▲▼▲▼▲▼▲▼▲▼▲▼▲▼▲

70 Why Fowls Scratch

Once there was a little boy. One day his mother said this boy should go with her to the farm. He said he wouldn't go. As soon as his mother was out of sight he got a cutlass and went to the bush and cut wood for a drum. He carved the drum and put it in the sun. The boy was called Kofi Babone. When his mother got back from the farm and saw the drum she asked him, "Kofi, didn't you say you couldn't go to the farm because you were ill? Why did you make this drum?" He said he wasn't the one who made the drum. His mother said, "All right then." She went off to prepare a meal, and after a little while called him to come and pound the food. He said, "I'm sick."

The next day his mother said she was going to the farm again, and Kofi must go with her. He said, "No, I'm sick." But as soon as his mother had gone, Kofi Babone went and got his drum. He said, "I am little Kofi Babone. I play for fowls to dance Kren Kren Ka! Kren Kren Ka! Fowls are dancing, Kren Kren Ka!"

So the hens danced, and Kofi drummed in the courtyard of his mother's house. He was happy.

When his mother got back she said, "Kofi, who was that drumming?" He said, "Mama, I don't know."

The next day his mother took her basket and said, "Come on, Kofi, let's go." He said, "I don't feel at all well." So his mother left him behind, but this time she went and hid behind a plantain tree. She saw Kofi go to his drum and recite, "I am little Kofi Babone. I play for fowls to dance Kren Kren Ka! Kren Kren Ka! Fowls are dancing, Kren Kren Ka!"

His mother was very angry. She rushed back, snatched up an old wooden pestle that was lying there, and hit Kofi on the head with it. He fell down dead.

Under the hearth where they light the fire they buried Kofi Babone. So anytime now that you see fowls scratching around a hearth, you must know that it is Kofi Babone they are scratching for—to come and drum for them to dance.

▼▲▼▲▼▲▼▲▼▲▼▲▼▲▼▲▼▲▼▲▼▲▼▲▼▲▼▲▼▲

71 The Hog's Magic

A long time ago there lived a chief who had a most beautiful daughter. She wasn't married, though there had been many suitors for her hand. There was a good reason for this. The daughter had a magic mirror, you see. Anything that happened anywhere, anywhere in the world at all, was shown in this mirror so that the chief's daughter could see it if she wanted, and was looking. She said, "I will only marry the man who can hide himself so well that I can't see him in my mirror." Every man who wanted to try his luck was given three chances. If he failed, and she saw him in the mirror, that was that. After the third attempt, the king had the man killed.

In another village lived a chief who had a son, and this son was very friendly with an animal, a red river hog, to be exact. This hog was a magician. The chief's son had caught him one day when he was out hunting.

This was how it happened, he was just going to kill the hog when it spoke and said, "Please don't shoot me. I can be very useful to you. In fact, there isn't anything I can't do for you." So the chief's son didn't kill the hog, and they became fast friends.

Now this young man had made up his mind to try for the girl in the next village. He told his father one day, "I'm going to try too." His father said, "Don't. You will be killed." So the son went off to his friend the hog and consulted him about the matter. The hog said, "Oh yes, I can help in this business."

The young man went off to the village where the beautiful girl lived, and he told the chief, her father, and the chief's wife, "Please, I've come to marry your daughter, so give me the tests." They didn't waste time at all, but started the competition that very day. The hog put the boy on the bed of the sea. The girl saw him in her mirror. The second time, the hog put the boy in a secret cave in a mountain. The mirror showed him there, and the girl saw him clearly.

All right! So now it was the third and last attempt, and if this one failed, the young man would soon be seeing his executioners. So the hog dug a tunnel from the place where they had lodged the young man in the village, right under the chief's house—in fact, under the room where his daughter kept the magic mirror.

Now, when the test began, the hog took the young man and positioned him in the tunnel so that he was standing just under the magic mirror. The girl was now at her mirror searching everywhere with it, looking over land and sea and even in the air. She didn't see the young man. After a while she got angry and broke the mirror. So the young man had won, and he came out of the tunnel and claimed the chief's daughter, and they were married that same day.

▼▲▼▲▼▲▼▲▼▲▼▲▼▲▼▲▼▲▼▲▼▲▼▲▼▲▼▲▼▲

72 The Bag of Salt

There was once a time when nobody had any salt in the village where Lizard lived. So Lizard traveled far and wide, and bought a sackful of salt. He tied up the sack with some rope and tied the other end of the rope around his neck. This was the way he began dragging the bag of salt behind him home to his village.

On the way he met Tortoise. They talked a bit and parted, but when Lizard was not looking behind, Tortoise cut the rope that held the sack and tied a stone instead to Lizard's end of the rope. Then he made off with the bag of salt himself.

After pulling for some time, Lizard stopped for a rest and turned around. There was no bag of salt! Just a big stone! Lizard did not know what to do, so he went to Anaanu, the Spider, and told him how he had bought this bag of salt and lost it. Anaanu listened to his story, and then told him not to worry but to be patient and wait, and Anaanu promised to find the bag of salt himself and bring it back for Lizard.

Anaanu went off looking for the bag of salt straightaway, and he soon caught up with Tortoise on the road. Tortoise, too, was dragging the bag of salt behind him. Anaanu, too, cut the rope holding the sack and started pulling the bag away with him. Tortoise turned round to Anaanu and asked him why he was doing that. Anaanu said the bag was his, because he was just sitting in a tree by the side of the road when he saw the sack lying on the ground, and he came down and claimed it. He said that if Tortoise did not believe him, he would take him up into the tree and show him where he had been when he saw the sack. Since he was carrying the sack, and climbing a tree was difficult for Tortoise anyway, Spider offered to wrap Tortoise up in some leaves and carry him up with the sack.

Tortoise said all right, and Anaanu took him and the sack up into the tree. But when they got there, Anaanu dropped Tortoise to the ground. When Tortoise hit the ground—it was hard and stony—his shell cracked in many places. That is why Tortoise has many lines all over his back.

▼▲▼▲▼▲▼▲▼▲▼▲▼▲▼▲▼▲▼▲▼▲▼▲▼▲▼▲▼▲

73 The Beaten Path

At first there was only one path in the whole world, and the reason why there are more now is as follows:

Grandfather Sky God had a daughter. He said he would give her to whichever man could tell her name. Of course, all the young men were eager to find out her name, and they asked all the elders of the town, but no one knew the name. One day when Spider was walking alone along the path, he said to himself, "I wonder what I could do to find out this girl's name so that I could marry her." The path replied, "I can easily tell you that, but then you will go and tell people who it was who told you, and they will come and beat me for telling you and not them." Spider said, "Oh, I would never do that. I swear." At this point Path told Spider what he would pay for the information. Path demanded a hare, a dwarf, and a python.

Spider said, "That is no problem," and he went off and returned shortly after with all that Path had asked for. Path now revealed the name of

Grandfather Sky God's daughter, "Mpensaaduasa." Spider said, "Oh, Oh! Thank you for that. Today I will be getting married."

Spider went off and told Grandfather Sky God that he would name his daughter publicly before all the elders, if Grandfather Sky God would convene a celebration for him on the next day. The Sky God, who had named his child secretly on the path before he brought her home, and did not know that the path had told Spider her name, thought Spider was bluffing. "Yoo!" said Spider. On the day of the celebration all the men present were invited to come out and speak the girl's name. No one could. Spider was called last, and he came forward and said straightaway that she was called Mpensaaduasa. Grandfather Sky God was very surprised but agreed that Spider had said the correct name. Everybody acclaimed Spider, calling out "Yee, yee! Spider O! Spider O!"

Then God said, "I will give you my daughter in marriage, Spider, but you must tell me who told you her name, or else I will have to deal with you." Spider wasn't happy about this, but at last he said, "It was the path, the path, the path." God then ordered all the people to go and beat the path.

Spider went ahead to show them Path's house, singing: "Path oh! God's Path oh! I thank you I've got Mpensaaduasa. I thank you, Path O, I thank you." They beat the path until it was broken up into many more paths. That is why we now have many paths.

▼▲▼▲▼▲▼▲▼▲▼▲▼▲▼▲▼▲▼▲▼▲▼▲▼▲▼▲▼▲

74 The Stone with Whiskers

One time, long ago, there was a famine, and all the animals were dying of hunger. Nobody had anything to eat. Bra Spider got up one morning and said, "Let me go and see if my trap has caught anything today." So he left his wife and family at home and went off.

On the way he saw a stone, but it was not an ordinary stone at all. It had a long, long beard. Bra Spider had heard about this stone, and he knew that if you said, "This stone has a beard," it would lift itself up, fall down on you, and crush you. So he didn't say anything. To himself, however, he said, "I know how to get meat now." He didn't even bother to go and look at his trap—he ran off to find his friend Bra Deer.

He said, "Bra Deer, my friend, come and look at my trap with me, eh? If I have caught anything, I will share it with you."

Bra Deer said, "All right, let's go, because my wife and children have nothing to eat."

So off they went. When they approached the place where the stone was, Bra Spider said, "Bra Deer, you go ahead. I'll let you pass."

So Bra Deer, so innocent, went ahead, Bra Spider showing him the way until they reached the stone. Just as they got there Bra Deer shouted to Bra Spider, "Bra Spider, come and look. Come and look at this stone with a beard."

No sooner had he said it than the stone lifted itself up, rolled over on him, and killed him. Bra Spider was delighted. He had some meat at last. He wrapped the carcass up in big leaves and took it home. His wife and children were overjoyed. In no time at all they had Bra Deer in a pot and were cooking him. They ate and ate.

The next day when Bra Spider was hungry again he said, "I'm going to try to get some more meat."

He went off and found Bra Antelope and invited him home with him. On the way he led Bra Antelope to the stone, and when Bra Antelope saw it he cried out, "Bra Spider, come and look at this stone with a beard." And the stone fell on him and crushed him. Bra Spider put the carcass in a bag and took it home for his wife to cook. Everybody was delighted. They ate Bra Antelope.

Well, Bra Spider made this into a regular job. Every day he would go call some animal and have the stone kill it—until only Cunnie Rabbit was left. Well, Bra Spider thought he was clever, but—as it turned out—Cunnie Rabbit was more clever than Bra Spider.

He went to Cunnie Rabbit one morning and said, "Bra Cunnie Rabbit, friend, come and look at my trap with me, eh?"

Bra Cunnie Rabbit replied, "Yes, friend, let's go. That would be nice."

Bra Spider chuckled to himself, thinking he had got more meat. When they got near the place where the stone was, Bra Spider instructed, "Bra Cunnie Rabbit, you go in front. I'll tell you which way to go."

They went on until they reached the stone. Bra Cunnie Rabbit didn't say a word. Bra Spider waited, but he said nothing. Then Bra Spider said, "Bra Cunnie Rabbit, don't you see. . . . "

Bra Cunnie Rabbit, who had his wits about him, said, "See what?"

Bra Spider said, "I said, don't you see what that stone has?"

Bra Cunnie Rabbit said, "No, what does it have?"

And whatever way Bra Spider put the question, Bra Cunnie Rabbit pretended he could not see anything on the stone.

Bra Spider said, "Say, stone with that thing that your grandfather has."

Bra Cunnie Rabbit said, "Stone with that thing that your grandfather has."

Bra Spider said, "Not that way, man. Say the thing's name. Say, stone with a bea——."

Bra Cunnie Rabbit said, "Stone with a bea——."

Bra Spider said, "Go on, then, say it. Stone with a bear——."

Bra Cunnie Rabbit said, "Stone with a bear——."

Bra Spider lost his temper and shouted, "Stone with a beard!" And immediately the stone rolled over and crushed him, and, as the others he had tricked, he died.

That is why it is not good to do bad things. When a cunning rogue dies, it's a still more cunning rogue who buries him.

▼▲▼▲▼▲▼▲▼▲▼▲▼▲▼▲▼▲▼▲▼▲▼▲▼▲▼▲▼▲

75 The Charmed Cutlass

There was once an old woman who did a lot of good. She fed the poor, especially the motherless children and the widows.

One day she went to cut the bush to make a farm, but she could only clear a little bit. So she went back on the following day. Well, there, to her surprise, a fairly large area had been cleared for her. She was very grateful and blessed the person who had helped her in this way. She said, "I will now cut down some trees." She cut down one little tree. The next day she went back to go on with the tree felling. She found when she got to the farm that all the trees had been chopped down. She was grateful and blessed the person who had felled the trees for her.

When the bush was dry she went to burn it. She lighted a torch and put it to a corner of the farm. Suddenly torches appeared all over the farm, and in no time at all the bush was burnt, and the farm was cleared.

A few days later rain fell, and the old woman went to sow corn. She couldn't do much. But when she returned to the farm to continue sowing, she found corn growing everywhere. The same thing happened when she planted cassava, rice, cocoyam, yams, pepper, and any other crop you can think of on the farm.

When the time for cultivation and weeding came, the same benefactor helped her with everything.

When the corn was ripe, she pulled a few ears for her breakfast. The following day when she visited the farm, all the ears of corn had been pulled off, and the stalks were standing bare in the field.

At harvesttime she built a little barn and filled it with a few things. The next day there was a huge barn standing on the farm, and it was filled with a rich harvest. The old woman was grateful and blessed the people who had worked for her.

Many months passed, and now there was a scarcity of food in the land. She distributed a few baskets full of grain to some poor people. When she visited the farm a few days later, she found the great barn empty. She was grateful and blessed the people who had helped her. She was closing the door of the barn to go home when she saw a little cutlass lying on the floor of the barn. She took it home.

The months went by. Another farming season came round. The old woman took the small cutlass to clear the bush. As soon as she started on the bush, the cutlass slipped out of her hand and started cutting all by itself. Every bit of work to be done on a farm was done by that cutlass. Cutting down trees, planting, harvesting. That cutlass did everything. It was easy!

In time, news of the wonderful cutlass spread, and when Ananse heard of it he came to see it for himself. He stayed with the old woman as a servant.

One day when the old woman was not at home, Ananse stole the cutlass and went back with it to his village. He made a big show. He invited all the villagers round about to come and see what his wonderful new cutlass could do.

All the people—men, women, and children—gathered in a big forest. Ananse took the cutlass and started cutting the bush. After a few strokes, the cutlass slipped out of his hands and went off on its own, cutting through the thick bush and chopping down the giant forest trees. The people shouted for joy. It was an amazing sight. The cutlass hacked and whacked and whacked and hacked. The thickest forest was no match for this magic knife.

At last there was no more bush to cut, so it started hacking and chopping the people. There was utter confusion. Within a short time not a single human being was left on the vast open space. It was total desolation! And since there was nothing else left to destroy, the cutlass started to chase Ananse. He ran, but it was too late. The knife hacked him to pieces.

Now there was absolutely nothing more it could cut. So it went round and round the clearing several times, and, finding nothing, it planted itself on the banks of a stream and grew into a plant which up to this day is called "The old woman's razor."

▼▲▼▲▼▲▼▲▼▲▼▲▼▲▼▲▼▲▼▲▼▲▼▲▼▲▼▲▼▲

76 Why Tortoise Is Bald

Tortoise one day went to visit his mother-in-law with two of his friends. At his mother-in-law's house, Tortoise and his friends were given porridge to eat. Although the porridge was very hot when it was set before them, they quickly finished it. But Tortoise was still very hungry. He therefore left his two friends and crawled into his mother-in-law's room, where he found the remaining porridge inside the pot, still very, very hot. Tortoise took his cap and emptied the porridge into it. That done, he put the cap back on his head with the hot porridge inside.

Tortoise came back to his friends, sat down for a little while, and stood up again. He was getting restless because of the hot porridge on his head. All at once he went and told his mother-in-law that he and his friends were going home. But his mother-in-law had messages for her daughter which she wanted Tortoise to take, and she detained Tortoise in conversation. He was growing more restless. He was suffering from terrible burns under his cap where the hot porridge was.

Tortoise finally managed to take leave of his mother-in-law. But as he was prostrating himself, bidding her goodbye in the traditional way, his cap fell off his head, and he was exposed.

This time the Tortoise had gone too far. His cleverness not only burned off all his hair, it shamed him in front of his friends and his wife's mother.

▼▲▼▲▼▲▼▲▼▲▼▲▼▲▼▲▼▲▼▲▼▲▼▲▼▲▼▲▼▲

77 Why Lizard Bobs His Head

Once upon a time there was a chief who had a very beautiful daughter. All the men wanted to marry her, but none managed to get her to be his wife because when anyone went forward, the first thing the chief did was to ask him her name. No one was able to give it because no one had ever heard it. So the young men pined, and the girl stayed beautiful and unmarried.

This same chief had a big and famous cock. The rooster was well known all over town because it always crowed loudly in the mornings and woke people up.

One day Lizard had gone to the beach and was basking in the sunshine on the sands, and suddenly, there was the chief's daughter coming to the beach along with her maid. Like everybody else, Lizard admired the girl and wanted very much to have her for his wife. He made up his mind to find out her name so that he could succeed where so many others had failed.

Quickly Lizard climbed up a coconut tree and hid in the branches. Soon the two girls arrived on the beach and sat under the coconut palm, talking and laughing. All of a sudden, Lizard dropped a coconut from the tree, and it fell near the two girls. The maid was surprised and pleased, so she called out the name of her mistress and said, "Oh look, a coconut!" They drank the coconut juice and went home.

After they were gone, Lizard, who had seen and heard everything from his hiding place, came down from the tree. He went to the chief's palace and said he wanted to marry his beautiful daughter. The chief said that he would give him his daughter to marry if Lizard could tell him her name. So Lizard went forward and told the chief the name. The chief was amazed, but he said he would get everything ready so Lizard could marry his daughter the following day. He gave Lizard a room in the palace and told him to spend the night there in preparation for the wedding on the morrow.

Now Spider, who was Lizard's neighbor, soon heard of his neighbor's good fortune, and he couldn't rest. He, too, wanted the girl. He decided to pay Lizard a call. In the night he crept into the palace carrying a pot of boiling hot water with him. He went to Lizard's room and poured the boiling hot water into Lizard's mouth. The water scalded Lizard's tongue and burned his throat. Then Spider slipped out, caught the chief's rooster, and killed it. He dipped it in the hot water, plucked off its feathers, and scattered the feathers all over the way into Lizard's section of the compound. Then he went away.

In the morning Spider went to the palace as though to visit the chief. He said that it was curious that he had not been wakened that morning by the rooster crowing. The chief also wondered why, and sent people round the compound looking for the bird. Spider went off to visit his friend Lizard, he said, and soon returned to tell the chief that he had seen lots of feathers round the entrance to Lizard's room.

The chief sent people to the place, and they brought Lizard up in front of him. He asked Lizard whether the feathers were those of his famous rooster. Lizard, whose voice had been scalded away, could only raise his head up and down. To every question, he could only nod. The chief really thought he had killed the rooster. He became very angry and announced that he would no longer give his daughter to Lizard to marry. Instead, Spider would marry the princess. Lizard was thrown out of the palace.

So Spider took Lizard's place, and married the chief's beautiful daughter. But whenever he came out of the palace, Lizard, who still could only nod, chased him. That is why the Lizard always bobs his head up and down, and why he is always chasing a spider to eat him.

▼▲▼▲▼▲▼▲▼▲▼▲▼▲▼▲▼▲▼▲▼▲▼▲▼▲▼▲▼▲

78 Spider the Swindler

One day a great famine came, and everyone had to search for food to eat. Spider, too, had to go out and look. By chance he came to a riverbank, where he could hear birds calling from a huge tree that grew in the middle of the water. When he looked more closely, he could see that the tree bore all the fruits that men and animals look for on land, as well as fufu, porridge, and bread, and all kinds of other things.

The birds could simply fly in and peck at whatever they fancied. Oh, how he longed for that food! But what could he do? How could he reach it? He gave up and was miserable. He had just begun to walk away when suddenly a bird flew by, plucked out one of its feathers, and fixed it firmly onto Spider. Then another came and another. Spider thought he might be able to fly. He tried to fly, and behold, he could fly! Joyfully, he flew straight to the tree and began to gorge himself.

After a while he noticed that the amount of food was dwindling. He became angry and accused the birds of greed. He claimed that the food was his and that they had no right to take any more. The birds became alarmed and flew off, each one taking back the feather he had given Spider. Spider was too busy eating to notice, but when he had finished all the food on the tree, he realized that he couldn't fly back. He sat down and thought hard about what he could do. He thought of a plan. He quickly plucked a leaf from the tree, wrote something on it, and dropped it into the river.

Now a big crocodile saw the leaf in the water and asked, "Who wrote on this leaf?"

"I did," said Spider from the tree, "and I have laid seven eggs, which I will keep for you if you will take me back to land."

Crocodile agreed. He agreed even when Spider demanded as part of the bargain that he should be given a new house, a new cooking pot, new cooking stones, and a brand new calabash. Crocodile went off and found all these things and then collected Spider and brought him to dry land.

As soon as he reached his new house, Spider went inside, cooked six of his eggs, and ate them. Then he took outside the one egg that was left to show Crocodile, and he wrote on it, "reserved for Crocodile." He took the egg back inside, washed off the writing, and reappeared to write on it again, "reserved for Crocodile." He did all this seven times, and told Crocodile that he was going to keep his eggs in the new pot for seven days, and that they must not be disturbed before then. He warned Crocodile that they would vanish if he did not obey these instructions.

Crocodile went back to the river, but after a while he began to have doubts and grew anxious in case he had misunderstood his instructions. When he returned, Spider had gone out, so he went and opened the pot just to check. But when he looked inside, the pot was empty.

In a panic, he ran out looking for Spider, and when he found him and told him what had happened, Spider was very angry, but said that he might just be able to bring the eggs back. In the meantime, he asked Crocodile to help him lift up a huge grindstone that lay nearby, saying that it belonged to his wife and that he had been instructed to bring it to her. While they were struggling to lift it, Spider asked Crocodile if any part of him was particularly vulnerable. Crocodile was very unsuspecting and believed Spider to be a friend he could trust, so he confided to him that the tip of his nose was very delicate, and any damage to it would kill him. Now, as Crocodile lifted up the heavy grindstone for Spider to carry, Spider deliberately knocked him off balance, and the stone came crashing down on his nose, killing him instantly.

Spider set to work at once to weave a long basket, into which he put Crocodile's body. Later, as he was carrying it through the forest, he met Hyena and Leopard. As soon as he saw them, he began to moan and weep, saying that he was mourning for his poor dead mother. Hyena was touched and expressed his sympathy. Leopard, however, was not so easily tricked. He knew Spider of old and he demanded to see what was in the basket. Hyena and Leopard claimed the crocodile, and Spider was already planning a way to get it back.

While Leopard and Hyena were preparing to cook the crocodile meat, Spider enlisted the help of Lizard to put his plan into effect. Lizard came to where the two of them were cooking and convinced them that the meat would not be tasty unless the crocodile's teeth were properly painted, and that the Spider was the only one to do it.

They agreed reluctantly, and Spider came to paint the teeth. As he set to work, he said that Hyena and Leopard were distracting him because they refused to sit quietly. He ordered them to go into the forest to get some vines off the trees. They were told to bring the vines back to make a platform for the meat when it was cooked. No sooner had they left than Spider and Lizard fell upon the meat, cooked it, and ate all there was.

Before the others returned, they ran off and hid themselves in the branches of a huge tree. Spider climbed higher and was perched among the leaves at the very top, high above the ground. Hyena and Leopard were very angry when they returned and found the meat gone. They immediately began a search in the forest, and enlisted the help of some of the other animals.

The sluggish Lizard was soon found sleeping in the lower branches of the tree. When he was caught and questioned, he became frightened and betrayed Spider's hiding place. Taken unaware, Spider, too, was bound and brought back to Hyena and Leopard. But Spider's bag of tricks was not exhausted yet. He already had another plan. As soon as he was brought down, he fell upon the ground and began to revile himself for the evil deeds that he had done. He said that he deserved the extreme penalty, and that they should take him and Lizard and throw them deep into the earth, where the land had been baked and cracked by the sun. Leopard agreed with the punishment, and both Spider and Lizard were untied and hurled into the deepest crack they could find.

Really, it was no trouble to them at all. Lizard's mother had her home deep down at the bottom of the crack, and Lizard was very welcome there. Spider, too, was not unused to wandering under the earth in cracks and crevices, and he crawled off to hide until the coast was again clear.

It is wrong not to show gratitude for a favor, the way that Spider had been ungrateful to the birds, even though they had done so much for him, and by his ingratitude, look what trouble he had made for himself.

▼▲▼▲▼▲▼▲▼▲▼▲▼▲▼▲▼▲▼▲▼▲▼▲▼▲▼▲

79 Tortoise Sheds a Tear

Tortoise was a very clever creature. He had a ready answer for any situation. He was never caught off guard. One day his wife's father died. He had to go with his friends to his in-law's house and perform his funeral duties as a good husband.

One of the very first things the Tortoise had to do upon reaching his in-law's house was to weep and wail with all his friends, and it was important that everybody should see that he was actually shedding real tears. Now, it is absolutely impossible for Tortoise to shed tears because of his naturally callous attitude to everything and everybody.

Tortoise thought up a clever trick to meet the situation. He was never at a loss. He boiled a certain vegetable and put it inside his cap. When he was near his dead in-law's house, he put the cap on his head with the boiled watery vegetable inside. He then told his friends that it was time to start weeping. Soon Tortoise was weeping most and crying loudest and shedding the biggest tears. The tears came from inside his cap. As he cried, he would put his two hands on his head like a man in deep agony and press down. Immediately, the watery vegetable inside his cap would drip big drops of water on his face, and Tortoise would pretend that these were actual tears. In this way the Tortoise escaped the ugly situation into which he was put by the death of his father-in-law—the position of a chief mourner who had no tears to shed.

Once again, Tortoise had demonstrated that he has an answer to everything.

▼▲▼▲▼▲▼▲▼▲▼▲▼▲▼▲▼▲▼▲▼▲▼▲▼▲▼▲▼▲

80 The Cunning of Galonchi

There was once a great rogue named Galonchi. He was highly skilled in the art of deception, and was completely impoverished, except that he owned a horse. He said to his wife, "Give me that gold earring of yours, and I'll give it to my horse." The woman gave it to him, and he gave it to the horse inside some food. The horse swallowed it, and when the food passed through the horse, the gold was stuck to the dung.

He took the horse and its golden dung to the chief and said to him, "Here you see my horse, whose dung contains gold."

The chief answered, "You are quite right." And he added, "How much do you want for the horse?"

The man said, "One hundred of whatever I name."

The chief promised him that, and the man said to the chief, "There is one thing I must tell you. You must put the horse in a stable for three months and let no one go near it."

The chief left the horse in the stable for three months. The horse was excreting steadily. The man came and said to the chief, "You must call all the elderly women of the town, and they must go and pound the dung, but you must send people to keep an eye on them, so that they don't steal all your gold."

And that is just what the chief did. They called all the women of the town, and they came and pounded and pounded that dung. Then they winnowed it, and nothing! They saw nothing! They went and reported to the chief, "We have seen absolutely nothing."

The chief said, "Go and call that man Galonchi for me."

As he was about to go to the chief, Galonchi said to his wife, "You and I are going together. When I am talking to the chief, you will contradict me. Then, I will say to you, 'Shut up!' and you must say to me, 'I won't shut up!'" He tied a blood-filled chicken's gullet to his wife's neck, and they set off.

The chief said to him, "Galonchi, didn't you say that your horse excretes gold?"

Galonchi said, "Yes, I did say that."

His wife said to him, "Ah, that's not true."

Galonchi exclaimed, "Shut up!"

His wife responded, "I will not shut up."

He flung his wife to the ground and cut the chicken's gullet so that blood came forth.

The chief said, "Goodness, Galonchi, you have killed the woman!"

Galonchi replied, "Tell me quickly why you have called me, for I must begin to raise her up immediately."

The chief said, "No, let's leave that matter. Let's talk about what you did just now."

Galonchi had a cowtail switch. He said, "Bring a new calabash." A new calabash was bought, and he put water in it, dipped the cowtail in it, and sprinkled it on the woman. The woman got up and exclaimed, "Atishoo!"

The chief said to Galonchi, "All right, let's leave that other matter. That cowtail of yours, that's what I want because I have seen this with my own eyes. How much is it?"

Galonchi answered, "One hundred of whatever I name."

The chief promised him that, and Galonchi gave the chief the cowtail, and off he went.

The chief's attendants were sitting chatting. He and his favorite wife were sitting chatting, when he said to her, "Now I'm going to cut your throat if you don't keep quiet."

They said, "Ah, the chief has said that he will cut someone's throat."

The chief said, "I will cut this woman's throat and then raise her up again." So it was that he came to throw his favorite wife to the ground and cut her throat with a knife.

They said, "Oh, the chief has killed someone, the chief has killed some-one!"

He said, "Come and let's chat. I'll raise her up again in a moment."

And so they chatted for a long time. Then they said to him, "Raise her up now."

He dipped the cowtail switch in water and sprinkled it on her. Nothing. He sprinkled it on her again. Still nothing. He shouted, "Go and bring Galonchi here. I'll kill him for this!"

They went and brought Galonchi. The chief said to his attendants, "Come and kill this big bull, and remove its skin. I'm going to put him inside it and go and throw him in the deepest part of the river. In the deepest part of the river, that's where he is going."

They killed the bull, removed its skin, seized Galonchi, and put him inside the skin and tied the mouth of it. The chief said to his personal soldiers, "Four of you take him to the river and throw him into the deepest part." They put a stone inside the skin bag and went on their way. After a time they left the road to go and relieve themselves.

A trader with a load of kola nuts was on a donkey, urging it on with shouts of "Ai! Ai! Ai!" When Galonchi heard that, he shouted, "Oh, I don't want to go to heaven. They say they are taking me to heaven. I don't want to go to heaven!"

The trader exclaimed, "Goodness, what sort of a person are you? Every-body wants to go to heaven, and you say you don't want to go!"

"Not me! *I* don't want to go," Galonchi declared. "Untie me, untie me. If you untie me, I will get out of the bag, and you can go."

The trader untied him and got inside the bag, whereupon Galonchi tied the mouth of the bag and then mounted the trader's donkey. The four men came out of the grass by the side of the road and loaded him on their heads, saying, "Aha, Galonchi, you've got away with it for a long time, but today we are going to throw you in the river."

The trader shouted, "It's me! It's me!"

They said to him, "No, no, today it's into the river."

They went and threw the man into the river and then went and reported to the chief, "We have thrown him in the river."

Some little time elapsed, but the sun was not yet hot when they saw Galonchi coming with the donkey, and with two loads of kola nuts on the donkey's back. When he saw the chief, he shouted, "Ai! Ai!" He urged on the donkey.

People said, "Isn't this Galonchi?"

They said, "It's him all right."

The chief said, "No, it's not him."

They said, "It *is* him."

He came and said to the chief, "The spirits of your mother and father send their greetings. It was they who gave me this kola to give you, but in any case you must go to shadowland, because there is silver there, and there is gold there in limitless quantity. You are not doing anything of consequence here. When they take you and throw you where they threw me—there is a fork in the road there—you will go to your mother and father, who are at peace there."

The chief sounded the drum, boom! boom! boom! The whole country assembled, and he said to them, "I have summoned you here. Galonchi has come from my father and mother, who say that I must go. Galonchi will sit on my throne until I return. I have given Galonchi three months. If anyone opposes Galonchi, it will be just as if he were opposing me."

They removed the skin from a big bull, put the chief in it, and tied it securely. Galonchi instructed the attendants, "Go and throw him where you threw me."

They went and threw the chief into the deepest part of the river. Galonchi sat on the throne. One month, two months, three months, the chief did not return, so Galonchi became chief.

▼▲▼▲▼▲▼▲▼▲▼▲▼▲▼▲▼▲▼▲▼▲▼▲▼▲▼▲▼▲

81 Tortoise Disobeys

Tortoise was a very clever creature. He claimed that he was the best doctor in the area. He claimed that he could cure sterility, leprosy, coughs, and colds. He also claimed that he could restore the hunchback, the dwarf, and the cripple.

Many of Tortoise's neighbors were bringing sick people to him to be cured. The very first case that was brought to him was that of a barren woman. After Tortoise had taken plenty of money, clothes, food, and drink from the relatives of the woman, he promised that he would cure the woman in seven days.

Tortoise then went during the night to a Divining Priest in the neighborhood. He gave the priest part of the money, clothes, food, and drink he had received. In return the priest promised to give him a medicine that would cure barrenness. But he warned Tortoise never to taste the medicine. The medicine was put in a pot, and Tortoise carried it home, glad that he had found a medicine that would cure sterility.

On the way home Tortoise noticed that the smell of the medicine was very pleasant. He placed the pot on the ground and sat by it to enjoy the pleasant smell. After some time, he dipped his fingers into the medicine, took a handful, passed it to his mouth, and started to eat it. It was only after he had swallowed it that he remembered the warning of the priest. He set off home again with the pot, and suddenly he noticed that his stomach had begun to swell. It swelled and swelled and swelled, until Tortoise could hardly walk. Tortoise was now forced to go back to the priest who had prepared the medicine for him.

On the way he started singing: "Divining Priest, Divining Priest, I come to beg you for mercy. As I was carrying home the medicine that you prepared for me last time, I slipped on the ground, fell down, accidentally dipped my fingers into the medicine, and unknowingly put it into my mouth. Then I noticed that my stomach had become swollen. Divining Priest, Divining Priest, I come to beg for mercy."

The priest blamed Tortoise for his disobedience, but he gave him another medicine to swallow. Immediately his stomach started to shrink. It shrank and shrank until it became flat. Then it shrank some more and became hollow. The Tortoise has had a hollow stomach to this very day.

▼▲▼▲▼▲▼▲▼▲▼▲▼▲▼▲▼▲▼▲▼▲▼▲▼▲▼▲▼▲

82 Dog Is Betrayed

Tortoise and Dog were friends. It happened once long ago that there was famine in the land where they lived, and food was scarce. The two friends therefore decided to go and steal yams on a farm far away from their homes.

They set out late at night and reached the farm while it was still dark.

They quickly gathered as many yams as they could carry, and they started back for home again. On their way home Tortoise, who was a very lazy person, started to complain. He complained that he wouldn't be able to move his legs unless Dog helped him to carry part of his own portion of the stolen yams. Now, the real reason why Tortoise wanted Dog to carry his yams for him was that he had noticed that it would soon be dawn, and they might be seen and captured. But Dog, who did not see the trick, helped Tortoise carry some of his load. A few minutes afterward, some people appeared from behind. They had been following Dog and Tortoise. Tortoise heard footsteps from behind, and suspecting they were being pursued, he passed on his remaining yams to Dog. By the time the pursuers actually appeared, Tortoise had slipped into the foliage beside the road and covered himself with leaves. Dog was caught with the stolen yams on his head and arrested, but Tortoise, who was now only a spectator to the scene, watched from his hiding place, safe and laughing.

Tortoise proves his cleverness one more time.

▼▲▼▲▼▲▼▲▼▲▼▲▼▲▼▲▼▲▼▲▼▲▼▲▼▲▼▲▼▲

83 The Wise Child and the Chief

Once upon a time in the olden days, it was the chief who performed the naming ceremony for newborn children, and it was he who gave them their names. Now it so happened that a woman who did not realize her time was so near went to her farm one day and was working in it when—suddenly—she gave birth to a baby boy. She lay exhausted, wondering how she was to let her husband know what had happened, when the baby said, "Look, Mother, why don't I go call Father?" And that is just what he did.

A few days later the baby was taken to the chief's compound for the naming ceremony, to be given his name, but no sooner had the ceremony started than he stood up and told the chief and the elders that he already had a name, and he didn't want another. When they asked him what his name was, he told them, "I am called Wiser-than-the-chief."

The chief thought, "All right, we will have to do away with this one," but he only said he would like to give the baby a test to see whether he deserved his name. He gave the boy a palm nut and said he wanted palm wine that evening to pour a libation. But this was impossible, wasn't it? To plant a palm nut, grow a palm tree, and tap it for palm wine, all in a single day! Nobody could do that. But, wait a minute, in the old days, you know, palm wine was collected in and drunk from a calabash. So what did Wiser-than-the-chief do? He went off and found the seed of a calabash tree and came back to the chief with it and said, "Grandfather, here is the seed that has to be planted to grow a calabash to drink your palm wine from tonight."

Well, of course, the chief couldn't do that, either. So he released the boy from his task. But he spent a month or so thinking of ways to get even with the boy—and the boy's family, too, because by now he was very angry. At last, he thought he had a good plan.

His plan was this. He had a bull from his own herd put among the cows that Wiser-than-the-chief's father was raising. (The father had only cows, no bulls.) Now the chief intended the next day to pretend to find the bull and accuse Wiser-than-the-chief and all his family of stealing it. But the boy saw what was in the chief's mind, so early the next day he went off to the chief's house with a cutlass and started to cut down the one good tree in the whole compound.

The chief came out to see what he was doing and asked him, "Why are you cutting down this, my favorite tree?"

The boy replied, "O my father has just given birth to a baby boy, and I need some leaves from this tree to make medicine for him."

The chief said, "What is all this nonsense? Who ever heard of a man having a baby?"

Wiser-than-the-chief said, "Well, whoever heard of keeping bulls with cows?" So the chief could do nothing. He accepted the boy for what he was and left him alone after that.

When someone is born into this world and says, "I am such-and-such!" it is best to believe him. One man cannot rule the whole world and judge all that happens in it.

84 The Drunkard's Wisdom

In the old days there was a woman who had two sons. One of them was a drunkard. The drunkard was useful about the house, though. He wasn't all bad. But one day he got drunk, and his mother lost her temper and told him to get out of the house. To tell the truth, this man lived for drinking! So now he had to go away and live on his own somewhere.

Well, some time after that, the mother became seriously ill. She took all sorts of medicine, but nothing seemed to do her any good. Her remaining son took her to an herbalist, who quickly diagnosed what was wrong with her. He told the son, "The only thing I know that will cure your mother's ailment is a certain fruit. Unfortunately, the only tree I know near here that bears this fruit is the one that grows on the little island in the middle of our lake. It's an evil lake, as you know. The water is poisonous, and if you even try to cross it, you will be killed. I also will remind you that in the tree lives a fierce old monkey."

The family was totally downhearted. There seemed to be no way at all of getting what the old lady needed. It meant that there was no hope for her.

Quite by chance, the drunken son was on his way to town and passing by the lake when he saw his family standing on the bank looking miserable. He went up to them and asked them what the matter was. They ignored him at first, and then, getting angry, they began to cast insults upon him. His brother said, "Oh, you, what can you do? Go and get drunk—it's all you are good for."

But he didn't get angry in turn. No, rather, he just said quietly, "Now, you just tell me what is wrong." So they told him how his mother had fallen ill, and they had taken her to an herbalist because nothing else had done her any good. He was told how the herbalist said that she needed the fruit of the tree that grows on the island in the middle of the lake, but there was no way to cross to the island because the lake was an evil one, its waters poisonous to man. They got angry again and shouted, "All right, drunkard, now you know. Now that we have told you everything, what are you going to do? What can you do?" And the drunkard said, "What am I going to do? I'll show you what I'm going to do. I'm not all that stupid, you know." He took a stone and threw it across the lake and hit the monkey with it. The monkey got annoyed, looked around for something to throw back at the man, and picked a fruit. He threw it at the drunkard. The drunkard threw another stone, and the animal threw another fruit back. Soon the drunkard had enough fruit. He gave them all to his brother and said, "Take our mother home now, and give her these and get her well."

And the mother did indeed get well. When she went to thank the herbalist for curing her, he said, "It isn't I you should thank, it is your own son. It was he who cured you, not I." So the woman was cured, and the drunken son was welcomed back into his family.

What the herbalist told the woman is true. A mother should love all her children equally and not choose among them. They are all her children, and even the worst is not all bad.

▼▲▼▲▼▲▼▲▼▲▼▲▼▲▼▲▼▲▼▲▼▲▼▲▼▲▼▲▼▲

85 The Wisdom of Aja

There once was a woman who was pregnant, and when her time came she gave birth to septuplets. This was unlucky, and the woman was ashamed. All seven were boys. The first boy was born with a gun in his hand, and the last boy held a cowtail switch. The woman reported these strange events to the chief as soon as she could, and he decided that the children should all be killed. His plan was to dig a pit with stakes in it like an animal trap. The trap was covered, and seven stools were set on top. When all the boys sat, the trap would be sprung. The chief summoned the brothers, but as they were setting out for the chief's house, the youngest saw what was in the chief's mind and advised the others not to sit when they got there.

What he said was, "When you have been born into this world, and there is someone who wishes to kill you, then you must all stand up."

They went and greeted the chief and kept standing. The chief called the mother and said, "I wasn't able to kill your children, what shall I do now?"

Now the mother wanted them to die because they had brought shame on her, so she told the chief, "Send them to cut seven sticks for you, and the place they will go for the sticks is where you should lay another trap." The chief said, "All right."

The next day the seven boys—Odebibi, Odebaba, Nyankoma, Kumachere, Cherebi-Akon, Kakajasa, and Aja—went off to cut the sticks, but Aja again saw the plot, and he said to his brothers, "Eh, Odebibi, Odebaba, Nyankoma, Kumachere, Cherebi-Akon, Kakajasa, when you have been born into this world, and your mother doesn't love you and wants you to die, then I, Aja, say that this wood should be cut into seven sticks, and these seven sticks should appear—now!" And he threw his cowtail switch against a log, and there were the seven sticks the chief had asked for.

When the brothers brought him the sticks, the chief realized his plan had failed and, moreover, he saw that it was Aja's doing. So he devised another scheme to get rid of Aja. Aja was to go to Death's Abode and bring back from there Death's snuff bottle, Death's snuff-grinding stone, and his fly switch. While Aja was away the chief would call his six brothers and kill them.

Aja set off. He took with him two loaves of bread and two fishes. No sooner had Aja left than the chief killed his six brothers and buried them.

Now along the way, Aja came to a small stream. The stream spoke to Aja. It said, "I'm hungry. Give me some of your food."

Aja gave the stream something. He went on and on and on, and came at last to a very small tree, and it, too, asked for bread and a little fish. He gave it some and went on till he came to a stone. He gave the stone food, too, because it, also, was hungry. Next he met a few ants, and they asked for food, and he gave them some. Now he had only a little food left, but he went on and on and on. A tsetse fly met him. It said, "I'm hungry; give me some of your food." Aja gave the fly all the food he had left and continued his journey.

Soon he came to an old lady sitting by the roadside. She asked Aja where he was going, and he told her he was looking for Death, but he did not know where Death lived. The old lady told him where Death's house was and how to get to it. Aja followed her directions and was soon at Death's house. Death greeted him politely and asked what he wanted.

"Oh," said Aja, "I'm only coming to visit with you."

"All right. I'll cook some fufu, and we'll eat," Death replied. "Then you can stay the night with me."

Before they went to bed, Death asked Aja, "Have you got a secret?"

"Oh, yes," said Aja, and told Death, "when I'm asleep I breathe quietly, but when I'm wide awake, I snore loudly." And Aja went off to sleep.

Now Death wanted to kill Aja, but whenever he went to where Aja was sleeping he heard snoring and thought he was awake (because Aja had told Death the opposite of what was true). At last Death got annoyed and said, "Aja, why are you still snoring? Why aren't you asleep?" And this woke Aja, and he said to Death, "I have a headache, and it's keeping me awake. If you would give me some snuff, it might get rid of my headache, and then I could go to sleep."

Death gave him his snuff bottle. A little bit later Death thought he would try again. He went to the place Aja was sleeping, heard him snoring, and said, "What is it now that is keeping you awake?"

Aja woke up quickly and said, "It's the flies, Death. They are keeping me awake."

Death gave him his fly switch and went back to his own bed. Soon Death came back to kill Aja, but Aja was snoring. Death was angry now. He said in a loud voice, "Are you still awake? What is the matter with you?"

Aja woke up quickly and said, "Oh, Death, there are insects on the wall. Give me your grinding stone to kill them." Death brought him the grinding stone. By now it was daybreak and too late to kill Aja. Death decided to wait until the following night.

Later in the morning, Death and Aja were sitting talking outside the house when the tsetse fly—the one I told you about, that Aja had befriended—came and bit Death. Death said, "So! I'm going to kill that fly!" He set off after it. While Death was chasing the tsetse fly, Aja got away with all the things he needed.

As he left, it was the old lady who saw him and gave the alarm. She called out, "Ho, Death, your visitor is leaving." Death heard her and left off chasing the fly to chase Aja instead. Before he caught up with Aja, he saw those very same ants that Aja had met on his way to Death's house. But they were many—many!—very many. They had multiplied. Death was fond of fried ants, and he couldn't resist these. He turned round and rushed back to his house for a frying pan, came back, made a fire, and ate the ants. Then he set off after Aja again. But now he came to a tree. It was the very same tree that Aja had befriended before, but it had grown big, oh, so big, and it blocked the road. Death went back for an axe to chop down the tree.

Aja was running, running all this time, and at last he came to the little stream and crossed it. No sooner was he safely on the other side than the stream flooded. Death was nearby this time, but when he saw that he could not cross the river, he went back again to his house to get a calabash. He had in mind to drink the river dry and cross. But he couldn't. He drank and drank and drank, but the more he drank, the wider the river grew. So this was how Aja escaped Death, and brought the chief all the things he had asked for.

On his way to the chief he saw the graves of his brothers, and he woke them all up.

The chief thought of another plan. He sent for a fetish priest who had powerful medicine. Aja told his brothers, "Eh, Odebibi, Odebaba, Nyankoma, Kumachere, Cherebi-Akon, and Kakajasa, when you are born into this world, and your mother doesn't love you and has sent for someone who is much more powerful than I am, then you should all run away and hide in a tree."

And they did. The fetish priest found them. He stood under the tree and called them one by one, by name. He called out, "Odebibi! I say come down." Odebibi fell out of the tree. Then he called, "Odebaba! I say come down." Thereupon, Odebaba fell out of the tree. Next he called Nyankoma and said, "Nyankoma! I say come down." And Kumachere, "Kumachere! I say come down." Kumachere, too, fell out of the tree. "And Cherebi-Akon! I say come down." Right then and there Cherebi-Akon fell out of the tree. And he called, "Kakajasa! I say come down." Kakajasa, too, fell out of the tree. Now he called Aja and said, "Aja, I say come down."

But Aja said, "Leaf, he says you must fall," and a leaf fell from the tree. The fetish priest made more magic and called out, "You, Aja, you come down!" And Aja said, "Leaf, he says I must fall with you." And another leaf fell from the tree, and Aja fell with it, and when they reached the ground, he hid under it. The fetish priest thought Aja was still in the tree, and he went on making magic until there was nothing left on the tree. It was bare, completely! But he still thought Aja was up there somewhere. So he left his box of magic at the foot of the tree and started to climb it to look for Aja.

But now it was Aja who had the box, and it was he who was calling, "You, fetish priest, come down." And the fetish priest fell down, bump, and he was dead. Now, in the box, Aja found a leaf that could bring people back to life. He touched his brothers with it, and they all got up and began to walk around. Aja threw away the leaf when he had finished with it, but it fell on the fetish priest, who also came back to life. The brothers started to run away again. But the fetish priest called out to Aja, "Aja, don't run away again. I don't bear you any malice for what you did. You killed me, and I was the greatest magician of them all. Rather, I respect you for that. But we can't go on like this. So your brothers can be tomatoes, onions, okra, and eggplants, and I'll be pepper. But you, you shall have the crown. You shall be hot pepper."

That was how vegetables and spices first came into the world.

Always remember that in this world of ours, if someone is born today, and he knows a good thing, someone else will always be born tomorrow—someone who knows something better.

▼▲▼▲▼▲▼▲▼▲▼▲▼▲▼▲▼▲▼▲▼▲▼▲▼▲▼▲

86 The Lion's Advice

There were once two friends, Kwasi and Kwaku, and one day they went to the bush. They had been playing there for some time when they saw a lion coming. Straightaway, Kwasi climbed the nearest tree. Kwaku tried to follow him, but he couldn't climb very well, and he had to give up. He was very frightened and called up to his friend, "Eh, Kwasi, I can't climb. What shall I do?" Kwasi said, "Ah, I don't know, you must look out for yourself."

Now Kwaku had heard somewhere that a lion doesn't eat dead meat, so he lay down and feigned death. The lion came up to him and sniffed around for a while and then went off. Kwasi came down from the tree and said to Kwaku, "Oh, Kwaku, I thought you were dead. What was the lion saying to you just now?"

Kwaku told Kwasi, "Well, Kwasi, he said a lot of things to me, but the most important one was that I should choose my friends better. So when we leave here, you and I will part company for good."

87 Choosing the Right Friends

A long time ago there lived a hunter. One day he was going to his farm when he met a man sitting under a coconut tree, and the man said to him, "Please let me go with you to your farm."

The hunter said, "But what could you do for me if I took you along?" The man said, "My name is Nose. If I blow my nose, mountains will fall." So the hunter said, "All right! Come along!" And they went on their way.

On their way they met another man sitting under an orange tree. He asked the hunter to take him, too. The hunter asked him what he would do for him, and the man said, "My name is Bag. When I slap the back of my neck, I vomit water." The hunter said, "All right, come along!" And they went on their way.

They had gone about a mile when they met a man sitting by the road-side, smoking his pipe. He said, "Please, won't you take me with you?" The hunter said, "Well, what can you do for me?" The man smoking the pipe said, "My name is Gunpowder. If you like, fire your gun, and I'll show you." The hunter fired his gun, and the man swallowed the bullets. The hunter took him along with him.

They had not gone far when they saw a man under a palm tree, husking palm nuts. "May I come with you?" the man asked. The hunter said, "And if I agree, what can you do for me?"

The man husking palm nuts said, "My name is Star. I am as quick as a wink. If you like, send me to your house, and I'll bring you some of your bullets!" The hunter tested the man, and it was as he had said. He was back with the bullets almost as soon as the hunter had finished speaking. So the hunter and these four men went on their way.

Eventually they came to a village. They went to greet the chief, and he gave them the news that there was neither food nor water in the village. For a long time there had been a severe famine and drought in the land. Now, this chief had a very beautiful daughter. This daughter used to fetch water for her father, and though she had to go a long way for it, she was very quick. She was so quick in this business of getting water, in fact, that the chief had boasted about it, offering a big prize to anyone who could get water faster than his daughter.

When the hunter heard about this, he gave the task to his friend who was quicker than a wink. In a flash, Star was off and back with water. The chief was annoyed and told the hunter that if he wanted the prize he must first dig a well, and when there was water in it, then he would get the money, and not a second before.

They dug a well, but they couldn't find water. So the hunter told his friend who could vomit water to do so. Bag slapped himself hard on the back of the neck and vomited a flood. The well was full to the brim with water, so the chief had to give them the money. He was annoyed, though—very annoyed. He got so angry that he ordered his soldiers to shoot the hunter and his friends. But Gunpowder—who could swallow bullets—saved them. He swallowed all the bullets the soldiers fired at them.

The five friends began to run, and the soldiers pursued them. Nose blew his nose, and the mountains fell, and that made it easier for them to get home quickly. But the soldiers kept following, so Bag vomited water—a sea of water—and that kept them back. Then Star put the hunter, Bag, Nose, and Gunpowder on his back and rushed them home at high speed.

Now they were safe, at last. They shared the money the chief had given them. They made five equal piles of coins, one for each of them. But there was one gold coin left.

Who do you think should have it?

▼▲▼▲▼▲▼▲▼▲▼▲▼▲▼▲▼▲▼▲▼▲▼▲▼▲

88 The Clever Boatman

One day Hyena, Goat, and Cassava met at the river. They all wanted to cross to the other side. Now there was only one boat, and because it was a little one, it could take only the boatman and one passenger. The boatman was worried because he knew Hyena and Goat were on very bad terms. For that matter, Goat was no friend of Cassava's. If the boatman left Hyena and Goat alone together and took Cassava across first, it seemed likely that by the time he got back, Hyena would have eaten Goat. Or, if he left Goat and Cassava alone, Goat might eat Cassava.

So what do you think the boatman did?

All right, I will tell you. The boatman first took Goat and left him on the other side of the river. Then he came back and got Hyena. He took him across and brought back Goat. He put Goat down and took Cassava to the other side and left him with Hyena. Then he went back for Goat.

▼▲▼▲▼▲▼▲▼▲▼▲▼▲▼▲▼▲▼▲▼▲▼▲▼▲▼▲

89 Why the Mason Wasp Has a Narrow Waist

There was once a Mason Wasp who had a farm. One day he said, "I will ask my friends Corn, Hen, Kite, Hunter, Snake, Stick, Fire, Water, and Sun to help me weed my farm."

So he set off to Corn's house and told Corn that he wanted to weed his farm the next day and please would Corn help. Corn said, "All right, I'll come, but don't ask Cock or Hen. If you invite either of those two, I'm not coming."

Mason Wasp said, "Oh, no, I wouldn't do that," but he did, and went straight from Corn's house to Hen's house and asked her if she would help him weed his farm the next day early in the morning. Hen said, "Yes, all right, I'll help you, but please don't ask Kite. I warn you, if Kite comes, I won't."

Mason Wasp said, "Thank you, I'll not ask Kite, then." But he did. He went to Kite and said, "Some friends are coming tomorrow to help me weed my farm. How about you? Will you come?" Kite said yes, he would, but he didn't like Hunter at all, and Mason Wasp shouldn't ask him. Mason Wasp said, "All right, if you don't like Hunter I won't ask him, but please, you come."

And Mason Wasp went straight off to Hunter and asked Hunter if he would help with the weeding. Hunter said, "Yes, I'll be glad to, but don't go and ask Snake, whatever you do. I can't stand him."

Mason Wasp went off to Snake's house and asked him, "Will you help me weed my farm tomorrow?" Snake said, "Yes, tomorrow will be all right for me, but you aren't going to ask Stick, are you? If you ask Stick, I won't be there." Mason Wasp said, "Oh, if that's how you feel, I won't ask Stick." But he did, and Stick said, "Well, all right, I'll come, but don't ask Fire, that's all." "No," said Mason Wasp, "I won't ask Fire."

And there he was at Fire's house almost the next minute, asking Fire to help him with his farm. Fire agreed, but only if Water didn't come.

So Mason Wasp promised not to ask Water, but he did, and Water said, "Very well, I can come tomorrow, but, look, you don't need Sun, do you?" "No, not if you would rather he didn't come," said Mason Wasp, and then went off to ask Sun, and he agreed to help, too.

The next day they all showed up for work in the morning: Corn, Hen, Kite, Hunter, Snake, Stick, Fire, Water, and Sun. A fine company! They started to quarrel straight off. Mason Wasp took ropes and tied each one of his friends to his waist—he thought he could control them better that way.

But Hen started it. She said, "Corn, you are too lazy. That's why I never liked you." Corn said, "Eh, Hen, is that so? But you are always saying bad things about me. Look to yourself." Hen got angry and pecked at Corn and ate him. Kite saw what Hen had done and said, "All right, Hen, if you can eat Corn, I can eat you," and he got hold of Hen and killed her. Hunter shot Kite, and Snake bit Hunter because he hated him. So Stick beat Snake to death, and Fire burnt Stick. Water put out Fire, and Sun dried up Water.

While all this was going on, the ropes tightened round Mason Wasp's waist as his friends ran around fighting and struggling. By the time it was over, Mason Wasp was squeezed in the middle practically to nothing.

That was how Mason Wasp got his narrow waist.

▼▲▼▲▼▲▼▲▼▲▼▲▼▲▼▲▼▲▼▲▼▲▼▲▼▲▼▲▼▲

90 The Fairies and the Flute

Once upon a time there was a man who had two wives, and each of the wives had a son. The elder wife's son was called Kwame Nomo, and the younger wife's son, Tetteh Nomo. Whenever the elder wife went to market she would come back with presents for her son, Kwame. She would bring nothing at all for Tetteh. The younger wife was different. She would always share everything between the two boys. In fact, she treated both equally well. Now, one day the elder wife went to market and brought back a flute for Kwame. Tetteh, too, would have liked a flute, and he cried a lot because Kwame wouldn't let him play his. So Tetteh's mother went to market, too, and brought back a flute for him. Oh, this boy liked his flute, I mean, he really did. He didn't leave it alone for a minute. He was always playing on it, and soon he could play some very nice songs. He played much better than Kwame.

It happened one day that the two wives and their children went to their farm, and on their way home in the evening Tetteh remembered he had left his flute behind. He told his mother what he had done, and she said that it would be all right where it was, and that she would fetch it for him in the morning. Tetteh wouldn't hear of it. But his mother insisted, and they set off again for home. After they had been home for a short time his mother looked round for Tetteh, but he was nowhere to be seen. He had gone back for his flute.

By the time Tetteh got back to the farm it was midnight. He went to look for the flute, and near the place where he thought he had left it he saw some fairies. They were fighting over his flute. Tetteh Nomo began to cry. The fairies stopped quarreling and asked him what he was crying about. He told them he had lost his flute. The fairies produced a gold flute as well as Tetteh's own and asked him, "Which of these do you want?" Tetteh only wanted his own flute, and so the fairies gave him a little magic pot to take with him. They let him go, and he was home before dawn.

Now, the pot the fairies gave Tetteh was wonderful! When he would play his flute, anything he could name would come out of the pot—anything at all!

When Tetteh got home, he called everybody to come and listen to his news. And he told them the secret of the little pot and showed them how, if he played his flute to it, all sorts of nice things would come out of it, and Tetteh gave everyone a present, sharing everything among the members of the family.

The elder wife was angry. The next day, Kwame and Tetteh and their mothers set off for the farm again. Kwame, in fact, left his flute in the house, but his mother went back and got it for him. She intended, you see, that he should leave his flute at the farm this time. When they had finished their work and were getting ready to return home in the evening, she made

Kwame leave his flute, and when they were halfway home she sent him back to get it.

When the boy got back to the farm he saw these same fairies fighting over his flute. He started to cry. The fairies stopped fighting and called him to come and tell them what was the matter. He told them about his flute, and again they brought two flutes and asked him to choose. One flute was his own, and the other was a gold flute. Kwame chose the gold flute, and the fairies gave it to him and left.

Now, all this time Kwame's mother had been standing at the door waiting for him. At last, she saw her son coming with the flute. She rushed to meet him, embraced him, and took him to her room and began to question him. He showed her the gold flute. She called all the family to come and see what her son had brought. So when they had all gathered, and Kwame had told his story, they asked him to play his fine new flute. No sooner had Kwame begun to play, than his mother turned into a snake and began to dance.

That is why snakes now like flutes. And, also, it is why when someone has something and gives you some, you should not want to get it all.

▼▲▼▲▼▲▼▲▼▲▼▲▼▲▼▲▼▲▼▲▼▲▼▲▼▲▼▲▼▲

91 Sophia and the Devil

There was a woman who had only one daughter. Her name was Sophia. This daughter was looking for a husband, and because she was good-looking, men came from everywhere, hoping to marry her. A boatman came one day. The girl refused him. She told her mother he smelled like fish. The mother gave up. She said, "You tell me whom you would like to marry."

A devil heard about all this. He went off and borrowed some clothes. Fine clothes they were, too. With diamonds and all. Even his shoes had diamond buckles. Now the devil went courting, and his borrowed shoes made a loud noise as he walked to the girl's house. Those shoes went "Clip! Clop! Clip! Clop!" The devil paid the girl several visits, until at last she agreed to marry him. They were married, and he took her away with him.

Now this girl, Sophia, had a little brother. When the two were leaving, the little brother asked his sister, "Sister, shall I come with you?" The devil said, "No." But the boy went with them just the same.

Along the road the devil's coat fell off. Just like that! The little boy said, "Sir, your coat has come off." The devil said, "Leave it where it is." They went on their way. Now, one by one, everything the devil was wearing fell off, and he left it on the road.

They reached the devil's home by nightfall and went to bed almost at once. Before she fell asleep, the girl saw the devil making fire and asked him, "Husband, why are you lighting a fire? It isn't cold." The devil said, "Oh, just in case it rains in the night. If we have a fire we won't be cold." And he went on with what he was doing, and soon he put a long crowbar in the fire to get hot. He was going to kill the girl, you see. When the devil took the bar out of the fire the little boy, who had been lying watching him, began to sing: "Oh, Oh, my craw-craw itches. Oh, where is my mother, oh?"

And the devil heard him and said, "What is all this about craw-craw? What are you using to cure it?" The little boy said, "They have been giving me water they bring from London in a fishing net. They wash my skin with it."

The devil decided to get the medicine for the boy, and he went off to London with his fishing net. It took him a long time to fill the net because at first the water wouldn't stay inside, but at last he was back before dawn with the water, and he dabbed the boy's sores with it and told him to sleep.

Once the boy was sleeping, the devil went back to his wife and was about to try to kill her for the second time. Again the little boy woke up and sang: "Oh, Oh, my craw-craw itches. Oh, where is my mother, oh?"

The girl, too, woke up when she heard the boy's song. The devil was angry. He said, "What now?" The boy said, "Please, sir, my craw-craw is itching again." "What can I do about it?" said the devil. "Please, sir, get a stone," said the boy, "and boil it till it is soft and then rub my sores with it."

The devil was boiling a stone all the rest of the night. It was dawn before he got it soft. With the dawn, the devil's mother came to call on the girl. She said, "Eh, little girl, I like you. Do you see all these heads around the room? My child and I have eaten all the bodies. So now you had better go. You see that cock over there, that big cock? Give it a bushel of rice and a barrel of palm oil and a can of water."

The girl did as she was told and ran off. She was far away before the cock had finished eating all that she had given it and began to cry, "Cock-a-doodle-doo, your wife has gone." When he heard the cock, the devil set off after his wife, saying, "Vugu vaga vaga we shall kill her today. Vugu vaga vaga we shall kill her today."

All the while he was pursuing her, the devil broke eggs, and, as each egg broke, the road was swallowed up in thick bush. But the girl also broke eggs, and as each egg broke, the road appeared again. So it went on in this way until the girl reached the river, and there was a boatman. She called out, "Oh, kind sir, please, come take me across. Oh, please!"

This boatman—it was the one who had sought her hand—said, "Do you remember when I came to ask you to marry me, and you refused? Now you want me to take you in my boat, do you?"

The devil by now had nearly caught up with them, and the boatman relented. He put the girl and her little brother in his boat and pushed it off from the river's edge. He began to paddle, singing, "It was my father who bought me this canoe."

They were soon across the river, and the girl and her brother reached home safely after all.

That is why it isn't good to be too choosy.

▼▲▼▲▼▲▼▲▼▲▼▲▼▲▼▲▼▲▼▲▼▲▼▲▼▲▼▲▼▲

92 Wonder Child and the Beast

A long time ago in a certain village in Krobo, a woman gave birth to a baby boy. Now the same day the baby was born—and I mean the very same day—he started talking. He was also born with a magic snuff bottle held tightly in his little hand. That was a rather unusual thing in that part of the world at that time. Moreover, a week later, the boy told his mother, "Look, Mother, I don't want to be taken out and given an official name. I have a name already." The name he told his mother was Kwaku Babone.

The chief heard about all this and became worried and annoyed. He ordered the child killed, but Kwaku Babone ran away and went to live in the bush. In fact, he went to dwell with a very old lady who lived all by herself in a village in the forest.

It happened that at about the same time there was a wild beast living in that part of the forest, and it was doing a lot of damage, but no one in the old lady's village could kill it. The chief of the village had offered a big reward for anyone who could kill the beast—half the land of his village, in fact—but so far no one had tried to claim it.

So Kwaku Babone was living with this old lady, and one day he was playing in the bush when night fell. He decided not to try to go back to the village in the dark, but instead he climbed a tree and went to sleep in its branches. In the middle of the night he was awakened by a loud noise. It was the beast coming, roaring and shouting, "I am coming. The Big One is coming. The King is coming!"

Kwaku shouted back, "I am coming. The Big One is coming. The King is coming!" Now this beast had a weak spot, which was in its very short tail. In fact, anyone who could get to its tail could get rid of the beast. All this Kwaku Babone knew because his magical snuff bottle had told him already. So he touched the beast's tail with the snuff bottle, and it died. Kwaku cut off the tail and went back to the old lady's place with it.

The next morning a farmer was going to his farm early, when he saw the carcass of the beast lying where Kwaku Babone had left it. He was a greedy, dishonest fellow, this farmer. He rushed to the chief's house straightaway and told everybody he had killed the beast.

The chief said, "All right, you have done well. You have earned the reward, and I will give it to you." He called all the people of his village together and, in front of them, gave half of his village to the farmer. But Kwaku Babone was there, and he stepped forward and said in a loud voice, "I killed the beast, not this man. He who killed the beast has the beast's tail."

Well, as it happened, you see, when they had brought the beast's carcass to the chief, he had looked everywhere for its tail because it would have been good for magic and medicine. But it was missing, and no one had been able to find it. So the chief said, "You are right, whoever you are, whoever brings me the tail will get the reward."

Kwaku Babone gave the tail to the old lady he was lodging with, and she took it to the chief, but she told him the truth about all that Kwaku

Babone had done. The chief was pleased. He summoned Kwaku to his house and told him, "You no longer need to hide. Because of what you have done I am going to make you my most trusted advisor, and I'm going to give you half the royal land, too."

And from that day on, Kwaku Babone was an important man in the village and did many wonderful things on its behalf.

▼▲▼▲▼▲▼▲▼▲▼▲▼▲▼▲▼▲▼▲▼▲▼▲▼▲▼▲▼▲

93 Crying for Yaka

A long time ago there were once twin brothers, Ate and Lawe, and these brothers had nicknames: Ate was called Yaka ("Useless") and Lawe was called Anani ("Spider"). Yaka had a wife, but Anani was a bachelor. Yaka was rich; Anani was poor.

One day the bachelor Anani came to Yaka's place to tell him he had just heard of a town where there were many unmarried women hoping for husbands. Anani said, "You must come with me, Yaka, and help me find a wife," he said.

Now, Anani hadn't any suitable clothes. He was so poor he practically dressed in rags. But when they set off to find Anani a wife, Yaka was wearing a very fine garment and Anani conceived a scheme to get it. They soon came to a stream and Anani said straightaway, "Look, Yaka, we had better take a bath in this stream because I hear there isn't much water where we are going."

Yaka said, "Oh, I've had my bath already. Why should I bathe again?" But Anani persisted, and Yaka said, "Oh, all right, if you think we should, I'll join you in the stream." They both took off their garments and started to wash. Anani wasn't a minute in the stream. He was out in a flash and had Yaka's garment in his hands, saying, "Oh, Yaka, I do like this garment of yours. Let me try it on and see if it suits me. You can have mine." And before Yaka could say a word, there was Anani all dressed up in his fine clothes.

When they got near the town they were going to, Yaka asked Anani for his garment back several times, but each time Anani put him off with one or another excuse, finally saying, "Oh, what does it matter anyway? Wait till we get there, and then you can have it." And Yaka gave up.

So they reached the town, and all the women came to greet Anani in his finery and ignored Yaka. Anani was happy, oh so happy, he soon had several wives. Yaka would not have got anything at all in that town—he was badly dressed—but at the last minute an old lady came to him and said, "Oh, I am sorry for you. You look neglected. So I'll give you a girl to look after you." And Yaka got a wife, too.

Now it was time to take the women home, and they set off. When they reached the road junction where Anani and Yaka would part, the women noticed that the path to Anani's house was overgrown with weeds, but Yaka had a fine wide road leading to his house. Yaka's house was much nicer than Anani's, too. Anani's wives became suspicious. Life at Anani's house turned out just as they had begun to suspect. The food was terrible. There was nothing to drink and no decent place to sleep. What was worse was that every day they heard sounds of drumming and dancing coming from Yaka's house. There was a lot of laughter, as if people were really enjoying themselves.

So the women said to Anani one day, "Look, why is it that there is always something going on at your brother's place and nothing doing here? We want to go and look." Anani took no notice. But soon the women got really fed up and were talking about leaving him. Anani thought, "This is all Yaka's fault. I'll kill him."

He went over to Yaka's house the next day and said to him, "Brother, we have been having a lot of bad nights at my place recently. A wild animal keeps visiting us. When you hear us shouting in the night again, please, come quickly and bring a gun."

That night Anani went secretly to Yaka's house, and when everyone was asleep he dug a big pit in front of Yaka's door, put sharpened stakes in it, and hid it all under piles of leaves. Anyone who fell in that trap, I tell you, was bound to die. Anani went back to his own house and a few hours later started shouting, "The beast is coming again! It's here, I tell you!" Yaka heard him and got up quickly, grabbed his gun, and rushed out of the house to go and help his brother. He fell in the trap and was killed.

Poor Yaka was buried, and he had quite a nice funeral. He had done nothing to deserve death, and our children are always crying for him to this day. For you know that in Krobo when a child cries for no reason we say *eye Yaka foe*, "He is crying for Yaka."

94 The Child's Vengeance

A long time ago there was a village, and one day soldiers from Ashanti came and killed everybody in it except one young man and one young woman. After the soldiers had gone, these two young people came out of hiding and got married, and soon they had a child. A little boy came out of his mother's womb and immediately asked her, "Why aren't there any people in our village, Mother?" His parents were astonished, but they told him the reason why they were the only two left in the village, how everyone else had been killed by the Ashanti king's soldiers. The little boy said, "Hmm."

The very next day he asked his mother to buy him a small knife from the market when she next went there. She said she would, but the first time she went to the market she forgot. Gbeseku—for that was the baby's name—was very angry and said he wasn't going to eat or drink anything at all until he got the knife.

His mother went back to the market and bought a little knife and brought it home for her baby son. He was pleased. Straightaway he began to sharpen it. He sharpened that knife until a fly couldn't land on it without cutting itself, and he still wasn't satisfied. He went on sharpening and sharpening. At last he threw the knife at a tree and sang a little song. The tree split right down the middle. Gbeseku was satisfied. He said, "Now I'm going to do something with this knife."

He went off and told his mother he was going to kill Boafo, the Ashanti king. She was frightened and begged her son not to go. She said, "The king is very powerful. You will never be able to kill him." Gbeseku said, "Oh yes I will," and off he went.

On his way he met a man planting yams on his farm, and the man asked him where he was going. Gbeseku said, "I'm going to Kumase to kill the Ashanti king."

The man roared with laughter and said, "You! Why you are only a baby! You can't do that."

"I can," said Gbeseku. He went on and met an old lady, and she asked him where he was going. Gbeseku said, "I'm going to Kumase to kill the Ashanti king."

The old lady was amazed. She said, "All right, then, go and kill him, and when you have killed him, come back and kill me." And she laughed and laughed.

Gbeseku said, "If you wish it, I'll do it."

Next he met a blacksmith working in his smithy. The blacksmith said, "Where are you going, little baby boy?"

Gbeseku said, "I'm going to Kumase to kill the Ashanti king."

The blacksmith said, "That's good! When you have killed him, come back here and show me his head, and then you can take my poker, make it red-hot, and shove it in my stomach."

Gbeseku said, "If you wish it, I'll do it."

Then he went on his way to Kumase. When at last he reached Kumase, he saw two boys. He went up to them and asked them where King Boafo lived. They took him to the palace, where the king welcomed him.

Gbeseku told the king, "I've brought you a nice present—this enchanted knife—but before I show you its magical power, which will make sure it will win any war you take it to, you must please call all your people together here." He did what Gbeseku asked, and when everybody was assembled in the courtyard of the palace, Gbeseku went and stood on a high veranda and told them, "Watch me. I am going to sing a song three times, and then you will see what this knife can do."

He began to sing. Three times he sang his song, and then—whoosh!— he threw the knife at the crowd assembled below. Everyone was killed except Boafo, who began to beg for his life. Gbeseku told him to bring out all his money, all his gold and silver, his worry beads, and every precious thing. The king brought out everything, and Gbeseku took the paper money and made a cloth of it, sticking some of the notes on his skin. The gold coins he threw all over the place, just playing with them. Then he cut off the king's head.

He took the king's head, put it in a basket, and set off back home. On the way, he saw the blacksmith working in his smithy. He went to him and said, "Is this not the king's head?"

The blacksmith said, "Yes, it really is." Thereupon, Gbeseku put a poker in the fire, left it until it was red-hot, and then shoved it in the blacksmith's stomach and killed him. Leaving the blacksmith dead, he went on his way until he came to the old woman who had told him to kill her. He did, and she turned into an anthill. Soon he came to the farmer, but he did nothing to him because he hadn't asked him to. When he finally got to his house he showed the head to his parents, and they were so impressed they called people from far and near to come to a dance in Gbeseku's honor. There was drinking and dancing far into the night.

The Ashanti king's head—well!—Gbeseku threw it away and it fell in the branches of a palm tree, and at once turned into a clump of palm nuts.

▼▲▼▲▼▲▼▲▼▲▼▲▼▲▼▲▼▲▼▲▼▲▼▲▼▲▼▲▼▲▼

95 Why Hippo Wears No Coat

A long time ago Hippo and Rat were friends. Now you must know that in those days Hippo was not like he is today. He had nice soft fur and lived on dry land. His coat was long and silky; he was really quite nice, you know, and he had a nice house, too. It was made of grass. Hippo liked to visit his friend Rat and play with him. They always had fun and enjoyed being together. But one day when they were playing, Hippo stepped on Rat. It was an accident, but Hippo failed to say he was sorry. Rat was angry about that.

One day, to get his revenge, he said to Hippo, "Look, Hippo, I visit Fire at his house, and he visits me at mine. My friendship with Fire is clearly better than your friendship with Fire. Why don't you ask Fire to visit you one day?"

Hippo said, "You are right," and he went off straightaway to Fire and asked him to come and spend some time with him. Fire said, "We are friends. You can come here any time. It isn't necessary for me to visit you." Hippo persisted, however, and at last Fire asked him, "Do you want to know why I haven't been to your place before? It is because you would run away, if ever I came to visit you."

Hippo was upset. He was jealous that Rat had a better friendship than he did with Fire. "That's nonsense," he said. "You are my friend, so why should I run away?" Fire said, "All I know is that whenever I go somewhere everything and everybody runs away from me—birds, snakes, everything—everything and everybody. So I don't visit people anymore."

Hippo wouldn't leave it be. He wanted to be as good as Rat. He kept on asking Fire, and at last Fire said, "Oh, very well, then—I'll come tomorrow." Hippo was pleased. He said, "That's good! I'll go home straightaway and get ready. We'll have a nice time with lots to eat and drink."

The next day, early in the morning, Hippo went to Fire's house and said, "Don't forget! You promised to visit me today. Are you coming?" Fire said, "Yes, I'll come."

Hippo ran home and spent the rest of the morning preparing food and getting everything ready for his friend's visit. When he was satisfied that he had done all that he could, he went off to his room to have a little rest and wait for Fire. Soon he heard noises. It sounded like birds shrieking and flapping their wings and flying away. He went to the door and looked out. Fire was coming! Hippo went to greet him. But before Hippo realized what was happening, Fire had burnt off all Hippo's hair and burned down his nice grass house—everything was burned. Now Hippo was really frightened. He ran away, and he ran and ran until he came to the river. He jumped in the river out of Fire's way, and he has stayed there to this very day.

▼▲▼▲▼▲▼▲▼▲▼▲▼▲▼▲▼▲▼▲▼▲▼▲▼▲▼▲▼▲

96 Foriwa's Beads

One day a long time ago there was a woman who had a beautiful baby daughter. Now, this woman was very possessive. She didn't want anyone else to have anything to do with her daughter at all. She built a house in the middle of the forest, and locked her daughter up inside. Every day she would go to the house to take her daughter food, and, so that the daughter would know that it was her mother coming to see her, the woman would stand outside the door and sing a little song: "My daughter, Foriwa, come out. Come eat, come talk."

She would sing this song three times, and the door would open. As I said, the woman did this every day. On her way to her farm she would pass by Foriwa's place and sing: "My daughter, Foriwa, come out. Come eat, come talk."

One day a leopard heard the woman. He went to tell his friends about it. He also told Tortoise. So they all decided that they would do exactly what the woman did, and when the girl opened the door, they would kill and eat her.

They went to the house, and Leopard sang first: "My daughter, Foriwa, come out. Come eat, come talk."

Nothing happened. All the animals tried in turn, but the girl did not answer. Nobody's voice was like the mother's. So Tortoise said he would try, too. The animals all laughed, but Tortoise sang: "My daughter, Foriwa, come out. Come eat, come talk." His voice was just like the woman's. He sang three times, and the door opened.

Leopard killed the girl. He gave the blood to Tortoise and shared the flesh with the other animals. They were all hungry because there was a famine in their land at that time. They ate everything, and soon only the poor girl's beads were left.

When the mother came the next day, as usual, she sang her little song, but the door didn't open. She sat down on a log and said, "Why is it that I sing my song, and my daughter doesn't come?" She sang again, but nothing happened.

Nearby was a palm tree, and in it was sitting a little weaver bird. This bird began to sing to the woman: "The room is all blood. The room is all blood. Only beads are there, only beads will you see."

The woman picked up a stone and threw it at the bird, but it went on singing: "The room is all blood. The room is all blood. Only beads are there, only beads will you see."

So the woman forced the door open and saw that what the bird said was true. The woman wept.

From this we see that there is danger in trying to protect children from all the evil in the world. Parents do not own their children.

97 The Tail of the Elephant Queen

A long time ago there was a woman who had twins, both of them girls. The elder girl was called Ataa Panyin and the younger one was called Ataa Kumaa. The woman died unexpectedly, and the girls were left with all her belongings: clothes, sandals, gold necklaces, and many other things.

One day, Ataa Kumaa foolishly went swimming with one of her mother's necklaces on, and she lost it in the river. She couldn't find it, and after a while she gave up looking and went back to tell her sister what had happened. The elder sister was furious. She told Ataa Kumaa to go back and find it at once, or she would be punished severely. The girl went back to the river and looked and looked and looked, but she couldn't find the necklace.

Because of this, Ataa Panyin ordered her younger sister out of the house and told her, "Don't come back until you bring with you—a leopard's paw, hyena fur, a plant with only two and three leaves on it, white sand from the River Denkyera, some yaws, and the tail of the Queen elephant."

These were all impossible things, of course, but the poor girl decided to try to get them for her sister, so that she could go back to living happily again in her mother's house. Before she set off to look for them, she cooked a meal of mashed yam and eggs and took it with her to eat on the way.

She hadn't gone far when she met a leopard lying in the sun outside his lair. She was about to run away when the leopard called to her, "Why do you come here, where nobody ever comes?"

So the girl greeted the leopard politely, and then began to cry as she told him how her mother had died and left all her possessions to her and her elder sister, how she had lost her mother's necklace while swimming in the river, and how her elder sister had sent her to get some impossible things as punishment. The leopard was sorry to hear all this, and he promised to give her one of his paws only if she could get the other things she needed. So the girl thanked him and went on.

Soon she met a hyena, and he asked her what she was doing so far away from home. She told him her story. The hyena, too, was sympathetic, and said she could have some of his fur if she could get the other things she needed.

She went on and on until she came to where the plants with only two and three leaves grew. She threw some of her mashed yams on the ground, and the plants thanked her and promised she could have what she needed on her way back.

Now she came to the banks of the terrible River Denkyera. She stood there weeping, and the god appeared and asked her what was the matter and why was she weeping so. The girl told him her story: how her mother had died and left all that she owned to her and her elder sister, and how she had been foolish and had lost one of her mother's necklaces because she had worn it while swimming in a river. And she told him how her sister was angry and had given her impossible things to find. The god was sorry for the girl, and the river parted to let her pass safely. As she crossed, the god promised her the white sand her sister wanted, and said he would give it to her on her way back.

On the other side of the Denkyera river was a house, and in this house lived a dirty old woman with yaws. This old woman looked after some elephants. When she saw Ataa Kumaa, she said, "Why do you come here where nobody ever comes?"

So the girl told the old woman her story.

"Well," the old woman said, "come over here and sit with me and see if you can treat my yaws. If you will do that, I'll give you some of my yaws, and, what is more, I'll show you how to cut off the Elephant Queen's tail." The girl cared for the old woman's yaws and was given some to take back home.

The old woman had been living with elephants a long time, and she knew an important secret of theirs. That is, when elephants were sleeping, they made a noise like "fifi toto." Sometimes they made a noise like "fi to," but this meant they were only half-asleep and would wake up easily. But if you heard "fifi toto," that was all right; you could do anything, and you wouldn't wake them. The old lady gave Ataa Kumaa a knife and told her the elephants would be coming home soon, so she should hide. But when the elephants arrived, they could smell that someone was in the house, and they asked the old woman who it was. She told them there was nobody there, and they believed her.

The girl waited until she heard "fifi toto, fifi toto," and then she went and cut off the Queen Elephant's tail, which was gold and had a silver bell on it. She did this without any trouble.

Before she left, the old woman gave a shining mirror to her as a parting gift. Now it was easy. On her way home, the girl collected all the things that had been promised her, and she gave them to her elder sister, who was very much surprised.

The elder sister had not seen a mirror before, so she spent a lot of time looking in it. When she put it down, she broke it. The younger sister said it was now her turn. She told Panyin that she, too, must go and get for her the same impossible things that she herself had just brought back from the land beyond the Denkyera.

The elder sister set off and met the leopard first. But she wasn't like Kumaa at all. When the leopard asked her who she was and why she had come to that place where nobody ever comes, she was insolent and offensive in her manner. She was just the same with all the animals and the plants and even the old woman. She didn't even take the old woman's advice properly. Just as the elephants came home in the evening, she came out of the place where the old woman had hidden her, saying she couldn't stay another minute in that filthy place. So the elephants asked the old woman why she kept the girl there and why she had said there was no one in the house when they had smelled the girl. They blamed the old woman for their queen's losing her golden tail. They killed her, and then they killed the girl, too. They cut the old woman into pieces and threw them all over the place. That is how old women were distributed around the world. And that was what brought mirrors, too.

This story teaches us that you should not punish your sister badly if she loses something of yours.

▼▲▼▲▼▲▼▲▼▲▼▲▼▲▼▲▼▲▼▲▼▲▼▲▼▲▼▲▼▲

98 Why Spider Is Bald

Anaanu and his wife Kornorley were living happily in a small town. One day just after Anaanu and his wife had returned from their farm, a messenger arrived from Kornorley's village and announced that Kornorley's mother had died. Kornorley undid her hair, threw herself on the ground, and wept long and loud. After some time Anaanu got her calmed down and said, "Since you are the eldest daughter, you must go and see to things. I will follow you immediately and do what I can." So Kornorley left to tend to her mother's funeral.

The following day Anaanu went and called some of his animal friends to accompany him to his mother-in-law's funeral, to give him support, and to let people see that he was a man of consequence. All his friends put on their mourning clothes and went with him. When they reached the funeral site, they were met by the men of Kornorley's family and given a special place to sit. Then they were served corn-beer, and the elders spoke to them about the traditions observed on occasions such as this in this village.

When this was over, Anaanu, too, addressed the gathering through Goat, his spokesman. He said that Kornorley had been a very good wife to him, and as the husband of the dead woman's eldest daughter, he would give a coffin for the burial of his mother-in-law, and he would contribute drinks and clothes and money to the family for the funeral.

In the evening, the elders took Anaanu and his friends to a special room and said they would give them something to eat. But Anaanu refused food saying, "My mother-in-law is dead. I cannot eat till a week after the funeral. I swear it: I will not eat. But my friends are just visitors who accompanied me. So kindly get them something to eat and let them return to their village." So Kornorley prepared something for Goat and the others to eat, and they left for home after the burial.

Two days later, Anaanu, who loved food and was very greedy, began to feel hunger pains. Try as he might, he couldn't think of anything but how hungry he was. By the fourth day, he couldn't stand it any longer. He looked out on a corner of the veranda and saw a pot of guinea corn cooking on the fire. Quickly, he sneaked out to the corner and poured the hot guinea corn into his hat. Just as he got back into the room and was about to eat the guinea corn, he heard steps and voices at the door, so he put the hat with its contents on his head. It was Kornorley and her brothers and some old men and women and other people.

As soon as they came in, Anaanu said, "Kornorley, I have to leave at once for my father's village, because I have just remembered that today they are holding a special festival there, and they cannot do anything without me. So I have to go."

Kornorley said, "Ah, but you haven't told me anything about this before. Since you came to your mother-in-law's funeral, you have been so sad that you have not eaten anything. You cannot travel on an empty stomach, and you cannot go to a festival without eating anything. So let me get you something to eat first."

But by this time, the boiling-hot guinea corn was really burning Anaanu's head. He couldn't wait. He walked out of the room, onto the veranda, through the courtyard, onto the road going to his father's village. On the way he danced and sang: "By this time at my village, they want to begin the festival, and they want to sing." And all the people ran after him trying to persuade him to take some food.

Suddenly, he could stand it no more. He pulled the hat off his burning head and threw it onto the path, and all the guinea corn fell out of it. The people saw the guinea corn and started ridiculing and mocking Anaanu. The guinea corn had burned off all his hair, and his head was bald and shining. Ashamed, he jumped into the grass at the edge of the path, and the grass hid him.

That is why Spider is bald and can always be seen hiding in the grass at the edge of a path.

▼▲▼▲▼▲▼▲▼▲▼▲▼▲▼▲▼▲▼▲▼▲▼▲▼▲▼▲▼▲

99 Spider and the Calabash of Knowledge

Father Kwaku Ananse said that all knowledge in the world was his alone. No one but he could have any knowledge. There was, indeed, no knowledge except that which he possessed. So he put this knowledge in a large calabash and sealed it. He decided to hang the calabash from the ceiling where no one save himself could get it. That way, no one else could have any knowledge.

With the calabash tied around his neck and hanging in front of him, off he went to climb a ladder to the ceiling, but he could not climb it. He tried and tried, but he could not climb it. The calabash full of knowledge got in his way every time.

His son Ntikuma stood behind him and called softly to him, "Papa."
"Yes, Ntikuma," he answered.

Ntikuma said, "Hang the calabash down behind you, and let's see if you can climb."

Kwaku Ananse put the calabash on his back. Up! Up! Up! Using Ntikuma's little bit of knowledge, he soon reached the ceiling. When he got there, he realized he hadn't captured and locked up all the knowledge in the world. Even his small son, living in his own house, possessed a bit of knowledge that Kwaku Ananse had failed to put into the calabash. Having failed at his task, and having seen the value of knowledge, he opened the calabash, and knowledge spread over the world.

▼▲▼▲▼▲▼▲▼▲▼▲▼▲▼▲▼▲▼▲▼▲▼▲▼▲▼▲▼▲

100 The Noble Adowa

There was once a great famine in the land. It was hot, and all the streams were dry. Ananse went to the bush in search of water. He came to a water hole where all the animals drank. As he stooped to scoop up some water, he noticed a heap of grayish matter lying not far from the water hole. He was curious and went to look at the heap more closely. As he was looking, something dropped on it from above. He looked up and saw a little bird, and in astonishment he cried, "Little bird, are all these your droppings?"

As he said this, something knocked him off his feet. Whump! He was flat on his back on the ground.

He got up and said, "Ah, what is this? Only when I ask, 'Are these your droppings?' then something makes me fall down." As soon as he said "droppings," down he went again. This happened a third time. He said, "This is very good. I know what I am going to do." He made a path from the bush to the water hole. Right in the middle of the path was the little bird's heap of droppings. No creature could walk to the water hole without noticing them.

Ananse hid himself in the bush, and along came Antelope. "Hello, Antelope," he said. "Where are you going?"

Antelope said, "Oh, I am just going to the water hole to drink."

"I am going there, too. Let us go together then. Ah, here is a new path some kind people have made for us. Let us walk on it." He fell in behind

Antelope. As soon as Antelope saw the heap of droppings, he looked up and saw the little bird. He said, "Little bird, are all these your droppings?"

Immediately, Antelope was flat on his back. Then Ananse hit him on the head with a club he was carrying, and Ananse took him back to feed to his family.

Every day Ananse lured more animals to the water hole—Warthog, Buffalo, Hippopotamus, Leopard, Porcupine, and even mighty Elephant. They all fell into Ananse's trap, and he killed them all. Only Adowa, the Royal Antelope, had not yet come to drink at the water hole. For days and weeks Ananse searched for the Royal Antelope. Then one day along came Adowa, looking fat and sleek.

Ananse addressed him, "Yie ee, my brother Adowa, how well you look! You are now more handsome than ever. Where have you been all these months?" Adowa did not look as pleased as Ananse thought he would. So he said, "Now, sir, I know you have come to drink. Let me show you where the best water hole is."

He led Adowa to the heap of droppings, but Adowa avoided it. Ananse pointed to it and said, "Do you see that little hill? What is it?" Adowa said he saw nothing. In spite of everything Ananse tried, Adowa wouldn't fall into the trap. Out of desperation, Ananse then pointed to the heap of droppings and said, "Don't you see that big heap of droppings made by the little bird?"

Immediately, Ananse was flat on his back on the ground. As soon as Ananse fell down, Adowa took the club and beat Ananse with it until he died. That was how the noble Adowa outwitted the deceitful Ananse.

▼▲▼▲▼▲▼▲▼▲▼▲▼▲▼▲▼▲▼▲▼▲▼▲▼▲▼▲▼▲▼

101 Spider's Funeral

For a long time Bra Spider and Cunnie Rabbit had been very close friends. But the way they lived their lives was not morally satisfactory. They were forever cheating and tricking people for the fun of it. They would go somewhere, and by any devious means that occurred to them they would deceive people in order to get what they needed to live on. As soon as people in one town caught on to their tricks, Bra Spider and Cunnie Rabbit would move on to another town. Soon news about these scoundrels spread far and wide, and everyone grew to expect these two to dupe all the people they met. Finally, the two lifelong friends decided it would be best to part. They could no longer fool anybody.

Bra Spider wondered what to do—life was hard for him now. In another town far away only white men lived, and Bra Spider decided that if he went there, he would be unknown, and he could start his tricks again. He went to the white man's town and, because he was a stranger and appeared to have money, he soon managed to gain the people's respect and confidence.

Whenever an important man died in the white man's town, it was the custom to bury him in a glass coffin, along with diamonds and many other valuable ornaments. One day, while things were still going well for him in this new town, Bra Spider feigned death. When the people heard about his death, they decided to bury him according to white man's custom, since he had seemed to be a man of consequence. They put him in a glass coffin with a large amount of diamonds and many other precious things.

In the meantime, Cunnie Rabbit had fared no better than Bra Spider. After a few months of wandering around, he began looking everywhere for Bra Spider, but could not find him. Suddenly he fancied that Bra Spider might have gone to the white man's town, so he headed in that direction. No sooner had he got there than he heard that a big funeral was taking place for a stranger who had died. When he asked who the stranger was, the people told him that it was Bra Spider. Cunnie Rabbit burst into tears, crying, "Oh, my uncle! I shall never see you again."

Then the people gathered around Cunnie Rabbit and said, "Thank God you have come. We have tried to get in touch with Bra Spider's family, but we couldn't."

Cunnie Rabbit inquired about Bra Spider's funeral and was told that it had been decided to bury him in a manner befitting an important man—in a glass coffin with diamonds and other valuable goods. Cunnie Rabbit was immediately jealous. He didn't at all like the idea of Bra Spider's good fortune—even though he was dead and couldn't enjoy it. But since they were birds of a feather and thought alike, he soon guessed that Bra Spider was playing a trick. He was going to rise from the dead, sell the diamonds and things, and make a lot of money.

Cunnie Rabbit shook his head and told the people they had made a bad mistake. He explained, "According to law, the white man cannot bury Bra Spider with the bag that is joined to his middle. If it bursts, everyone in the town will die. Bra Spider was a chief, and chiefs in their own country are buried under special laws."

So the white men got Bra Spider and got ready to cut off the bag that was joined to his middle. He immediately opened his eyes when he heard that they were going to cut him in two and shouted, "You, Cunnie Rabbit. Who invited you to my funeral? I don't want this kind of funeral at all— I'm leaving!" As Bra Spider got up to run, the townspeople—having quickly recovered from their shock—got hold of him and gave him a good beating!

That is why they say that the left hand shouldn't know what the right hand is doing.

▼▲▼▲▼▲▼▲▼▲▼▲▼▲▼▲▼▲▼▲▼▲▼▲▼▲▼▲▼▲

102 Who Is the Greatest Magician?

Three magicians were traveling together one day when they came to a flooded river. They each used a different kind of magic to get across the river.

The first magician cast a thread across the river between two trees. He drew it tight, and without even taking off his sandals, he walked across on the thread.

The second magician put all the water into his little snuff bottle, crossed the dry riverbed, and put the water back into the riverbed.

The third magician made a huge fire, so hot that it caused the waters to evaporate, and he walked straight across.

Now, which of these three was the greatest magician?

103 Tortoise and the Stew Bowl

There was a fine palm tree which bore the best and tastiest fruit, but there was no one who could climb it.

The people of the village in which this palm tree stood looked and looked for someone who could, but there was no one. They decided to ask the animals to help. They called them all. Monkey, the best climber of all the animals, couldn't climb the tree. Many other animals tried and failed just as Monkey had failed. Then Tortoise tried, and he was able to climb the tree. He climbed and climbed until he got to the top and got the fruit. So they gave him the king's daughter in marriage.

The first thing she cooked for him was stew. Tortoise liked stew very much. So in the middle of the night, when he got up to relieve himself, he climbed up the post of the cooking shed and into the shed itself, and ate up all the stew. He was just licking the bowl when it overturned and covered him. When day broke, and she couldn't find him, his wife had them beat the gong and look everywhere for him. They couldn't find him. It was only when the woman went to find something to eat herself and lifted the bowl that she found Tortoise there, under the bowl! As she looked at him, he covered his face with his hands in shame. From that day Tortoise has had a large bowl on his back!

▼▲▼▲▼▲▼▲▼▲▼▲▼▲▼▲▼▲▼▲▼▲▼▲▼▲▼▲

104 Crab and Guinea Fowl Part Ways

Crab and Guinea Fowl were very good friends. Crab used to visit Guinea Fowl in the bush, and Guinea Fowl used to visit Crab in the river. Sometimes Crab would send one of his children to Guinea Fowl to ask for grain, yams, and other food. Guinea Fowl would also send one of his children to the river to ask Crab for water.

It is sad that after many years of friendship, a quarrel developed between Crab and Guinea Fowl. It happened like this. Guinea Fowl sent one of his children to the river to fetch some water from Crab, but since water was scarce at the time, Crab would not allow the child to draw water. Crab and especially Crab's children, have to have water around them, not just inside them. Crab claimed that there was just enough water to keep his own family alive, so he couldn't share it with anybody.

In the following month there was a shortage of food, and Crab was forced to send one of his children to Guinea Fowl for food. When the child got to Guinea Fowl's house, he knocked on the door. Guinea Fowl called out, "Who is asking for me?" Crab's son replied, "It is I, the son of Crab. I have come to beg for food."

Guinea Fowl and his children all replied in one voice and cursed Crab's child, "When you get home, tell your father that we have no food for him. Tell him we said that he is ugly and has ridiculous long thin legs, and silly-looking long thin arms. He is burdened with a rock on his chest and heavy armor on his back. Instead of walking straight on the road like a sensible creature, he walks sideways on it." These cruel words and those that came back from Crab to Guinea Fowl turned Crab and Guinea Fowl into bitter enemies.

From that time the Crab has stayed near the water and has never gone into the bush. That is also the reason why the Guinea Fowl never goes to the river to drink.

▼▲▼▲▼▲▼▲▼▲▼▲▼▲▼▲▼▲▼▲▼▲▼▲▼▲▼▲▼▲

105 The Gift of the Wicked Old Woman

There was once an old woman who had several children. Any time the children were naughty the woman would say to them, "Wait there, and you will see." One day one of the children—Asamaniwa—who was a bad child said, "Today I want to go and find out about this 'wait-there-and-you-will-see' that you are always talking about because I, for one, don't know what it is." Her mother said, "All right, come, let's go."

They went off, and after a while her mother said, "Sit down, I'll be back shortly." But she had no intention of coming back at all. She ran away and left her daughter to wait and see.

Now, as the child was sitting there, she saw an old woman coming toward her, and the old woman had very long breasts that hung down almost to her feet. She came up to the child and said, "Granddaughter, why have you come to this place where nobody comes?"

The child replied, "My mother said I should sit here if I wanted to know about 'wait-there-and-you-will-see,' of which she is always talking." The child went on, "My mother always says, 'wait-there-and-you-will-see.' So I said, "Today I am going to find out about 'wait-there-and-you-will-see.' That is why I came."

The old woman said, "Come and stay here with me. When you live here you will see wait-there-and-you-will-see." So the child stayed with the old woman. Now, this old woman was very strange, and she would often change her shape. One day she would turn into a four-legged animal. On another day into a snake. Other days she could be almost anything.

After a while the child said, "I cannot endure any more of this." One day when the old woman was going to work at her farm, she said to the child, "Granddaughter, cook something for us to eat while I am gone." But soon after the old woman left, the child decided to run away, and she quietly left the house and began the journey back to her home. It was a long way back, and on the way she was surprised to hear the old woman coming after her and calling, "Asamaniwa e! Asamaniwa e!"

"Yes, ma'am," the child replied, continuing to run.

The old woman called, "What happened that made you run away?"

The child called back, "I was frightened. I had a dream of an old woman with long breasts, but one of them had been cut off."

And the old woman shouted and shouted after her, "And so you ran! Go on then, Asamaniwa, I'll catch you if I can, Asamaniwa! I'll catch you if I can!"

After a time, the child met a man who asked her, "What is the matter?"

Exhausted, the child said, "An enchanted old woman is chasing me."

The man took a magic switch and put it behind her so the old woman couldn't follow her farther.

But behind her she again heard the old woman calling, "Asamaniwa e! Go on, then, I'll catch you if I can." But now she had nearly reached home, and as she did, her father came to meet her, and she told him about the enchanted old woman.

He said, "Stand where you are, and let me see who is chasing you." And they stood there till the old woman came plodding along with her long breasts dragging about her feet, plop, plop.

As soon as her father saw the old woman he killed her. Then he cut up the enchanted body and the enchanted breasts in many pieces and scattered them all over the world. The result of this was that breasts came into the world. If it hadn't been for that enchanted old woman and the loving father, we would not have been given breasts.

▼▲▼▲▼▲▼▲▼▲▼▲▼▲▼▲▼▲▼▲▼▲▼▲▼▲▼▲

106 The Honest Finger

The five fingers were brothers of the same mother. One day their mother left before dawn to go to the market, and she was not to return until late at night. When the five brothers woke up, they could not find anything to eat. After they had waited a long time for their mother to arrive from the market, and she did not return, they started to grumble.

The little finger started the grumbling. He said, "As for me, I am hungry." The ring finger replied, "But mother is not at home." The middle and tallest finger said, "I have a bright idea. Let us go and steal some food." Then the index finger said, "But if we steal we will be caught by the king."

The thumb, who was the eldest and most experienced finger, saw that his brothers were so hungry that they would do anything in order to find food to eat. He warned them that stealing is bad, but they would not listen to him. Then he said, "I refuse to steal. I do not want to associate with thieves. I had better stay apart from you."

From that day until now, the thumb has been separated from the other four fingers.

107 Cat and Rat Have It Out

Cat and Rat were friends. They lived near one another in the same town. The friendship between them was so close that neither could go a day without visiting the other. They were very fond of each other.

One day the two of them cooked a very sweet porridge. Cat was gone from the room just at the time the porridge was ready. Before he came back, Rat began eating the porridge hot from the fire. He ate more than half of it while Cat was watching him from a hole in the ceiling.

When Cat came back into the room he asked Rat what had happened to most of the porridge. Rat claimed he did not know, and he denied eating any part of it. The result was an exchange of strong words between the two friends. First there was a loud argument that could be heard in all the village. Then there were curses and threats. Finally, Cat and Rat had a terrible fight, which Cat won.

Soon after that day, Rat moved out of town into the bush. Cat was so angry and resentful that he decided never to forgive Rat or his wife or his children. From that very day until this very day, all Cats have been enemies of Rats, and they begin to fight all over again whenever they meet.

▼▲▼▲▼▲▼▲▼▲▼▲▼▲▼▲▼▲▼▲▼▲▼▲▼▲▼▲▼▲

108 The Hunter's Best Friend

A certain brave hunter had three dogs who were his best companions, and he almost always took them hunting with him.

One day he went to the forest, and for some reason he failed to take his dogs along. He saw an animal and shot it with his gun. The animal fell to the ground, and to the hunter's great surprise, it changed into a fairy. The fairy chased the hunter, and the hunter ran as fast as he could. He ran and ran and ran, until he came to a very big river. Because he could not swim across the river without being caught by the fairy, the hunter climbed a tree. Not deterred, the fairy began to chop down the tree with a cutlass.

The hunter's thoughts turned to his three dogs at home, and he began to sing: "My dogs, my dogs, my hunting dogs. Where are my dogs, my hunting dogs?"

By this time the fairy had cut halfway through the tree. The helpless hunter sang again, more loudly than before. The tree, meanwhile, was just about ready to fall. But just when the hunter thought his end had come, his three dogs appeared out of the distance, running very fast. Just as the fairy was about to strike the blow that would bring down the tree, the dogs rushed up, pounced on the fairy, and devoured him. The hunter was saved.

This shows that a hunter without dogs is not a hunter. Dogs are a hunter's best friend.

▼▲▼▲▼▲▼▲▼▲▼▲▼▲▼▲▼▲▼▲▼▲▼▲▼▲▼▲▼▲

109 The Vultures and the Liver Cave

Once upon a time there was a town that was plagued with famine. No one had any food to eat, so a young boy called "Yonkon-pass-me-dollar-loss" made up his mind to go into the bush to look for food.

He walked and walked until in the distance he saw a big cave with a stone blocking the entrance. As the boy was looking at the cave, he noticed a lot of vultures hovering nearby. He immediately hid so that he could both protect himself and watch them. Each of the vultures approached the entrance to the cave and said, "I haven't eaten liver yet." As soon as the last one had said it, the stone moved aside, and the vultures went into the cave, one by one.

Some time went by, and after all the vultures had come out and gone, Yonkon-pass-me-dollar-loss decided to have a look inside the cave. He repeated the phrase uttered by the vultures, and the stone moved aside for him. Once he was inside the cave he found some liver, and he ate some immediately. He put some of the liver in his bag and took it home for his family.

When his father heard what had happened, he decided to fetch his own meat. In fact, this man wanted to take this cave away from the vultures. The next day the father went to the neighborhood of the cave and began to boil some water during the time when the vultures were at their meal.

When the vultures finished and were sound asleep, he caught them, one by one, and dipped their heads into the boiling water.

As their heads came in contact with the boiling water, their head feathers fell out. The terrified vultures flew away for ever, and the clever man claimed the liver cave and all the meat inside it for his own.

Since that time, Vulture has had a bald head.

▼▲▼▲▼▲▼▲▼▲▼▲▼▲▼▲▼▲▼▲▼▲▼▲▼▲▼▲▼▲

110 The Nefarious Fly

Once upon a time there lived a man who kept many dogs. The dogs went hunting for him every day. Each dog would bring back home whatever it caught in the forest. Eventually the man became rich.

One day while the dogs were all out hunting, their master planned a special feast for them. He wanted to show his gratitude to the dogs, so he hired many cooks to prepare huge quantities of food and reserve it all for the dogs.

Some time before they were due to return, when all the food had been prepared, Fly took some nice hot soup and gave himself a bath. Later he came across the dogs on the road, and spoke to them saying, "Go back home," he said, "and see what your master has done. He has prepared a lot of food and given it to me, and I have eaten it all up. But I think it is unfair, and I think you should have a say in what is done with the food you catch."

The dogs were enraged, and immediately seized the game they were taking home and devoured it all. On reaching home, they did not wait for their tempers to cool, but fell upon their master and devoured him, too. Then they looked round and saw all the food that had been prepared for them—more than they had ever thought possible. Their anger was turned against Fly, for it was he who had caused them all their problems.

From that time on, therefore, dogs have never trusted flies, and so it happens that every time a fly tries to land on a dog, the dog will snap his jaws and try to bite the fly, just as he would any other thing.

From that day on, then, dogs and flies have never been friends.

111 The Hunter's Daughter

One day a hunter went hunting. He took along his daughter to cook for him. They made a hut in the thickest part of the forest, and made it their base. In the olden days they called such a camp "the place of meat." Each day the hunter went to the forest to hunt. In the evening he brought back what he had killed. He cut it up and sent the meat to the village to be sold, but the skulls he left on a platform near the hut as a way of showing the number of animals he had killed.

In the course of time, the platform was full of skulls, and the hunter had to build an extension to it. At about this time he killed and brought to the place of meat a leopard, a female leopard. Its skull was also preserved. The child knew the names of all the animals whose skulls had been preserved on the platform, except that of the leopard.

Meanwhile, the husband of the leopard was searching for her. He searched everywhere in the forest—without success. At last he came to the hunter's camp. He inspected the skulls on the platform, and then, putting his face up close to that of the hunter's daughter, he began to question her.

Smiling, he held up the skull of Adowa, the Royal Antelope, and asked, "What animal's skull is this?"

She sang: "This is Adowa, poor dear Adowa, Adowa, noble Adowa, When the gun goes off, I say, 'That means trouble for father.'"

Smiling and pressing closer, Leopard lifted the head of the porcupine. "And what is this animal, my dear?"

"It is Porcupine, peaceful Porcupine, Porcupine, poor Porcupine. When the gun goes off, I say, 'That means trouble for father.'"

One by one, Leopard indicated the heads of all the animals on the platform, and asked the name of each animal. The girl named the owners as before. When he came to that of the leopard he asked, "What is this animal?"

The child said, "As for this animal, my father has not told me the name."

Staring deep with his fiery eyes, Leopard said, "All right, I am going away. When your father returns, ask for the name of that animal. I shall come back tomorrow to find out." And he was gone.

The hunter's daughter did not tell her father about the leopard, and she did not learn the name of the skull she could not identify.

Next day the leopard arrived as he had promised. He asked for the name of the animal that had the leopard's skull. She could not say it because she did not know it. So the leopard went away. This went on for a long time. Then one day the leopard said, "Tomorrow, if you do not tell me the name of that animal, I shall kill you."

When the hunter returned home, his daughter told him everything. He told her the name.

When the leopard came the next day, he asked, "What is the name of the animal whose skull this is?" She sang so sweetly: "This is Kotwiamanse, the leopard's wife. When the gun goes off, I say, 'That means trouble for father.'"

The leopard stood still, for the child's song had entered both his ears, the right ear and the left ear. It had entered both ears and gone on into his head. He stood there for a moment, and then he moved back a little, and he sprang into the air and was about to pounce on the child. This frightened child made herself very small, for she could not run away. She knew her time had come, and she must die.

Just as the leopard was about to fall on the child, Hunter made the gun speak, BANG! Leopard flew over her and fell down, THUMP! The hunter came out of the bush with smoke coming out of his gun. He ran and embraced his daughter. This is why we do not leave a child alone in any deserted place.

▼▲▼▲▼▲▼▲▼▲▼▲▼▲▼▲▼▲▼▲▼▲▼▲▼▲▼▲▼▲

112 The Gluttonous Monkey

I wasn't living then, but Monkey was, and there was a famine at that time. Monkey made an enormous pot of red porridge. He took it to the village meeting place and sat down right in the center and began to eat his porridge. People going to their farms came by and begged him for a bit of porridge. He wouldn't give them any. He just sat there eating and eating until his belly got very big and swollen. He was almost too full to get up. He went on eating. If a tiny ant on the ground managed to get a little of Monkey's porridge, he would kill it and squeeze out the porridge and eat it. This went on for a long time. By and by Monkey wanted to get up and couldn't, he tried and tried to get up, but he couldn't. He was right in the center of the meeting place and was in everyone's way. So the people beat the gong, and they put their heads together to try to figure out a way to help Monkey get up. They quietly made a plan. They put a spade in the fire, kept it there for a very long time, and then put it under Monkey's bottom.

He got up very fast and yelled, "Oh, I'm cooked, I'm burned, Skreeee! I'll never be the same!" Since that time Monkey has had a red bottom.

▼▲▼▲▼▲▼▲▼▲▼▲▼▲▼▲▼▲▼▲▼▲▼▲▼▲▼▲▼▲

113 Why Singing Tortoises Are Solitary

Once upon a time there lived in a certain village a very poor hunter who had a large family. He had to go into the bush many times, because he had to hunt a great deal.

One day when he was out hunting alone, he came upon an open space in the middle of the forest. There was a tortoise in this place. This tortoise was standing upright on its hind legs and playing a fiddle with its forelegs.

While it played it sang a song, the gist of which was: "Trouble never goes looking for Man. It is Man who always goes looking for Trouble."

The Hunter was amazed at what he heard, and he moved out of the trees toward the tortoise. The tortoise stopped singing.

Then the hunter said, "What a wonderful tortoise! A singing tortoise! I shall take you home with me, and all my family and friends will hear you sing. I will become rich and happy because I have a singing tortoise."

When the tortoise heard this, he begged the hunter not to take him to the village where there were lots of people, but to leave him alone in the bush. The hunter, however, would not listen.

The tortoise begged and begged again, but the hunter would not agree. So the tortoise said, "All right, Hunter, I will go with you. I will bring my fiddle, and I will sing for you. But for you alone. If you want me to sing, you must shut your door, and I will sing for you in your room. But you must not tell anybody that I can sing. I do not want other human beings to know." So the hunter took the tortoise to the village and put the tortoise in his room. The tortoise's music made the hunter very happy.

Now people in the village began to see that the poor hunter had changed, and he was now very happy. When he went hunting he always came back with plenty of game. Soon afterward he would lock himself in his room and would stay there alone for a long time. Always when he came out, he looked very happy. So the people of the village started paying attention to him, and they talked about him. One day when he was very happy, he boasted that he was the most wonderful hunter in the world. So he and his friends started arguing, each one of them claiming to be the most wonderful hunter in the world.

The hunter said, "I have captured what nobody else ever had, a singing tortoise." His friends were astonished. Nobody believed him. But he insisted that it was true and that not even the chief had anything so fine.

This story soon got to the ears of the chief. He did not believe it. He sent people and messengers to the hunter, saying that the hunter should make his tortoise sing before the court. If the tortoise sang, he would give the hunter one of his daughters to marry. If the tortoise did not sing, the hunter would be killed.

So that morning, all the people came out into the marketplace. The hunter, all dressed up, came out with his tortoise and its fiddle, and he set them down in the middle of the gathering. Everybody became silent.

Then the hunter commanded, "Sing for them, my dear little tortoise!" But the tortoise would not sing. "Sing!" the hunter commanded again, but again silence. The hunter ordered the tortoise to sing again and again, but all for nothing. The tortoise wouldn't sing.

Then the people shouted and hooted at the hunter. The chief's servants took him and chopped off his head. But no sooner had he been beheaded than the people were amazed to hear a high, thin, sweet voice. It was the tortoise, singing: "Trouble never goes looking for Man. It is Man who always goes looking for Trouble." And as he sang he played his fiddle, just as the hunter had said.

So they took the tortoise to the chief. The chief asked him why he had not sung when the hunter had commanded him. The tortoise replied, "I told him that Trouble never looks for Man, but Man always looks for Trouble, and still he did not listen."

The chief became very pensive and remained silent for a long time. After a while, he told his people to take the tortoise back and leave him in the same clearing in the middle of the forest from which he had come.

▼▲▼▲▼▲▼▲▼▲▼▲▼▲▼▲▼▲▼▲▼▲▼▲▼▲▼▲▼▲

114 The Price of Eggs

One day the yellow-backed duiker's hen laid a lot of eggs. Duiker went off to farm, and when he got back he saw that someone had taken the eggs. He asked everyone who had taken them, but no one paid any attention to him. This sort of thing went on for a few days. The hen laid eggs, and someone stole them, but Duiker couldn't find out who it was. So he told the chief, and the chief beat the gong all round the village, but no one paid him any attention either. The chief had a big fire made and called all the animals of the forest to come and prove their innocence by ordeal. The idea was that the animal who could jump over the fire and not fall into it wasn't the one who had taken the eggs. The animal who fell would be identified as the thief.

Adowa, the Royal Antelope, who is chief of all the animals of the bush, stood there and began to sing: "Duiker's hen has laid many eggs. If even my eyes have seen these eggs—if my hands have touched these eggs—pick me up and put me in the fire. Here I go!"

And Adowa jumped over the fire. They all shouted together, "Congratulations, Adowa!" and praised him.

The gray duiker stood there and sang the same song: "Duiker's hen has laid many eggs. If even my eyes have seen these eggs—if my hands have touched these eggs—pick me up and put me in the fire. Here I go!"

And, bump! He jumped over and was standing safe on the other side. They cheered. Elephant jumped, Bushbuck jumped, Bongo jumped, Porcupine jumped, Black Duiker jumped. Almost all the animals jumped.

Now it was Leopard's turn. He stood there and sang: "Duiker's hen has laid many eggs. If even my eyes have seen these eggs—if my hands have touched these eggs—pick me up and put me in the fire. Here I go!"

And he jumped. Oof! There he was, smack in the middle of the fire.

That is why a part of the leopard is white, a part is red, and a part is black, too. The part where the charcoal touched him is black; the part where the fire touched him is red; and the part that wasn't touched at all is white.

▼▲▼▲▼▲▼▲▼▲▼▲▼▲▼▲▼▲▼▲▼▲▼▲▼▲▼▲▼▲

115 The Coffin of God's Daughter

Once upon a time God had a daughter called Asiedua. Near the town in which God and his daughter lived were many delicious snails. One day Asiedua and her friends decided to go and gather some of these snails. They went a long way and got hungry, tired, and thirsty. They came to a village in which there was only an old lady.

The old lady asked them, "My granddaughters, why do you come to this village, where no one ever comes?"

They answered her, "Please Grandmother, we were looking for snails, and we got thirsty, so we came to beg you for some water." The old lady was delighted, showed them to her kitchen, and gave them a cup of water. Asiedua said she didn't like drinking from that sort of cup. Her father, she said, always gave her a gold one. She kicked the old lady's cup and broke it. So the old lady just looked Asiedua in the face and winked at her. Asiedua fell to the floor and died. This old lady did not know that winking carried a fatal curse for Asiedua.

Her friends rushed to the chief of the animals and told him the story— how they had gone for snails and met an old lady who had winked at Asiedua, and that Asiedua had died. The animals made a basket, put the corpse in it, and made the old lady carry it.

She started to sing: "Grandfather Sky God's daughter was the girl Asiedua. She came and asked me for water. I gave her some, but she kicked my cup and broke it. I winked at her, and Asiedua died on the spot."

And she went to Grandfather Sky God's village, still carrying the corpse and singing her song: "Grandfather Sky God's daughter was the girl Asiedua. She came and asked me for water. I gave her some, but she kicked my cup and broke it. I winked at her, and Asiedua died on the spot."

When God heard all this, he called a celebration, a big one, of course, and ordered his men to fetch the old lady. The old lady told him the full story: how his daughter was gathering snails with her friends and got thirsty and asked her for water. She told how his daughter would not drink from the cup she gave her, but kicked it and broke it because she said she usually drank from a gold cup, and how she winked at the girl, not knowing about the fatal curse, and how the girl died. She told how the animals had made a basket for her to carry the corpse in, and bring it to the father. God took revenge by having the old lady killed. He made a nice shiny coffin for his daughter and kept it in his room, under his bed. When he thought of his beautiful daughter he would bring out the coffin to see her.

Anytime there is lightning in the sky, that is God pulling out the coffin. The noise of thunder is God pulling the coffin from under the bed.

▼▲▼▲▼▲▼▲▼▲▼▲▼▲▼▲▼▲▼▲▼▲▼▲▼▲▼▲▼▲

116 The Quarrel Between Heaven and Earth

There was a very, very big forest. This forest was so big that people thought it must be full of many different kinds of animals. There were then two very important beings in this region. These two were Earth and Heaven. They were living peacefully together with all the animals, birds, men, and women.

These two, Earth and Heaven, called a conference of the people of the area and named a date to burn the bush. On the appointed day the bush was burnt, and after the burning of the bush, all the birds, all the animals, and all the people went in to see what animals they could capture.

But they were surprised. They searched between the rocks, they searched the nests of the birds, they searched in every nook and corner of the burned bush, but they could not find a single animal to kill.

At the end of the long search only a small rat was killed. The small rat that was killed was taken before the two important beings of the area, Earth and Heaven. They started to quarrel over it. Earth said that he was the older, and as such he had a right to the rat. Heaven said that he was the older, and as such he had a right to the rat.

When no agreement could be reached, Heaven refused to acknowledge anyone's right to the rat, and he left the place in anger.

That was how Heaven left Earth and removed his house far, far away into the sky, above the reach of all men, all birds, and all animals.

For a few days, and then a few weeks, Earth and all the animals and birds and people living on earth didn't feel Heaven's absence from Earth. But after some time they noticed that there was no rain, and all the trees had started to shed their leaves, all the rivers and ears of corn had started to dry up, and the ground itself had started to crack. The singing birds could not sing anymore because they had no water to drink. The children could no longer laugh and be merry, because they were hungry and thirsty. So Earth, who was the remaining being in the area, was forced to call a conference of the birds and animals and people, and he asked them what they thought was responsible for the famine and drought that were creeping over the face of the earth.

Fortunately, a Divining Priest was there, and through his divination he was able to find out that the drought and famine that were then afflicting the people of the earth were brought upon them by the quarrel between Earth and Heaven.

Then he prescribed the remedy. The remedy was that the rat in dispute should be sent back to Heaven. So Earth called another conference of all the birds and told them that one of them must take the rat back to Heaven. Each of the birds tried to lift it.

The first bird to try it was the Hawk. Hawk said that he was a brave bird, a bird that could fly for days in the sky without resting on a branch. He picked up the rat from the ground, and he started to go off with it to Heaven, while all the birds and the people and the animals watched him.

As he soared higher and higher into the sky, they all sang: "Earth and Heaven fought over a rat. Earth said he was the older one, and Heaven also said he was the older one. Heaven withdrew to Heaven, and the face of the Earth was covered with drought and famine. Pregnant women no longer delivered, barren women had no chance to bear children. Small rivers were covered with dust and leaves. Ears of corn stopped growing. Small tubers of yams dried up."

As Hawk was about to go out of sight, his strength gave out; he could go no farther, and he dropped to the ground. The rat was still there to be carried to Heaven.

Then the Hornbill picked the rat up and soared into heaven, singing in the same way. He, too, could not get too far with the rat before he dropped out of the sky.

The birds each had a turn, and none got the rat anywhere near Heaven, and Earth was becoming very depressed. It was then that Vulture stepped out of the crowd. Everybody started to laugh at him because the vulture, as we all know, is neither a clever bird nor very bright. But Vulture insisted that he was the one that would take the rat to Heaven. When he said this, all the birds laughed again. But Earth said that they should give the vulture a chance to take the rat to Heaven. So Vulture picked up the rat from the ground and took it into the sky, singing the same song that the other birds had sung.

After a few minutes, Vulture was out of sight, and the people were wondering whether Vulture had reached Heaven, or whether he would soon drop down like all the other birds. But after a few more minutes they heard thunder in the sky, and all of them agreed, "Oh yes, Vulture has reached Heaven."

When Vulture reached Heaven he knocked very hard at the gate. The Gateman of Heaven asked, "Who are you?"

He replied, "I'm Vulture, the emissary of Earth. I've come bringing the disputed rat to Heaven."

Then the Gateman of Heaven opened the door for him, and Vulture entered into the palace of Heaven.

When he entered he inquired about the abode of Heaven, and he was shown into his presence. He knelt down and prostrated himself in front of Heaven, and then said that Earth had sent him to give the disputed rat back to Heaven. He said that Earth now realized that he was wrong, and had now conceded seniority to Heaven.

When Heaven heard this he laughed and laughed, and then he said, "Then you will have rain again, and all your fields will be full of green again, and all your children will laugh again, and all your barren women will have a chance to produce children again, and everybody will be happy again upon the face of the earth."

He showed the Vulture into his backyard. In the backyard, Heaven asked him to pick up three small gourds. He instructed him to break one of these gourds on the ground as he was leaving the gates of Heaven, and to break the other one when he was midway between heaven and earth, and to break the third one when he reached earth.

Then Vulture thanked Heaven and left upon his journey back to earth.

At the gate he broke one of the gourds, and straightaway thunder and dark clouds started to gather in the sky. All the animals, birds, and men watching the return of Vulture from heaven said, "Now we are quite sure that the vulture has reached Heaven."

When the vulture got halfway he broke the other gourd, and small showers of rain started to fall on earth. In great confusion, everybody rushed home to repair their broken roofs, and some went to gather other things that might get wet. It was while they were doing these things that the vulture reached earth.

When he reached earth he broke the other gourd, and rain started to fall. Vulture could find no shelter. As he stuck his head into one home after the other, looking for shelter, people threw stones, pebbles, and sticks at his head. He tried all the houses in the neighborhood, and all the nests of birds, and all the holes and burrows of animals, but nobody would give him a place in which to protect himself against the rain. They all knocked him very hard on the head.

Then, when the vulture could find no place in which to rest and shelter from the rain, he went to rest in the top of a tree, and pronounced a curse upon the face of the earth. He said, "From now on, all of you will pay very dearly for any good turn that anybody does for you."

Since that day, Vulture has had a very bald head, caused by the stones, pebbles, and sticks with which his neighbors hit him.

▼▲▼▲▼▲▼▲▼▲▼▲▼▲▼▲▼▲▼▲▼▲▼▲▼▲▼▲▼▲

117 The Cry of Sasabonsam

All the beasts and the birds came together in a great council to choose a king. They sat in a circle. Sasabonsam sat on a silk cotton tree with his thin legs dangling, and Leopard sat on a log and kept an eye on the fat antelopes. The birds clung to trees and vines.

Owl, sitting on a dead branch, proclaimed, "I kill the mighty!"

The elephants and the other giants of the forest were startled. But the Gray Mona monkey shouted his agreement.

Hyena was so afraid that he pretended to be making a fire. He began to break pieces of wood to start it. He then accidentally got hold of Sasabonsam's legs and began to break them. He thought they were dead twigs.

Tree bear, who doesn't see too well by day, thought it was the Royal Antelope's legs that were being pulled, because Adowa, the Royal Antelope, also has thin legs.

Tree bear screamed, "Father Elephant! Father Elephant! They are breaking Adowa's legs, Adowa's legs."

Sasabonsam thought he was being attacked and cried out, "Eee Yaowow!"

His cry was heard all over the forest. The animals thought it was an alarm being sounded, and they stampeded away through the thick undergrowth, leaving Sasabonsam alone. Every time you hear "Eee Yaowow!" in the forest, it is Sasabonsam crying from the pain of the Hyena's grip.

▼▲▼▲▼▲▼▲▼▲▼▲▼▲▼▲▼▲▼▲▼▲▼▲▼▲▼▲▼▲

118 Adowa and the Leopard

Adowa, the Royal Antelope, was frolicking in the sun in a grove of young trees. Nearby, three leopard cubs were playing. Adowa joined them. During the course of their play, Adowa kicked the cubs on the head with his hoofs and killed them.

When he saw the mother leopard, Kotwiamansa, coming, he ran away and hid among the buttress roots of a huge tree. Kotwiamansa followed him, and when she caught up with him she said, "Hee, Adowa! Is that you? Was it you who killed my children? If so, you are as good as dead."

Adowa replied, "No, not I! The Adowa who killed your children is different from Roots Adowa. I am Roots Adowa."

As soon as Kotwiamansa had rushed off, Adowa went and sat on a hillock. When Kotwiamansa came up to him she said, "Hee, Adowa! Is that you? Was it you who killed my children? If so, you are as good as dead."

Adowa replied, "No, not I! Roots Adowa is different from Hillock Adowa. I am Hillock Adowa."

So Kotwiamansa went away to search for the Adowa who had killed her children. Adowa slipped away and lay in a grove of reeds. When Kotwiamansa found him she said, "Hee, Adowa! Is that you? Was it you who killed my children? If so, you are as good as dead."

Adowa looked at her lazily and said, "No, not I! Roots Adowa is different from Hillock Adowa. Hillock Adowa is different from Reeds Adowa. I am Reeds Adowa."

So Kotwiamansa ran off. It wasn't long before she saw Adowa busily cultivating a guinea corn field. She shouted at him, "Hee, Adowa! Is that you? Was it you who killed my children? If so, you are as good as dead."

Adowa jumped about crazily and said, "No, not I! Roots Adowa is different from Hillock Adowa. Hillock Adowa is different from Reeds Adowa. Reeds Adowa is different from Guinea Corn Adowa. I am Guinea Corn Adowa."

Kotwiamansa turned away sadly and continued her search. Meanwhile, Adowa had fixed himself up in a pepper plantation and was grinding red-hot pepper.

Kotwiamansa also reached the pepper plantation. She said, "Hee, Adowa! Is that you? Was it you who killed my children? If so, you are as good as dead."

Adowa replied in a very serious voice, "No, not I! Roots Adowa is different from Hillock Adowa. Hillock Adowa is different from Reeds Adowa. Reeds Adowa is different from Guinea Corn Adowa. Guinea Corn Adowa is different from Pepper Adowa. I am Pepper Adowa."

Poor Kotwiamansa, what could she do? She went away to find the Adowa who had killed her children.

Now Adowa ran and ran. There was no place left for him to hide. Now that she could see who he was, Kotwiamansa ran after him. Now she could hear him. Now she was close to him. Now her breath was all over him. Now she was ready to spring on him. But Adowa rolled over on the road and lay on his back with his legs pointing up. He pretended to be asleep. Kotwiamansa said, "Hee, Adowa! Is that you? Was it you who killed my children? If so, you are as good as dead."

Adowa just opened his eyes and said rather sleepily, "No, not I! Roots Adowa is different from Hillock Adowa. Hillock Adowa is different from Reeds Adowa. Reeds Adowa is different from Guinea Corn Adowa. Guinea Corn Adowa is different from Pepper Adowa. Pepper Adowa is different from Road Adowa. I am Road Adowa."

Kotwiamansa went on down the road thinking she was chasing the real Adowa until she came to the end of the road. Then she said, "Hee, it *is* Adowa. There was Road Adowa. Road Adowa is the same as Pepper Adowa. Pepper Adowa is the same as Guinea Corn Adowa. Guinea Corn Adowa is the same as Reeds Adowa. Reeds Adowa is the same as Hillock Adowa. Hillock Adowa is the same as Roots Adowa. Roots Adowa is the same as the Adowa who killed my children."

She bounced back, and she ran and ran, but when she came to the middle of the road, the real Adowa was gone.

▼▲▼▲▼▲▼▲▼▲▼▲▼▲▼▲▼▲▼▲▼▲▼▲▼▲▼▲▼▲

119 Ananse and God's Business

Kwaku Ananse made a bargain with God, and as part of the bargain, God gave him a fine loud crowing cock. In return, Ananse said he would get God many people. Ananse was going along the road with his fine fowl when he saw some sheep. He said, "God's cock doesn't sleep with other fowls. He sleeps with sheep." And he put him next to a large ram. Night fell, and at midnight Ananse went and killed the fowl, took its blood and smeared it all over the ram's horns. Then he cooked the fowl and ate it. It was this same Kwaku Ananse who killed the fowl and ate it and plastered its blood all over the ram's horns who went to the owner of the sheep and complained about the ram. The man said, "This is God's business. I can't do anything about it, so take the ram and go." Ananse took the ram and left.

He went on and came to a bull grazing. He said, "This ram doesn't sleep with sheep; it sleeps with cattle." And again when night fell, Ananse killed the ram, smeared the bull's horns with blood, cooked the ram, and ate it. Again the bull's owner could only say, "This is God's business, I can't do anything about it. Take the bull and go." And Ananse went off with the bull.

Later he met a man carrying a corpse. He said, "Give me the corpse; you take the bull instead." The man at first said no, and then said, "Give me your bull for this corpse." As it was agreed, Ananse handed over the bull and took the corpse. He brought it to a town, where he said he would lodge the night. Before he slept he told everybody in the room, "This is God's son, and he breaks wind at night, so if you beat him for it, beat him gently or he may die." And they all slept, and Ananse broke wind all night long. When the smell rose, the people got up and beat the corpse and beat it hard. The next day, Kwaku Ananse took the corpse to the chief and lodged his complaint. The chief replied, "This is God's business. I can't deal with it. Take all the people and go."

▼▲▼▲▼▲▼▲▼▲▼▲▼▲▼▲▼▲▼▲▼▲▼▲▼▲▼▲▼▲

120 Why the Sky Is High

A certain man, living in a small town with his mother, was very much blessed by God. He was happy and rich, and his mother was happy. They lived happily together.

Now, one day this man decided to find himself a wife. He and his mother looked all around the whole town and surrounding districts, and at last they found a young and very pretty girl for him to marry.

This young wife came to live with him in the house, but unfortunately she did not turn out to be a very good wife. She did not respect the man's mother, her mother-in-law. In fact, she did not seem to have respect for anybody at all, even her husband. She would never do what her mother-in-law asked her and sometimes, even when the mother-in-law was speaking, she would laugh out loud and mock the older woman.

This wife got worse and worse and could get along with no one. Very often when all the women were together and cooking the day's meal in the kitchen, this young wife would take her coal pot and her cooking utensils and her food, and move outside on her own and start cooking there. The mother-in-law tried to reason with her and plead with her to be civil and sociable.

She told the young wife, "You must not cook outside, it is simply not done. We have always cooked inside the kitchen, and that is the way that cooking is meant to be done." But this young and pretty girl wouldn't listen. She just went right on cooking outside.

Then, one day, she again did what nobody had ever done before. She carried her mortar and pestle outside the kitchen and got ready to pound the fufu in the open air. Her mother-in-law told her not to do it, but the young girl wouldn't listen. The mother-in-law told her that food was always pounded inside the kitchen, and that is the only place that food is meant to be pounded. The mother-in-law also told her that God wouldn't like it, but the young wife would not listen. She started pounding.

Even in those days God lived in the sky, but the sky was much closer to earth. In fact, the sky was just above the roof of the kitchen and the houses. A very tall man could almost touch it, in fact. God who sees everything used to watch the mother-in-law and all the other women cooking, and he smiled upon them and made them happy. But when the young wife started pounding the fufu, she boosted her pestle higher than the roof of the kitchen, and the end of the pestle hit God right in the face. So God got angry and frowned. Then the young girl pounded again and hit Him a second time, and then a third. Now God became so very angry that He pulled Himself far, far up—away from this selfish and stubborn girl. He took the sky with him, too. He was never seen again. This is why the sky is so far away.

▼▲▼▲▼▲▼▲▼▲▼▲▼▲▼▲▼▲▼▲▼▲▼▲▼▲▼▲▼▲

121 The Gifts

A hunter went off to hunt in the bush. He roamed the whole day without killing or even seeing an animal. He said, "I will go back home to enjoy my hunger and my poverty."

It was getting dark so he hurried along. He had not gone far, however, when a voice from the side of the path cried, "Please pull us out, pull us out!"

The voice seemed to come from the ground, so he stopped to investigate. He cocked his gun and cautiously went toward the voice, which was still pleading, "Please pull us out, pull us out!"

He found a large, deep pit. Inside he found a rat, a snake, and a man. "Take us out of here, we beg you!"

The hunter replied, "You, Rat, you have been destroying my crops and stealing my seeds. Why should I help you? You are safe where you are, and my seeds are safe too. It is better that you stay where you are."

The rat pleaded again, and promised to tell the hunter where he could find a pot of enchanted gold. "Tell me first, before I pull you out." The rat told the hunter where there was an enormous pot of enchanted gold. The rat also told the hunter that the gold would belong to the hunter as long as the hunter told no one where he got it.

Then the hunter said, "And you, snake! You bite my kind, and they die. You must remain where you are. You are safe in there, and all people are safe from you while you are where you now are." Snake said, "I will be good and bite only when it is to save someone, and thus will I reward your kindness."

The man did not need to plead, for he was, after all, the hunter's own kind. He pulled all three out. They thanked him and went on their way. Snake said, "Take this, it is snakebite medicine. You may find it useful."

At dawn the next morning Hunter set out to find rat's enchanted gold. He found it after much digging. In time, Hunter became very rich. He was made a subchief and became very powerful and influential. He used his money to do good deeds, helping the sick and the poor. He built a beautiful house and lived in it with his family. Everybody liked and respected him—except a few wicked people who were jealous of his prosperity.

One day it was announced that the great chief of the land had lost some money, which was, of course, gold in those days. Since a chief is not careless, it was thought that the gold had been stolen from him. He sent messengers to all the villages and towns to find the thief. The chief promised a big reward to any who could give information leading to the recovery of his gold.

One night the man whom the hunter had rescued went to the chief's messenger. "I know who stole your gold," he said.

"Tell me then," the messenger of the chief demanded. This thankless man did not really know who had stolen the gold, but he wanted the reward. He also wanted to disgrace and harm the hunter who had pulled him out of the pit, because the hunter was rich and powerful, and he was not.

The hunter was arrested and brought before the chief. He was asked to account for his sudden wealth. Of course, he could not disclose the source of his prosperity because the rat had told him that the day he told his secret he would lose all his property, because the gold was enchanted gold.

The chief therefore ordered him to be executed. He was put in chains, and a large crowd followed him to the outskirts of the town where criminals were executed. The executioners danced and performed many acrobatic tricks. They sharpened their bloodstained knives and rehearsed the execution. They did somersaults and, contorting their bodies, danced in narrowing circles until they could touch the hunter with their knives.

Suddenly, a great cry arose from the quarters of the chief's wives. The chief's favorite wife had just been bitten by a deadly snake. There was great clamor and confusion. The crowd moved toward the new scene of excitement. Poor Hunter was left alone with only one guard to watch him. Messengers were sent to all villages and towns demanding that all the medicine men come and try to cure the chief's wife. Famous and powerful medicine men rushed to the chief's house, but they shook their heads. "She will not live," they all declared. The chief went mad with grief. He tore off his clothes and put on mourning cloth. He proclaimed a fast.

The situation was now very serious. Hunter sat there in the hot sun, wishing that he was dead. He remembered toward evening that the snake he rescued from the pit had given him some medicine. He asked if the guard could seek permission from the chief to try the medicine of the hunter on the stricken wife. The chief was ready to try anything, for he was desperate.

Hunter was led to his house to fetch the medicine. When he arrived at the chief's house he said, "O great and powerful one, I am sure I can cure your wife, but one important ingredient is lacking for mixing the medicine."

"Whatever it is, it will be supplied," said the chief eagerly.

Hunter said, "I must have the arm of a treacherous man." The chief was puzzled. Where on earth was he to get the arm of a treacherous man? One of the chief's elders who believed the hunter was innocent said, "What of the man who betrayed Hunter?"

"You are right," said the chief. He sent messengers to fetch Konkon, for that was the man's name. When he was brought in, the executioners cut off his arm. The snakebite medicine and blood and sinew from the arm were applied to the snakebite. Instantly, life began to flow in the chief's wife's veins. She recovered in a short time.

The hunter was released. The chief apologized for the bad treatment he had given him and asked him to name a reward.

The man said, "I have already been rewarded, chief, for you have spared my life."

The chief ordered Konkon's arm to be tied to a post on the path leading out of town, to serve as a warning to other treacherous people. So it was that when children passed that way, they pointed to the arm and said, "Nea konkon sa," which means "Look at Konkon's arm."

Before then, the Akans had had no word for treachery, but as people repeated, "Konkonsa, Konkonsa," it became the word for treachery.

▼▲▼▲▼▲▼▲▼▲▼▲▼▲▼▲▼▲▼▲▼▲▼▲▼▲▼▲▼▲

122 The Necklace

There were once two co-wives, Musu and Kema, who loved each other very much. They ate from the same dish, they slept in the same bed, and they visited each other's families. One day Musu went with Kema to visit the latter's hometown. On arriving, Kema planted a seed of the kola tree, and then they returned home. They both went back later to Kema's hometown, and they saw that the kola seed had sprouted and was growing well. Musu said, "I have a brass kettle with no bottom which I'll put over this kola tree to protect it while it is young."

They remained close friends for a long time till their husband died, and then they parted, Musu going to Kema's hometown, and Kema going to Musu's hometown. They continued good friends, then Kema seduced Musu's new husband. Musu gave up her husband to Kema, and they never mentioned the subject again.

One day Musu said, "Now that Kema has taken my husband away from me, I'll get even with her."

Therefore, Musu went to Kema's town to pay her a visit. Kema prepared a fine meal, and they slept till dawn. At daybreak Musu explained, "Remember that brass kettle I gave you? I've come back for it."

Kema said, "What can we do? You see, the kola tree has grown up inside the kettle."

Musu replied, "Dear sister, I want my kettle."

Kema answered, "All right. I will try."

Kema went and explained the situation to the elders, and they questioned Musu and asked her, "Is this story true? Have you really come for your kettle?"

She replied, "Yes, I have come for my kettle."

They told all this to Kema, and she said, "Plead with her, please."

Musu said, "Plead with me if you like, I will not relent; I want my kettle."

They returned to the house, and Kema pleaded with her for a long time, but she would not relent. There was nothing that could be done, so Kema had the kola tree cut down. They cut down the tree and gave her her kettle, and off she went.

A long time elapsed, then one day Kema heard that Musu was pregnant, and she thought to herself, "I will get my revenge on this woman." The two women resumed their friendship. Kema went to Musu's home and said, "Let's forget what has happened, and let's be friends again." Then Kema went and made a necklace without an opening in it—just a solid circle. As soon as she heard that Musu had had a baby, a girl, and that they were to name the child in two days' time, she went with the necklace. On arriving, she showed Musu the necklace, and put it around the child's neck. At daybreak they named the child. Kema slept till dawn, then said her farewells and went off.

They were now good friends. Musu forgot what she had done to Kema, but Kema did not forget.

One day when the child was grown up and was able to fetch water, Kema went to Musu's hometown. When she arrived she greeted Musu, and Musu treated her hospitably. They slept till dawn. At daybreak Kema explained to Musu, "Remember that jewelry I gave you for your daughter's naming ceremony. I have come for that."

Musu said, "Oh, it is on the child's neck, and she has grown up now. What are we meant to do, cut the necklace?"

Kema replied, "No, we're not cutting it! I want it exactly as I gave it to you."

Musu said, "Oh, what am I going to do?"

Kema answered, "That's your problem. I want my necklace."

Musu went and laid the matter before the elders, and they called Kema and questioned her and asked her, "Kema, is that how it is?"

She replied, "Yes, that's how it is. I want my necklace just as I gave it to her."

The elders said, "If she offered you money, wouldn't you accept it? Look now, the child has grown up and goes and fetches water for her mother."

But she said, "I won't agree to anything except the return of my necklace intact."

The elders pleaded with her earnestly and appealed to her sense of compassion, but she would not relent, and they gave up.

Musu begged her and begged her, but she would not relent. They returned once more to the elders, and they said, "What we must do in this case is to cut the child's throat." And they cut the child's throat and removed the necklace and gave it to Kema, and Kema went away.

Wrongdoing is not good. The one who strikes the blow forgets, but the one who receives it does not.

▼▲▼▲▼▲▼▲▼▲▼▲▼▲▼▲▼▲▼▲▼▲▼▲▼▲▼▲▼▲

123 The Tale of Aso Yaa

Ananse was handsome. He loved the girls. The girls loved him. They really loved him. He had many wild adventures in the north country and brought many lovely girls home. It was on one of these adventures that he found Aso. She was lying by the side of the road. Her body was covered with ulcers. There was not one part of her body that was free of them.

Ananse looked at her. She was beautiful. She seemed beautiful even though she was covered with sores. Her eyes were big and full of hope. Ananse said, "Will you marry me, woman?"

"Don't mock me, man. How can I marry you with all these sores? When I am in this sad state?"

"Will you marry me?" Ananse said again.

"No, but I will be your servant forever."

Ananse took from his bag a calabash. Into this he collected all the ulcers on Aso Yaa's body. All of them. He did not leave even one single sore to annoy her.

By my white hair, I swear you never saw a more beautiful girl. She was more beautiful than the orb of the morning sun. Certainly more beautiful than any of your modern girls, Aso Yaa was. Yes, she was beautiful.

Ananse took Aso Yaa to town and bought her a cloth. He bought her jewels and beads. She was beautiful in her new things. When Ananse had finished all his business in town he came back to his own village with Aso Yaa. He built a two-story house for her and provided her with every luxury. She lived like a queen. Her happiness was complete.

Now Ananse was once again seized by the spirit of adventure and went off on another wild adventure. He traveled to a far country and came home three years later with a lot of money and many slaves. He brought with him many valuable and beautiful presents for Aso Yaa. He looked forward to a warm welcome from his beautiful wife. He was very happy that he was coming back home.

Ananse's arrival was heralded by a caravan of drum beaters and horn blowers. This was followed by a caravan of his spoils—the goods and the slaves. At last Ananse himself arrived. To his surprise, it was no warm welcome he received. There was no one in the house to meet him. When he asked the servants, they told him Aso had gone off drinking with some men she had been living with in Ananse's house.

Ananse was very wise. What would you do if you were Ananse? Don't tell me you wouldn't beat Aso. No, Ananse didn't beat Aso. He was very patient. For two days Aso was away with her lovers. When they arrived back Ananse received his wife kindly, but she was very rude and demanded that Ananse should leave her house, for she was now married to another man.

Ananse quietly left the house. He left all his things at home, however, for he knew what he would do. What would you do? Wait! Don't you tell me. You will soon know for yourself what Ananse did. For several days he stayed out of the town. The eighth day was a national festival. Thousands of people put on their best clothes and paraded through the town. Aso and her friends were among the people. Her dress was of the purest silk—one that Ananse had brought from the eastern countries.

Ananse, accompanied by a crowd, was playing his musical instrument. Holding it against his chest he sang in a melodious voice: "Have you seen my Aso Yaa, the proud and radiant Aso Yaa? You have never seen beauty until you have beheld my Aso Yaa."

Again Ananse sang, playing: "Have you seen my Aso Yaa, the proud and radiant Aso Yaa? You have never seen beauty until you have beheld my Aso Yaa."

The whole crowd joined in the song. Many danced to its rhythm. Aso was very much flattered. She danced gracefully among the beauties of the town. At the height of this delightful episode, when everybody was enjoying the music and dancing, Ananse drew from his bag a calabash—the calabash in which he had put and kept Aso Yaa's ulcers. Like a flash of lightning he threw the calabash at Aso Yaa. Instantly, every kind of ulcer spread on Aso Yaa's body. She fell down and crawled on the ground just as when Ananse had first met her on the road. All her fine clothes disappeared. Her jewelry disappeared. Her servants vanished, and all that she possessed became nothing at all.

She cried and pleaded with Ananse for mercy, but he continued to play and sing: "Have you seen my Aso Yaa, the proud and radiant Aso Yaa? You have never seen beauty until you have beheld my Aso Yaa."

All the people danced away. Aso Yaa's friends danced away. Her men friends danced away. As the music died away far, far on the outskirts of town, Aso Yaa looked up and saw that she was left all alone in the world. The whole town had gone, and she had a fitting reward for her ingratitude—the deserted streets and her ulcers.

NOTES

▼▲▼▲▼▲▼▲▼▲▼▲▼▲▼▲▼▲▼▲▼▲▼▲▼▲▼▲▼▲▼

The numbering of the notes corresponds to that of the tales. The language in which the present version of the tale was originally told is listed after the title, followed by the country where the tale was told. The initials that follow refer to the collector or transcriber of the tale; the full name of this person appears in the Acknowledgments section. This information was not always available. Many of the tales begin and end with traditional opening and closing formulae; these are listed in the Notes at their first use. (See nos. 1, 2, 4, 13, and 29.)

1. The Scarecrow – Ga (Ghana). N.A.K. This scarecrow is analogous to the "tar baby" in the famous Uncle Remus tale. Spider's wife, Kornorley, is the same as Konole in nos. 18 and 98. The standard Ga opening formula is: STORYTELLER: Shall I tell you or shall I not? AUDIENCE: Yes, tell us! The typical closing formula is: STORYTELLER: If I get another [story] I'll stick it behind your ears.

2. The Wise Fool – Sefwi (Ghana). T.Y.E. These particular fairies or elves are identified as little men with backward-pointing feet. The standard Sefwi opening formula is: STORYTELLER: Now this story—I didn't make it up! AUDIENCE: Who did then? The typical closing formula is: STORYTELLER: This is my story which I have now told you, whether it is sweet or whether it is not sweet, take a bit of it and keep the rest under your pillow.

3. Why We Tell Stories About Spider – Ga (Ghana). N.A.K. See no. 22 for another version. This is a widespread tale, usually involving three seemingly impossible tasks. Opening and closing formulae at no. 1.

4. How Tortoise Won by Losing – Yoruba (Nigeria). W.A. Tortoise frequently receives punishment or personal injury. The standard Yoruba opening formula is: STORYTELLER: Once upon a time; a time passes; a time is coming; a time will never finish upon the face of the earth.

5. The Power of the Temper – Ga (Ghana). N.A.K. See the tale of the fish child in no. 67. Also similar to the pineapple child motif. See Index: Pineapple child. Opening and closing formulae at no. 1.

6. The Contest Between Fire and Rain – Yoruba (Nigeria). W.A. See fire personified in nos. 89 and 95. Opening formula at no. 4.

7. The Constant Parrot – Yoruba (Nigeria). W.A. Opening formula at no. 4.

8. Aja and the Enchanted Beast – Krobo (Ghana).

9. The Elephant, the Tortoise, and the Hare – Yoruba (Nigeria). W.A. Similar to the Western fable of the race between the tortoise and the hare. See nos. 41 and 44. Opening formula at no. 4.

10. The Snakebite Medicine – Ga (Ghana). N.A.K. See similar story in no. 121. Opening and closing formulae at no. 1.

11. What Spider Learned from Frog – Adengme (Ghana). The frog actually said, "Woya."

12. The Magic Contest – Language not known.

13. The Greedy Dog – Vane Avatime (Ghana). The Avatime opening formula is: STORYTELLER: Hear my tale! AUDIENCE: Let the tale come! A typical closing formula is: STORYTELLER: At the bottom of my story, at the top of my story, here, there: all is ended.

14. Adene and the Pineapple Child – Ga (Ghana). See no. 32 for a version about Adele. See the fish child version at no. 67. Opening and closing formulae at no. 1.

15. Sasabonsam's Match – Sefwi (Ghana). T.Y.E. See Index: Sasabonsam. Opening and closing formulae at no. 2.

16. The Jealous Wife – Sefwi (Ghana). T.Y.E. The original tale contains a song that is repeated a number of times. Opening and closing formulae at no. 2.

17. A Mother's Love – Yoruba (Nigeria). W.A. See no. 26. Note the motif of inequitable treatment of children, as in no. 70. Opening formula at no. 4.

18. Spider Finds a Fool – Ga (Ghana). L.L. Spider's wife, Konole, is similar to Kornorley in nos. 1 and 98. Opening and closing formulae at no. 1.

19. The Locust-Bean Seller – Yoruba (Nigeria). W.A. See the "river judge" in nos. 35, 47, and 97. Opening formula at no. 4.

20. Magotu and the Devil – Mende (Sierra Leone). A.S. See also no. 24. Note the wisdom of the twin.

21. Leopard and the Son of the Hunter – Larteh (Ghana). B.J. See no. 111 for a similar tale concerning a hunter's daughter.

22. Spider's Bargain with God – Sefwi (Ghana). T.Y.E. See no. 3 for a similar tale. Nana Nyamee is Grandfather Sky God. The tale is told with much singing. Opening and closing formulae at no. 2.

23. Python Meets His Match – Krio (Sierra Leone). S.M. This may also serve to explain the great length of the python.

24. Big Man and the Chimpanzee – Krio (Sierra Leone). S.M. See another tale of chimpanzee strength at no. 23.

25. The Sacrifice – Larteh (Ghana). B.J. The food she took him is called *oto*. Concealed people and secret words are common motifs. See Index: Hidden people, Open Sesame for other similar tales.

26. The Cruel Mother – Yoruba (Nigeria). W.A. The sinking child is similar to the departing pineapple child. See nos. 14, 17, and 32. Opening formula at no. 4.

27. The Orphan's Revenge – Vane Avatime (Ghana). Underlings are singled out for extra hand-washing before eating. See no. 41. Opening and closing formulae at no. 13.

28. The Sacred Bowl – Yoruba (Nigeria). W.A. The voice may be the voice of the river. Opening formula at no. 4.

29. The Wise Child – Twi (Ghana). G.O.B. There may be an element of wordplay in the business about hair-cutting and the eating of the ear of corn. This child is identified as Kwaku Babone, the wonder child, in other versions. See the hair-cutting motif again in tale no. 57. A similar tree-chopping episode in no. 83. The typical Twi opening formula is: STORYTELLER: Hear my tale! AUDIENCE: Tell us! Typical closing formulae are: STORYTELLER: This story I have told you, whether it is sweet or not, take some and bring some. STORYTELLER: My story that I've told is this: let some go and let some come! STORYTELLER: So if this, my tale, is good or not, we leave it up to you to bring your own.

30. The Headstrong Bride – Yoruba (Nigeria). W.A. The headstrong bride discovers that her husband is really something other than what he appears to be. See no. 58. The serpent in human form is a very old motif. See Old Testament, Genesis. Opening formula at no. 4.

31. The Pact – Cameroon Pidgin. C.G.

32. Adele and the Pineapple Child – Ga (Ghana). N.A.K. See the version with Adene at tale no. 14. Opening and closing formulae at no. 1.

33. The Voice of the Child – Sefwi (Ghana). T.Y.E. Kwasi again, as in no. 3. A cow- or horsetail switch is the equivalent of a magic wand. See Index: Switch for other tales mentioning the switch or whisk. Akokoaa Kwasi Gyinamoa is another name for Kwaku Babone. Opening and closing formulae at no. 2.

34. The Yam Farm and the Problem Tongue – Ga (Ghana). L.L. The use of a trick to learn a secret is a common motif. See Index: Name-guessing test, Open Sesame for similar tales. The lethal word appears again in no. 54. Opening and closing formulae at no. 1.

35. The River's Judgment – Sefwi (Ghana). T.Y.E. The original tale begins with a song. See the "river judge" motif in nos. 19, 47, and 97. Opening and closing formulae at no. 2.

36. Who Has the Greatest Love? – Ga (Ghana). A cow- or horsetail switch is the equivalent of a magic wand. See Index: Switch for other tales that mention the switch or whisk. Opening and closing formulae at no. 1.

37. Tortoise Buys a House – Yoruba (Nigeria). W.A. Tortoise is slow but clever. He is often associated with magical music, either hypnotic or diverting. Opening formula at no. 4.

38. Why Bush Pig Has a Red Face – Ga (Ghana). N.A.K. The grasscutter is a cane-rat or the bush-rat. Opening and closing formulae at no. 1.

39. Spider and the Nightjar – Sefwi (Ghana). T.Y.E. A fetish priest is a sorcerer whose power derives from a fetish or charm. Opening and closing formulae at no. 2.

40. Spider Learns to Listen – Sefwi (Ghana). T.Y.E. Neither "Food Pounder" nor "Pounder" are exact translations, but they allow the necessary sense of the wordplay to be retained. This whip is similar to the cutlass in tale no. 75. The whip is also reminiscent of the brooms in the Walt Disney version of "The Sorcerer's Apprentice." Opening and closing formulae at no. 2.

41. Tortoise and the Singing Crab – Vane Avatime (Ghana). Tortoise is weak but clever and triumphs. See also nos. 9 and 44. Tortoise is typically associated with the use of music to accomplish his ends. See no. 27. Opening and closing formulae at no. 13.

42. Spider Meets His Match – Sefwi (Ghana). T.Y.E. The reference to killing two birds with one stone is T.Y.E.'s rendering of an expression in the text meaning, "while one is off urinating, it is a good opportunity to break wind." It can be taken to mean: "How convenient; why not?" Opening and closing formulae at no. 2.

43. The Enchanted Loom – Sefwi (Ghana). T.Y.E. In his greed for more cloth, spider forgets the magic word for stopping the loom. The same word, "Adwebreww" is used in no. 40 to stop the beating whip. Opening and closing formulae at no. 2.

44. How Tortoise Got Water – Yoruba (Nigeria). W.A. See also nos. 9 and 41. Tortoise uses music to divert the animals into dancing. Opening formula at no. 4.

45. The Cloud Mother – Krio (Sierra Leone). See Index: Hidden people, Open Sesame for tales with similar motifs.

46. Spider the Artist – Ga (Ghana). N.A.K. This is a tale of Spider's greed made into a how and why tale. Opening and closing formulae at no. 1.

47. Ata and the Messenger Bird – Krobo (Ghana). See other cases of the "river judge" in nos. 19, 35, and 97. Ate and Lawe are found in tale no. 86. See also the tales of the pineapple child at nos. 14 and 32.

48. Who Is the Greatest Thief? – Mende (Sierra Leone). A.S. A contest to settle competing boasts.

49. The Song of the River – Twi (Ghana). B.J. Also called "The Gift of Densu." Opening and closing formulae at no. 29.

50. The Most Suitable Name – Fula (Nigeria). D.A. The cake of pounded grain is millet flour, which is formed into balls and then stirred into milk.

51. Who Is the Most Helpful Lover? – Sefwi (Ghana). T.Y.E. A cow- or a horsetail switch is the equivalent of a magic wand. Opening and closing formulae at no. 2.

52. What Spider Knows – Sefwi (Ghana). T.Y.E. The magic word is mostly nasal: [hũã]. A similar "hunting nose" is found in no. 68. In general, fairies or elves have big noses. Opening and closing formulae at no. 2.

53. The Tale of the Enchanted Yam – Sefwi (Ghana). T.Y.E. The name Dagraga is in the original tale, but the others are substitutes. See Index: Name-guessing test for tales with similar events. Opening and closing formulae at no. 2.

54. The Most Powerful Name – Avatime (Ghana). W.G. This Mawu is also God in Krobo stories. The tale uses the element of a lethal word that backfires. Opening and closing formulae at no. 13.

55. The Return of Ananse – Sefwi (Ghana). T.Y.E. Spider's greed leads him to a feigned death so he can eat all the beans. See no. 1 for the same motif. Opening and closing formulae at no. 2.

56. Spider Gets Cured – Vane Avatime (Ghana). The overly particular bride gets seduced. Opening and closing formulae at no. 13.

57. The Wise Man Takes a Wise Wife – Language origin not known. The tale has three parts. The third part is a typical Kwaku Babone tale. See no. 29.

58. The Spoiled Bride and the Python – Language origin unknown. Important motifs are the disguised groom and the bride who strikes her parents when she decides to marry. See the latter motif in no. 65.

59. The Dishonest Wife – Yoruba (Nigeria). W.A. Opening formula at no. 4.

60. Ananse Is Put in His Place – Sefwi (Ghana). T.Y.E. The name of the slippery herb is *efiandoro*. Opening and closing formulae at no. 2.

61. Wonder Child and the Talkative Woman – Ga (Ghana). The name Sosorisu is a "funny name," and stands for Kwaku Babone. "Throne" here is a translation of "stool," the symbol of power for a chief. "Dethroning" is a translation of "destooling." Opening and closing formulae at no. 1.

62. Greed Makes a New Friend – Krio (Sierra Leone). S.M.

63. How Crab Got His Shell – Language unknown (Northern Ghana). Name-guessing is often used to incite a dispute.

64. Tortoise and All the Wisdom in the World – Yoruba (Nigeria). W.A. The collecting of wisdom in a gourd or calabash appears in many tales. See no. 99. Opening formula at no. 4.

65. Dede and the Leopard – Ga (Ghana). L.L. See Dede again in no. 5. Opening and closing formulae at no. 1.

66. The Master Trickster – Hausa (Nigeria). D.A. The Hausa Spider has a cleft palate, which affects his speech with heavy palatalization. It appears here as a lisp.

67. Asiedo and the Fish Child – Sefwi (Ghana). T.Y.E. and J.Y.E. (J.Y.E. is the six-year-old son of T.Y.E.) Compare to the pineapple child stories at nos. 14 and 32. Opening and closing formulae at no. 2.

68. The Incredible Nose – Sefwi (Ghana). T.Y.E. The word is mostly nasal: [hũã]. A similar "hunting nose" is found in no. 52. Opening and closing formulae at no. 2.

69. Rat's Vanity – Ga (Ghana). N.A.K. An all-female-animal cast is not common. Opening and closing formulae at no. 1.

70. Why Fowls Scratch – Twi (Ghana). H.M.. Note the motif of the inequitable treatment of children, as in no. 17. This also points out the immortality of Kofi (or Kwaku) Babone. Opening and closing formulae at no. 29.

71. The Hog's Magic – Yilo Krobo (Ghana). The Red River Hog is the *patafo*.

72. The Bag of Salt – Ga (Ghana). N.A.K. Opening and closing formulae at no. 1.

73. The Beaten Path – Twi (Ghana). H.M. Opening and closing formulae at no. 29.

74. The Stone with Whiskers – Krio (Sierra Leone). E.J. Tale revolves around greed and a lethal word.

75. The Charmed Cutlass – Sefwi (Ghana). T.Y.E. See a self-planting whip in no. 40. The cutlass is reminiscent of the brooms in Walt Disney's "The Sorcerer's Apprentice." Opening and closing formulae at no. 2.

76. Why Tortoise Is Bald – Yoruba (Nigeria). W.A. Hot food in hat motif again in nos. 79 and 98. Opening formula at no. 4.

77. Why Lizard Bobs His Head – Ga (Ghana). N.A.K. Name-guessing motif is common. See Index: Name-guessing test for similar tales. Opening and closing formulae at no. 1.

78. Spider the Swindler – Sefwi (Ghana). T.Y.E. The punishment is of the Briar Patch type in Uncle Remus tales. Opening and closing formulae at no. 2.

79. Tortoise Sheds a Tear – Yoruba (Nigeria). W.A. Hot food in hat motif in nos. 76 and 98. Opening formula at no. 4.

80. The Cunning of Galonchi – Mandinka (Gambia). G.I. The exchange of bodies to be put in the drowning sack is a common motif.

81. Tortoise Disobeys – Yoruba (Nigeria). W.A. The plastron of the males of many species of tortoises is slightly concave. Opening formula at no. 4.

82. Dog Is Betrayed – Yoruba (Nigeria). W.A. Opening formula at no. 4.

83. The Wise Child and the Chief – Adengme (Ghana). The child's name is actually Olenopematse. A similar tree-chopping episode in no. 29.

84. The Drunkard's Wisdom – Ashanti (Ghana). An herbalist is essentially a medicine man.

85. The Wisdom of Aja – Krobo (Ghana). A cow- or horsetail switch is a magic wand.

86. The Lion's Advice – Ashanti (Ghana).

87. Choosing the Right Friends – Avatime [?] (Ghana).

88. The Clever Boatman – Krobo (Ghana). See Index: End in question for tales that ask a question.

89. Why the Mason Wasp Has a Narrow Waist – Krobo (Ghana). See fire personified in nos. 6 and 95.

90. The Fairies and the Flute – Adengme (Ghana).

91. Sophia and the Devil – Krio (Sierra Leone). L.T.

92. Wonder Child and the Beast – Krobo (Ghana). Kwaku Babone can also be called Kofi Babone in this tale.

93. Crying for Yaka – Krobo (Ghana).

94. The Child's Vengeance – Krobo (Ghana). The name Gbeseku is a funny-sounding one similar to Kwaku Babone, one of the wonder-child names.

95. Why Hippo Wears No Coat – Krobo (Ghana). See fire personified in nos. 6 and 89.

96. Foriwa's Beads – Akan (Ghana). See Index: Bird messenger, Open Sesame for other tales using these motifs.

97. The Tail of the Elephant Queen – Ashanti (Ghana). See the "river judge" again in nos. 19, 35, and 47.

98. Why Spider Is Bald – Ga (Ghana). N.A.K. Kornorley is the same as Konole in nos. 1 and 18. Hot food in a hat motif in nos. 76 and 79. Opening and closing formulae at no. 1.

99. Spider and the Calabash of Knowledge – Twi (Ghana). B.J. See no. 64. Opening and closing formulae at no. 29.

100. The Noble Adowa – Sefwi (Ghana). T.Y.E. Adowa, the Royal Antelope, is different from other antelopes. Opening and closing formulae at no. 2.

101. Spider's Funeral – Krio (Sierra Leone). S.M. This "Bra" is "Brother," the same as "Br'er" in Uncle Remus tales.

102. Who Is the Greatest Magician? – Ga (Ghana). These magicians are herbalists, or medicine men. Opening and closing formulae at no. 1.

103. Tortoise and the Stew Bowl – Ga (Ghana). G.A.

104. Crab and Guinea Fowl Part Ways – Yoruba (Nigeria). W.A. See Index: Food dispute for other tales with this common motif. Opening formula at no. 4.

105. The Gift of the Wicked Old Woman – Twi (Ghana). G.O.B. The old woman is addressed as Nana, a term of respect. Opening and closing formulae at no. 29.

106. The Honest Finger – Yoruba (Nigeria). W.A. Opening formula at no. 4.

107. Cat and Rat Have It Out – Yoruba (Nigeria). W.A. Food disputes are a source of animosity in many tales. See Index: Food dispute. Opening formula at no. 4.

108. The Hunter's Best Friend – Yoruba (Nigeria). W.A. Opening formula at no. 4.

109. The Vultures and the Liver Cave – Krio (Sierra Leone). S.M. There is another tale of how the vulture became bald at no. 116. See Index: Open Sesame for the other tales using secret words to gain entry to something.

110. The Nefarious Fly – Sefwi (Ghana). T.Y.E. See Index: Food dispute for other tales using this theme. Opening and closing formulae at no. 2.

111. The Hunter's Daughter – Sefwi (Ghana). T.Y.E. See no. 21, which is a similar tale told about the hunter's son. The bang of gunfire is rendered as "Tomm!" Opening and closing formulae at no. 2.

112. The Gluttonous Monkey – Avatime (Ghana). Opening and closing formulae at no. 13.

113. Why Singing Tortoises Are Solitary – Ga (Ghana). N.A.K. Tortoise is often associated with hypnotic music. Opening and closing formulae at no. 1.

114. The Price of Eggs – Sefwi (Ghana). T.Y.E. The yellow-backed duiker's name is Ekwaduo. The original tale is filled with words for the various sounds made by the animals leaping and falling. Opening and closing formulae at no. 2.

115. The Coffin of God's Daughter – Twi (Ghana). G.O.B. The old lady is a witch, of course—an opponent of God. Opening and closing formulae at no. 29.

116. The Quarrel Between Heaven and Earth – Yoruba (Nigeria). W.A. The separation of heaven from earth is also in tale no. 120. Opening formula at no. 4.

117. The Cry of Sasabonsam – Sefwi (Ghana). T.Y.E. Opening and closing formulae at no. 2.

118. Adowa and the Leopard – Sefwi (Ghana). T.Y.E. Most of this tale is to be sung. I have deviated from the translation in order to provide more symmetry for this tale. Opening and closing formulae at no. 2.

119. Ananse and God's Business – Larteh and Twi (Ghana). B.J. Opening and closing formulae at no. 29.

120. Why the Sky Is High – Ga (Ghana). N.A.K. Includes a moral about obedience in women. See also no. 116. Opening and closing formulae at no. 1.

121. The Gifts – Sefwi (Ghana). T.Y.E. The man in the pit is probably Kwaku Babone. See also no. 10. Opening and closing formulae at no. 2.

122. The Necklace – Mende (Sierra Leone). G.I. The term "elder" is used here for the literal "big man." The underlying moral is that co-wives should not be jealous.

123. The Tale of Aso Yaa – Sefwi (Ghana). T.Y.E. The original song was: "Aso Yaa, eee! Sodene. Aso Yaa, eee! Sodene!" Opening and closing formulae at no. 2.

INDEX

▼▲▼▲▼▲▼▲▼▲▼▲▼▲▼▲▼▲▼▲▼▲▼▲▼▲▼▲▼

Topics, motifs, and names are listed in alphabetical order in this index. The numbers of the tales containing the topic, motif, or name appear immediately after the entry phrase. Some of the index entries include brief notes.

Some expressions in the index are followed by a suggested English pronunciation—adapted from the African language word—in phonetic respelling. In these respellings, the capitalized letters indicate stress or accent. These transcriptions provide a useful, English approximation of the original African languages of the tales. They are meant to serve only as a guide and a model for the English-speaking reader, not as authentic samples of African languages. The respelling system is explained in the chart that follows the index.

Beard, 61, 74

Beast, 5, 28, 45, 52, 53, 92, 93, 117.
  A large animal or a monster

Bed, 8, 55, 56, 58, 61, 65, 85, 91,
  115, 122

Beer, 98

Bees, 3, 22

Beggar, 62

Belly, 1, 11, 15, 33, 39, 42, 46, 54,
  59, 60, 81, 112. See also Stomach

Berries, 47

Bigbelly, 40. Proper name

Bighead, 40. Proper name

Bigman, 24. The leopard

Bignose, 52. A proper name

Bird, 6, 7, 25, 37, 40, 47, 49, 52, 63,
  77, 78, 95, 96, 100, 116, 117

Bird messenger, 96

Blacksmith, 31, 94

Blood, 25, 31, 59, 80, 96, 119, 121

Boafo [bow AH fo], 94. Proper name

Boasting, 6, 37, 39, 48, 68, 87, 113

Boatman, 88, 91

Boiling, 38, 77, 91, 98, 109

Bongo [BAHNG gow], 114. A forest
  antelope. See also Antelope

Bottle, 49, 85, 92, 102

Bowl, 1, 28, 59, 103

Box, 15, 68, 85

Boy, 21, 25, 29, 31, 33, 34, 40, 47,
  49, 52, 57, 70, 71, 83, 85, 90, 91,
  92, 94, 109

Bread, 78

Break wind, 42

Breasts, 105

Bride, 6, 57, 58, 65

Bride hits parent, 58, 65

Broken spell, 8, 113, 121. See also
  Spell

Broomstick, 33

Broth, 33. See also Soup

Brother, 9, 40, 54, 65, 69, 84, 85,
  91, 93, 98, 106

Bruku [BRU ku], 33. Proper name of
  a fetish

Buffalo, 100. See also Bush cow

Bull, 80, 83, 119

Bullet, 15, 61, 87

Buried, 8, 27, 28, 35, 51, 55, 70, 85,
  93, 101

Burn, 6, 53, 75, 76, 77, 89, 95, 98,
  112, 116

Bush, 8, 20, 31, 33, 34, 39, 40, 41,
  43, 44, 46, 47, 50, 52, 53, 55, 60,
  70, 75, 86, 91, 92, 100, 104, 107,
  109, 111, 113, 116, 121

Bushbuck, 52, 114. A small antelope.
  See also Antelope

Bush cow, 44. The short-horned
  buffalo

Bush pig, 18, 38. The wild pig

Butter, 30

Buttocks. See Backside

Cage, 24

Calabash, 3, 19, 33, 59, 60, 63, 78,
  80, 83, 85, 99, 123

Cannibalism, 31, 45. Humans eating
  humans

Canoe, 29, 52, 91

Caravan, 123

Carcass, 15, 74, 92

Cassava, 75, 88

Cat, 107

Cave, 71, 109

Celebration, 12, 29, 73, 115

Charcoal, 60, 114

Charm, 51. See also Fetish

Chemist, 31. A druggist (U.S.)

Cherebi-Akon [CHE ree bee ah
  KON], 85. Proper name

Chest, 32, 47, 64, 68, 104, 123

Chest hair (male), 14, 32, 47

Chicken, 80

Chief, 2, 8, 10, 12, 16, 29, 34, 39, 48, 57, 61, 71, 77, 80, 83, 85, 87, 92, 101, 113, 114, 115, 119, 121. *See also* King

Chimpanzee, 23, 24

Cloth, 34, 37, 42, 43, 57, 65, 69, 94

Clothes, 10, 16, 26, 37, 53, 66, 68, 81, 91, 93, 97, 98, 121, 123

Cloud, 6, 45, 116

Coat, 91, 95

Cobra, 22, 33

Cock, 77, 89, 91, 119. Cockerel or rooster

Coconut, 77, 87

Codfish, 49

Coffin, 1, 98, 101, 115

Coin, 62, 87, 94

Compound, 16, 34, 77, 83. Cluster of dwellings

Contest, 6, 8, 9, 12, 48, 71, 73, 114

Corn, 4, 29, 35, 54, 57, 75, 89, 116. Maize. *See also* Grain

Corpse, 51, 115, 119

Coucal, 18. A larklike bird of the cuckoo family

Court, 57. A court of law. *See also* Wooing

Cow, 18, 42, 44, 58, 83. *See also* Bush cow

Co-wives, 16, 17, 28, 32, 36, 59, 69, 90, 122

Crab, 41, 63, 104

Craw-craw [KRO kro], 91. An itchy skin disease

Cricket, 56. The insect

Criminal, 28, 121

Crippled, 81

Crocodile, 78

Cunnie Rabbit, 45, 74, 101. The rabbit; a coney

Curse, 53, 55, 104, 107, 115, 116

Cutlass or Machete, 11, 31, 45, 70, 75, 83, 108. *See also* Knife

Dagraga [dah GRAH gah], 53. The name of a magic yam

Dance, 20, 37, 39, 70, 90, 94, 98, 121, 123

Daughter, 10, 17, 26, 29, 30, 32, 35, 39, 56, 57, 58, 63, 71, 73, 76, 77, 87, 91, 96, 98, 103, 105, 111, 113, 115, 122

Death, 10, 11, 42, 57, 69, 79, 85, 86, 89, 93, 115

Deceive an animal in order to eat it, 46, 54, 74, 100

Deception, 4, 8, 9, 11, 29, 31, 37, 42, 45, 48, 59, 60, 66, 70, 72, 77, 78, 79, 80, 81, 82, 89, 90, 93, 95, 98, 100, 101, 110, 118, 119

Dede [DE de], 5, 65. Proper name

Deer, 74

Densu [DEN su], 49. The name of a river

Dessert, 34

Devil, 20, 91

Diamonds, 91, 101

Dig, 40, 49, 85, 87, 121

Digirigi [dee gee REE gee], 53. A nonsense name (for a yam)

Dilemma tale. *See* list at End in question

Disgrace, 1, 4, 18, 42, 55, 60, 76, 85, 98, 121

Dish, 40, 42, 57

Disobedience, 81, 120

Dispersion, 53, 99, 105

Divination, 81, 116

Tar-baby analog, 1

Teeth, 15, 20, 53, 60, 61, 78

Test, 71, 83, 87. *See also* Contest; Guessing test; Name-guessing test

Tetteh [TE te], 90. Proper name

Theft, 1, 4, 38, 48, 66, 82, 106

Thief, 1, 4, 48, 55, 114, 121

Thinlegs, 40. Proper name

Thread, 22, 102

Throne, 61, 80, 124. A translation of stool, the seat for and symbol of the power of a chief

Thumb, 35, 106

Thunder, 115, 116

Tobacco, 68

Tomato, 38, 55, 85

Tomm [TOM], 111. "Bang!"

Tongue, 33, 34, 46, 77

Tortoise, 4, 9, 37, 41, 42, 44, 64, 72, 76, 79, 81, 82, 96, 103, 113

Transformation, 8, 14, 15, 32, 58, 65, 108, 123

Trap, 18, 24, 74, 85, 93, 100

Treachery, 35, 121

Tree, 2, 3, 4, 6, 7, 12, 15, 16, 21, 22, 25, 29, 40, 43, 48, 49, 52, 54, 55, 58, 61, 64, 66, 70, 72, 75, 77, 78, 83, 84, 85, 86, 87, 92, 94, 96, 102, 103, 108, 113, 116, 117, 118, 122

Trial by ordeal, 114

Triplets, 47

Triumph of weakness, 9, 41, 44, 57

Tunnel, 71. *See also* Cave

Twi [CHWEE], 29, 49, 70, 73, 99, 105, 115, 119. Tales told in this language

Twins, 20, 93, 97

Ulcers, 123. *See also* Sores; Yaws

Verandah, 94, 98

Voice, 7, 14, 15, 16, 17, 28, 31, 33, 38, 42, 45, 52, 55, 69, 77, 96, 98, 104, 113, 118, 121, 123

Vomit, 42, 49, 87

Vulture, 49, 109, 116

Wart hog, 100

Wasp, 89. The Mason wasp

Water, 6, 8, 14, 19, 22, 25, 26, 28, 30, 31, 32, 33, 34, 38, 41, 44, 47, 53, 56, 57, 61, 63, 66, 69, 77, 78, 79, 80, 84, 87, 89, 91, 93, 100, 102, 104, 109, 115, 116, 122

Wealth, 5, 62, 121

Weed, 75, 89, 93

Whip, 40

Wicked, 17, 28, 57, 63, 105, 121

Widow, 69, 75

Wife, 1, 4, 11, 14, 15, 16, 17, 18, 28, 29, 32, 33, 34, 35, 36, 49, 50, 52, 55, 57, 58, 59, 60, 66, 67, 68, 69, 71, 74, 76, 77, 78, 79, 80, 90, 91, 93, 98, 103, 107, 111, 120, 121, 123. *See also* Co-wife

Wind, 49, 119. *See also* Break wind

Wisdom, 2, 7, 41, 44, 54, 57, 64, 84, 85, 99

Wiseman, 54. A name for the spider. *See* Spider

Witch, 17, 25

Witchcraft, 35

Wonder child, 15, 29, 33, 61, 83, 92, 94. Typically the wonder child has a "funny sounding" name: Gbeseku, Akokoaa Kwasi Gyinamoa, Kwaku Babone, Sosorisu

Wooing, 6, 8, 20, 60, 71, 73, 77, 91

Wordplay, 54, 74, 93, 121

Yaka [YAH kah], 93. Proper name

Yam, 1, 4, 15, 17, 34, 38, 41, 53, 55, 75, 82, 94, 97, 104, 116

Yaws, 33, 65, 97. *See also* Sores; Ulcers

Yonkon [YONG kong], 109. Proper name

Yoruba [YO ru bah], 4, 6, 7, 9, 17, 19, 26, 28, 30, 37, 44, 59, 64, 76, 79, 81, 82, 104, 106, 107, 108, 116. Tales told in this language

GUIDE TO PRONUNCIATION

▼▲▼▲▼▲▼▲▼▲▼▲▼▲▼▲▼▲▼▲▼▲▼▲▼▲▼▲▼

The transcriptions in the Index provide an easy-to-pronounce, English approximation of the original African languages of the tales. They are meant to serve as a guide to the English-speaking reader, not as authentic samples of African languages. The following chart shows International Phonetic Alphabet (IPA) and American English values for each of the symbols used in the pronunciation guide. The letters in boldface type indicate where the sound in question is found in the English keyword.

[ah] = IPA [ɑ]
shop
stop
top

[b] = IPA [b]
boot
bubble
tub

[ch] = IPA [tʃ]
cheese
church
cinch

[d] = IPA [d]
dead
leader
bad

[ee] = IPA [i]
feet
sleek
seat

[e] = IPA [ɛ]
let
met
set

[f] = IPA [f]
frog
feel
if

[g] = IPA [g]
get
giggle
frog

[h] = IPA [h]
hat
hold
who

[j] = IPA [dʒ]
joke
judge
Jim

[k] = IPA [k]
cat
keep
sneak

[l] = IPA [l]
feel
yellow
law

[m] = IPA [m]
slam
family
mouse

[n] = IPA [n]
soon
net
funny

[ng] = IPA [ŋ]
bring

singer
ring

[o] = IPA [ɔ]
raw
caught
yawn

[ow] = IPA [ow]
cloak
vote
coal

[p] = IPA [p]
people
sip
pillow

[r] = IPA [r]
rack
berry
heart

[s] = IPA [s]
pass
sun
fasten

[sh] = IPA [ʃ]
sure
fish
mush

[t] = IPA [t]
Tom
Pat
twist

[u] = IPA [u]
stew
moon
blue

[v] = IPA [v]
saver
give
voice

[y] = IPA [j]
you
yankee
yellow

[w] = IPA [w]
wound
will
wallet

[z] = IPA [z]
zebra
fuzzy
buzz